SHADOWBORN

You want me, come and get me, Kael thought as he turned away from the knight and pushed the throttle. His wings hummed, then screamed as he touched his light element with his mind. Subtle shifts of his shoulders and hips swayed him side to side, a tiny curl of his back lifting him higher. Blast after blast of fire raced through the air like burning spears, before fading away with their power spent. Kael had thought the knight would turn and give chase to the cargo platforms the farther away from the battle they traveled, yet each fire bolt confirmed that would not be the case. Platforms be damned, the knight was coming for him.

By David Dalglish

Shadowdance

A Dance of Cloaks

A Dance of Blades

A Dance of Mirrors

A Dance of Shadows

A Dance of Ghosts

A Dance of Chaos

Cloak and Spider *(e-only novella)*

Seraphim

Skyborn

Fireborn

Shadowborn

SHADOWBORN

SERAPHIM: BOOK THREE

DAVID DALGLISH

www.orbitbooks.net

ORBIT

First published in Great Britain in 2017 by Orbit

1 3 5 7 9 10 8 6 4 2

All characters and events in this publication, other than those clearly in the public domain, are fictitious and any resemblance to real persons, living or dead, is purely coincidental.

A CIP catalogue record for this book is available from the British Library.

ISBN 978-0-356-50653-1

Printed and bound by CPI Group (UK) Ltd, Croydon CR0 4YY

Papers used by Orbit are from well-managed forests and other responsible sources.

Orbit
An imprint of
Little, Brown Book Group
Carmelite House
50 Victoria Embankment
London EC4Y 0DZ

An Hachette UK Company
www.hachette.co.uk

www.orbitbooks.net

For Morgan, my littlest
and most important beta reader

CHAPTER 1

Eyes closed. Breath steady. The cold floor beneath his knees and elbows smooth, immovable, like his faith. Like his heart.

"I am the blade of the angels," Liam Skyborn whispered. "I am the flesh on their bones. I am the blood on their feathers. What is holy must never break."

The litany soothed him as it always did. There could be no turmoil in his heart if he were to fulfill his task. This was too important for hesitation. Much too dangerous for doubt. Humanity's continued existence depended on his success. One task. Two lives.

"I am the blade of the angels."

He would kill the little girl who had once sat on his lap begging for more stories of his battles as a Seraph. The girl who had asked him what it was like to fly. Who dreamed of soaring over green lands and blue ocean waters. He'd bring her down in a fiery blaze, all in the name of salvation. He would kill the boy who had carved "mommy is pretty" a dozen times on his bedroom wall as a surprise birthday present. He would put his sword through the child who had once clung to his neck and demanded to be carried up Market Road to the open stalls for sweets.

Liam's teeth clicked as he ground them together. His children were heretics. Blasphemers. Deniers of the Speaker, and therefore deniers of God himself. Their actions enabled the remaining four islands, Center's little children, to rebel. A message had to be sent. The angels would not be mocked.

His hand passed over his eyes. Wet? But why? He clenched his hand into a fist, crushing the emotion that threatened to corrupt him.

"I am the blade of the angels," he said, louder and with a rasp. "I am the flesh on their bones. I am..."

The door creaked. Liam's eyes opened as he sat up from his crouched prayer. The holy Speaker for the Angels stepped inside.

"Are you prepared?" Marius asked, arms crossed over his chest. Liam frowned, and he glanced over himself. He was naked but for a pair of simple gray pants, the many crisscrossing scars of his flesh his only decoration.

"I thought my squadron left tomorrow night?"

"I've not come for your squadron," Marius said. "Only you."

Liam obediently rose to his bare feet.

"I am ever your servant," he said, bowing.

Marius led the way back up the stairs. He did not speak, or reveal their destination. Liam kept his mind focused on a song to the angels instead of pondering the reason for Marius's nocturnal visit. It didn't matter where they were going, or why, so why wonder? Liam would perform without question whatever the Speaker wished of him.

They passed between two armed soldiers at the top of the

stairs as they exited into the grand halls of Heavenstone. Red banners dozens of feet long hung from the ceiling. Stone pillars braced the ceiling, its height so great, the pillars so wide, it was as if Heavenstone were built for giants instead of men. Marius led them down the crimson carpet, through guarded doorways and halls covered with enormous paintings of ancient lands. Snow-capped mountains, endless deserts swirling with sand in great dunes, forests with trees so tall and branches so thick the sun struggled to pierce through to the exotic life hunting and hiding beneath the canopy. The world prior to Ascension. A vital reminder of all the beauty they'd lost.

At last they stopped before a simple wooden door guarded by a knight armed with a halberd. Liam kept his frown hidden. He'd passed this unassuming door many times but had never seen anyone going in or out. The guard swung the door open for Marius while keeping his eyes straight ahead. The two stepped inside, the door shutting behind them with an echoing thud.

"We go where few ever go," Marius said, and Liam felt his heart seize up. The undecorated room was far larger than he'd expected. Four more soldiers stood guard at the end, barring the way to an ornate lift. The white of its marble and the gold of its decorative writings were a stark contrast to the barren gray of the room. To either side of the lift were large gears with cranks attached.

"My lord," Liam said as the guards stepped aside, "where is it we go?"

"To the heart of Heavenstone," Marius said, stepping onto the lift and beckoning him to follow. "Hurry. The night is late, and I do not wish to delay."

Liam's meager clothing suddenly felt shameful and disrespectful for where they were headed. He stepped onto the lift while avoiding the gaze of the soldiers, fearful of their judgmental gazes. Once they boarded the lift, two soldiers began cranking, setting chains to rattling and stone to grinding. The lift jolted a moment and then descended down into the stone floor. For a long minute total darkness overwhelmed them, and Liam closed his eyes and meditated on his breathing. He hated darkness. Darkness meant being alone with his thoughts.

A sudden blast of light washed over them. Liam squinted in an attempt to see but found it hopeless. It was as if he stood within a star.

The brightness lasted only a moment before it subsided. Liam glanced above his head, and through the colored blotches he saw the dimming light of more than thirty light elements embedded into the wall.

"A necessary precaution," Marius said, answering his unspoken question. "The shadowborn can take many forms, but none will survive the holy light of our beloved angels."

The lift slowed, revealing their destination. It was a single room, with little space between them and the twelve soldiers bowed low in respect. Filling the entire wall opposite the lift was a massive pair of doors. So great was its size that twelve silver chains, six on either side, were required to open it. Its stone was pure white marble and heavily decorated with gold leaf. Liam felt his knees go weak. There were many names for this place. The holy gate. The heart of Center. The angels' cathedral. All words for a place Liam never thought he'd lay eyes upon.

"At ease," Marius told the twelve. He exited the lift. Liam followed two steps behind.

The closer he approached the doors, the more Liam was overwhelmed by the sight. He stared at the swirling gold lines, thin and finely carved. They looped and twisted unendingly, patiently spelling out words of worship and praise to the heavens above, unceasing no matter how long one stood before the doors and read. Liam fought an impulse to touch his own tattooed head. His marks were similar, but they were not written with the purity of gold, nor were they words of worship. Their ink was black as sin, and they spoke warnings against open minds, wandering eyes, doubtful tongues, and hesitant hands.

At Marius's request the dozen guards took up the silver chains attached to the rungs upon the door. Once braced, they turned their heads aside, as if unworthy of even looking upon the light from within the sealed room. With but a word from Marius, they would open the gates.

"Shall I wait here?" Liam asked as Marius put a hand on the door.

"No, Liam," he said. "You're coming with me."

Liam's heart seized.

"But within—" he began, but was quickly cut off.

"Within is every reason you must succeed in the task I have given you," Marius said. "This gift is offered to precious few. I pray you cherish it forever."

Liam swallowed down a stone in his throat thrice the size of Center.

"I am unworthy to be in their presence," he said. "My heart is weak and my mind sinful."

"We're all unworthy," Marius said. "That's why it's a gift. Now hold your head high and step inside."

The soldiers pulled their ropes, splitting the doors open with a stomach-trembling grinding of stone and gears. Light flooded out the crack. Bright. Pure. Squinting, Liam choked down his fear and entered the greatest and most secretive cathedral buried deep in the heart of Center.

Despite all he knew, all he'd read, Liam was still not prepared.

The cathedral opened out immensely, a tremendous sphere of white marble stretching out hundreds of feet in all directions. Gold and silver ran like rivulets across the walls, winding and dancing like a heavenly spiderweb. An overwhelming beauty, the sight of those walls, but it meant nothing to Liam's eyes when compared to the otherworldly presence of the three lightborn. They hung beside one another in the center of the vast cathedral, their arms at their sides, gilded manacles clamped about their wrists and ankles. Several more chains looped about their waists, their arms, holding them so that their feet hovered mere inches above the stone floor. It was a vision of imprisonment, but also one of support. Without those chains, the lightborn could never rise at all.

A new servant comes before us?

The voice echoed in Liam's mind, soft, gentle, tinkling like glass. Liam forced his fearful eyes to meet the gazes of the three. They were giants, incredible beings of crystal and marble and all things good and pure. Their humanoid shapes were flawless. Neither the sky nor the ocean could compare to the blue intermixed with flecks of shining gold in their eyes. Beautiful, yet terrifying. With a clenched fist the heavenly figures could crush Liam's mortal shell.

"A servant most humble," Liam said, dropping to his knees.

The middle of the three leaned closer, her form slenderer, somehow more feminine than the other two. He glimpsed the hundreds of tubes piercing her spine. Pearlescent blood flowed through them, vanishing into a hundred holes in the cathedral walls. It was that blood that kept Center floating above the Endless Ocean. The life-giving blood that spared mankind from extinction.

The lightborn's face was perfectly smooth, without mouth or nose, but he heard her voice as if she whispered beside his ear.

Many men and women are humbled before us, she said. *You tell us nothing, so tell us instead your name.*

Liam resisted the urge to glance over his shoulder to see if the Speaker was with him.

"Liam Skyborn," he said. "Knight of Center, follower of God, and obedient servant to his angels."

"And a fine servant at that," Marius said, putting a hand on his shoulder. Liam flinched at his touch. "He will be spearheading our retaliation for the outer islands' blasphemy. I would like you to show him the true threat we all face. I want him to know why we must perform such desperate measures in these trying times."

A second lightborn stirred, his chains thunderously rattling as he stretched them to their limits. His voice sounded in Liam's head, its tone deeper than the other's, like a different-sized bell.

It is a risk to give such knowledge. Not all are strong enough to withstand it.

"I am strong enough," Liam said, a bit of his sinful pride igniting. "After all I have endured, the truth is the last thing I fear."

The middle lightborn narrowed her eyes and her giant hand floated toward him, her forefinger pointing. The chain on her wrist flexed, the heavy bolt securing it to the wall groaning.

Then endure, she said. *See through the eyes of a man just as ignorant, and just as proud.*

The slightest kiss of her finger touched his forehead. Every muscle in his body clenched tight. His vision blanked, and then he was falling, twisting, becoming someone else.

Lord Commander Alexander Essex stood atop the ramparts of the castle overlooking the sandy coastline. The sun shone bright on his dark skin. He smiled and felt alive. The Oceanic Wall quivered a few miles beyond the edge of the rocky shore, its translucent surface cracking with a thousand silvery spiderwebs.

"The theotechs estimate the wall will collapse before the week's end," First Seraph Kaster said, climbing the stone steps to join him on the rampart. His armor, like Alexander's, shone a brilliant gold in the sunlight.

"And what does Y'vah say of this?" Alexander asked.

"The lightborn says nothing." Kaster shook his head. "I don't think he has the strength."

A grin pulled at the right half of Alexander's mouth. He turned and clasped Kaster's armored shoulder with his hand.

"Let it fall," he said, and he gestured across the shoreline. "What does it matter when we have such power ready for L'adim's monsters? They'll never reach a single stone of this castle."

Kaster said nothing. Alexander pulled him closer, pointing him west. The castle was built upon a high cliff overlooking the smooth shore to the east, the waves having won their war against the stone over the centuries. Golden armored men scrambled over the cliff's edge like ants, and farther inland, tents formed a haphazard city. Five thousand men armed with spears and shields, the finest Europa had ever crafted, but beyond that front line of foot soldiers waited his pride and joy—the dragoons.

"The shadowborn has never faced the likes of our dragoons," Alexander said. "Let him come. We shall crush him beneath our heel."

Still Kaster did not respond. Alexander sensed an uneasy question lurking within him, and he had no patience for it on this fine day.

"What bothers you?" he asked. "Spit it out already before it eats a hole in your stomach."

"Commander... there are many wondering if we should use

the time before the Oceanic Wall collapses to retreat further inland."

"Retreat?" Alexander asked, stepping closer. "And where shall we retreat to?"

"Just a few dozen miles toward Odeon," Kaster said, refusing to back down. "If we can meet with Commander Torman, and unite Y'vah with Gh'aro, our forces will—"

"Our forces will hold their ground here, where the terrain is favorable and our supplies plentiful." Alexander snorted. "Besides, Commander Torman is an idiot, a member of the Appeasers before this war started. How he's kept his position after that, I don't know." He glared at the cracking wall. "We will not appease those monsters and their shadowborn master. We will grind them to ash and crystal and build our world anew with their blood."

Kaster bowed low.

"As you wish," he said. "Am I dismissed?"

Alexander waved him off. He had more to worry about than the minor rumblings of fear from the more cowardly soldiers under his command. Arms crossed over his chest, he turned east, his smile growing. The castle had been considered a relic of wartime past, but now its sturdy walls would be of great use. Ten dragoons—magnificent mixtures of man and machine sprung forth from the combined minds of himself and Y'vah's escort of theotechs—waited atop the ramparts, with twenty more on the beach below.

"Come get us, you bastard," Alexander whispered. "We're ready."

Time loosened. Liam felt its passage across him like a blur, its length unchanged but its speed a thousandfold higher. The sun rose and fell, dancing with the illustrious moon, until it slowed, time hardening, the world resuming its proper way...

Fire blanketed the Oceanic Wall. Every few moments, the fire parted and something struck the other side, creating silver cracks in the wall that spread thousands of feet. With night fallen, that fire, and the shield struggling to hold against it, were more than enough to clearly see the thousands of soldiers forming defensive lines across the beachhead. Alexander imagined what might be large enough to cause such impacts against the wall, decided not to bother. With demons, one never knew for certain their form, let alone their size.

"Are your Seraphim ready?" he asked Kaster, who patiently waited beside him.

"We are."

"Then take to the skies and ready your elements. Make them suffer long before setting foot on dry land."

"Will you not watch from the castle?" Kaster asked.

"Here is where I belong. Now go, and ensure your stone casters remember their role."

"They will," Kaster said, bowing. "May the angels ever watch over you, Commander."

"No angels will take me tonight," Alexander said. "And none are coming for you, either. We're putting an end to this war."

Kaster's wings shimmered, and with a deep, pleasant hum he lifted to the skies to join the one hundred others of Europa's Second Seraphim Division. Their wings shone like golden stars of the night sky, and their glow strengthened Alexander's resolve. Not as much as the presence of his dragoons, though.

Alexander walked to five neat rows of his dragoons behind

the shield wall at the beachhead and stopped beside the nearest of the machines. The dragoon was a culmination of two years of work, a grand creation of gold and steel. The wide bottom was spherical, and it shimmered white from the power of five light prisms embedded within the protective metal that kept it afloat. The rest resembled a chariot with a cramped space in the center for the driver. The upper half of a golden dragon was carved across the front, its legs reared up, its mouth opened in a snarl. On either side of it, braced to the metallic chariot, were cannons shaped like the naval weapons of old.

A pale bare-chested man sat in the dragoon's cushioned middle, five tubes sunk into his back. His blood flowed through the clear tubes, traveling to the ten elemental prisms powering each of the two cannons. A seeing eyeglass was strapped to a pole beside his head to aid with aiming long distances. Iron clamps around his waist kept him steady. Dozens of wires controlling the dragoon's movement sank into the man's waist, his legs surgically removed upon his acceptance of such a crucial role in the war against the shadowborn.

"Are you ready, Tarkir?" Alexander asked.

The man lowered his head in a respectful gesture.

"We have all suffered much," Tarkir said. "Now is our time to pay it back."

The commander grinned.

"That's the spirit."

Alexander patted the side of the dragoon lovingly, eager to see its full fury unleashed. Soon. So very soon.

The Lord Commander joined the rest of his army in watching the assault upon the protective dome. L'adim's army raged on the other side, flinging its might against the lightborn's defenses. The silver cracks spread wider and wider, so thick they appeared like frozen strikes of lightning. A deafening screech of glass scraping against glass emitted from the wall, coupled with what sounded like ice breaking atop a frozen lake.

And then the wall broke. A deep rumble replaced its glow, strong enough to rattle bones. Wind blasted across the water, angering the surface and knocking helmets off Alexander's soldiers. The great burning fire fell to the water, momentarily extinguished, but its fall revealed the vast demon horde, so numerous it took Alexander's breath away.

The iceborn led the way, dozens of giants twenty feet high lumbering across the ocean. With every step the water froze, granting passage to the army that followed. Among them came the stoneborn, even taller than the iceborn, vicious creatures made up of boulders cracking and twisting together into a humanoid shape. The fireborn and stormborn lurked behind, waiting for their time.

Alexander raised his arm and shouted his command. Few would hear his voice, but they'd hear the battle cry of the dragoons.

"Adrian," he shouted. "Show them humanity's anger!"

The rider put his hands to the controls. The light beneath his dragoon brightened as the vehicle lifted higher into the air. Crackling sounds swelled from within the cannons, power building, building, until Adrian released it with a single press of a button. Twin lightning blasts surged forward in great swirling beams, rocking the dragoon backward several feet. The beams dwarfed any a single Seraph could manage and contained power Alexander knew nothing could withstand.

The lightning blasts struck the center of an iceborn giant, and it roared as its torso shattered. Thick chunks of ice fell to the frozen ocean, blue blood flowing in streams down its waist and legs. The thing managed a single step before collapsing to its knees and crumbling.

Alexander could hear the cheers of his soldiers at the demon's demise even amid the chaos. The battle begun, the rest of dragoons unleashed their fury. Streams of lightning and fire shredded the iceborn, melting limbs and blasting holes through their elemental bodies. Ice and stone struck the stoneborn, cracking the boulders of their bodies and ripping off limbs. Ten dragoons atop the nearby castle joined in, assaulting the fireborn and stormborn lurking behind the initial wave of giants. The frozen ocean steadily cracked; the blasts that missed the stoneborn were often still enough to break the ice nearby and send them into the waters below. All in all, it was a blinding display, and Alexander was forced to shield his eyes to watch the battle unfold.

Still the giants came, though far fewer in number. The first of the iceborn touched shore, and it howled as twin beams of fire slammed its neck and face. Its upper half melted and it dropped dead to the hard ground. But the bridge to shore was finally complete, and with a sudden surge the fireborn and stormborn rushed past the dying giants to the shore, eager to battle the thousands of men with their shields and spears.

Now's your time, Alexander thought, looking to the sky. Kaster's Seraphim swirled above the battlefield, and when the horde of smaller demons approached, fifteen Seraphim dropped low into a strafing run. Stone flowed from their gauntlets in steady streams, forming a three-foot-high wall protecting the entirety of the shoreline. Alexander's soldiers rushed to it, spears thrusting up over the top of the fortification at the incoming tide of elementals.

The first few moments of battle were a slaughter, and not in the demons' favor. The fireborn and stormborn flung themselves against a wall of stone and spears, having to climb one and avoid the other to even begin their attack. Their speed was their only advantage, but with five thousand men pressed shoulder to shoulder and shields at ready, there was no room for the demons to pass, no way for them to dodge.

Alexander's smile grew as his dragoons continued to sing. Giants littered the horizon, a number that would have terrified any regular force of ground troops but meant nothing to him. His dragoons would crush them before they ever neared his soldiers. His Seraphim circled, blasting the smaller demons with their elements while leaving the giants for the dragoons.

Slowly men died along the barricade, but with each one that fell another was waiting to take his place. There would be no break in the shields, no gap in the defenses for the demons to exploit. This was it, their breaking point. Despite the countless lost battles other nations suffered, the proud men of Europa would show the world how it was done. It was all a matter of escalation. Soldiers weren't enough. Seraphim weren't enough. Machines of war, the greatest mankind had ever seen, were the necessary tools to crush the demons. The nearby dragoon launched another terrifying volley of lightning, and Alexander beamed at his creation.

The dragoons were but the beginning. Now that his original concept had proven superior on the battlefield there'd be architects and theotechs flocking to his aid. How much grander might these war machines grow? What of one piloted by several men, all with different elemental affinities? Gun platforms, airships manned by hundreds of Seraphim, grand cannons rolling on wheels... there'd be no limit. L'adim's rebellion would be crushed, and through the horrors of war amazing new inventions would emerge for the betterment of mankind.

A strange rumble returned Alexander's attention to the battlefield atop the frozen ocean. The bulk of the demons were in retreat, something that hardly surprised Alexander, but the iceborn giants stood still, collapsing in on themselves, breaking as if from within.

"What's happening?" Alexander asked Adrian.

The dragoon rider pressed his face to the eyeglass and held it there.

"They're splitting apart," he shouted over the chorus of dragoon fire. "They're becoming smaller iceborn, hundreds of them."

Alexander stared at the battlefield, contemplating. If the iceborn giants were suddenly numerous and small, it would nullify the effect of his dragoons. A clever strategy, but it would only make them weaker to the Seraphim strafing them from above. And why just the iceborn? The stoneborn continued their lumbering approach. True, the stoneborn were more resistant to the dragoon barrages, but only by a small margin. Why not change as well?

"Commander?"

Alexander turned his attention back to Adrian, and he didn't like the worried look on the rider's face.

"What is it?" he asked.

Adrian squinted into the eyeglass.

"A shadow's coming."

So, it seemed L'adim would finally make his appearance as his army was being destroyed. This sounded excellent to Alexander, not worrisome.

"Where from?" he asked, thinking his dragoons could concentrate fire on the shadowborn.

Adrian pulled away, shaking his head.

"Everywhere."

"Every—?"

Alexander grabbed the edge of the dragoon and pulled himself up. Adrian backed away as best he could to make room. Shifting himself half onto the seat, Alexander looked through the eyeglass, though truth be told the shadow had grown so close he didn't need its aid. Adrian was right. It didn't approach from any one direction. Instead, roaring dozens of feet high from horizon to horizon came a tsunami of darkness.

"Nothing we cannot handle," Alexander said, hopping down. "Stay strong and unleash hell, rider. That's an order!"

The dragoons blasted their elements into the distance, ignoring the stoneborn. The ice, stone, and lightning vanished within the shadow, while the fire broke into momentary swirls of flame. Nothing slowed it. Alexander's heart fluttered as the tsunami approached. He'd never before witnessed L'adim in person, only heard rumors of his power. Was this it? Was this overwhelming wave his true presence? So be it. The demons could bleed, and they could die. The shadowborn was no different.

The wave of darkness curled as the shore neared, and with chilling silence it slammed downward upon itself and flooded against the stone barricade, hiding the smaller demons from view. The soldiers braced themselves, but no attack came. The liquid darkness pooled and curled at the barrier, licking it, teasing it, but not passing over. The stoneborn giants were the only demons left visible, the shadow up to their chests as they lumbered onward. Dragoons focused their fire upon them, the battery steadily wearing the giants down.

What was the point of this? wondered Alexander. *To hide their retreat?*

And then a torrent of fire erupted several hundred feet away from the barricade. It moved through the shadow, the fireborn hidden within its chaotic inferno. Stormborn joined them, their lightning crackling through the fire and shadow. It seemed a cloud of hell had risen before their defenses, and within it hid all sorts of monstrosities. The shadow wasn't there to hide the demons' retreat. It was there to disguise their attack. When the fire and lightning reached the wall, the demons leapt over the barricade, assaulting the shield wall with renewed frenzy.

The dragoons resumed firing upon the stoneborn, but the creatures endured, not caring for their losses. They bent to the darkness at their feet, hands scooping. Alexander's eyes widened with horror as he realized their plan. The stoneborn giants hurtled dozens of demons through the air in a single, smooth pitch, aiming for the row of twenty dragoons behind the embattled defense line.

The demons landed and scattered in a rolling chaos. Their high-pitched laughter grated up and down Alexander's spine as they jumped up to attack. Soldiers scrambled, dragoons firing even as fireborn sank their molten teeth into their flesh and stormborn flooded their bodies with electricity. A few Seraphim broke ranks to help defend, the rest too busy holding back the tremendous tide slamming into the defensive barricade.

Alexander climbed onto Adrian's dragoon and drew his sword.

"Keep firing," the commander shouted. "I'll keep us safe!"

The dragoon's cannons sang as Alexander swung his sword, slicing a fireborn in half. Its burning blood splashed the ground beneath the dragoon, hardening in the soft white glow of the dragoon's engines. A stormborn sparked below them, zipped to the side nearest Alexander, and then leapt up at Adrian's throat. The tip of Alexander's sword greeted it, piercing through its open mouth and out its belly. The yellow corpse collapsed over the side.

"Fly higher!" he shouted to Adrian. The light beneath the dragoon beamed brighter, steadily lifting the vehicle. Another stormborn lashed at Alexander, white and gold light swirling around its reaching hands. Alexander pulled away his leg, grimacing as a claw made brief contact with his ankle. Electricity traveled all the way to his hip, firing off muscles and flooding him with pain. He returned the favor with his sword, slashing off the stormborn's jaw and then kicking the damn thing to the ground.

Another volley of demons arrived, but the Seraphim were ready, and there were fewer of the battered stone giants now to throw them. Men died by the hundreds along the barricade, but Alexander held out hope. This was the demons' last hurrah. They just needed to survive a little bit longer. His eyes searched the battlefield, a troubling question tickling his stomach. The fireborn and stormborn were racing through the liquid shadow to attack the ground troops. The stoneborn had assumed the form of giants, doing their best to besiege the dragoons behind the front lines. But what of the iceborn? Where had they gone after breaking apart and vanishing beneath the crawling darkness?

The ground shook, an earthquake thrice the power of when Y'vah's shield had collapsed. Alexander gripped the side of the dragoon, his jaw falling slack. It couldn't be. His eyes must be deceiving him.

Shadow and water rolled off the creature rising from the waters beside the tall castle cliff. Its head was the size of a cottage, its broad shoulders little blue hills. It continued to rise, higher and higher, four arms digging into the steep cliffside as it pulled itself up from the ocean. The gargantuan creature was beyond anything Alexander had ever seen. Its three-fingered hands bore enormous spikes of ice, and they slammed into the hard stone, pulling itself toward the castle. The creature had milky white eyes, no mouth, and a crown of horns formed by nine jagged spikes of frost. Long, thick icicles trailed from its head down to its waist, frosted white and shimmering like frozen hair.

"The iceborn," Alexander whispered, still in shock. "It's all of them together. Every last one."

The cliffside began to crumble under the gargantuan's weight, but it kept digging deeper, pulling itself higher as boulders crashed into the ocean below. The dragoons turned their fire toward it, needing no order to prioritize such a terrifying monstrosity. Fire, lightning, and stone struck its arms and sides, sending showers of frost flying in small white puffs. They were but bee stings, inconveniences as the iceborn climbed, and climbed, until it reached the castle and the dragoons stationed atop.

It took less than a minute for the iceborn to smash the ancient fortress to the ground. Its four arms thrashed and grabbed, walls crumbled by its strength, towers collapsed like they were made of glass instead of centuries-old stone. Alexander watched it all with newfound horror in his gut and tears threatening his eyes. The ice of the creature's face split wide, giving it a mouth with which to speak. The creature's voice thundered across the countryside like a volcanic eruption.

YOU ARE CHILDREN WITH TOYS. BREAK THEM. BREAK THEM ALL.

The entire cliff collapsed, castle and iceborn crumbling together to the ocean. The iceborn's laughter was still audible over the roar of the stone and the splash of the water.

Alexander climbed down from the dragoon, his hands shaking and his knees weak. The plan had been to retreat to the castle should the battle turn ill, but there would be no retreat. There was no castle. The gargantuan iceborn had crushed it to rubble with its mere fists. The soldiers had lost the stone barricade along the beachhead, forced to engage in scattered duels without shield brothers to rely upon. The stoneborn had stopped flinging demons and instead were throwing enormous chunks of ice and stone at the Seraphim in the sky, scattering them out of their tight formations.

No hope left. The battle was lost. Alexander reached into his pocket and pulled out a heavy gold cylinder. He twisted off the top, then pushed the bottom, connecting the light element inside to the many wires built into the cylinder. A thick beam of light focused by a series of mirrors across the top shone into the air. Alexander held the light aloft, waiting. Within moments one of the golden wings curled his way, a Seraph coming to answer his summons.

"Our forces are broken," First Seraph Kaster said, landing before the Lord Commander on one knee. "What are your orders?"

"Take me to Y'vah," Alexander said. A hard look crossed Kaster's face, one Alexander could not decipher. The Seraph dipped his arms underneath Alexander's shoulders and wrapped his hands together in a tight lock across his chest.

"As you wish, Commander."

Together they fled high above the pathetic remnants of Alexander's army. They left behind dying men who'd thrown down their arms in retreat from the demons swarming them. They left the broken remains of Alexander's dragoons, the mighty machines turned to wasted junk with massacred drivers. Stony hills and village hamlets replaced swirling shadow as they traveled. The rushing wind was a haunting tone in his ears. They flew, and flew, until arriving at a simple, elegant shrine. Nine stones formed a circle atop a hill, each side carved with golden runes facing east. In the very center, his light visible from more than a mile away, floated Alexander's only remaining hope for survival.

Y'vah hovered several feet in the air, his arms stretched toward the ground. Golden mist fluttered into the air from underneath his closed marble eyelids. A great beam of light shone from his legs, steady like a waterfall. The light struck the ground and rolled in all directions in barely visible waves for several hundred feet before rising up to form a newly summoned protective dome over the surrounding area. Eight theotechs knelt between the pillars, heads bowed in prayer, their red robes fluttering in the ethereal wind swirling around the white beam.

"Y'vah!" Alexander shouted as Kaster set him down. "Our defenses failed. We need you to resummon the wall farther inland to protect our retreat!"

The lightborn tilted his head toward him, and his eyes opened. No mouth creased his perfectly smooth face, but he spoke nonetheless, his words clear in Alexander's mind.

I cannot. I must first rest.

"Rest? How long?"

Several days.

Alexander fought against the steadily growing panic inside him. He felt it flickering, a small fire eager to burst into an inferno.

"We don't have several days," Alexander said. "I doubt we have several hours."

The time I have does not change the time I need, Alexander.

The commander's mind raced as he scrambled for a solution.

Perhaps he could order Y'vah to retreat, but he doubted the celestial being would care for an order given by a human. The only potential reinforcements were in Odeon, but it would take days for them to arrive, not that Alexander believed they'd answer a summons. They'd protect the capital, not die in fields attempting to save a desperate few who'd survived the battle at the beachhead.

"Kaster, what is your..."

Alexander stopped, stunned to see his First Seraph no longer at his side. Instead he saw him far to the east, the gold dot of his wings a shining insult of cowardice. Turning back to the west, Alexander saw the first hints of the shadow wave crashing toward them. The liquid darkness bathed the land, covering grass and tree, a demonic flood approaching their meager little shrine.

"What do we do?" Alexander asked aloud. He spun to the theotechs, maddened by their constant, steady prayers. "What do we do!"

It seemed even Y'vah would not listen. Panic continued its spread throughout his body, tightening his throat, cramping his stomach, and layering his skin with cold sweat. With a sudden quiver in Y'vah's protective dome, the shadow arrived. It surrounded them, completely covering the barrier.

It's a smaller shield, Alexander thought. *Hundreds of miles smaller than the Oceanic Wall. Maybe it will hold. Maybe Y'vah can endure.*

The shadow burst into flame. Alexander flinched despite not feeling a lick of heat. The fire rolled around them, smothering, flooding their enclosed space with crimson light. Alexander watched in awe and then terror as the first of many cracks flickered across the lightborn's barrier. How many demons were out there? Alexander could almost feel their claws ripping into his flesh. Would their teeth pierce, or would they burn? Would he die of pain before they finished eating?

"Y'vah!" Alexander screamed at the lightborn. "Get us out of here!"

There is nowhere to flee. We are surrounded, and my shield shall soon fall.

The panic burning in Alexander's veins was now a wildfire. He spun, eyes wide, the spiderwebs of cracks beginning their dance across the dome as the demons flung their bodies against it. The eight theotechs sang their prayers louder, begging for safety and absolution.

"It can't end like this," Alexander shouted. "You're God's angel! Do something!"

The lightborn tilted lower, his arm stretching out at a calm, careful pace.

I shall remember you, Y'vah said, the smallest tip of his forefinger gently brushing Alexander's face. *And as I remember you, so shall my brethren remember you.*

"Remember me?" Alexander asked. "But what of heaven? Will we not die and ascend?"

I do not know, said Y'vah. The shield vanished, and his toes touched ground. *Let us find out together.*

Liam gasped as the lightborn's finger pulled away from his forehead. It felt like she'd brushed him for a moment, but the vision, no, the *experience* he'd lived had lasted hours. The sensation of his own body was welcome, and he closed his eyes while struggling to control his breathing. So much he'd seen. The incredible might of the pre-Ascension armies, and how little it had mattered against the power of the shadowborn and his demons. The breaking of the protective dome. The death of a lightborn. But most painful was the beauty of the old world, the shorelines, the hills, the land stretching far beyond what the eye could see. All lost.

Marius's hand rested against Liam's back, the touch gentle, reassuring, like a father's.

"Now you see," Marius said. "The Ascension spared us from extinction. The dome saved us from the demons' nightly assaults. But our realms squabble while all we've ever accomplished hangs in the balance. There is no measure that goes too far. There is no risk we cannot take. Our islands must be united if we are to be victorious."

Liam rose to his feet and wiped the beginnings of tears off his face.

"I understand," he said. "No threat is greater. All must be sacrificed."

Marius lingered closer, those sapphire eyes piercing deep into him.

"Even kin," he said.

A blasphemous shiver of fear ran through Liam but he nobly banished it from his mind. He fell to one knee, lifted his hands up, and bowed his head in supplication. When he spoke, his words were steady, his heart true. Before his Speaker, and the angels of God, he made his vow.

"I swear upon our God, who is faultless and mighty," Liam said. "I swear upon the angels, who speak God's voice to the chosen. I swear upon the Speaker, who shares the angels' will with the people. My heretic children must die. Their blood will paint my swords, and their wings shall fall from the sky. So shall it be, until my final breath and the angels take me away."

A hand touched Liam's chin, lifting his head. Marius knelt before him. Pride beamed from his steady gaze.

"I know of no finer servant," the Speaker said. "So shall it be, my friend. So shall it be."

Liam returned his eyes to the floor to hide the sudden resurgence of tears.

I am the blade of the angels, he shouted inside his mind. *I am the blade of the angels. I am the blade. I am the blade. I am the blade.*

CHAPTER 2

Kael stood beside Weshern's edge, feigning calm. The midnight shadow rolled over the Endless Ocean far below while the stars speckled the nighttime canvas above. Despite the weeks since the dome collapsed, revealing the starry sky, the pale light of the moon remained strange to Kael. He'd grown up seeing red and orange hues of the midnight fire bathe Weshern outside his window. True, he'd never been too fond of it, but it had still been normal.

A bit of hope struck Kael as he waited alongside the seven other Seraphim calmly watching the two platforms loaded with barrels and crates filled with fish that grew only in Weshern's lakes. The midnight fire had been normal to him, but once this was all over, his children, and the thousands of children growing up on the other islands, would find the calm white of the moon and stars soothing. Its soft glow would be their normal. Perhaps that was the best result he could hope for as they fought their war.

"Ready to use that thing again?" Bree asked, leaving her conversation with Olivia West to join him.

Kael tapped the large shield strapped to his left arm, Weshern's blue sword vibrant against the painted black interior.

"I am," he said. "Though hopefully I won't have to tonight."

Bree smiled a half smile.

"Agreed."

Kael returned his attention to the platforms. They were hasty, ugly constructs compared to the aged elegance of those used by the ferrymen, but the ferries had ceased travels the moment the fireborn fell and the outer islands declared their war. Weshern had already begun to suffer from the sudden halt of trade, with rationing growing stricter by the day. The acres of crops burned by the fireborn assault certainly hadn't helped.

Twelve fishermen waited in a group separate from the Seraphim, six for each platform. Their words were quiet, nervous. Should a Center patrol discover their delivery of goods to Candren the fishers would be helpless in battle, fully relying on the Seraphim to protect them. Kael hardly blamed them for their nervousness.

"Ready up," Olivia said, joining Bree and Kael by the edge. "Elern's Seraphs are almost here."

Kael looked to the horizon, seeing no sign of them. Bree nudged him and pointed lower. Seven flew along the ocean surface, keeping just above the swirling black mist. There was no hiding the gold of their wings, but keeping low at least made it more difficult for patrols to spot them. Kael felt his own nerves tensing, and he grinned at Bree to alleviate them.

"See, this is why I keep you around," he said. "You have the better eyes."

Bree laughed.

"I guess I shouldn't be the Phoenix then," she said. "Just call me the Owl."

"Makes sense to me. Not quite as intimidating, though. Maybe 'Fiery Owl' or 'Burning Owl' would work better."

Bree nudged his side and shushed him. Olivia stood in the center of their group, addressing all Seraphim.

"If the night is kind, this trip will be uneventful, but we'll prepare as if it's not." Olivia gestured to the approaching Elern Seraphs. "Elern will form the far outer perimeter of our convoy, engaging any of Center's knights before they can get close to our platforms. If they do break through, our first priority is protecting the fishermen. Stone and ice wielders, use screens to stop any long-distance shots, then engage our foes hard and relentless. If they're constantly on the defensive, our fishermen will have a chance. Once our cargo is delivered, we'll switch roles for the return trip."

"What are we taking back with us?" asked Amanda, the diminutive girl lurking at the far edge of group. "If I'm allowed to ask, of course."

"Salt," Olivia answered. "Lots and lots of salt."

She broke from the group to join the fishermen. A word from her, and their small, stubby wings shimmered with light. They took up the six thick ropes tied to the sides of each platform, looping them about hooks on the front of their harnesses. The men barked orders among themselves, expertly coordinating the upward rise as if carrying the most important catch of their lives.

Kael flicked his own wings on, then swallowed down the rock that had formed in his throat. He had accompanied several messengers, even carried a royal decree to Sothren not a week back, but never a cargo delivery of such size. Between the platforms and the accompanying Seraphim, the odds of traveling unnoticed between the islands was worrisomely slim. Hopefully the one or two knights on patrol would be far too outnumbered to consider engaging in battle.

The Elern Seraphim never landed when they reached Weshern, only circled once overhead and then fanned out. Olivia led the way, her and Chernor the front point of the diamond formation surrounding the platforms. Kael and Bree took the left, hovering side by side, their speed slow enough that they were more upright than horizontal. Elern's Seraphs hovered high above and below, keeping a watchful eye for golden wings from afar.

The lumbering pace left Kael feeling like an easy target for Center's knights. Surely if spotted, the knights would have time to return to Center for reinforcements? Annoyed by his own nerves (he'd fought battles against knights, Seraphs, and fireborn after all), he did what he always did when nervous: ramble to his sister.

"Do you think we'll get to visit one of Center's royal conservatories after the war?" Kael asked as they flew. "I bet they have tons of owls there. Supposedly lions, panthers, and snakes, too. Maybe even a real phoenix."

"The closest thing to a real phoenix is a fireborn," Bree said. "And I pray I never see one of those again."

"Always the downer when it comes to these things, aren't you?"

Bree laughed. The murky shadow slowly passed beneath them.

"Fine. If we do ever visit a conservatory, I'm not interested in lions and snakes. I want to see an eagle, especially in flight. I bet we could learn a few things from it."

"Like how it's smarter to use feathers for wings instead of metal?"

"That's a start."

Elern crept closer, the white of its shimmering Beam a beacon. The soft thrum of their wings formed a steady song as the Seraphim approached. Kael looked to the west, to where no island floated, just seemingly endless waters.

"Do you think there are any animals out there?" he asked. "Land, even? Given all the other lies the theotechs told us, I doubt the Endless Ocean is truly endless as they claim."

"I don't know," Bree said. "Would the demons have let any animals live?"

It was a good question. The demons were such a mystery, and they had limited information to go on.

"You saw their hatred," Kael said. "I wouldn't be surprised if they burned everything to the ground just for the pleasure of it."

Bree didn't look satisfied.

"Then what world do they desire?" she asked. "Why wipe out humanity just to rule a barren wasteland of rock and dirt? Is there even a purpose to such an existence?"

"Maybe for them," Kael said. "I don't even know if they have a purpose beyond hating us. How would we even find out?"

"We could ask L'fae."

This only soured Kael's mood further. Johan Lumens had barred all entrance into the wrecked Crystal Cathedral, the reason supposedly to prevent any chance the island might fall. Maddeningly enough, the Archon had supported the decision, though Kael suspected his true motive was to keep on Johan's good side. Right now, the supplies and network of spies provided by the man were too important to put at risk.

"We'd need to convince Johan first," he said. "And he's not one to be easily convinced."

A shout from Olivia alerted them to the convoy's rise. They approached Elern from far below, again hoping to make it that much more difficult for a Center patrol to spot them. Kael and Bree tilted their wings up, beginning their ascension.

"Johan has no right to bar you from L'fae," Bree said, her voice dropping softer as if afraid ears lurked even in the air. "I don't like how much power he's started to wield. There's hardly a moment he's not whispering in the Archon's ear."

"One problem at a time," Kael said, sighing. "Let's just get home safely first."

Dozens of soldiers armed with spears and shields waited upon the soft grass of Elern's edge. Nervous fishermen surrounded stacks of small barrels nearby. The delivery exchange was planned at an empty field instead of a dock in the hopes that any Center patrols would be focused elsewhere. The Elern Seraphim landed and shut off their wings, and the Weshern groups did the same. All elements had to be preserved as much as possible. Center certainly wouldn't be trading them any new ones.

Kael and Bree stood by the edge, waiting as their cargo was unloaded and replaced with barrels of salt. Olivia, having spoken briefly with the leader of the Elern Seraphim, walked among the Weshern Seraphs, giving out instructions.

"Our turn for outer defense," she said. "You two will take the low point beneath the platforms. Stay just above the water, and whatever you do, do not touch the crawling darkness."

"Understood," Bree and Kael answered in unison. A fisherman had flown down on a dare a week before, dipping his hand into the murky black that washed atop the ocean. He'd returned to the surface vomiting, his hand pale and withered. Kael didn't want to imagine what would happen if he fell through with his entire body.

Olivia hesitated, a shadow passing over her pale brown eyes. "Chernor swore he saw a far-off pair of wings when we first left Weshern," she said. "We've seen no other sign since takeoff, but be wary. If a knight did spot us, they'll have had more than enough time to prepare for our return trip."

"We'll keep our eyes open," Bree said. "No matter what they try, we'll be ready."

Olivia left to join the Elern Seraphim leader beside the loading platforms.

"Looks like our return trip won't be as peaceful as we hoped," Kael said.

"We've fought them before, and we've won before," Bree said. "Nothing's changed."

"Such confidence," Kael said. "It must come with such owl-like vision."

Olivia called out a signal and the Elern fishermen backed away, their job done. Weshern's twelve fishermen took up their ropes, their wings humming back to life. Together they lifted off, and the Elern Seraphim in their white jackets and golden wings positioned themselves in a similar diamond pattern about them. Kael and Bree took their own positions far below the platforms, skimming above the hidden ocean.

The shadow must be L'adim's, Kael thought. They flew closer to the murky black than he'd ever flown before. It shifted and swirled like a heavy smoke, wisps floating off it to vanish in the air. There was a flow to the darkness. Like a river, Kael decided. A shivering thought occurred to him. Was the shadow created by L'adim, or was it L'adim himself? Did a part of the mysterious enemy of all humanity, destroyer of the entire world, creep mere feet below him? And could it reach up to pull him below its depths to drown...

Cut it out, Kael ordered to himself. Now was not the time to drift off into pointless conjecture and horror. There were real threats to keep an eye out for.

"See anything?" Kael asked his sister, grabbing a hold of a wing and pulling himself closer so she would hear.

"Nothing," she responded. "Not a single light anywhere."

Though the ocean and the darkness layered over it were several hundred feet below, Kael inched his wings higher.

"Maybe tonight we're just lucky," Kael said. Bree responded to his grin with a roll of her eyes.

"When have we ever been lucky?" she asked.

"Well, they say there's a first time for everything."

Weshern slowly grew in their sight as the caravan made its way home. Kael kept his head on a swivel. No wings. No messengers. No anything. The night was dark, quiet, and something about it didn't sit right with Kael's nerves.

"Chernor said he saw wings," he said, once again pulling closer to Bree. "But why haven't they returned?"

"Maybe they didn't belong to Center, but one of the other islands?"

It had to be. Kael refused to believe the knights of Center would be afraid to ambush any sort of potential trades. Sure, they had a significant escort, but did that really mean anything to the total might the angelic knights could bring to bear? Even a quick hit-and-run could do some damage without any losses.

"This isn't right," he whispered aloud. Bree glanced over at him, caught sight of his worry.

"This really bothers you, doesn't it?" she asked. She waved

about with her left arm. "Look. No lights. No knights anywhere. We'd see them coming, Kael. There's no midnight fire to disguise the glow of their wings. Just stars."

"I know," Kael said. "I know. But I still can't—"

An impact sent Kael into a spin, the sound of ringing metal flooding his ears. Panic threatened to overwhelm him, but he fought it down and forced his mind to react properly. A lance of ice had struck his wings. He had to protect himself. He had to move faster.

They were being ambushed.

Despite the disorienting rotation of ocean and stars, Kael jammed the throttle with his thumb. His wings thrummed to their fullest, the restraints of his harness digging into his shoulders and chest as he soared in a corkscrew. He briefly saw Bree from the corner of his eye, her wings shimmering and her swords burning brightly as she danced and dodged through the stone- and ice-filled air.

Where? wondered Kael as he lifted his shield to cover his chest, a faint shimmer of white light glowing from its silver edges. He still saw no ambushers.

Lightning flashed upward, the bolt striking from the ocean below. Kael avoided it on pure dumb luck, having started to turn just before it fired. He winced against the brightness, then spun for the source. A plume of flame roaring straight up toward him was his reward. Kael shut off his wings, braced his shield, and trusted its power. He felt a tug on his mind as the light across the shield flared just before contact with the fire. The light shone even brighter as flames washed over the shield, flickering and dying into a deep black smoke. Kael felt the heat on his skin, felt the strength of the blow on his arm, but he survived, something he highly doubted the angelic knight below him expected.

"My turn," Kael whispered as he rotated to face downward and punched his wings back to life. He could see the knight by the starlight reflecting off his golden armor, but not his wings. What should have been a vibrant gold glow against the crawling shadow was instead two vague shapes equally dark. They were muted somehow, their glow completely hidden. Kael didn't even know that was possible. The power of the light prisms always surrounded active wings, passing through layers of steel, silver, and gold with ease.

No time to think on that. Kael tracked the knight as best he could, following the shape against the black backdrop that was the ocean. The knight fled, and Kael spotted two more with him angling to drop behind Kael should he pursue. Except Kael had one more trick left.

Momentarily closing his eyes, he sensed the connection between the light prism in his gauntlet and the wings granting his flight, sensed it like Bree sensed the fire about her swords. The moment he felt it, he ignited the connection. His throttle was already pushed to maximum, the theoretical limit his wings could carry him. It didn't matter. His speed dramatically increased, his wings shining with light as if they were a newly awakened star. Gauntlet ready, Kael caught the fleeing knight in mere seconds, soaring overhead before he even sensed danger. Kael made only minimal shifts with his shoulders, glad for all his time chasing after Bree during training. Even the slightest error now would send him careening wildly. Control. It was all about control.

With such proximity and advantage, Kael didn't bother with lances. Instead he fired a single enormous stone of ice twice the size of a grown man. It slammed into the knight, crushing his black wings and flipping him head over feet toward the ocean.

Lightning and fire missed to Kael's either side, the knights greatly misjudging his distance due to his speed. Kael arched his back and rose higher to the rest of the Seraphim. A glance over his shoulder showed Bree doing the same, twin trails of fire marking her upward passage.

In but a moment the Elern Seraphim had joined them, and Kael slowed so he could turn and face their foes. Together they unleashed a barrage upon the knights who responded in kind. Stone and ice slammed against one another, bolts of lightning illuminating the battlefield alongside streams of flame. Kael stayed defensive, keeping his speed in check as he formed a wall of ice to stop a twin barrage of stone boulders. For the first time he saw how many had waited in ambush and it frightened him. Eight knights, all with disguised wings. That he and Bree were alive at all felt like a miracle.

The head-to-head collision was brutal. Several of Elern's Seraphim died, crushed by the elements. Two knights fell, one punctured by multiple ice lances, the other ripped in half by Bree's vicious twin blades. Despite knowing they were his enemy, he prayed both were dead before they touched the shadow on the water.

Their forces now intertwined with one another, Kael searched for Bree, found her chasing after a knight. He shifted his aim, reigniting his light prism to its absolute fullest. He shot through the battlefield, eyes wide, the wind tearing at his clothes and limbs. Once he neared his sister's fire trails he shifted alongside her in her chase.

I'll protect, he signed to Bree when she quickly glanced his way.

Affirmative, she signed back.

The fleeing knight was clearly skilled, using even the slightest motions to make aiming difficult as he performed a wide spiral. Bree twisted and mimicked the spiral, but tighter, straining both body and wings to perform the feat. Kael kept a dozen feet beyond her, his turn wider and easier. He didn't need to chase the knight as viciously. He just needed to keep his sister safe. His eyes locked on the two enemy knights flitting nearby, waiting for the chance to strike.

There. One broke off, abandoning the engagement with two Elern Seraphs to come to his comrade's aid. His gauntlet shimmered a faint red, the only warning Kael had of the blast of fire coming their way. Kael punched his throttle, mentally touched the prism for his wings, and then plunged ahead of Bree with his shield raised. The bolt of flame slammed his shield, a sound like thunder echoing in his ears as the attack crackled and died.

The maneuver cost him speed, and with Bree still chasing, Kael was left to face the knight solo. It wouldn't be long, he knew. The other Weshern Seraphim would join the fight in moments, but that wouldn't matter if Kael died before then.

You want me, come and get me, Kael thought as he turned away from the knight and pushed the throttle. His wings hummed, then screamed as he touched his light element with his mind. Subtle shifts of his shoulders and hips swayed him side to side, a tiny curl of his back lifting him higher. Blast after blast of fire raced through the air like burning spears before fading away with their power spent. Kael had thought the knight would turn and give chase to the cargo platforms instead of abandoning the battle, yet each fire bolt confirmed that would not be the case. Platforms be damned, the knight was coming for him.

Kael craned his neck to see his chaser steadily falling behind. Two Weshern Seraphs in the far distance followed as well, but they would never catch up unless Kael or the knight turned. Kael glanced at his wrist, felt his throat tighten. Before the battle they'd traveled dozens of miles back and forth between Weshern and Elern, and it seemed that pushing his wings far beyond their limits, coupled with the defensive abilities of his shield, had finally taken their toll. Kael could barely see the white glow of the prism.

There's still enough, he thought as he shifted his course back around for the cargo platforms, and a head-to-head battle with the knight. *I just have to reach my friends.*

His chaser never slowed, nor showed fear that Kael might be preparing a counterattack. Kael prayed that lack of fear would work in his favor. Ice gathered in his gauntlet. As the two approached one another at incredible speeds Kael swung his hand wide, forming a wall of ice that arced forward as it fell. Two quick bursts of fire struck the other side and then the knight dipped low to avoid being crushed. Kael touched his prism with his mind, craving speed beyond his wings' limits... only this time nothing happened. There wasn't enough left besides a few scraps to keep his wings powered at normal speed.

Kael looked to the reinforcements and knew he didn't have enough time. One last gamble. He shifted his path, rocketing toward the sky like a shot. If the knight wanted to kill Kael, he'd have to do it in the wide-open air, clearly exposed to the other Seraphs in the starlight.

You kill me, then you'll die, too, Kael thought. It wasn't exactly a pleasant thought, but he'd take his victories wherever he could.

The knight maneuvered around the ice wall and took up the chase. Kael grabbed his right wrist with his left hand, bracing himself as he unleashed barrage after barrage downward. He'd barely used his ice this battle but he planned on draining that prism dry. Walls, boulders, lances: he blasted every kind of attack at his pursuer. The knight abandoned retaliating, instead dodging and weaving with all his concentration. The distance between the two steadily closed, Kael's terror increasing with each passing moment.

What'd I ever do to you? he wondered as he released his ice in a wide arc in hopes of bathing the knight in thin, deadly shards. It might have worked if not for one thing: Kael's wings suddenly grew silent, their glow vanishing as the last of his prism drained dry.

Oh shit.

Kael misjudged the spray, not expecting the sudden drop in speed. The knight twirled below it, then arced straight upward. Kael braced for the killing gout of flame. Defeating a knight in battle was a difficult task even in the best conditions. Fending one off while hovering helplessly? Not a chance.

The knight drew closer. His blades remained sheathed, and before Kael even thought to draw his own, the man's hand was around his throat. Kael clutched at the man's arm, gasping against the pain as he kept them both aloft with an iron grip. He caught a brief glimpse of the knight's face through the red of his vision, felt a spark of familiarity in his dying brain.

"Is this all you are?" the knight asked, voice nearly drowned out by the hum of his wings. His hand clutched tighter around Kael's throat, choking, turning the red of his vision into yellow splotches floating over a pulsing darkness. The other hand kept a solid grip on Kael's right wrist, keeping his firing prism safely pointed away from the knight's body. Kael could feel the thin needle of the knight's firing prism pressed against his neck. All it would take was a single release of flame and he'd be dead. He waited for it, one long agonizing second after another.

The fire never came.

"The water take you," the knight said. And just like that, he let go. Kael plummeted headfirst, the wind whipping his body.

That one sentence echoed in Kael's head, the words strange, the voice not.

The water take you. The water take you.

"Keep calm," he told himself as his vision slowly started to return. He had no time to panic. The others were too far away. If he was to survive, it would be on his own. Eyes closed, Kael sensed the light prism tucked into the thick metal of his shield above the handle. There was no throttle to activate that prism, just a single on-and-off switch to remove the bulk of the weight through a slow, steady drain of the light prism. Except Kael didn't need a slow and steady drain. He needed to fly.

Kael felt a click in his mind, the connection made. Just as with his wings, he demanded it surge far beyond its limited constraints. Immediately Kael felt the shield turn weightless, and then with a painful jerk it became lighter than air, pulling against his descent, nearly ripping his right arm out of its socket. Kael screamed through clenched teeth, using the combination of pain and adrenaline to keep himself focused. His descent slowed by half, but the heavy shield was certainly no set of wings.

Not enough, Kael thought. He could feel the prism draining, its presence in his mind dwindling rapidly. Still, it might buy him the time he needed. Kael jammed the metal loop of his gauntlet atop the ringed hilt of his sword, locking them together, and then flung the sword out of its sheath. The coiled cord in his gauntlet stretched out a foot, the sword twisting in air briefly before the cord began to retract. Normally one would catch the handle to resume battling, but that wasn't what Kael needed.

Kael's fingers closed around the blade, and he screamed as the sharp edge sliced into his skin. He released immediately, telling himself whatever damage he'd done was preferable to slamming into the cold ocean waters. A glance down showed the churning shadow surface terrifyingly close.

There's still time, Kael told himself. Likely a lie, but by God he was going to believe it to keep sane. He reached for the gauntlet holding his shield above his head and yanked the compartment containing the depleted light element open. The prism slid free, and for one awful moment Kael watched it fall before his face and then fumble through his bleeding fingers. His heart frozen, he saw it tilt end over end past his chest, past his waist, down to his knee…

And then Kael shut off the element in his shield while simultaneously lunging downward. The ocean was suddenly above him, filling his vision with impending death, but the prism was close, so close, his fingers almost touching. A bloody fingertip brushed the prism, and it suddenly flashed white, the crystal sticking as if his blood were glue. Kael clutched it in his fist. His blood soaked the prism, and he felt strength flowing out of his body and into the crystal. Filling it. Recharging it.

No time to risk a glance at the ocean. Kael jammed the now-glowing element into the open compartment of his gauntlet, slammed it shut, and then powered his wings while simultaneously reactivating the prism in his shield. The wings flooded with life, giving Kael control.

Proper procedure would be to power them up gently to prevent loss of control into a death spiral. The ocean filled every bit of Kael's sight. To hell with proper procedure. His thumb pushed the throttle all the way to its maximum. Pulling his shield to his chest, he touched both prisms in his mind, demanding they flood his ancient technology with power. The straps of his harness dug into his skin, and Kael shrieked as his lower back strained with agony from his body pulling out of the dive. The entire world rotated, the ocean and the layer of shadow above him, before him, and then with a glorious blast of wind and spray of salt water across his legs, below him as he soared back into the air.

"The ocean take you?" he shouted, pumping a fist to the air. "Not fucking today!"

The reinforcements closed in, but there was no one to battle. Kael twisted in search of the knight. Faint golden wings in the distance flew to Center. Kael watched, the man's voice repeating in his head. It was familiar, so hauntingly familiar, but it couldn't be. It wasn't possible.

It must be coincidence he spoke with his father's voice.

Kael's adrenaline faded, and he breathed in and out with a rasp from his swollen throat. He touched it with his fingers, winced at the tenderness. That was going to leave one hell of a bruise. Bree raced ahead of the others, and Kael slowed his speed to a hover for her arrival. She practically collided with him in midair as she wrapped her arms around him in a vise grip.

"I was so sure, Kael," she said, fighting back a sob. "I was so sure I was watching you die."

Kael pulled away from her and he gave her his best grin, given the circumstances.

"Give me some credit, sis," he said, his words cracking. "You're not the only one capable of pulling off miracles."

Bree laughed despite her tears.

"Follow me," she said. "A medic needs to look over your wounds."

Kael didn't have the energy to argue. Exhaustion and pain quickly replaced the exhilaration of battle and the terror of the long, long plummet. As the two carried him toward Weshern, and presumably safety, Kael craned his neck for one last look at the vanishing knight who had dropped him to his death.

Or maybe not death, he wondered. The knight could have executed him with a single swing of his sword or burst of fire from his gauntlet. Instead he had let go, for Kael to fall. For him to survive.

It's not him, Kael told himself as Weshern steadily approached in the calm starlight. *Stop kidding yourself, Kael. It can't be. It can't.*

Not once did he completely believe his own words.

CHAPTER 3

I'm fine," Kael said as he lay in the tiny bunk, his shirt beside his bed, a loop of bandages encircling his chest.

"Your purple neck says otherwise," Bree said, hovering at the foot of his bunk in the small tent. They were in one of the temporary camps housing both soldiers and Seraphim set up across Weshern. In the days following the fireborn's fall, and Center's removal from Weshern grounds, Rebecca Waller had organized their placements and set up a chain of supplies throughout, the camps forming a loose perimeter along the outer ring of the island. The goal was to be able to respond quickly to an attack no matter the direction it came from, but the added benefit was that after a patrol or skirmish, the flight back to safety was always a short one.

"Only a little sore," Kael said, and the left side of his face curled up in a grin. "Don't worry. It'll be a day or two at most before I'm out there getting myself killed alongside you."

Bree was still not convinced. Kael's grin had vanished the moment he stopped talking, and she knew her brother too well to think it was because of the pain. Something bothered him. Telling herself it was only because of his close brush with death, she patted his leg and headed for the tent's open flap.

"At least try to rest for a little bit," she said. "Oh, and I'll let Clara know where you are. I'm sure some snuggle time would do wonders for your health."

Kael flung his shirt at her. It thudded against the tent flap as she closed it behind her. Bree thought Clara would be with the other Seraphim relaxing around a small bonfire in the middle of the street, but she was not. A few larger tents were to either side of her, also propped up in the center of the road, but they were filled with rows of bunks for sleeping. It didn't feel right that Clara would turn in for the night so quickly, especially not without seeing Kael first. The only place left to look was the home nearby that had been claimed by the royal family to be used as an armory. Bree ducked inside, saw the walls and tables filled with shields, spears, and a few precious sets of wings, including Bree's. Noticeably absent was Clara's set.

I guess she went home, Bree decided. Not a bad idea, and she wished she could return to her bed at Aunt Bethy's, but if everyone else had to sleep on uncomfortable cots in their stationed camps, she was certainly no different. Bree walked to the large northern tent, the appointed women's tent, but was stopped halfway there by a Seraph landing from the sky.

"Breanna?" the man asked, squinting in the dim blue light.

"Yes?" she asked.

"Your presence is requested at the holy mansion."

"Are you to carry me?" she asked.

"You're to fly," the Seraph answered. "Now make haste."

Bree kept her face passive despite her concern. By the sound of it, either Rebecca, Argus, or the Archon wished to speak with her at the mansion. For what reason? And more important, with crystals so scarce, why would they require she have her wings with her?

Bree returned to the armory and donned her black jacket and silver wings. The light element within the left gauntlet had been removed, and she grabbed a replacement before heading outside. The Seraph nodded to her, then began walking toward the bonfire when she powered on her wings.

"Are you not coming with me?" she asked.

"Others here are also invited," he said. "Go on ahead. You know the way."

Bree's worry only grew. Why the urgency? Why the vague orders?

"Yes, sir," she said, softly lifting into the air. Once above the roofline she rapidly increased the throttle until she was soaring toward the holy mansion in the heart of Weshern. Her imagination bounced between a dozen reasons why she could have been summoned. Likely her every guess would be wrong, and she was worried over nothing. For all she knew, Rebecca Waller had cooked up another publicity stunt for her to perform. Keeping the Weshern people's morale high seemed more important to Rebecca than the actual war itself.

Bree landed at the outer gate surrounding the mansion, knowing that flying any closer would risk inviting an arrow from the archers posted throughout the building's many barred windows. The gate itself was twisted and broken from the assault to save the royal family from their prison. Two soldiers with spears and shields guarded it nonetheless.

"Welcome, Phoenix," said one as they made way for her passage. "You're expected."

Bree smiled politely at them as she passed. She didn't know

their names but she recognized their faces. Ever since the fireborn's descent, she and her brother had become regular visitors to the holy mansion. Bree crossed the walkway, walked up the steps, and met the waiting servant at the mangled front doors.

"Follow me, please," said the smartly dressed man. They traveled down empty halls, the damage from the attack still evident. Shadowed squares marked removed paintings, too damaged to repair. Curtains were burned, walls knocked in from stone and ice boulders, and everywhere it seemed there was a stain of blood. The servant walked straight ahead of her, back stiff, arms behind him. No small talk. Bree wished he'd at least try. They weaved through the halls in silence, ending at the enormous dance hall.

The great hall no longer held extravagant parties with dancers floating above one another on golden discs raised to the ceiling. Bree felt a stab of sorrow seeing those discs. A lifetime ago, she and Dean had danced above all others on one such platform, a magical night she wished she might return to every time she lay down her head to sleep. Back then she'd viewed the great field of stars powered by light prisms to be one of the most beautiful things she'd ever witnessed. Those light prisms were gone, delivered to the war effort, but their loss didn't sting like it should have. Those stars were no longer a historical echo of the past. Now the true stars shone their beauty every night, the lone joy brought about by all the ugliness, war, and death.

Instead of dances and feasts, the hall was now Rebecca Waller's permanent home, and had been so since the Archon named her head of defense after all her work building up the resistance. The tables were covered with maps, charts, and lists of supplies attached to the various encampments. Rebecca sat with Argus Summers and Avila Willer at a smaller, circular table. The Archon's wife had slowly taken on more duties as her husband focused on maintaining public appearances while recovering from his many injuries.

Just a normal meeting, Bree told herself as she slowly breathed out her nerves. *Nothing to worry about.* She joined the table, the echoes of her footsteps disturbingly loud in the quiet.

"Thank you for coming, Bree," Rebecca said. Her hands were crossed in her lap instead of holding a pencil or pad. Not a good sign.

"Indeed," Argus said, fidgeting in his chair. His face was a mess of bruises, and a long scar cut across his forehead to the back of the skull, pale and white and disrupting the neatly cut trim of his hair. So far as Bree knew, he'd recovered from his injuries inflicted during his capture and imprisonment, but the legendary Seraph was yet to return to battle.

"While Center's obvious lies and abandonment should have drawn the remaining islands into war, the situation has not proved that simple," Avila said. "None of the other islands have suffered as we have, nor have invading boots marched across their streets. Some have hedged their bets, acting cautiously instead of pledging their support outright. The most troublesome one has been the Dayans, the rulers of Candren."

"Are they afraid of Center?" Bree asked.

"Not afraid. I think all of us in power have moved past that. The trouble with Candren is that despite their willingness to resist Center's control, they want to do it alone instead of in a cohesive alliance with all four islands."

"We were at war with them when Galen fell," Argus said, cutting to the point. "And that war has not officially ended. That's what we're here to accomplish. We're sending a delegation to formally declare peace, opening the door to an alliance against Center. However, there's some significant distrust toward us from their populace, and we're worried things might turn sour."

It made a little bit of sense, though it still troubled Bree. Were there really so many people out there willing to turn a blind eye to all of Center's crimes just to be spiteful toward Weshern for what amounted to a handful of battles in the sky?

"How do I fit into this?" Bree asked, glancing between the three. "Am I to protect a delegation while there?"

"In a way," Avila said. She leaned back in her chair, hands folded over her dark blue dress. "You will actually be an integral part of that delegation, Breanna."

Bree blinked a few times, tried to get her brain to function.

"I can't," she said.

"You can," Argus said.

"No, it's... I'm not any good with this sort of thing. You can't have this pressure on me. I'll botch the whole thing, and then what? We lose out on a potential ally?"

"Calm down," Rebecca said, her scolding tone like that of an annoyed schoolteacher. "Your responsibilities are minimal. Archon Dayan personally requested you make a visit to the island. You'll greet a few crowds, have an audience with the Archon, and overall be there to help nudge the public's opinion. We need them to see us as friends and the theotechs as their true enemy."

It sounded like a thoroughly miserable time to Bree. Yet again she'd be propped up and paraded about like a trophy. Instead of flying across the sky with her burning blades she'd be in tedious meetings and dinnertime discussions, perhaps even a literal parade through the streets. *Look at the Phoenix, Mommy,* thought Bree. *Isn't she scary?*

"I have no choice in this matter, do I?" Bree asked.

"No, you don't," Argus said, rising to his feet. "Consider it an order from your commander, and be annoyed with me if it will help you cope."

Bree clipped her heels together as she stood straight and saluted her fist against her breast.

"Yes, sir," she said. "When do we leave?"

"Right now, actually," a voice called behind her. Bree turned to see Chernor Windborn enter the room. He was dressed in his Seraphim uniform, his wings and harness strapped to his giant frame. His enormous maul hung loosely in his left hand. The Seraph nodded his respects to Avila, then looked to Argus.

"I assume she's heard the whole spiel?" he asked.

"More or less," Argus said.

"Good. We're moving out when the sun starts to rise. We don't have the midnight fire to hide our wings anymore but the first sharp rays of sunshine might do the trick. I expect you to be on your best behavior, Bree, and follow orders to the letter. Argus has put me in charge of your ass while we're on Candren, so don't make me regret the decision."

"You're not coming with?" Bree asked the commander.

"I am," Argus said, pushing in his chair. "But I'll be discussing strategy and doing my own meet-and-greet among their Seraphim. I can't afford to keep an eye on you while we're there. Try not to be shocked, Bree. You're not the only one with a reputation here on Weshern."

He smiled at her to show he wasn't truly serious, and Bree smiled back, glad for anything to help ease her nerves.

"Perhaps," she said. "But I'm the only one with a *good* reputation."

"Smart-ass newbies," Argus said, and he shared a grim shake of the head with Chernor. "Always quick to dismiss those who actually know what the hell they're doing."

"Don't worry about it, Argus old buddy," Chernor said, smacking him hard on his uninjured side. "Reality's usually quick to slap them around a few times to show them what's what. And if reality won't, my maul will."

Together Chernor, Argus, and Bree traveled down the hallway, though not to leave the premises, she noticed. They were heading toward the walled-off garden built into the very heart of the mansion. No meeting up at a dock, then. Perhaps they feared potential spies. Given their ambush on the return trip home, it was certainly a possibility.

A pair of glass doors blocked the entrance to the garden, and even before they opened, Bree recognized the blurry silhouette of her brother. Clara stood beside him, the two wearing silver pairs of wings. Kael's giant shield rested in the grass beside him, the bottom digging a half inch into the dirt. Saul lingered nearby, and though he looked tired she was surprised at how eager he seemed. Several other members of Wolf Squad chatted with one another separate from the three, and they fiddled with their wings or checked the straps to their harnesses for a third or fourth time.

"Finally she appears," Kael said when he heard the door open. "Looks like I won't have much chance to rest, will I?"

"They not give you a choice in the matter, either?" Bree asked him as she joined his side.

"A direct order from Argus," Kael said. "So no, not really."

"You're there to be a backup Skyborn in case the first one disappoints," Saul said, and he winked at Bree. She punched his arm.

"Dick."

Bree's attention stole toward the stone path winding off through the painstakingly organized collections of flowers. Argus's wings were waiting on a bench, and the man slowly took them into his arms. He paused, a fleeting look of hesitation passing over his face, and then his hands were a blur. In a flash the buckles were secure, the gauntlet cinched tight, and the wings shimmering a soft silver as he tested his equipment. Bree saw an immediate change in him, a relaxed confidence he'd not had since his capture. Argus was at home in the skies, no different from Bree.

"Do you think he's nervous?" Kael asked when he realized where she looked. His voice dropped low to avoid being overheard. "I heard he was tortured pretty badly before the Speaker tried to drop him in a well."

"No," Bree said, remembering that fleeting look. "Not nervous. I think he's relieved."

A black square hovered over the mansion rooftop, six fishermen carrying another platform. Bree frowned, confused.

"Who's the platform for?" she asked as it settled to the ground.

"We aren't traveling alone," Clara said. "This is a formal declaration of peace. We'll have a few lords with us, as well as myself to act in my father's stead. Plus, Rebecca's coming to be the master of this parade."

A worried look crossed her brother's face. They'd just been ambushed accompanying a platform traveling to nearby Elern. There was no guarantee a similar fate didn't await them on their way to Candren.

"We'll be fine," Bree promised. It offered about as much comfort as she expected.

"Sure we will," he said, clearly not believing a word of it.

The door to the garden reopened, and seven men and women exited in an unsteady trickle. Their clothes were immaculate, steel cuffs and black buckles for the men, silver trim for the women in their blue dresses. Despite their importance, Bree recognized none of them. These were the landowners, the maker of laws, the controller of trade and tax, and Bree couldn't name a one. Just another reason she was painfully unfit for any sort of role in the peace negotiations.

But perhaps it didn't matter. She wasn't there to argue or inform, only to look pretty as she let the people of Candren gawk at her and her burning blades.

Rebecca was the last to arrive, three folders tucked underneath her left arm and a single long pencil held in her right hand. She tapped the pencil against her leg with speed rivaling the wings of a bird, and Bree wondered if the woman even realized she carried it.

"It's time we leave," she announced to the gathered crowd. "Best we not keep Candren waiting."

Argus ordered everyone into a single formation of nine, with him at the lead and Bree at his side. The nobles piled onto the platform, looking awkward and uncomfortable with how close they stood to one another. Rebecca remained at the side of the platform holding one of the protective ropes. She looked almost bored.

The fishermen raised the platform into the air on the count of three. It rocked unsteadily for a moment, then smoothed out as they coordinated their lift. Bree admired how quickly they'd taken to the work. Their previous cargos were nets full of fish, and it wasn't like they had needed to worry about jostling the occupants flying back to land.

A single twirl of Argus's finger and the formation lifted, flying much higher above the platform. Bree wondered why they flew with such a small escort as they slowly drifted to the northwest. Surely their passengers were more worthy of protection than the two platforms full of salt they'd escorted earlier.

She needn't have worried. Rebecca had mentioned not

keeping Candren waiting, and she understood what the woman meant as they neared Weshern's edge. Forty Candren Seraphs hovered in six scattered formations, the rising sunlight reflecting off their yellow jackets. They looked like an impatient swarm of hornets, Bree decided. Not exactly a pleasant sight.

"Don't be so nervous," Kael said as they approached the island home of their former enemy.

"Who said I was nervous?" she asked.

"I was talking to myself."

The ocean steadily passed beneath them as Candren neared. The only excitement came from two knights who flew nearby and quickly retreated. Bree knew they were too close to Candren for any reinforcements to arrive, particularly in numbers high enough to challenge such a strong escort. That fact only mildly calmed her nerves.

They did not land at the docks, nor anywhere near the edge. Bree kept an eye on the ground beneath them, taking in what she could of Candren. It lacked the plentiful rivers and waterfalls of Weshern, but in that drier landscape she noticed vegetation she'd only previously seen in books. Tall cliffs lined with pale yellow vines. Valleys filled with mushrooms growing in the shade of curled trees with wide, flat leaves. What Bree would give for a chance to wander among its wilderness. Only the scars of ash from the fireborn ruined the splendor.

Their capital steadily neared. The sprawling city was built upon all levels of an extremely steep hill, one long road curling around and around its circumference. Tightly packed houses littered the way, many carved into the earth itself. Long rope ladders hung from short wood planks, offering a shortcut to the next circular revolution of road above or below.

At the bottom of the hill was a structure both familiar and

yet not. It looked akin to the Crystal Cathedral, but instead of painted glass it was built from the dark clay of Candren's land. They flew too high for her to get a proper look at it, but she made sure to note its location in her mind.

Last was Candren's holy mansion and seat of power, built upon the very top of the capitol hill. The Candren Seraphim led the platform of diplomats toward a clearing upon its eastern end. Soldiers waited in long lines stretching from a set of well-lit doors. Bree landed among the rest of their Seraphim, quickly falling to one knee out of respect for the waiting Archon Evereth Dayan and his wife, Lucia.

The Archon was a hard-looking man, his jaw and forehead square, his hair and beard neatly trimmed. His wife appeared the exact opposite, all soft lines and curved features highlighted by twin braids of blond hair trailing down her neck and chest. They both wore sharp black suits, Evereth with a bright yellow tie, Lucia with ribbons of gold throughout her hair, neck, and waist.

"Welcome to my home, people of Weshern," Candren's Archon said with a smile. "Release your weapons. Calm your nerves. You come as enemies, but I pray you leave as friends."

CHAPTER 4

The dining table made the one in the holy mansion seem small by comparison. It wound through the grand room in two slow curls, forming a gigantic S. Golden cloth covered its every inch. The wood of the eighty or so chairs was stained exceptionally dark, and the cloth covering their cushions was solid black. Chandeliers hung from long golden chains, their interconnected circles of gold and crystal holding dozens of candles. Real candles, not the false ones the Willers had used. The walls had six gigantic paintings that flowed from one into the other. Candren Seraphim flew over a peaceful spring valley that slowly became an orange and red harvest season, which then melded into a snow-covered wilderness. Above the frost-tinted trees the Candren Seraphim warred in the skies against an invading Sothren army. Corpses littered the ground in the melting spring snow, only to loop back around to the peaceful valley, protected by the ever-present Seraphim.

"Really puts you in the eating mood," Kael whispered to his sister. He needn't have bothered to keep his voice down. By his best guess there were eighty people seated at the table and many more servants hustled about, carrying trays of food and baskets of wine bottles.

"You're right," Bree said. "The demons on the ceiling of our holy mansion are much more suitable for a feast."

"Fair enough."

Kael and Bree were seated near the upper half of the S, at an awkward distance from the Archon so they'd need to speak just shy of shouting to be heard over the hum of conversation. Kael felt a hint of jealousy toward Clara seated opposite him. Of course she'd look calm and relaxed while eating and conversing with the two Candren lords on either side of her. The lady to her left was absolutely fascinated by Clara's story of her parents' rescue and the battle that followed in the streets against the fireborn giant.

"It can't possibly be as big as that," insisted the balding man to Clara's right. His gray mustache looked about as puffy as his attitude.

"It was," Clara insisted. "I watched it throw house walls made of solid stone. At one point it tore up the road itself as if it were a simple carpet."

"But how could a fireborn become so big?" asked Lady Clairmont, if Kael remembered the name correctly from their brief introduction. "Do they grow over time? Or did it perhaps eat more than the others? Though of course that begs the question, do the demons even eat?"

"And *what* do they eat?" Mustache Lord added.

Clara smiled pleasantly enough.

"I'm not sure what or if they eat, but we did see how the giant fireborn was created, didn't we, Kael?"

Kael felt a cold slap across his face as he realized he was being dragged into the conversation.

"Not exactly the happiest of memories," he said, bothered by how both the husband and wife appeared so amused. Likely they'd spent that harrowing night safely hidden inside their giant mansion, personal guards protecting their lives and possessions. If they'd walked amid the burning towns, heard the screams of the dying, perhaps they'd not view the fireborn giant as a theoretical fascination.

"Of course not," Lord Clairmont said, and he twirled his fork in his fingers. "Little of that night was a joyful affair. But the horror of the past is now in the past, and we may continue ever stronger into the future."

Another little prick against his skin. The past was the past? Perhaps there was something Kael could do to at least dampen a bit of their excitement.

"Except it's not the past," he said. "The threat is real, Lord and Lady Clairmont, and very much here. The protective dome around us is gone, and after all these centuries the demons can finally reach us. How many of the fireborn wait to attack again, this time with stormborn and iceborn at their sides?"

Both looked greatly upset by his outburst. Lady Clairmont took a long drink from her glass and then addressed the man beside her as if she just noticed he was there. Mustache Lord's face reddened as he frowned deeply at Kael.

"He's still upset about all the trauma he witnessed," Clara said, smoothly gliding into the conversation to pull it away from Kael's prophetical warning. Only her sideways glare revealed her true feelings. "I don't blame him, either. That fireborn giant was birthed from dozens of the creatures melding together with the bones of the innocent. It was terrible to witness, and I pray that the angels are kind to me so I never see such a monster again."

Mustache Lord accepted the pseudo-apology and quickly switched topics. Now thankfully ignored, Kael decided it was a fine time to eat something of the extravagant feast laid out before him. Bored and annoyed as he was, the least he could do was enjoy foods he might never taste again. He sucked on little berries with juice so dark and purple it was almost black. The sweetness awoke a bit more of his hunger. Next was a flat cake with some sort of cream baked into a glaze. One small bite led to him wolfing down the rest. Was this how the wealthy ate every day? Kael decided he should visit Clara more often, particularly during mealtime.

The conversation dulled around them. Kael glanced up to see the grim-faced Archon Dayan risen from his chair, a wineglass in his left hand, the knuckles of his right steadily knocking against the table. He had begun lecturing those nearest him, and all down the table others strained their ears to hear. With each practiced word, Kael felt more certain this seemingly impromptu speech had actually been carefully rehearsed.

"Not since the rise of the ocean waters have we ever faced such a threat," the Archon said. "But together we faced it nobly and cast those demons back to the hell they escaped from. The stars are free. The crawling shadow no longer burns. Let us turn our focus from the past to the future of our people. *All* our people, of all islands, from the eldest of men to the children yet to be born. Center has held us in a stranglehold for too long. They whispered lies in our ears and left us to die when those lies fell from the skies like fire. Our squabbles between us must end. We battled like dogs over the scraps the theotechs gave us to survive. No longer. Let us turn on our abusive master and with our fangs tear free the key to a better, more prosperous life."

Scattered applause and stomping feet soon grew into a

standing ovation from the entire room. Rehearsed or not, Kael agreed with the need for a united front, but he disagreed that Center was their only enemy. The shadowborn lurked somewhere in the hidden spaces of their islands. The other troubling thing was how similar it sounded to Johan's speeches. Did the man whisper in the ears of Candren's Archon as well?

Archon Dayan barely reacted to the applause. Instead he took a sip from his glass, nodded to the others around him, and then slid back into his seat. It was as if he fully expected the applause.

"Truly we are blessed with the greatest Archon of all the islands," Lady Clairmont said. She was practically beaming with pride.

"I respectfully disagree," Clara said, "but our Archon is my father, so I must admit I am biased in the matter."

The two laughed politely. Kael took a bite from a buttered roll and wished they could be eating alone, just him, Clara, and Bree. Nothing in the world was so terrible as forced small talk.

To Kael's right sat a heavyset man, his belt strained by the stomach it tried to keep in. Unlike the Clairmonts, he hadn't introduced himself when he sat down, and for the most part he had kept to himself. The man took Kael's awkward silence as an opportunity to jab Kael's side with his elbow.

"It was a nice speech, wouldn't you say?" he asked, an eyebrow raised. His face was as round as the moon and featured an equal number of blemishes and craters.

"Yes, it was," Kael said, figuring politeness was his ticket to survival.

The man wiped at his mouth with his cloth, his green eyes locked on to Kael's.

"Of course it's easy to say things like that now, after Weshern proved such resistance is possible by defeating Center's initial invasion."

That was about the last thing Kael expected, and he nervously glanced about to see if any others had overheard.

"We've just tried to do our best," he said, unsure where this was going.

"Of course, of course." The man leaned closer, his voice still deep and pleasant but his eyes hardening. "But we both know that Weshern is not the reason our islands are preparing for conflict. Another's been prophesying this war for years."

Kael sipped his chilled water, trying to wet his suddenly parched tongue. Johan had always insisted he had people in every corner of every island, but some part of Kael had never let that sink in; it was easy to forget Johan's influence extended beyond the boundaries of Weshern.

"Another has indeed," Kael said, not wanting to be the first to say his name. "Do you know him well?"

"I've spoken with Johan on many occasions. He's even told me about you, Kael Skyborn." The man offered his hand, and Kael reluctantly shook it. "My name's Bartley Harran. I'm Candren's master of trade."

"Pleased to meet you," Kael said, his voice conveying quite the opposite.

"And I am quite pleased to meet you," Bartley said. "I've heard you were one of the biggest reasons Johan's movement was able to unite with the royal family."

Not exactly how Kael remembered it. He'd been little more than a go-between, perhaps a glorified messenger at best.

"Whatever aids Weshern," he said, not wishing to discuss it.

"And a strong alliance with Johan aids us all, Weshern included."

There was a twinge of fanaticism to his every word. Kael wished he could somehow trade seats and escape the conversation.

"Right now I'd rather focus on our newly built relationship here," he said. "A unified Weshern and Candren is a powerful thing."

"Powerfully irrelevant," Bartley said. "This meeting here is all show and little meaning."

"A formal alliance between Candren and Weshern means plenty," Kael argued. "We're stronger together. Elern should quickly follow after Candren joins us and Sothren. Center will almost certainly barter for peace once we are united."

"But why should we barter for peace?" Bartley asked. "Peace isn't what we need. Alliances mean nothing if we return to the old status quo, quarreling for power among ourselves while Center's chains hold us like puppets. Truth be told, I wouldn't mind if all four minor islands stopped pretending at being separate nations and instead formed an alliance ruled by a governing council of our Archons. We must sacrifice everything, perhaps our very sense of identity, to ensure we bring Center to her knees."

"But what of the fireborn?" Kael asked. "Should we not prepare for another attack?"

Bartley smirked.

"I'm sure Marius would love us to focus on licking our wounds and burying our dead. In some ways you could say the fireborn helped him. We're weak and we're scared. The Speaker's likely hoping we don't notice how badly Center suffered that night. No, we should act now, Kael. Opportunity is before us, just as Johan has predicted. Center and her theotechs are our one true enemy."

Anger pulled him from his seat. His hands slammed the table in frustration.

"You're wrong," Kael said, voice so loud he surprised himself. "Center is not the only threat, nor the greater one. Fire demons fell from the sky. Why the hell does everyone think that's the last we'll see of them?"

Those seated nearby quieted, and Kael caught an embarrassed look on Clara's face.

"Sit down, Kael," Bree whispered beside him.

"Mr. Skyborn," Evereth said. His cold tone jammed an icicle into Kael's heart. "Is there something you'd like to share with the rest of us?"

"No," he said. "Though I would like to make a request of you, Archon, while I still have your attention."

"Please, ask, and I shall do my best as host to accommodate."

If the people of Candren were to believe him, he'd need proof, substantial proof. The threat of Center was very real while L'adim was a bedtime story, or at best, a cautionary lesson mentioned in theotech sermons. To obtain such proof, Kael could think of only one location.

"I'd like entrance into Candren's holy cathedral," he said.

"Why is that?"

His throat was cracked stone. Kael could barely swallow before he spoke.

"To visit with the angel inside."

Silence thundered around him. A few looked astonished at the very idea. Others stared at him as if he were insane. The worst was the soft, barely hidden laughter of many.

"The angel," Evereth said, his voice surprisingly even. "You believe the theotechs have an angel here in their Clay Cathedral? I'm sorry, Mr. Skyborn, but I believe you've taken the teachings of the theotechs far too literally. God and his angels lifted us up from the Endless Ocean, yes, but they did so through the technology he gifted to us. The stories of a legion of angels pulling the earth heavenward with silver chains is a beautiful but fanciful retelling."

More snickering set Kael's blood to boil. This was it, he realized. This was what L'fae had asked of him. God help him, he was really going to do it, and on Candren of all places.

"I don't just believe it," Kael said. "I know it. I've spoken with the angel L'fae in the heart of Weshern, and through her I witnessed our Ascension as we fled the forces of L'adim."

Again the room was shocked into silence.

"L'adim?" asked the man seated on the Archon's right, his advisor, if Kael remembered correctly. "Who is L'adim?"

"The shadowborn," Kael said. "The true enemy we face. We should not war among ourselves, perhaps not even with Center. We should make peace before the true threat arrives. Already he has struck against us, slaying the angel within Galen to bring the island crashing down. He destroyed the dome protecting us from his forces. The fireborn are his servants, and we are yet to face the iceborn, the stormborn, and the stoneborn. Killing each other only weakens us for the shadowborn's final assault."

His neck was flushed red, and he felt its heat upon his cheeks. All eyes were on him now, the people listening to the stark ravings of a lunatic. What could they possibly think of him? Jealous of his more famous sister, perhaps? Even Archon Dayan looked baffled as to how to reply, but try he did to respectfully address the Phoenix's brother.

"The theotechs are still in control of the Beam," he said. "They have pledged to remain neutral in the conflict between us and Center so long as we leave them be. I will... ask them about your theories, and see if they are comfortable in letting you beneath the Clay Cathedral to search for your 'angel.'"

The Archon's dismissal stank on every word. Kael slumped to his seat, avoiding all eye contact.

“Thank you,” he said.

“No, thank you,” Evereth said. “Every day we must challenge our preconceptions or the world remains the same, forever and on.”

Bartley shuffled beside Kael, cleared his throat.

“Peace with one enemy to fight another that does not exist,” he said. “A shame, Kael. I thought you one of the more levelheaded ones at this table.”

Kael stood, his neck flushing red.

“I’m sorry, I don’t feel well,” he said, addressing no one in particular. He caught Clara’s pitying look and Bree’s smoldering frustration. But it wasn’t their eyes he felt on his back as he fled to his room, but those of dozens of others snickering as he passed, his name whispered as the punch line for a terribly unfunny joke.

CHAPTER 5

Liam stood before Speaker Marius and his right hand Er'el, the icily calm Jaina Cenborn. The three were alone inside Marius's royal cathedral hall, their voices casting long echoes. Liam kept his arms crossed behind his back and his spine rigid. His military experience locked his face into a calm, confident mask. Everything was meant to convey complete control over his emotions, a mastery of body and mind. Anything at all to help achieve the lie.

"You had Kael in your hands," Marius asked. It was the first thing he'd said since Liam began detailing the battle against the Weshern and Sothren Seraphim. "Yet you let him go?"

"I did no such thing," Liam said. "His prism was depleted and no rescuers were close enough to reach him before he hit the water."

"Yet he survived," Marius said. His voice was soft, his tone inquisitive. Liam believed none of it. "Why kill him with a fall instead of your fire or sword?"

Liam straightened further, if that was even possible. He met the Speaker's gaze without flinching, all the better to sell the lie.

"Because Kael is a heretic and a disgrace to my legacy. I did not wish him to die a warrior's death. He deserved to drown—the fate of an incompetent fisherman."

Marius glanced at Jaina. Her own face was as carefully disguised as Liam's.

"A fitting, if unnecessary, decision," Jaina said. "But your task was to eliminate the Skyborn children. We did not request anything beyond that."

"My apologies," he said. "If I'd have known somehow Kael would survive—"

"You'd have done it anyway," Marius interrupted. "Wouldn't you have?"

That was it. The truth behind the lie. Liam debated continuing the charade, to deny it as forcefully as possible, but what was the point? The Speaker for the Angels carried their blessing. His ears were gifted with God's wisdom, and no lie would ever escape their detection.

Liam dropped to one knee, hands flat against the crimson carpet. He kept his eyes low, refusing to meet the Speaker's gaze.

"Yes," he said, barely above a whisper. "I fear I would have."

He heard the Speaker walk around his lectern and descend the five steps to the walkway.

"And why is that, Liam?"

Liam lowered his head farther. Heat flushed up his neck, and he felt his insides tremble.

"It was the shock of it," he said. "I swear, that is all. I have not seen my children in years. To be face-to-face with Kael and see who he has grown up to become was enough to stir my compassion."

"And so you let him live."

Anger surged through him, whether at himself or the Speaker, Liam wasn't sure.

"I dropped him to die," he said, rising back to his feet. That anger gave him the strength to meet Marius's eye. "I could not bear to witness his death, so I let the ocean have him. It was still to be his death, Speaker. That moment of weakness was never meant to compromise the task given to me. I saw the panic in his eyes. His element was dry. How was it his wings suddenly gained new life?"

The two shared another look, one that confused Liam greatly. If it were so simple as an extra light element secreted somewhere, this wouldn't be a question of any significance. Yet clearly it was.

"You know of your daughter's blood," Marius said. "And how she wields the flame in a most unnatural way?"

Liam nodded. Of course he knew. The whispers and rumors were everywhere on Center.

"Your son appears to share a similar power," Jaina said. "His entrance tests for the Academy showed him to be of light affinity. Just as his sister uses her blood to control flame, Kael used his own to power his prism before he struck the ocean waters."

"Power," Liam said, dumbfounded. "And how do they possess such a power?"

Marius put a hand on Liam's shoulder.

"They rebel against everything sacred," his Speaker said. "And with the dome's collapse, the shadowborn rises. There is no elegant way to put this, Liam. Your children are powered by the blood of demons."

Even his experience and training weren't enough to keep the shock and horror off Liam's face.

"I . . . do not know what to say."

"Then simply listen," Marius said. "There is a reason I brought you before the angels. There is a reason I let their light shine upon you as you witnessed the destruction that befell our world before the Ascension. Your will must be strong. Your heart must be stronger. When I said your role was vital, I did not lie, nor did I exaggerate. Your children are to somehow play a key part in the shadowborn's plans, and no matter the cost, they must be stopped."

Liam bowed his head low, and stubborn tears spilled free of his eyes. For the first time he truly understood how great the task granted to him, and the utmost faith the Speaker had in both his mind and heart.

"Forgive me," he said. "I was ignorant of the true threat my children represent. I will fare better our next confrontation."

"I believe you will," Marius said, and he smiled. "And do not think this is a total loss. Kael has now seen your face, has he not?"

"I believe so."

"Then the doubt and confusion will begin. We are not without gains made, even if more should have been accomplished."

Jaina reached into the neck of her robe and pulled out a gold key on a thin silver chain.

"And so we have the truth at last," she said to Marius. "Shall we proceed to the armory?"

Marius smiled at Liam and released his shoulder.

"Yes," he said. "It is time."

The three exited the royal cathedral through a side door, Jaina leading the way. Beyond it was a much smaller room stationed with two knights to protect the Speaker on his throne should the need ever arise. The two saluted, eyes to the floor as Liam passed. The three exited into a long hallway, the main passage throughout the ground floor of Heavenstone. Liam kept to himself as they walked, servants and soldiers quickly parting to make way. He yearned to ask where they traveled but did not dare, given their clear displeasure with Kael's survival. What he did know was that there were two armories for knights in Heavenstone, one in the eastern wing, the other the west. The soldiers' armories were near the front gateway on either side. Jaina, however, led them to the far back of Heavenstone, to a silver door he'd never noticed before. Heavenstone had many secrets, and Liam wondered which would soon be revealed to him.

Jaina unlocked the door with her key and pulled it open. Inside was a thin, circular staircase descending into the bowels of Heavenstone. Liam felt a twinge in his throat. The last time he'd traveled deep into the fortress he'd been given audience with the three blessed angels keeping Center afloat.

"Stay silent, and touch nothing," Jaina said as Marius led the way. "We will explain your visit shortly."

"Yes, Er'el," Liam answered with a dry tongue.

The stairs looped down and down, periodically lit by small square light prisms set into the brick. Liam was glad he wasn't wearing his wings. There'd have been no way to fit them. He wondered if that was coincidence or purposeful construction as he counted the steps down. They passed no doors, no exits, just a continual descent.

It wasn't until the hundred and fiftieth step that they reached another door. This one wasn't silver but instead thick iron with heavy bolts and lacking any decoration. Jaina used the same gold key, which looked an odd contrast to such a door. The lock clicked and Jaina stepped aside so Marius could enter.

"Which armory is this?" Liam asked, unable to help himself.

"The Ancient Armory," she said. "Do not ask questions, knight. Use your eyes instead."

Liam accepted the rebuke, ducked his head, and passed through the door to the room beyond.

And what a room it was. The ceiling vaulted at least a hundred feet above their heads, if not more. Liam could see only a hint of what he believed to be the opposite wall. Thick stone pillars formed a series of even lines supporting the high ceiling. No decoration, no fanciful artwork. Just smooth, strong stone with light elements fitted into them at set intervals. The number was staggering, more than a thousand needed to light the room with a soft glow.

All of it paled in comparison to the machines of war that filled the armory.

"God in heaven," Liam said, frozen in place. "What are these monstrosities?"

The nearest was a vehicle on six wheels, the front four wood, the back two larger and of stone. It was stocky and square, and also seemingly made of stone. The corner had been smoothed, covered with painted wood and shaped to look like wings. Nearly all of it was trimmed with gold. Mounted atop that bulk was a thick cylinder, open and hollow at the end. It was a cannon, Liam realized, a cannon like in the old stories his mother read to him when he was a child. Red light shone from the cylinder, so bright he knew at least a dozen fire prisms had to be powering it.

Lined up neatly in a row, a pillar between each one, were nineteen more. Theotechs scurried about them, cleaning, checking, and fitting with elemental prisms.

"These monstrosities are the firepower once wielded against the demons as they destroyed our civilization," Marius said as he led them deeper into the armory. "We had no need of their power after the Ascension. Our wars were settled elegantly with duels in the sky, without need of wanton slaughter and lengthy, brutal sieges."

More such vehicles filled the next row, smaller, more mobile versions of the cannons. Liam examined one closely, saw hooks and latches near the front. To be pulled by horses or oxen, then, not light elements. Next were a few vehicles that looked more like men, with arms made of silver pipe. Others looked like roaring beasts, or a spinning top made up of blades. Liam's head spun trying to take it all in. Some he could guess their function; others, such as the enormous humanoid machines, left him baffled.

"Speaker, may I ask a question?"

"Go ahead, my friend."

Liam gestured to the ancient war machines.

"Why did you bring me here to show me this?"

The Speaker turned to him, and he smiled like a proud parent who knew something his child did not.

"Not yet," he said. "You will see your purpose shortly."

Theotechs bowed in respect to their Speaker before resuming their work. More than a hundred of the red-robed men and women scattered about, bees filling up a grandiose hive. Occasionally Liam would pass a chest atop a wheeled cart. Inside would be dozens of elemental prisms, each carefully wrapped in velvet cloth. He imagined the countless elements locked into each and every one of those machines, imagined the destruction they could unleash. It terrified him.

"There," Jaina said, pointing. The walls, while mostly smooth, weren't always so. Stone boxes jutted out from the rest of the stone, little rooms attached to the great armory. Each had square windows cut into them, their interiors lit with lanterns powered by light elements. A single number marked their wooden doors, and it was to number six that Marius led them.

"The team is already prepped," Jaina told Marius as they neared. "Er'el Xann is quite excited."

"He shouldn't be," said Marius. "This isn't a game. It's a necessity forced upon us by the minor islands' reckless ignorance."

"My Speaker," Liam said, anxiety rising as Jaina knocked twice on the door. Liam spotted at least five waiting theotechs through the window, plus a scattered assortment of unknown machinery.

"Stay calm, knight," Marius ordered. "We come to give not punishment, but a gift."

The door opened, and with a gesture of the Speaker's hand, Liam led the way.

Inside was more cramped than Liam expected. Stacked along the walls were rows and rows of shelves lined with baffling instruments. He saw parts of wing harnesses, sharp blades, jagged blades, gears, and wires. One wall had a pegboard holding more than one hundred elemental prisms, each of them cut and filed into bizarre shapes. In the center of the room, surrounded by five waiting theotechs, was a thick, slanted table with leather straps. Liam recognized Er'el Iseph Xann, who had been the one to painstakingly apply Liam's many tattoos over the years.

"Remove your shirt and lie down on the table," Iseph said.

Liam berated himself for his distrust. God's chosen leader had personally brought him to be granted a gift from the ancient technology of the pre-Ascension world. He would not whimper in fear of that gift, nor the process required to give it.

Liam lay down upon the table. The theotechs shifted around him, and despite his attempts to remain calm, a spike of fear jolted him as the first of the five leather straps looped around his wrists and ankles. The last was about his throat, pinning his head. Liam forced his breathing through his noise while suppressing a gag reflex.

"Are the straps necessary?" he asked. "What is it you fear from me?"

"We fear nothing," Iseph said, his voice astonishingly deep. Liam had listened for hours to that baritone calmly listing off a litany of Liam's sins and failures as the tattoo needle pierced his skin. The few knights Liam had regular contact with insisted the long-haired man had performed experiments upon his own throat to achieve such a depth of sound.

"Then what are they for?"

Iseph leaned over his head and squinted a moment.

"To keep you still while we work."

One of the theotechs wrapped a second strip of leather around Liam's right arm below the elbow and then looped it through a buckle attached to the table and pulled. It tightened to the point of cutting off circulation, and Liam grimaced as pain fought against the spreading numbness. The theotech put a foot on the table, bracing his weight to pull even harder until it finally locked in place.

"What is this?" Liam asked Marius, who stood with Jaina on the opposite side of the room. His right arm was starting to turn purple. Spiking sensations of pain traveled up his arm to his neck.

"Like all gifts of God, this one comes with a price," Marius said. "A blessing and a punishment, one and the same. I hold the highest hope for you, Liam, but I also see the weakness in your heart. You still cling to emotion over reason. We face extinction. Such weakness must be eliminated at all costs."

Jaina shook her head in disgust beside him.

"We should have bestowed this upon a better man," she said.

"Perhaps," Marius said. "But I give it not to the better man, but to the one most deserved."

Iseph stepped out of Liam's view. He heard rattling of metal from a nearby shelf, followed by a chilling scraping sound. When Iseph stepped back into view, he held a metal saw.

"My Speaker," Liam said, straining against the leather straps.

"Shush, child," Marius said. "The pain will be over soon."

The saw pressed against his skin below the tightened belt, the slightest contact with its sharp teeth puncturing his skin. Liam felt it like the touch of a ghost, a certainty of pain in his mind that somehow did not match the numb sensation dominating his entire right arm. Iseph nodded to one of the theotechs, who grabbed Liam's shoulder and held him down. And then began the cutting.

Liam watched, detached, confusion and shock overwhelming his emotions. Was this a betrayal? A deserved punishment? Why sever his arm and declare it a gift? The muscle separated, and the easy motions of the saw suddenly turned erratic upon hitting bone. Pain finally pierced the numbness, and Liam screamed at the agony blasting up his entire right side. He gasped and clenched his eyes, fighting to regain control. He was a soldier, damn it, a knight of Center and warrior for the heavens.

What is holy must never break, he silently echoed, desperately clinging to the mantra to calm his pain-fevered mind. The saw cut deeper and deeper.

"Hold him still," Iseph said. "This cannot be delayed."

More hands pressing against him, his chest, his legs, everywhere. Liam looked to Marius to see if the Speaker showed remorse for his decision, perhaps doubt or a sliver of compassion. Instead he saw an ice-cold stare and a face as numb as Liam's arm had been.

"The separation is complete," Iseph said, pulling back the saw. One of the theotechs fumbled with the buckle to release the severed arm's wrist. Iseph grabbed the arm and tossed it aside. Liam heard it thud against something metallic.

"Is that it?" Liam asked between gasps of pain. "You wanted my arm?"

"Please do not make guesses," Iseph said, his back to Liam. "It is distracting and pointless. We do not want your old arm, Seraph Skyborn. We wish to give you a new one."

He turned about cradling a thick golden cylinder. One side tapered and ended in four smaller cylinders that looked like stubby fingers—or a miniature version of the cannons that Liam had seen earlier. Wires trailed out the bottom of the other end, each one ending with a fine needle carved from either a light or lightning elemental prism. Iseph gently placed it below Liam's stump of an elbow.

"Try to relax," Iseph said. "I expect the amputation was the easier part."

Liam didn't know how that could possibly be true until Iseph slid the first of the needles into his flesh. Blood quickly stained the immaculate gold and pain blasted through him, so hard he nearly blacked out. There was no numbness to aid him, nor any visible source for the pain. It felt like the bones of his now nonexistent arm were being repeatedly shattered. More needles, one after the other, some inserted into the marrow of the bone, others into his weeping flesh. Liam cried out with tears streaming down his face. He didn't care to act the strong, controlled Seraph. This was torture. The fifth needle entered, and he screamed. It felt like his fingers were being pulled all the way back, the tendons tearing as his joints snapped. He knew it made no sense. He didn't have fingers. There was nothing to break.

His mind seemed not to care.

"Someone gag him," Liam heard Iseph's deep voice grumble. "I cannot concentrate."

A thick cloth jammed into Liam's mouth, and he bit down on it with all his strength. Another needle, this one different. Electricity sparked through him, his legs kicking against the restraints on their own accord. It felt like his body was no longer his own. His other arm tensed and flailed. His neck pulled so hard against the restraint he nearly vomited. Iseph continued patiently through it all. Needle after needle. Liam felt his mind close to breaking. The seventh needle pushed deep into bone, flooding his vision with a rainbow of swirling colors.

Twenty needles, Liam's voice sounded distantly inside his own skull. *I saw twenty needles.*

If only he could black out. If only he could wake when the pain was gone.

Tenth needle. This time Liam did vomit, and he choked until someone pulled the gag from his mouth and turned his head to the side. Fifteenth needle. Liam begged for death, for salvation, for rapture. Anything other than this suffering. What crime had he committed? He didn't even remember. Through blurred eyes he saw Marius watching him. Tears streamed down Marius's face as well. Why did the Speaker cry? Liam tried to think, failed. More pain. Another needle. God help him, if only he had a blade to sever his own throat. If only . . .

The twentieth needle awoke him, and he screamed a long, single tone of agony. He tasted blood on his tongue, felt vomit on his face and neck. The theotechs spoke among themselves, working as if Liam were a machine instead of a human being.

"Easy now," Iseph said as he and another lifted the blood-stained golden cylinder and pressed the nub below his elbow through the hollow end. Liam heard whirring, tightening, felt each and every one of those twenty needles digging deeper into his flesh and bone. Liam thought the pain would have lessened by now just from the sheer weakening of his mind. He was wrong.

The gold locked tight. More theotechs leaned in, jamming long, thin pieces of metal into small indents of the cylinder and twisting. Liam felt a tightening sensation across his skin, the machine bolting into his living arm. There were two knobs near the center of the new mechanism, and Iseph began tweaking them in turn. Each time a strange, awakening sensation filled the area.

"I believe this will suffice," Iseph told Marius. "Now we wait for the body to adjust."

The Speaker drew a small bottle from a pocket of his robe as he returned to Liam's side.

"It's over," he said. He tipped the bottle to Liam's lips. "This will help you rest."

Liam drank the mixture greedily. It tasted of copper and cloves, and it burned all the way down. Immediately his mind began to swim, overcome with an overpowering need to sleep.

"Why?" Liam asked, his speech slurred. "Why didn't you give me this before?"

Marius gently patted his uninjured shoulder.

"A gift and a punishment," he said as sleep began to take Liam away. "Each must be given their turn."

Liam felt his world slowly return to him, his mind awakening from a drugged stupor. His entire left side ached, and every inhalation scraped air across his raw throat. He tried to sit up. Restraints held him down.

"Hold still a moment," a voice spoke from the haze that

clouded his vision. "You were thrashing in your sleep and we wished to prevent injury."

Iseph's voice. Even in his confusion he recognized that deep rumble. Liam closed his eyes tightly and then reopened them. Clearer now. He was in the same room, though the blood was cleaned from his table. Iseph stood beside him while Marius lurked in the corner. Jaina was gone, as were the other theotechs. The leather buckles rattled as Iseph removed them one by one.

"My arm," Liam said. Talking hurt, but he could withstand a bit of pain. After the surgery he'd just endured, a sore throat felt like a soothing breeze. "What did you do to my arm?"

"Once you've recovered, I'll be happy to show you," Iseph said.

"No," Liam said, pushing off the bed and onto unsteady legs. "Now."

Iseph looked to Marius, who nodded in affirmative.

"Very well," Iseph said. "First, let us confirm the basic functionality. Can you move your right arm freely?"

Liam looked to the golden contraption bolted to his elbow. It was strange, so strange. As he moved it about it felt normal somehow, only muted, like it had almost fallen asleep. The top bit with the four smaller cylinders were where his hand should be, and somehow he felt those four as if they were his own fingers, currently pressed together into a fist.

"Very good," Iseph said. "Now hold still."

The Er'el tapped the golden arm with his finger several times, spacing the taps out every few inches.

"Do you feel that?" he asked.

"I do," Liam said. "I feel it like it was my own arm."

"That's because it is," Marius said from the corner. "You will move and control your gift like it is a part of yourself."

Interesting, Liam decided, but he still failed to see how it was a gift. There must be something else this new arm could do, but what?

"Follow me," Iseph said. "If you insist on testing it now, then we need more space."

They exited into the great cavern full of ancient weaponry. Iseph led the way, Liam trailing a few steps behind. They followed along the wall, for which he was thankful. Every few moments he'd rest his shoulder against it and gather his breath. His new arm occasionally brushed the stone, sending a shiver all the way up his neck. Liam could only guess how long it would take for him to adjust. His eyes saw a foreign chunk of golden metal, but his body felt a new arm and a clenched fist.

Iseph took them all the way to the far end of the cavern, which still stunned Liam with its size. Here there were fewer machines, but that didn't mean fewer theotechs. One machine in particular had more than two dozen theotechs hovering around it like little worker ants. It looked like the other cannons, only far greater in size and far more ornate in its decorations. Before passing the machine, Iseph stopped at one of the ten chests of elements stashed beside it and pulled out a handful of fire elemental prisms.

"This way," the Er'el said, gesturing to the massive empty wall towering ahead of them. "You may fire at the door."

Fire? Door?

Liam saw only the wall, perfectly smooth and flat all the way up to the ceiling, at least a hundred feet high. He nodded as if he understood and followed. When they were within fifty yards Iseph halted and offered Liam one of his prisms.

"There is a compartment on the underside of your new arm," he said. "You'll open it similar to a gauntlet."

Liam rotated his arm, and sure enough, he found the faint

indentations of a compartment opening. He pushed it down and in with his left hand, popping it free. Instead of space for a single prism Liam found three separate slots. After putting in the first, Liam accepted two more, carefully inserting them into the contraption and then snapping the compartment shut. Liam immediately felt better with it closed. His mind wasn't quite sure how to interpret the open compartment, and he couldn't get the unpleasant image of his flesh opening up to leave his thoughts.

"Your new arm will function as a superior form of gauntlet," Iseph said, stepping behind him. The theotech put his hands on Liam's new arm and extended it forward, his fingers tracing the four cylinders at the end. It felt as if Iseph were touching Liam's real, flesh-and-blood fingers. "Each of these will fire a burst of flame when you make the mental connection. Combined together, and harnessing a trio of linked prisms, this should give you vastly greater range and force than any other knight."

Liam closed his eyes, keenly aware of the Speaker quietly watching him. He needed to concentrate. Unleashing fire from his gauntlet was second nature to him, but after the drugs and the pain he felt rattled, and this was no ordinary gauntlet. This was a part of himself, akin to unleashing fire from his bare palm. Taking a slow breath in and out to calm his mind, Liam began to feel the soft presence of the fire prisms. When he opened his eyes, he braced his legs, tightened the muscles of his right arm, and envisioned the burst of flame roaring from the golden barrels.

A tremendous burst of fire shot from his arm, the power rocking his entire body sideways. It shrieked forward like a comet before slamming against the stone wall with a roaring explosion. Liam felt the strain of it on his mind, but it was different somehow. More natural. More free.

"Excellent," Iseph said. "Beyond expectations, even. You will need to relearn how to control your fire as well as brace your body for each attack, but I expect you will pick up these skills with ease."

"Perhaps," Liam said, staring at his golden arm. "It kicks harder than a mule."

"A worthy price for such power," Marius said. His arms were crossed over his chest, and unlike Iseph, he kept his face passive. "Show him the blade."

"Blade?" Liam asked.

"In case there are times where melee is necessary," Iseph explained. "There is a blade hidden within your arm. To activate it, I believe you must try to open your fingers as wide as possible."

"I don't have fingers."

"You once did, and that mental order is what the device will interpret. Now try it instead of arguing."

Liam nodded and turned back to the wall, now blackened in a large circle from his first attack. He might have four little barrels at the end of his arm instead of fingers, but they did indeed feel like a closed fist. Imagining it as such, Liam tried to open those fingers and spread his palm. Not much happened at first. He concentrated harder, prying open this fingers. The four barrels spread wide with a sudden snap, and from their center punched out a long blade. One side was thin and sharp, the other cruelly serrated.

"You will need practice with this new blade," Iseph said. "The sword is now a part of you, and as such, you'll lose much of the mobility of a twisting wrist. However, you no longer need to fear losing your grip, nor the strain of impact while striking in flight. This should more than compensate in most battles."

Liam shifted his arm, trying to get a feel for this new blade. It was thicker than a normal sword, more spearlike, too. He swung it a few times and was pleased with the sense of power and weight it carried. He thought to ask how to retract it but Iseph had pulled back to speak with an older theotech who'd joined him. Marius ignored both, and looked as if he were holding back a grin.

"There is one more surprise left," he said. "Aim at the wall and release your fire while keeping the blade extended."

Intrigued, Liam extended his arm once more. He felt the click in his mind, the activation of the prism, and then fire bellowed forth. Unlike the first release, which shot a thick, streaking projectile, this explosion sprayed a massive cloud of fire from the four spread barrels. It didn't reach the wall, instead consuming air in the space before him in an inferno and fading into smoke.

Iseph broke from his conversation and clapped excitedly.

"As I said, close quarters only. But even the glorified Phoenix will struggle to match the power you'll wield."

Liam shook his head in awe. He still mourned the loss of his arm, and the pain of the surgery haunted his waking thoughts... but he could not deny the raw power of the weapon granted to him.

"It is a fine gift," he said, bowing before Marius. "I pray I use it to its utmost capabilities to repay such trust."

"I send you to hunt the most frightening of foes," Marius said, bidding him to rise. "I will not do so without sending you prepared."

Iseph bowed to the other theotech, who stepped back to give them privacy.

"Er'el Modwin says all preparations for departure are ready," he said. "Shall we begin?"

Marius's smile vanished.

"Yes," he said. "Consider the order given."

Iseph relayed it to Er'el Modwin, who bowed low and then rushed away shouting. Liam watched as all throughout the cavern the theotechs set their machines to life with a hum of a thousand light prisms.

"How will we get the machines out?" Liam asked.

Iseph gave him a look.

"Are you deaf?" he asked. "I told you we were at the door."

Liam turned to the giant wall he'd blackened and refused to believe it. Only when the sound of tremendous gears turning assaulted his ears, coupled with the deep grinding of moving stone, did he understand.

A thin line split the wall from floor to ceiling, and outside light bled through, blinding in the gloomy cavern. Liam watched with mouth agape as the crack steadily widened. It was a door for giants, perhaps even gods. He squinted against the light, trying to see what lay on the other side. At last his eyes adjusted, and he saw a long, wide road leading down a large slope. Rocky outcroppings stretched far to either side, with the closest rocks carved into statues of angels with arms raised in supplication. He recognized that path and those statues. They were at the western base of Mount Vassal. An entire mountain, carved hollow to hide Center's might? The thought was overwhelming. Gears groaned and turned, and theotechs rushed about shouting excitedly. Both the Speaker and his Er'el could not appear more pleased.

"The vault of Heavenstone awakens," Marius said as daylight streamed through the ever-widening doorway. "Weshern's rebellion is at an end."

CHAPTER 6

Bree knocked on the door to their appointed room within the Candren royal mansion.

"Come on in," Kael said from the other side.

She saw exactly what she expected when she entered, a miserable-looking Kael lying on his bed, hands behind his head, eyes locked on the ceiling.

"How was dinner?" he asked. He didn't bother to look her way.

"You missed dessert," Bree said, sitting on the bed opposite his. "I think it was a bread roll of some sort. Was a little hard to tell. The entire thing was practically buried in honey."

Kael didn't respond. Bree frowned. She knew he'd been humiliated at the dinner, but this wallowing seemed a bit much. She opened her mouth to berate him, then paused. No, Kael wasn't moping. His brow was furrowed, his lips locked in a tight frown. He was debating something. Determined to suss it out, she stood and walked to his side.

"What is it?" she asked.

"You'll think I'm insane."

Bree smiled.

"The rest of Candren already thinks so. What does it matter if I do as well?"

He threw his pillow at her, which she easily could have dodged but didn't. It smacked her in the face and then dropped into her lap. Bree immediately flung it back into his stomach. Kael exaggerated a grimace, but he was smiling now, and he sat up.

"Fine," he said. "I want to break into the Clay Cathedral."

Bree lifted an eyebrow at him.

"You're right," she said. "I do think you're insane."

"Wait. Hear me out. You heard Evereth during dinner. He thinks I am a lunatic. There's not a chance he actually grants me permission to go beneath the Clay Cathedral."

"He'd probably think you were trying to blow up all of Candren," Bree said.

"Exactly. So we need to sneak in ourselves, tonight, before we perform the signing ceremony and leave for home. This is important, Bree. I don't feel like we have any other choice."

Bree crossed her arms and sighed.

"All right, I'll bite. Why is it so important?"

Kael stood and began pacing, his voice rising with excitement.

"Johan's banned all entrance into the Crystal Cathedral back home, even to me, and I've already spoken with L'fae. He's claiming it's to keep Weshern safe, but I'm not so sure anymore. There's so much we don't know about L'adim, what he looks like, how he'll attack, or how we're to defeat him."

The mention of Johan soured Bree's already exhausted mood. She remembered how pleased the man had looked capturing the Crystal Cathedral, how banishing the theotechs seemed to be Johan's personal victory instead of all of Weshern's.

"Johan asked you to tell no one about the lightborn," she said. "He's starting to act no differently than the theotechs."

"To be fair, he said I'd be mocked and disbelieved," Kael said, and he rolled his eyes. "He was right on that point, at least."

"All right, so say we decide we'll go into the Clay Cathedral. Care to tell me *how* you plan on doing that? We don't know the land, nor the layout of the cathedral, nor how well it's guarded. It's not like we can just strap on a pair of wings and fly over there without causing a ruckus."

Kael flung his arms up.

"That's what I was pondering when you started asking questions," he said. "You interrupted my planning. Don't blame me for not having everything figured out yet."

"One thing at a time, then," Bree said, sitting back down on her bed. "We need to get out of the mansion without being noticed first."

"Can't we just say we want to go sightseeing?"

Bree chuckled.

"Evereth kindly requested we stay inside the mansion grounds when he dismissed everyone from dinner. For our own safety, of course. He feared some lingering bad blood might cause an incident between us and the populace."

"Wonderful," Kael said. "So now we need a way to escape the mansion *and* sneak into the Clay Cathedral without drawing attention to ourselves." He sighed. "Maybe I am insane, Bree. The odds of us—"

A loud knocking at the door interrupted him, and the two stiffened and shared a look. Neither had been trying to keep their voice down. Had a passing soldier heard their plotting, or worse, Rebecca Waller herself?

"It's me." Saul's muffled voice came from the other side of the door. "I'm not a guard or assassin or whatever else you're worried about. Now let me in."

Kael sighed with relief. Better Saul than all the other possibilities. "One moment," he said.

Kael crossed the room and flung the door open. Saul stood before it, his Seraphim uniform untucked and his jacket unbuttoned. He held a dark red clay goblet in his left hand. A goofy smile covered his face.

"You left too soon, Bree," he said as he stepped inside.

"The Archon dismissed us."

Kael shut the door behind him while Saul cast her a wink.

"That was the polite way of saying people could leave when they wished. It was after that they brought out the wine. The *good* wine."

That explained the goblet, as well as Saul's goofy smile. He'd always been a stiff asshole since the first day she met him. To see him so loose and relaxed felt... unnatural. Kael and Bree awkwardly waited, unsure of what Saul wanted. Saul seemed not to care, sipping from his goblet while leaning against the wall.

"So," he said, glancing at Kael. "What you said about angels and the cathedrals and all that... is true?"

Bree felt her spirits dip. Was that all Saul wanted, to come and offer Kael some additional mockery?

"Every word," Kael said, and it looked like he was trying not to grit his teeth.

Saul took another sip.

"Every word," he repeated. A laugh escaped his lips. "Every goddamn word, eh? Damn. Couldn't you have just lied to me, Kael? I'd not have minded, but now I have to help you."

Bree couldn't be more confused.

“Help us what?” she asked.

Saul wagged a finger her way.

“Get out of here and into the Clay Cathedral, of course.”

Bree felt her neck flush, while opposite her, Kael’s hands balled into fists.

“You were eavesdropping on us?” he asked.

“Well, I wouldn’t have if you two weren’t so loud,” he said, taking another sip. “But it’s clear you both mean what you say. I don’t think you’d be risking your life for some garbage nonsense, right? So if there’s goddamn angels keeping our islands afloat, we should hear what they have to say about all this, and not whatever shit the Speaker claims is what they’re saying.”

Bree and Kael shared an incredulous look. It seemed they had an ally in their plotting, though hardly the one they expected.

“Do you, uh, have anything in mind?” Kael asked.

Saul grinned at him.

“Oh yes, yes I do. But first, we need one more Seraph, someone older than us recent grads. Got anyone in mind?”

“Chernor,” Kael said. “If I ask Chernor, I think he’ll help us.”

Saul emptied the rest of his goblet, red drops dripping down his neck to stain his white shirt.

“All right!” he said, wiping his chin with the back of his hand. “Time to go humiliate myself.”

A massive fenced-in garden filled with hedgerows, intricate wire animals made of flowers, and numerous secluded benches and gazebos surrounded the entire eastern half of the mansion. Perfect for meetings, gossiping, and drinking fine wine while gazing at the newly revealed stars. Tonight, it was also the perfect place for Bree and Kael to slip out while the patrolling guards were distracted. The two sat on a bench beside the spiked iron fence that formed the perimeter of the gardens. They'd shed their jackets on the bench and untucked their shirts, to make their Weshern allegiances less obvious. They'd carried their swords with them, and placed them beside the iron bars within easy reach.

"So say this works," Kael whispered to her as they watched Saul pace before one of the large gates where two Candren guards were checking all who entered and exited. Weshern guests might be forced to remain on grounds, but there were more than a hundred high-class men and women of Candren eager to stargaze while discussing the upcoming treaty and war against Center, and to catch a glance at their former enemies. Bree had kept her head down and shoulders hunched, hiding lest anyone notice she was the Phoenix they all loved to gossip over.

"It *will* work," Bree whispered back.

"All right. It works. Now how do we get back inside when we return?"

"We'll dump our swords here through the fence and then go through the front gates. Security will be far more lax come morning. Stop worrying so much."

Kael hardly looked convinced, but it was better than nothing. He kept an eye on Saul until Chernor exited the mansion nearby.

"Get ready," he said.

Saul had been mostly keeping to himself, but when he spotted Chernor he began to guzzle his drink while drifting toward a group of three men, their eyes lit by the glow of their long pipes. They seemed to pay Saul no mind, at least, not until Saul directly bumped into the tallest of the three, spilling his wine across the man's sleeve.

“Hey!” Saul shouted. “Watch where you’re going. Shit, you spilled my drink, too.”

The three looked flabbergasted by the sudden berating. Saul began muttering as he walked the pebbled path toward the mansion. The Candren man with the stained sleeve broke from his spell and hurried after Saul.

“Wait one moment,” he said with raised voice. “Weshern Seraph, I said wait!”

Chernor’s cue. The giant man intercepted Saul’s path and grabbed him by the shoulders.

“What the hell are you doing, Seraph?” Chernor asked.

Saul grinned up at him.

“Uh... walking?”

Either Chernor was a phenomenal actor, or he honestly was disgusted by how drunk Saul appeared to be. The Seraph back-handed him across the mouth, mixing a bit of blood with Saul’s wine.

“You’re a disgrace to Weshern,” he said. “Get back to your room this instant before I carry you there myself.”

All eyes were on the pair now, their focus intensifying when the Candren man arrived with his two friends in tow.

“A disgrace indeed,” said the man. “Will Weshern also pay to replace the garment he ruined?”

Kael tugged Bree’s arm, and together they rose from the bench and started walking alongside the iron fence. They kept their arms crossed and their eyes on the confrontation, pretending they wanted nothing more than a closer look at what was going on.

“Pay for what?” Chernor asked, spinning to face the newcomer. “It’s a few drops of wine on a brown coat sleeve. I’d hardly call that ruined.”

“Yeah, don’t get your pipe all twisted in a knot,” Saul added, a line they hadn't rehearsed in advance. Chernor gave him a death glare.

"That's enough out of you," he said. "Now go."

"Not before he gives me an apology," the Candren man said, reaching for Saul's arm. Chernor deftly stepped in, his voice lowering, his words deceptively calm.

"The peace treaty's not signed yet," he said. "I suggest you keep your hands off my Seraph no matter how badly you think you deserve an apology."

With the veiled threat given, the two guards at the gate hustled to intercede, their hands on the hilts of their swords. Bree tugged Kael's sleeve, urging them onward.

"Come on," one of the man's friends said. "It's just a young brat with too much wine in him. Let it go."

"Wise advice," Chernor said. He looked to the approaching guards. "Come to escort these gentlemen away?" he asked them.

They certainly didn't look ready to escort anyone but Saul and Chernor—exactly what Saul had predicted would happen. As both men began to protest their treatment at the hands of the guards, Bree slipped her arm around Kael's, leaning against him as if she'd had a bit too much to drink herself. Unnoticed, they passed through the gate and out into the streets of Candren and cut immediately to the left. Casting a glance to the commotion, she saw Chernor and Saul yelling and flailing, their voices exaggeratedly loud. Every soul was looking their way.

Bree reached through the bars, grabbed their swords, and then together they dashed down the street. By the time the royal castle was far behind, Bree and Kael were laughing.

"I didn't know Saul had it in him," he said. "I've always seen him with a frown on his face and a stick up his rear."

"Let's just hope Chernor doesn't get into an actual fistfight with anybody," Bree said. "It might look bad for diplomacy if he breaks a few noses before signing the treaty."

"Look bad here, maybe, but he'll be a hero back on Weshern."

Bree laughed again.

"Too true."

She buckled her swords to her waist as she walked. The long road down the capitol hill awaited them. Her fingers tapped the hilts. Instead of feeling comforted, they made her only feel more exposed.

"We won't be able to cxplain having these if we're caught," she said.

"Then we best not get caught."

They kept to one side of the road, eyes open and ears attentive. The hour may have been late but plenty were still drinking at the castle. Others could be on their way home, and all it would take was a quick shout for their plan to be exposed. The road gradually sloped downward, and twice Bree and Kael descended one of the rope ladders to bypass much of the walk. At the bottom of the hill, they spotted the Clay Cathedral rising up from a perfect circle of cleared earth. As with the Crystal Cathedral, it bore no protective walls or fences. Getting inside, however, would be the trick.

"No outside guards," Bree said as they neared.

"Good," Kael said. "It'd be nice if something went right for once."

Pride had convinced Bree that nothing could compete for beauty and majesty with the intertwining layers of glass of her home cathedral, certainly not something as meager as clay. But standing before Candren's cathedral, she thought otherwise. The building was perfectly square, all four sides lined with massive columns cut from the earth. Some were covered with painted carvings, detailing miracles of healing by the theotechs, people in worship, and great crowds kneeling in prayer as they listened to the words of the Speaker. Bree wished she could look upon the breathtaking detail in the daylight instead of the dim starlight. Instead of pictures, other pillars bore lines and lines of text traveling in a tight, circular path down the pillar that seemed to echo the road down the capitol hill. Bree brushed the words with her fingers, staggered by their density. They were divine words of various Speakers throughout the ages. Each carved recess was colored with paint, so that when Bree stood before the pillar the words formed the beautiful image of a pre-Ascension knight kneeling before a silver-winged angel.

"How long do you think this took to make?" Bree asked.

"It must have been years. Decades even," Kael said.

The makeup of the cathedral was different compared to Weshern's in that it had three entrances instead of one, grand double doors at the top of the steps on the east, west, and south sides. Kael tested one of them, not surprised to find it locked. No guards patrolled the grounds, either. The cathedral's security likely remained inside, for how could one break through such grand doors? It was impossible.

Which was why they had no intention of breaking in.

Kael slipped to the side, while Bree rapped against the door with her knuckles. It took a dozen tries but finally a tiny window slid open and a young, tired face peered out.

"Come back when it is daylight, child," the theotech said. "No matter your deeds the angels will wait to hear them."

"But I won't be able to wait until daylight," Bree said, leaning closer and speaking quickly lest the man close the window. "We return to Weshern come the morrow."

This seemed to catch his attention.

"Weshern?" he asked.

"I . . . my name is Breanna Skyborn," she said, feeling a shiver of nerves at revealing her identity. "I wish to pray for the angels' guidance, for much has been placed on my shoulders and I fear to make the wrong decision."

"Skyborn?" the theotech asked, his eyes narrowing in the dim light. "As in the Phoenix of Weshern?"

She meekly nodded.

"Well then, that is a different matter entirely," he said. "Have you any proof you are who you claim to be?"

They'd worried whoever greeted them might not believe their identities, especially since they were dressed in plain clothes and not their official Weshern Seraphim uniforms. Kael had come up with the simple answer, an ability only the Phoenix could possibly perform. Bree told herself to remain calm as she drew her sword. The theotech stepped back, clearly frightened. Bree ignored his reaction, pretending she was unaware of a reason for him to be worried. She carefully pricked the tip of her middle finger, nothing deep. She only needed a single drop of blood.

"I am the Phoenix," Bree said, sheathing her sword. "For who else might I be?"

The trickle of blood swelling across her finger shone a dull red in her mind. She focused on it, igniting the lurking demon blood within. The drop ignited, a softly flickering flame like a candle. Bree held it for only a second before extinguishing it.

"Who else indeed?" the theotech breathed. He was pretending to be calm but she saw the heightened fear and excitement in his eyes. "Please," he said. "Come inside."

Bree steeled herself as Kael sank farther back into the tiny alcove beside the door. They'd prepared an alternate plan should she be rejected, but this was their desired scenario. The door creaked open a few feet, granting narrow passage. The young theotech gestured for Bree to enter. She stepped just inside the door, ensuring it could not be closed. Open space greeted her, but it was dark compared to the Crystal Cathedral.

"Please, no swords," commanded the theotech.

"Of course."

Bree unbuckled her swords and placed them against the wall, purposely keeping herself between the theotech and the door so he could not close it. Done, she smoothed her clothes and stared at the vaulted ceiling far above her. Dozens of lanterns hung from wires so thin they seemed to float in the air. Still she refused to move.

"If you would, take a seat," the theotech said, and he gestured to the three different sections of benches that faced the raised center dais. Bree could sense the impatience in his voice. Another good sign. The best, though, was the way he kept his right hand close to his side, and the faint glint of steel he failed to hide among his red robes.

Exhaling slowly, she bowed her head and walked past him. She kept calm, her body relaxed. Unsuspecting. She did not hear his footsteps following her, for they walked upon thick red carpet, but she could imagine the eagerness in the young theotech's eyes. Here was the blasphemous Phoenix of Weshern, alone and on foreign soil. What fame might he receive should he bring her low? What reward would the Speaker offer for such a kill?

Bree halted abruptly in the middle of the aisle, knowing it would both surprise him as well as spur him into acting. She didn't turn or brace for the coming blow. Her trust in her brother was absolute.

She heard a gurgle and Bree turned to see Kael's left hand pressed against the theotech's mouth, the right jamming a sword through his posterior ribs and into his heart. Kael held him still until his last shudder and then gently lowered him behind one of the benches.

"Here," he said, handing over her swords. "Keep a lookout for more while I shut the door."

Bree belted her swords around her waist and then quietly dashed to the dais. The cathedral bore entrances on three sides, but she could now see two more. One door to the left of the dais stood slightly ajar, probably dorms for lower-ranking theo-techs and servants. The other was carefully hidden from view of the pews behind the dais and locked shut. She suspected this door led to the secret passage that would eventually take them down into the bowels of Candren. If it were anything like the Crystal Cathedral's, it would first lead to rooms for the theo-techs, followed by bunks for the angelic knights stationed on guard. After that would be the true secret rooms, places like where they experimented on her. Most important, there should be the grand door Kael described housing the lightborn within.

Bree placed her ear against the unassuming door. Soft breathing and muted conversation could be heard from the other side. She bit her lip as she pondered a way to catch them off guard.

At least two, she mouthed.

Kael tapped her shoulder, alerting her to his arrival. She wordlessly nodded, then gestured to the door. It bore no decorations, only a long, dark iron handle and a slender hole for a key. He crossed his arms and frowned at the door. Bree let him think. Hopefully he'd have a better idea than hers, which was to simply knock and hope they answered.

Suddenly Kael waved a finger, mouthed he'd be right back. He vanished up the steps. Bree shifted her weight from foot to foot, growing more anxious with each passing moment. When Kael returned, he sported a wide grin. Bree raised an eyebrow to communicate her curiosity, and in answer, he twirled his right finger, spinning the thick steel key on its metal loop.

Dead guy had it, Kael mouthed to her. He slowly drew one of his swords, careful to prevent any noise, as Bree did likewise. She braced herself before the door, both blades at ready. Kael shifted to the side, inserted the key, and then looked to her.

Ready?

She nodded in affirmative.

Let's do this.

Kael turned the key. A heavy, satisfying click marked the opening of the mechanisms. Before the guards on the other side might think anything of it, Kael pulled on the iron handle, flinging open the door.

Two soldiers stood opposite one another, leaning against the sides of the long, stone hallway, their arms crossed over their chests. On sight, their boredom vanished instantly, their hands scrambling for weapons. Bree assaulted the man on the left, jamming the tip of her sword into the base of his throat. She continued inward, pulling the blade free while spinning to face the other. Her left hand swung, but the soldier reacted in time, his sword parrying away the strike. He pressed her, taller, stronger, his blade hammering down upon her swords. Frantically she dove aside, unable to endure. The tip of the soldier's sword cut across her arm, splashing blood across the dark stone floor.

The soldier moved to follow but stopped, howling in pain. Kael had struck him from behind, his thrust cutting through a gap in the chain mail at his armpit. Now flanked on both sides, the man realized his doom and lunged at Bree with a desperate overhead chop. She ducked low and spun away. Kael's sword sliced the man's heel, dropping him to one knee. The guard swung his fist wildly behind him, trying to chase Kael off, but missed. Bree feinted an attack, retreated instead. It stole his attention once more, and Kael ended his life with another stab through the back.

The body collapsed to the floor, metal rattling against stone. Bree winced at the noise as she collected her breath. Together they waited perfectly still for alarms, doors opening, angered men rushing their position. Nothing. Only silence.

"Luck's with us tonight," Kael whispered, grinning nervously.

"Says you," she whispered back, looking at her injury. The cut didn't appear too deep, thankfully. Trying her best to ignore it, she gestured for Kael to take lead. He'd been inside the Crystal Cathedral twice, while she'd been there only the once, blindfolded and drugged for much of it. Kael started off at a slow walk, then sped into a quiet jog. Bree followed, her hands on either hilt to prevent her swords from rattling. They passed closed door after closed door, none apparently the correct one.

The hallway lowered at a steady slant, the ceiling lit with soft glowing light elements embedded into tiny holes surrounded with runes. After several hundred feet, it hooked to the left. Kael slowed at the corner, and after listening a moment, looked around it.

"Hurry," he whispered, gesturing for her to follow.

Bree turned the corner to see an immediate junction. The path traveled both left and right, continuing on to doors and rooms best left undiscovered. Before them, though, were the grand double doors, exactly as Kael had described the ones in Weshern. The ceiling vaulted suddenly, making room for the marble opening. Golden runes lined the sides, some she could read, most not. They were terribly imposing, these gates sealing away a giant otherworldly being. Most frightening were the sensations of awe and power emanating from the other side. Even without Kael's stories, she'd have sensed something incredible within.

"Here we are," Kael said, no longer whispering. His eyes locked on the doors, and he looked as if lost in a daydream.

"Are you sure we'll be welcomed?" Bree asked. It had seemed a silly question to wonder beforehand, but now that she sensed the presence of the lightborn, she feared its anger, feared its very attention.

"I promise you we will," Kael said as he grabbed the enormous handle with both hands and pulled. "They're creatures of light and grace. Don't be afraid."

Bree breathed in deep and slowly let it out.

"Easier said than done," she whispered as the door creaked open a sliver.

Kael gestured she enter, and steeling herself for the unknown, Bree took that first step into the lightborn's chamber.

CHAPTER 7

Kael watched Bree's enraptured visage and wondered if his face had born a similar look when he first gazed upon L'fae in the deep heart of Weshern. The cavernous room was almost identical, the ceiling dozens of feet above him and curled into a dome. Chains and tubes latched around the vaguely masculine lightborn. He stared at the siblings with his frozen marble face, his emotions radiating curiosity.

"You are not theotechs," the lightborn spoke into their minds. "Have you come to speak with me, or do you bring news to share?"

His clear words carried a purity to them, and an earnestness that was almost painful to hear.

"Kael?" Bree said. She was hearing the words, too, and for the first time.

"It's all right," Kael said. He stood as tall as he could and met the lightborn's gaze. "We have come to speak with you, for we have questions I believe only you can answer."

The walls groaned and the chains rattled as the lightborn leaned closer.

"I am A'resh," the lightborn said. "Who are you two?"

"Kael Skyborn," he answered. "And this is my sister, Bree."

The lightborn didn't smile, but the emotions rolling off him shifted slightly, including an aura of welcoming that relaxed Kael greatly.

"Welcome, Bree and Kael Skyborn," he said. "Welcome to my home." Another shift in the aura about the lightborn, this time of worry. "You are injured, Bree."

Bree pulled her bleeding right arm tighter against her stomach as if embarrassed by the injury.

"It's nothing," she said. "I'll be fine."

"Indeed, you will," A'resh said. His hand extended, light wafting off his fingers like mist over a lake. "Be healed, child."

The misty light swirled as it danced toward Bree. His sister tensed, clearly afraid. The light settled on her body, much of it focusing on her arm. It faded away but for a blazing section across her wound. Kael heard a sound like a soft bell ringing a constant tone, and then the light was gone, as was the cut. Clean skin remained, not even a scar to show the injury had ever existed.

"Thank you," Bree said, holding the arm before her. Wonder drenched her every word. "I'm . . . I'm grateful."

A'resh straightened in his chains, then sagged down, letting them hold his weight. The liquid light pulsing through the tubes momentarily dimmed.

"It has been many years since an injured was brought before me," said the lightborn. "I do not miss the praise, but I miss the smiles of gratitude."

A fresh wave of anger mixed with Kael's relief. How many sick and dying could have been saved on Weshern if the angels' presence hadn't been hidden from them? More dead on the Speaker's hands, if only by inaction.

"A'resh, our questions," Kael said. "Might we ask them?"

The lightborn nodded.

"Speak them, child," he said. "And I will answer as best I can."

Kael took in a deep breath. Where to even begin? He wasn't certain of A'resh's relationship with the theotechs. Did he view them as helpers and servants, or prison keepers? Still, there was one name Kael knew would be viewed as enemy no matter what. Perhaps that could ensure he received all the aid the lightborn could offer.

"Your ancient enemy has returned," Kael said. "The dome has fallen, and L'adim has already attacked our islands with his fireborn."

A'resh's aura immediately changed. Kael felt anger and disgust, coupled with an overpowering impulse to drop to his knees in supplication. He glanced at his sister, saw her hands trembling.

"I know of Ch'thon's death," A'resh said. "I felt his presence die as if it were my own. The fireborn accosted our protection nightly, and when our dome fell, so too did they fall. But who are you to know of L'adim if you are not a theotech?"

"I spoke with L'fae," Kael answered. "She showed me the time of Ascension, and the battle waged against L'adim's forces."

A'resh's aura softened slightly. Kael detected a wave of contentedness wafting over him. It was like feeling the sun on his skin after a swim, or smelling the scent of a freshly bloomed flower.

"L'fae was the kindest of us," A'resh said. "The most hopeful for your race. It would be grand to be in her presence again." His attention seemed to tighten, returning to the present. "Still, if you have spoken with L'fae, what questions might you have that she did not answer?"

Kael remembered the shock he'd been in, the overwhelming awe of L'fae's presence. When she'd granted him the experience of the Ascension, it had almost been more than he could handle. Only after having days to ponder, and subsequently being denied entrance by Johan, did he regret not asking many more questions.

"She did not answer because I did not ask them," Kael said. "Tell me, who is L'adim? What is he? How do we kill him?"

A'resh settled deeper into the chains. His glow cooled, the color remaining the same but the power of it dulling. Kael winced when he heard the ceiling groan under the angel's weight.

"L'adim is our most brilliant mind and greatest betrayer," the lightborn said. "But for you to know who L'adim is, you must know who we ourselves are." A'resh's hand stretched toward them with a great rattle of metal. He turned it palm upward, fingers spread wide. "Take my hand. I will show you pieces of the past so you might better understand."

"Is this safe?" Bree whispered beside Kael.

"So long as you trust him," Kael said. "Do you?"

Bree frowned as she stared up the enormous lightborn.

"They're suffering for us," she said. "Yes, I do."

Together they stepped closer to the lightborn and gently clasped his fingers. Kael expected the same jolting transition as when L'fae showed him the Ascension but instead he felt images building before him. They floated up from the palm of A'resh's hand, coalescing into colors and shapes so finely detailed it was as if they truly existed, held together in a thin circular frame of shining light. Kael and Bree watched stars dance around a dozen suns, some the color of their own, others deeply red or a chilling blue.

"We do not remember who we were," A'resh's voice echoed in their heads. "Nor the worlds we traveled before entering yours. But we feel it, all of us, so strongly in our essence. A million worlds, and they were all merely stepping-stones. Whatever those travels, and for whatever their reason, that age is lost to us. All we remember is this very first moment..."

The scene changed to flowing fields of grass beneath a clear blue sky. Puffy white clouds swirled together, and in their center broke a beam that ripped apart the sky. It was but a flash before it vanished, and there appeared more than fifty lightborn. To see so many standing together nearly took Kael's breath away. Their figures were similar, bearing slight variations, but somehow Kael immediately recognized both L'fae and A'resh from among their number.

"*Why are we here?* we wondered," A'resh continued. "We had no answer. No explanation. But the humans did. They had one clear answer, and they praised us with it without ceasing."

The clouds shifted, time passing as the image realigned itself. The lightborn were still together, but now scores of people surrounded them on all sides. The image swooped closer, turning and shifting to show a dozen sights at once of this frozen moment in time. Sick and injured numbering in the hundreds waited before nine lightborn, eager to receive the misty white light to heal their ills. Another tableau showed men and women with their heads bowed and their arms raised. Kael heard the softest of hymns, as if the combined choir of that legion of people were still singing from that far distant age. Another twist and Kael saw two lightborn speaking with rulers of nations, unwanted gifts of gold and silver strewn about the lightborns' feet.

"Who were we to deny them?" A'resh asked. "We could not explain where we came from, nor how our mere presence could spare the humans from death. Your people crave presence with divinity. To behold us in our splendor, and call our very existence miraculous, filled their hearts with joy and ours with peace. I still believe they were right. What is an angel to mankind but a being from a time and place far beyond their own?"

The hovering image shifted, seasons changing with a slow and steady march of time. Brick by brick, cathedrals rose from the ground, adorned with the silver and gold the lightborn refused. Existing places of worship tore down their old symbols and replaced them with the wings of the lightborn and their solemn, crystalline faces. More scenes showed the lightborn addressing tens of thousands in the streets of a wondrous city, and another lecturing in the center of an amphitheater that looked greater than all of Lowville.

"We accepted the role given to us and took upon our shoulders the grand task it represented," A'resh continued. "We did not know our own creator, but our hearts were not filled with hatred, nor prone to temptation of war. The ravages of time meant little to us. Humanity walks a path with their heads down, staring at the few steps ahead of their feet, but we witnessed the great length of the path they walked upon, and we knew the direction they headed. Endless conflict over borders, wealth, place of birth, and color of skin. There would always be the hungry, always the poor. Our lightborn gathered together, and after seven years, we reached our decision."

A'resh swirled his hand, sending the images scattering out in all directions only for them to suck back into one another, revealing an entirely new image. This time the lightborn addressed the people not as messengers or travelers, but as rulers. Kael saw untold years pass before him, overwhelming in detail, yet a soft voice hummed in the back of his mind, like an echo of a whisper from A'resh, and it guided his thoughts along, giving him understanding. Kael watched the dismantling of armies. The tearing down of the very foundations of societies. And then, at the end, the first drop of blood dripping from a lightborn's cut finger. Kael watched as it fell to the ground, crystallizing into the elemental light prism he was so familiar with.

"Humans were primitive creatures scrambling in the muck and dirt," A'resh said. "Yet their hearts were so determined, their will so powerful, they built grand empires despite the death and bloodshed. Or because of the death and bloodshed, my friend L'adim often said. His words should have been warnings to us all, but we did not listen."

Another shift. Kael gaped in wonder as he watched the light elemental prisms scatter throughout hundreds of nations. From them came the structures, the floating buildings of steel and glass, the heavy platforms carrying travelers heavenward, and the very first suit of Seraphim wings.

"Those first few decades were full of joy and splendor," A'resh said. His entire presence exuded a feeling of longing and sadness. "We should have known it was only temporary, but we believed the change we desired was coming to pass. The wonder of the light elements, and the imagination it sparked in your greatest thinkers, made us believe the discovery would aid your evolution. And so . . . we opened the rifts."

Another change. Kael felt Bree's hand slip into his, and he shared her fear and awe. The lightborn gathered together in a circle, speaking words that were older than humanity itself, and the air between them ripped open. The rift burned with fire near the outer edges, framing a center of perfect darkness. From that rift marched a legion of fireborn. They cowered before the lightborn, unable to move as holy men in red robes shackled them with chains of iron. A'resh sighed, and despite a clear hesitance, he showed more rifts opening, flooding the world with fireborn.

"We remembered nothing of ourselves prior to setting foot upon your land," A'resh said, "but we remembered worlds unlike your own, ones with creatures of fire and frost, planets of swirling ash and thunderous storms. Your people still shivered in the cold and starved in the winter months. But with all we'd seen you build with our blood, what might you do with access to fire, or ice, or the ferocity of a storm?"

They need not wonder, for A'resh showed them. Step by step Kael watched the old world begin to match theirs. Machines shifted and whirred, imbued with the power of the stormborn. Kael saw homes of ice in snowy landscapes, the people within warmed by lanterns powered by fire prisms. He saw elemental furnaces melt the earth into unknown metals. Simple platforms used to carry men and women became complicated vessels with enormous wings and domes of protective glass.

And then the images darkened, and A'resh's frustration and sorrow washed over all.

"As the centuries passed humanity did change, but not in the way we hoped. We became... *normal* to them. They believed our words were those of God, and surely the wonders and peace we brought to them proved it, but we found the ears of leaders becoming more and more deaf to our wishes. The urgency and fervor with which your people had tried to build our peaceful future gave way to the daily needs to live and thrive. And from that came the wars."

Kael had seen the destruction of battle before; L'fae had shown him the chaos of the Ascension, the lines of brave men lining up to die. And, after witnessing the fall of Galen and the furious fireborn wantonly burning villages, Kael thought he knew what A'resh would show them next.

It didn't even come close.

"Dear God," Bree whispered.

Two armies faced one another, thousands of Seraphim filling the moonlit skies on each side, thousands more soldiers stretching for miles in either direction huddled inside trenches fortified with spikes and wire. Some held bows, others carried long spears and thick shields upon their backs. Machines the likes of which neither Kael nor Bree had ever seen before rolled through the back lines. Some appeared to be cannons, others like metal humans with skin of gold. Great ten-wheeled contraptions powered by the roaring heat of a dozen fire prisms rolled over the ground between the armies, making a mockery of the trenches both sides had dug.

The Seraphim opened fire. The dark night sky turned bright as day. Barrages of fire slammed walls of stone and ice, lightning piercing through it all as if a hundred furious gods were conducting a hurricane. How the Seraphim could track one another or keep in formation was baffling. Perhaps they didn't. The dead rained from the sky, hundreds at a time. The boulders and ice shattered the bones of soldiers below who were locked in a deadly clash of shields and spears. Cannons punctuated the cacophony, each firing blasts of elements so powerful that a dozen coordinated Seraphim could not match in size or strength. When they struck, little remained of the bodies.

Kael felt tears running from his eyes. The sorrow radiated off A'resh like a cold wind, and he felt powerless to contain his own grief. The image swooped through the battle, miles upon miles, nations against nations in a war scorching green fields and quaint towns to ash and ruin.

"That battle was not the first," A'resh said as he dashed the images away. "But it was the grandest, known to the world as the Slaughter at Wolf Crossing. When the elements were dry and the blood drained from their soldiers, neither side claimed victory. Neither wanted it. The war ended, but the damage was already done, for L'adim had watched from afar."

Kael was curious to see this fabled terror, but L'adim appeared before him as any other lightborn, not at all like the crawling shadow L'fae had shown him. Eight other lightborn stood around him as he lectured atop a hill far from civilization. A'resh did nothing to shield the Skyborns from the aura of rage emanating from L'adim.

"We are not the voices of God," he shouted to his lightborn followers. "We are not the bringers of peace. We are enablers of suicide. We are the heralds of death. Witness the destruction humanity wreaks upon itself. Our gifts have not brought them up from their pathetic existence. It has only given them grander, wider, and more efficient ways to kill. We have dressed a rabid dog in a suit of gold and expected it to obey."

"Our very blood heals their wounds," one argued. L'fae, Kael realized. "Our commands are that they live in love. If we do not speak the words of God, then whatever God exists is undeserving of their faith."

"You misunderstand me," L'adim said, turning to her. "I say not that these principles are wrong, or our message was false. I say we are wrong to treat the humans as superior to all else. Why do we assume they are the chosen over all beasts by our God? Why coddle them and protect them yet let the eternal-born bleed daily for their trinkets and weapons? Because they were the first to worship us? What if our arrival had not been to this plane, but to the plane of the fireborn? Would we enslave humanity to further the fireborn's survival? Would we have them suffer in chains, their flesh cut, their blood drained, only to suffer anew the very next day?"

Kael could feel the frustration and confusion of the silent others.

"All I have are questions," L'adim said. "Yet you give no answers. Despite our best efforts, we do not have peace. We have warring nations built upon the suffering of thousands of eternal-born. The fireborn are our equal. The iceborn are our equal. They all bear a life far beyond the limits of the humans we have coddled. I say we free the eternal-born so they may return to their own worlds. In their absence we will force humanity to live in peace despite their meager protests. Perhaps, in the decades that follow, they will understand our wisdom is superior to theirs."

"We would tear entire societies to the ground," A'resh argued in the shimmering past. "We would bind humanity in chains and deny them their own choices. This is heresy."

"Tell me," L'adim asked as he whirled upon A'resh. "How is what you describe worse than the torture we inflict upon our fellow eternal-born?"

From both then and now, Kael felt the shame burn in A'resh's breast. He had no answer. None of them did.

"We cannot delay," L'adim insisted. "Our unwillingness to fully assume control has already cost lives. Humanity will not change. Not if it has a choice. So let us make that choice for it."

He paused. The auras of the lightborn overlapped one another, debating without words. Each of their opinions was perfectly clear to the other, and L'adim sadly shook his head.

"A shame," he said. "I thought you among the more open-minded of our brethren. It seems I was wrong."

A'resh closed his fist, ending the images. Kael wiped the tears from his eyes. Bree squeezed his hand once, then released, and together they gazed up at the towering lightborn.

"You need not see the rest, for L'fae has shown it to you," A'resh said. "L'adim closed the rifts to the other worlds, then freed the legion of eternal-born from their encampments. We had brought in too many, far too many. By our own hand we gave L'adim an army we could not stop. As the light faded from him, and he spilled blood with his own two hands, he lost the luster we all shared. He became twisted and cruel, his form turned to shadow instead of light. His very face became a lie, able to assume the shape of whoever he wished. No place was safe, and many a stronghold fell to his deceptions."

Kael remembered well those images of the Ascension. The chaos and destruction would stay with him to his deathbed. Having glimpsed the grand cities and inventions, Kael felt the loss of the prior world all the keener. The sheer scale of death, the millions upon millions of lives swept away in an instant, overwhelmed his ability to comprehend.

"Thank you," Kael said. "Thank you for giving us our answers."

"We once offered our knowledge to kings and lords," A'resh said. "But we also spoke with the least among you, and our healing blood cleansed the poor along with the powerful. I miss those days."

Kael glanced to his sister. They'd pushed their luck already with how long they'd visited, and he'd gotten far more than he'd ever hoped for when they started this foolhardy task.

"Are you ready to go?" he asked her.

Bree shook her head, and she stepped closer to the lightborn.

"L'adim swore you were not the voice of God," she said. "But what do you believe? Are you angels of heaven?"

A'resh sank his weight into the chains, setting them to rattling.

"Yes," he said. "I still believe. Daily my blood is drained, my eternal form bound to keep your last vestige of safety afloat. I endure this because I believe your people are sacred, and it was our responsibility to guide you, and our horrendous failure that led to your near extinction. The guilt is on our shoulders, and so I bear the weight of your world upon those very same shoulders."

Kael's insides quivered at the aura washing over him. There was so much guilt and confusion overwhelming him, mixed with a throb of pain and sorrow. But there was hope deep within, small but powerful. Kael wished to grab that faith and hold it inside his own breast.

"Thank you," Bree said. "I don't know why, but I needed to know. We're lost as well."

"The shadowborn walks among you," A'resh said. "Tread carefully, and with eyes wide open. Warn the people. Tell the deaf ears. There are no more miracles left within us to save you should the second apocalypse come."

A'resh suddenly stiffened, and his gaze lifted to the doors behind them. Kael and Bree spun. Two furious theotechs stood in the open doorway.

"Blasphemers!" one shouted. "Only the holy may look upon the angels."

He drew a knife from his pocket, as did the other. Kael braced for a fight, for he saw no way past the two.

"*KNEEL!*" A'resh thundered. His voice shook the very walls, his fury making Kael's bones rattle within his body. The theotechs immediately collapsed to their knees. Meager cries escaped their lips as their faces pressed to the cold stone. The lightborn rose higher in his chains, the glow of his body seeming to brighten with his rage. Kael had always felt comfort in the presence of the lightborn, but this was a facet of them he'd seen only glimpses of during his visions of the Ascension, and the battles against the shadowborn's forces. His limbs trembled. An impulse to kneel alongside the cowering theotechs filled him.

"It is time you leave," A'resh said.

"What of the theotechs?" Bree asked. Kael was impressed how steady her voice remained, for he himself was still reeling from shock at the outburst. "They've seen us. They'll know what we did."

A'resh leaned closer, one of his hands stretching closer. Chains rattled, a heavy, metallic thunder. The theotechs did not respond. They looked like they couldn't even move.

"Just as they may enter my mind, so may I enter theirs," the lightborn said. "They will remember only my face. Now go, and share what you have seen."

The two bowed in unison, and with a shiver of regret, Kael led the way out from the hall, and from the lightborn he knew he would never visit with again.

CHAPTER 8

Bree awoke to a rapid knocking on her door. She grimaced against the noise, every part of her desperately begging for another thirty minutes of sleep.

"One moment," she mumbled, sitting up in her bed and rubbing her eyes. Light shone through the window. Morning then, but how late? Bree dropped to her feet and walked to Kael's bedside.

"Wake up," she said, shoving Kael's shoulder until he began to grumble and curl up in retreat below his blanket.

The knocking continued in small, rapid beats. It sounded like an angry hummingbird was attempting to rouse them from their beds.

"What?" Bree asked, flinging open the door and staring bleary-eyed at Rebecca Waller. The icy look on the woman's face immediately jolted Bree awake.

"We need to talk," she said.

"Sure," Bree said, stepping out of the way. "Come in."

Rebecca entered as Kael was smoothing his bed-mangled hair in vain.

"Something wrong?" Kael asked.

"Something is very wrong," Rebecca said. She crossed her arms, her fingers clutching her elbows in iron grips. "Pray tell me what madness possessed you last night to break into the Clay Cathedral?"

The siblings exchanged a look.

"I don't know what you're talking about," Bree said.

"Don't," Rebecca snapped. "Don't even try. I know it was you two. Who else would be reckless enough to disobey a direct order by Candren's Archon during what was supposed to be a calm, diplomatic affair?"

Bree's cheeks were burning, and Kael was doing no better at hiding his embarrassment.

"Would you mind telling us how you know this?" Kael asked.

Rebecca glared.

"The theotechs have been raising a ruckus about this all morning. Someone broke into the Clay Cathedral, slew one of their own as well as two guards on duty. They're demanding a trial, and you can imagine who they believe to be the primary suspects."

"They can demand one all they want," Bree said. "Have they any proof?"

"What proof do they need when you openly proclaimed your desire to enter the Clay Cathedral in front of hundreds?" Rebecca asked. "Now answer my question, you foolish Skyborns. What possessed you to do this?"

Kael glanced to Bree, and she gestured for him to speak freely.

"We needed answers," Kael said. "The royal family wasn't going to give them to us, and the theotechs sure as hell weren't going to, either."

Rebecca looked ready to tear down the walls.

"You asked for permission and were denied," she said. "By going there you disobeyed the Archon as well as murdering three innocent men."

"Innocent?" Bree said, unable to keep anger out of her voice. "They were servants of Center! Has everyone forgotten that they're our enemy?"

"Except Evereth has given them clemency to perform their duties," Rebecca shouted right back. Well, for her it was shouting. Her words came out quieter than Bree's, but the tone was one of barely controlled rage. "The theotechs are furious, and they're threatening to cut off all clean water for two days if you are not punished."

"What stops Evereth from executing all of them if they do?" Kael asked.

"Nothing," Rebecca said. "But the only other person who knows how to operate the deep machinery is Johan, and I don't believe the Archon is too keen on granting that power to him, either."

The woman sighed and leaned back against the closed door. She rubbed her eyelids with her thumb and forefinger, refusing to look at either Kael or Bree with her amber eyes.

"Archon Dayan has ordered your arrest," she said. "And I have agreed to hand you over without incident. Your trial will be held later today, after we've signed the peace treaty. We'll have this resolved one way or another so we may return home."

Bree could hardly believe what she was hearing. Her and Kael on trial for killing servants of their enemy on their way to discovering the truth?

"You won't let them imprison us, will you?" she asked.

Rebecca finally looked back up. Her face was hard, but her words were harder.

"Their lack of hard proof or witness will make things difficult," she said. "But that doesn't mean the Archon won't rule against us. I'm sorry, Bree. If forced to choose between all of Candren's support and two Seraphs... the times are dire. As much as it pains me, I have to consider it as a possibility."

So that was it, then. One moment she was being praised as Weshern's grand symbol of hope, and the next she was an expendable asset in a political gambit. Goddamnit, why couldn't she just have remained a soldier? At least in the air she knew what she was doing.

"When do we turn ourselves in?" Kael asked softly.

"There are soldiers waiting outside," Rebecca answered.

Bree felt fear trickling down her chest to settle as a rock in her stomach.

"May we at least dress first?" she asked.

Rebecca nodded.

"Don't take long."

When she left, the two looked to one another, unspoken fears passing between them.

"We could try to escape," Kael said. Bree shook her head.

"No," she said. "We'll have to trust that Rebecca knows what she's doing. Fleeing only proves our guilt."

"All right then," Kael said, sliding open the door of his closet. "Prison and trial it is."

They emerged from their room fully dressed in their Seraphim attire. A dozen Candren soldiers waited in the hallway, six on either side of the door. Bree held her arms out to them, and wordlessly they slapped manacles on her wrists. They did the same to Kael, and then linked their two sets with a long thin chain.

"Say nothing," Rebecca told them as they were led away. "Save your words for the trial."

The soldiers led them down the hallway and toward the front of the castle to a locked and guarded door. Past it were stairs leading down into the deep, sunless parts of Candren. Dully burning torches lit their way into a foul-smelling dungeon. Many of the cells were full of prisoners, and Bree noticed several wore the distinct robes of Johan's disciples. It seemed Evereth was as distrustful of Johan's movement as he was of Center. No wonder he let the theotechs continue their duties so long as they promised neutrality.

At the far end of the dungeon, where only the light of the carried torches shone, the soldiers dumped them into the barred cell and slammed the door.

"Will you remove our manacles?" Kael asked as they heard a key turn.

"Manacles stay on," one muttered, and then the twelve headed back to the entrance. Bree took a quick assessment of their surroundings as the light of the torches faded. No windows, no furnishings, just a stone floor and a bucket in the corner for them to do their business.

The guards vanished up the distant stairs, bathing the two in complete darkness.

"I hope you're not afraid of the dark," Bree said, and she heard Kael laugh.

"It could be worse," he said. "At least we're not hanging by our feet or something."

Bree smiled despite her exhaustion and worry. Yes, it could indeed be worse. The two could be separate instead of together, unable to ease each other's worries and aid in the passing of time. She sat on the floor and leaned against the side bars of the cell, her manacled hands resting atop her knees. From the dull thud, she guessed Kael did the same opposite her.

Time crawled, without marker to acknowledge its slow passage. Bree tried to sleep, found herself too nervous to relax. She slowly tapped her manacles against the iron bars, the soft clink somehow calming in the pitch black. Dressing in her Seraphim outfit had proven a blessing, for at least the thick jacket provided some protection from the cold that seemed to seep from every surface.

"So," Kael said. Though he whispered, the sound of his voice was a startling thunder in the quiet. "What'd you think of the lightborn?"

Bree chuckled. They'd not had much time to discuss the encounter on their hurried trip back to the mansion.

"I think he was amazing," she said. "There's something... awe inspiring about being in their presence. And honest. They hide nothing. Their every emotion, it's just...there. You're bathed in it, invited to share without shame or embarrassment."

"Yeah," Kael said after a moment. "It's sad people aren't like that. It would probably solve a lot of fights before they ever started."

"It's also sad no one else will ever get to experience that feeling," Bree said. More and more she saw the terrible sins of Center in keeping the lightborns' existence a secret.

Kael kept to himself, the silence descending back over them for several long minutes.

"They won't really convict us, will they?" he suddenly asked.

Bree wished she had a better answer.

"I have no idea," she said. "But what will we tell them? That we were determined to visit an angel? You heard Evereth's mockery of the very idea. How do we convince him otherwise?"

"We bring him to the Clay Cathedral," Kael said. "That's all we need, right? It's so simple. Once he sees A'resh for himself he'll understand why we did what we did."

Bree was glad for the darkness, for at least Kael wouldn't see her bitter smile.

"Yes, so simple," she said. "But what if he refuses to go?"

Kael sounded baffled by the idea.

"Why wouldn't he?" he asked.

"Because the Archon doesn't just believe he's right," she said. "He *knows* he is right. To visit the cathedral is to entertain the idea he's wrong. Some people are willing to learn and accept their knowledge is not absolute. I think Evereth's quite the opposite. The theotechs will insist we broke in to tamper with the ancient machinery, endangering all of Candren. Our only counter is to claim wc wished to speak with an angel. Which do you think he'll believe, especially in open court?"

Bree heard Kael knock his head against the bars twice.

"There's still a chance he goes, right?"

"There's always a chance. I just don't like my life riding on a chance."

More silence. Bree felt bad for her pessimism, but she didn't want to inflate Kael with false hopes. Her impression of Evereth Dayan had been one of a tightly closed mind. The jailing of Johan's disciples, despite Johan being provably right about Center's aggression, showed how unwilling the man was to have his wisdom questioned. Perhaps the Archon would visit the Clay Cathedral and demand entrance, but he would do it quietly, and long after the trial was over.

Bree resumed tapping her manacles against the bars, using it as an indicator of time. A tap every few seconds. Every twenty taps about a minute. Every thousand an hour. It seemed silly to consider counting that high, but she was up to six hundred and seventeen when Kael spoke again.

"Bree . . . I have an idea."

"Let's hear it," Bree said. "Not like we have much else to do."

Bree heard shifting, some scraping of clothing. It sounded like nervous fidgeting, but what would Kael be so nervous about?

"I've been thinking about your blood," he said. "Our blood, really."

"What about it?"

"Well, we know yours restores a fire prism, and mine a light, but there's clearly more to it than that, right? I mean, look at your swords. No one else knows how you do it, but you do. You have control over the element in ways that don't require a Seraph harness."

"My blood," she said, remembering her battle against Nickolas Flynn on the steps of the Crystal Cathedral. "I ignited my blood with just a thought."

"Exactly," Kael said. "We know plenty of what your blood does, but what of mine? If I have lightborn blood in me, what else can I do that we've not even thought to test?"

It was an interesting idea, and Bree told him so.

"What is it you're currently thinking?" she asked.

"I'm thinking I need a way to cut my hand."

Bree stared around the room despite being unable to see anything. The only tool they had at their disposal was the manacles locking their wrists together. Slowly she pressed her cheek against the sides of the manacles, searching for a sharp edge. She found one near the keyhole, a small jut of worn metal.

"I can do it," she told Kael. "Scoot closer and give me your hands."

He did, and his manacles rattled as he extended his arms in the dark. Bree searched until she found them, then pulled both his hands down to his lap.

"I can't see what I'm doing," she said. "So, uh, please keep still."

"Whatever you say. Just try not to cut too deep, all right? I'll haunt you until eternity if I suffer an ignoble death bleeding out on the floor of a Candren prison."

"At least we'll still be together."

Bree twisted her elbows so the sharp metal bit faced downward. Using her knee to hold his hand in place, she pushed the manacles against his palm as hard as she could. It didn't draw blood at first, but then she dragged her arms along his skin. Kael cried out instinctively and pulled his hands from her lap.

"Sorry," she said. "Did it go too deep?"

"We're about to find out."

The dark cell went quiet, not even of the sound of their breathing. Bree waited, wondering what exactly her brother intended.

Her answer came in the form of a sudden twinkling of light in the center of their cell, like a newly born star. The light was blinding, but Bree forced herself to stare at it. The glow dwindled down until it shone like pale white embers hovering atop Kael's cut hand. In the pitch darkness, that somber glow was more than enough for them to see one another.

Bree winced at the sight of her brother's hand. She'd only meant to scratch him lightly, but the jagged slice looked in danger of leaving a scar. Blood pooled across his hand, which he held palm upward, soft light shimmering and glowing across its surface.

"Well, so far I'm one for one," he said, grinning. "Now for idea two. Bree, this will sound crazy, but I want you to put your hand in mine so you're touching my blood."

Bree frowned.

"Uh . . . gross?"

"Oh, so now you're suddenly squeamish about a bit of blood?" Kael asked, and Bree felt her cheeks flush.

"Sorry," she said. "Fine. I'll do it. But what are you hoping to accomplish?"

"Just close your eyes and keep still. I'd rather not say in case I fail miserably."

Bree put her hand in Kael's, and she felt the warmth of his blood spread across her palm. Kael closed his eyes, his face scrunched in deep concentration. Bree watched, curious as to his plan. Was he hoping to make her float above the ground like the lightborn? His hand tightened around hers, and Bree heard a strange ringing sensation in the back of her mind. Was that part of what Kael . . . ?

A memory returned to Bree, of the two of them playing in the backyard. Kael was "it," and Bree fled from him through a fallow field, dodging and weaving whenever he lunged. The smell of dirt filled her nostrils, the sway of the grass a phantom kiss on her hands. The careless joy of those years flooded her chest, and she smiled despite the tears rolling down her face.

The memory vanished as rapidly as it came, returning her to the somber white light of their prison cell. Bree pulled her hand free and attempted to wipe away the blood on the stone floor. To her surprise, her hand was dry, the blood already flaking off her skin.

"Did you see anything?" Kael asked. She could hear his nervous optimism, and she laughed as she wiped away her tears.

"I saw us playing in the grass when we were seven," she said.

Kael pumped his fist and grinned like a maniac, a celebratory *whoop* barely held in check.

"I knew it," he said. "I just knew it."

"How'd you do it?" Bree asked.

Kael glanced at his palm, and the slow trickle of blood from his cut.

"It's . . . it's a little like activating the ice prism in my gauntlet," he said. "I can feel the connection, but instead of trying to shape ice into a sphere or cone, I'm focusing on a memory. After a moment, it just . . . flows. Does this make any sense?"

Bree nodded. It was similar to how it felt when she bathed her swords in flame.

"So this is your plan to convince Evereth?" she asked.

"Yeah, that's it."

"What if you can only show people what they've already experienced? We were both there in the memory we shared. What of something only you have seen?"

Kael flexed his hand a few times, setting the blood to flow anew and brightening the cell further.

"I've got an idea," he said. "Let's try again. This time close your eyes, all right?"

Bree took his hand and obeyed. She kept her breathing steady and did her best to empty her mind. She didn't know how difficult this was for Kael but she'd try to help in any way she could. A minute crawled by without vision or memory, setting Bree to worry.

"Kael?" she asked.

"There," Kael whispered back. "There it is. Bree, open your eyes."

A vibrant blue sky spread before Bree when her eyelids parted. A sense of motion overcame her, wind blasting through her hair and swirling beneath her Seraphim wings. Sounds followed, the mighty roar of battle. Bree tried to look about, but her eyes were fixed ahead. She was part of a formation, her shoulders and back twisting to keep pace with her leader.

Lightning crackled through the air, ice and stone a destructive rain plummeting to the ocean below.

Where am I? Bree wondered as her formation curled back around the edge of the battle to dive straight in. They fought against people of Galen, she realized. Her gaze shifted upward, and before her blazed a twin trail of fire. Bree's heart caught in her throat. She saw from Kael's eyes in Phoenix Squad, and before her was the Phoenix.

Bree watched this phantom version of herself dodge and weave through the chaos of battle, fire dripping off her blades. Time seemed to slow as she watched herself dip below stone and then soar above a plume of flame meant to char her flesh to the bone. Horror flooded Bree. She didn't want to watch. Every attack showed how close to death she skirted. Every instinctual movement was now revealed to her, and it only frightened her further.

Then her eyes pulled away, and she was diving, turning, all her skill pushed to the limit to keep up with the madwoman that was the Phoenix. Dawning dread seeped through Bree's mind. She knew when this was. She knew where it led. Scattered from the formation, the dead raining down, she caught sight of Galen's weak, flickering Beam.

No, her mind shrieked. Not again. Never again. She tore her hand back, the vision rupturing as she broke contact. The comfortable darkness returned, lit by only the last flickering embers of Kael's shimmering blood. Kael slumped before her, a guilty expression on his face. He knew the demons the vision had stirred in her memory, yet he'd done it anyway.

"Why?" Bree asked.

"I'm sorry," Kael said. "But I had to know. I had to see if I could give a vision and have it inspire the same fear and confusion that I felt."

Bree shivered, trying to stomp down the memories of collapsing nets full of villagers and crowds of people plummeting off the side of the doomed island.

"It did," she said.

Kael reached out for her, and she instinctively pulled away. Catching herself, she paused, let him wrap his arm around her.

"Sorry," he whispered.

Bree leaned against him, accepting his comfort.

"I know. Now let me rest for a bit."

She closed her eyes and steadied her breathing. The vision had left her body drained and her mind lit. Kael clenched his cut fist tight, ending the light.

"Think it'll work?" Kael asked after a moment. His voice was a calm reassurance in the darkness.

"I'm not sure. The Archon might not be willing to touch your blood and wait. It's a bit . . . strange."

Kael actually laughed.

"We're desperate, Bree, so we're not exactly overflowing with options. I more meant if he does see a vision, will it convince him of the truth of our claims?"

Bree settled deeper into her brother's lap, her tense muscles and tired bones relaxing.

"The Archon? Trust me, Kael. He won't know what hit him."

CHAPTER 9

Bree didn't know how long she slept, only that when she woke, guards had come to escort them. The two left the cold, dark corridors surrounded by spears and shields and stepped into painfully bright hallways. Bree squinted, relying on the jostle of soldiers to keep her walking the right way. Through blurry eyes she saw both nobles and servants staring as their group passed. Bree tried not to be angry with them. Of course she and Kael were a sight to see. Here they were, heroes of Weshern, on their way to trial. Who wouldn't stare?

The guards took them to the Archon's grand throne room. The wide balconies were empty, the side tables seating only a few. Long curtains stitched into figures of war hung from the rafters. Archon Dayan sat in his gilded throne. His stone face revealed nothing. Beside him stood his royal advisor, arms crossed and mouth locked in a tight frown. On left side of a dais stood Rebecca, her fingers nervously tapping her clipboard. On the right waited two theotechs, their eyes wide with zealous fury.

"Leave us," Evereth ordered the guards. They left Kael and Bree standing before the raised dais, and did not release their manacles. Evereth kept ramrod straight in his chair, staring at the two of them as if he could drill the truth out with his eyes.

"The theotechs of the Clay Cathedral have made damning claims against you Skyborn twins, claims that Rebecca Waller has not directly denied."

"May we hear those claims for ourselves?" Kael asked.

The older of the two theotechs stepped forward.

"You knowingly broke into the cathedral without either our or the Archon's permission," he said. "You killed three men and injured two more, putting all of Candren in jeopardy with your recklessness. The inner mechanics of the Beam are protected inside the cathedral, and I fear the damage you may have caused if you'd ventured deeper within."

"You two were also present for Galen's collapse," said the other theotech. "I now wonder if that were merely coincidence."

Bree bristled at the accusations. The theotechs were clearly lying, but their counterargument would involve insisting the lightborn existed within the cathedral... something the two theotechs were clearly betting on the Archon not entertaining in the slightest.

"These Weshern Seraphs are not on trial for Galen's collapse," Rebecca interjected, and she sounded none too pleased. "Would you like to blame the rain of demons from the sky on them as well?"

"Both of you, hold your tongues," Evereth ordered. He leaned forward, gaze narrowing. "I have been within the inner workings of the Clay Cathedral," he said. "I have been shown the complicated machinery that powers the Beam. I have seen the veritable river flowing through the pipes, filtered of salt and sent to our fountains and lakes. All this I was shown when I took my seat on this throne, but what I never saw was an angel keeping our island aloft."

"That is because these children are deluded," said the older theotech. "Given to fantasy and legend, and because of that, our own paid with their lives."

"Of which you have no proof," Rebecca said.

"What proof do we need?" the theotech snapped. "Kael Skyborn here demanded entrance into the Clay Cathedral and was denied. That night, two guards and a theotech inside the cathedral are then slain. Who *else* would have attempted such an act, plus possess the skill to kill our trained people?"

That was the biggest crux of the argument, and one they could not easily refute. Bree nudged Kael in the side. Best to not let the point linger, and instead turn the conversation onto the lies of the theotechs. Her brother shot her a wink and then stepped forward into a bow before the Archon.

"Might I speak now that others are done speaking for and against us?" he asked.

Evereth waved a hand, and he glared at the theotechs when they started to protest.

"You say you have seen the secrets of the theotechs within Candren," he said. "So before I continue, I must ask, what if there *were* an angel hidden within the confines?"

Evereth frowned.

"Then it would mean I was lied to," he said, glancing to his left. "And it would mean the nonsense you spoke of at dinner might be true."

Kael lifted his bound hands. The rattle of metal echoed in the grand hall.

"I don't need to make an argument," he said. "I don't need

words. I have a gift, Archon. I will show you the angel, whose blood and sacrifice keeps your people safely above the Endless Ocean's waters."

Bree carefully watched the reactions to their planned gambit. Rebecca kept her face passive, but she clearly wasn't pleased. The theotechs appeared nervous. They likely knew what Bree could do with her blood. Perhaps they had an inkling of what Kael could do as well? Evereth, meanwhile, looked mildly disgusted.

"I have no interest in petty tricks," the Archon said.

"No trick," Kael said. "Cut my palm, and touch the blood with your hand. You will see the truth."

"And if I see nothing?"

Her brother didn't miss a beat.

"Then we will confess our guilt before the court and accept whatever judgment you see fitting for our actions."

Rebecca's displeasure turned to full-blown shock. Even the theotechs appeared confused if they should be worried or pleased by the gambit. Bree held her breath, waiting for Evereth to make his decision.

"Kahlil," he said. "Do as the boy asks."

"Of course, my Archon," he said, bowing low before descending the steps. The slender man drew out a knife from a pocket and held it above Kael's open palm. "How deep shall I cut?"

"Just enough to draw blood."

"Very well."

The advisor sliced across the skin, and pocketed the dagger as quickly as he'd drawn it. Kael grimaced in pain but did not cry out. Bree tried to appear confident despite her worry. Their lives were in Kael's hands, and in his ability to use a power they'd only recently discovered.

Bree rolled her eyes, realizing how ridiculous her feelings were. Was this any different from Kael entrusting her flaming blades after she'd spent an entire year overwhelmingly incompetent with her fire?

"I am ready," Kael said, looking to the Archon.

"Not me," Evereth said. "Kahlil shall witness while I watch for tricks and lies."

Kael tried, and failed, to hide his initial disappointment. Turning to the advisor, he offered his hand. When the man accepted, his palm sliding into Kael's bloody palm, Kael ordered him to close his eyes. Kahlil shuffled foot to foot, looking awkward and impatient as he obeyed. Time slowly ticked away, with the theotechs appearing more relieved with each passing second. Bree waited, trusting her brother. He'd shown her two visions. He could manage this third.

Kael suddenly relaxed, and a look of peace washed over his face.

"Open your eyes," he said.

To Bree's surprise, Khalil's eyes stayed shut. His entire body locked tight, and his mouth dropped open in awe. A few words strayed off his tongue, too soft to be heard. The advisor's legs weakened. He dropped to his knees. Kael held on to his hand, calm before the advisor's fright, steady before the advisor's trembling. It took only a moment before Khalil broke free, but in that span the entire room had been shocked silent.

Khalil turned to the Archon as he slowly rose to his feet.

"Well?" Evereth asked. He sounded angry that he didn't know what was happening.

"My Archon," a winded Khalil said. "I beg of you, accept this man's hand."

"This is merely a trick," one theotech said. "A false power of the demons. Do not fall for the illusion."

"Be silent," Evereth said as he descended the steps. "I have trusted you since the day of my coronation. I will spare this young man a moment of that same trust."

Kael offered his bleeding hand, and the Archon placed his bare fingers into the blood. He closed his eyes without needing told, and Kael did likewise. Her brother's face became one of concentration, searching for the connection.

It took far less time than it did for the advisor. Kael's face relaxed, his eyelids fluttering.

"Open your eyes," he told the Archon. "Behold his majesty."

The Archon's body locked tight. His jaw trembled. His knees shook. Bree knew what he was showing him. They'd discussed it before sleep had overcome them. Kael would share the memory of that first moment they stepped into A'resh's grand chamber. They would share the emotions of peace and awe. With borrowed eyes, the Archon would stare into the face of a lightborn, and who could deny their existence after such a sight?

The Archon slowly lowered to one knee. The throne room remained awkwardly silent, the only noise Evereth's labored breathing. The vision lasted a full minute before Kael pulled away. The Archon's eyes snapped open, and Bree saw tears in them.

"God in heaven, forgive me," he said, rising to his feet. His voice firmed, and a flood of anger overwhelmed him as he turned to the theotechs.

"Guards, arrest them both," he shouted and pointed at the theotechs. "And send word to General Viker. I must speak with him immediately."

Guards hidden behind curtains and disguised doors burst forth, surrounding the theotechs.

"It is a lie," the older theotech shouted. "A lie they have fed you, a tool of the demons to destroy our unity and threaten our islands. Do not believe, Archon, do not believe!"

Evereth never even looked at him. He motioned for a guard and ordered Kael and Bree to be freed.

"I have seen a great many things in my life," he said. "But that is a sight nothing has prepared me for. I shall meet with A'resh myself. Such a being shall not suffer in our stead without our praise and thanks."

Kael couldn't contain his smug grin.

"So you're saying we're *not* to be executed?" he asked.

Evereth cracked a smile.

"No, Skyborn children. You aren't to be executed. You'll go home with the rest of your Seraphim, and you'll go with my heartfelt blessings."

CHAPTER 10

The Speaker walked through the enormous grass fields along the eastern side of the holy island. Soldiers bowed their heads and raised their spears, their number in the thousands. They stood in five-by-five blocks atop wooden platforms, eagerly awaiting the ferrymen to come and carry them across the Endless Ocean. Their polished gold armor shone in the warm morning sun.

"Sing praises to the angels," Marius shouted to them when he stood in the center of the gathering. "And do not doubt the importance of your place in this battle. Seraphim may rule the skies, and the siege engines of old may carve the earth, but you are the bones that shall hold our army together."

The soldiers cheered, a chant of "The Speaker Reigns" echoing behind Marius as he continued down the wide dirt road carved by the weight of Center's army. Marius felt the warmth in his breast, weeks of nerves steadily easing. Everything had come to this. The rebellions would be crushed, the minor islands subjugated, and order restored in their little place above the Endless Ocean. The next time L'adim dared to attack he would face a united humanity instead of the squabbling tribal mess it was now.

Er'el Jaina Cenborn met Marius at the gathering of angelic knights. She stood prim and calm with her hands crossed behind her back, but her eyes sparkled with excitement.

"Measures are proceeding without incident, though we lag significantly behind schedule. Our chance for attacking at dawn are long behind us."

"It is no matter," Marius said, the two passing between groups of knights milling about. The soft hum of their wings, numbering in the hundreds, filled Marius's chest with a pleasant vibration. "Dawn, afternoon, midnight: it will all end the same."

Knights quickly crossed their arms over their chests and bowed low as the two passed. Marius dipped his head in return, ensuring each group received his acknowledgment.

"We've used every single ferryman for this invasion, putting a halt to our trade and travel," Jaina continued. "The other islands will likely sense something is amiss."

"And what will they do if they know?" Marius asked. He gestured to the army of angelic knights surrounding them. "Will they ambush us on the way despite being thoroughly outnumbered? Or will they gather armies together to challenge our landing?" He laughed. "Let them, Jaina. Let them bring the entire forces of all four islands together to face us. Victory will still greet us."

The two approached the final stretch of land prior to the island's edge. Ferrymen buzzed through the air like an angered swarm, hundreds of them coordinating liftoffs and assigning positions. All across the ground dashed the theotechs with cloths, prisms, and tools. Their work was almost done. The engines waked.

Towering over all were the weapons of the ancient world. Grand cannons on wheels. Turrets laced with slender steel pipes to funnel the barrages of coordinated fire. Wall breakers powered by fire in their bellies and light elements in their battering rams. Marius's favorite were the five machines that resembled metal men. Each one required fifty light elemental prisms to power, but they gave their controller unmatched precision and control. They were the knight giants, and Marius had personally assigned the five theotechs that would pilot them.

"Breathtaking, isn't it?" Marius asked. Theotechs swarmed over the machines, cleaning, tweaking, and latching chains to the enormous platforms beneath them.

"They are an impressive sight," Jaina admitted. "But their cost is extraordinary. I find it no surprise our ancestors gravitated toward Seraphim warriors. They are far more efficient in prism usage."

"Now is not the time to count the cost," Marius said.

"I find the moment before the battle the perfect time to count the cost," Jaina said. "Otherwise how can you be sure you are willing to pay?"

Fair enough. Marius continued toward the edge, his imagination growing wild. He'd witnessed only a few of the ancient weapons tested to ensure their proper functionality. What might it be to hear the song of a hundred cannons? Such a beautiful destruction, that horrible symphony. Despite the heavy cost, Marius knew in his heart there was no other way. After today it would be centuries before another minor island thought of rebelling.

"Where is my transport?" Marius asked.

"There," Jaina said, pointing. "At the very edge."

They passed one of the knight giants, and Marius paused beside it. The machine was designed to look like one of the knights from the ancient stories, every inch covered with shining silver steel. In its right hand it held a sword the size of a man. Its left hand was empty, the center of its palm an interlocking pyramid of six focal prisms. Marius climbed atop the enormous platform of logs lashed together with iron so he might touch its armored leg. What had the world been like before the Ascension? What mighty empire crafted such deadly creations? How many once walked the earth, for Center only held tiny remnants of weaponry from the ancient civilizations. As much as the potential destruction frightened him, he could not deny the awe-inspiring sight of those metal monstrosities slowly crossing the battlefield.

"Soon," Marius whispered.

A few knights and theotechs stood around the marble platform, waiting for Marius's arrival. The Speaker stepped between them, accepting their respectful, if impatient, bows. His custom platform was simple in design, though extravagant in decoration. A golden chair rested atop a thick slab of marble. All across the platform's sides blazed runes and angelic images drawn with melted silver and gold. Eight pairs of small silver wings marked the thick steel rings drilled into the marble. Silver chains looped through the rings, awaiting their ferrymen to lift them up and carry Marius into battle.

"I apologize for the delay," Marius told them as he settled comfortably into the throne. "But I found myself admiring the work of our theotechs. They have done a marvelous job restoring the ancient weapons to prime condition."

"That they have," said General Garnett. He was a burly man, with a thick black beard braided down to his belt. It was his responsibility to command the ground forces come landfall, and such responsibility left him in a near-constant sour mood. "But I still beg of you to reconsider their use. Too many of these machines aren't tested, and my soldiers have no experience fighting alongside such firepower. They're an unnecessary risk. My men will crush Weshern's ground forces with ease, as will our angelic knights. Leave the machines here, and carry them in only if you must."

Not a new argument by the general, but the most passionately given.

"I hear your worries, and I ask that you believe me when I say I do not take them lightly," Marius said. "But we have underestimated Weshern before, and we cannot risk doing so again. We will go in with all our strength."

"My men will die from friendly fire," Garnett said. "Know that their deaths are not on my head."

"Nor are they on us theotechs," Jaina said, frowning at him. "This is war, General. I would think you well aware of the risks all that entails."

"Enough," Marius said, cutting both off. "This is an hour for sacrifice and triumph, not bickering. If everything is prepared, summon the ferrymen and let us take to the air."

General Garnett bowed before leaving in a huff. Marius was more amused than upset by the lack of respect. Garnett was a temperamental sort, but his soldiers loved him, and they would die for him. In return, Garnett fought for their safety, feeling all too often that the ground forces were overlooked in favor of the more famous and legendary fighters in the air.

"The soldiers are ready," Jaina said. "And I believe most of the war machines are prepared for flight."

"And the knights?"

Jaina pointed to the sky.

"I think we're about to have our answer."

A golden-winged knight flew low overhead, and she twirled while descending to land in a kneeling position before the Speaker.

"My lord," Knight Master Allison Trevarch said with bowed head.

"Rise, Allison," Marius said. "Are my knights ready?"

Allison stood, her hands on the hilts of her two swords. She was tall even among the men, her hair a fiery red and her left cheek marred by a long scar traveling halfway down her neck. Allison wasn't the most skilled of his knights, but she was the keenest mind and the strongest leader.

"We await your command," Allison said. "My knights are eager for a taste of battle. Our spars and training do not do the exhilaration of war justice."

"Indeed," Marius said. "The Weshern Seraphim have proven admirably resilient, and there is a high chance the other islands will come to their aid. Are you ready to face such a force on enemy territory?"

Allison smirked.

"We are knights of Center. Let them come. All traitors to God will fall before our blades."

Marius waved her away.

"Return to your knights," he said. "We leave in but a heartbeat."

She bowed low.

"To a glorious battle," she said.

"And a peaceful end," Marius responded.

Allison's wings shone with light, and then with a jump she soared into the air. Marius glanced to the side, seeing Jaina conversing with several young theotechs. She finished speaking, then returned to Marius.

"It appears all divisions are reporting ready for liftoff," she said. "We await your order to begin."

"Consider it given."

Jaina's calm veneer momentarily broke into a smile.

"We start a new age, Speaker," she said. "History will remember this day as the day our islands unified as one."

"Worry not for history," Marius said. "Only for survival."

The Er'el returned to the younger theotechs and gave her order. They scattered, rushing to spread the word. Marius tapped the arm of his chair with his fingers, telling himself to be patient. It would take some time for the legion of ferrymen to carry the incredible number of forces to Weshern.

The roar started weak at first, then built and built as wings of both knights and ferrymen hummed together. Eight descended around Marius's platform, taking up the chains and staring skyward for orders from their supervisors to lift. Jaina stepped atop the platform beside Marius, arms crossed as she coolly watched the proceedings.

"This must have been what the Ascension was like," she said as countless platforms steadily rose into the air.

"I have witnessed the Ascension," Marius said. "And it was far more beautiful, and far more terrifying."

The knights flew overhead, taking up the vanguard to protect the slower, vulnerable platforms carrying soldiers and machines. The last time Marius witnessed so many was during a military parade through Center's capital. It failed to compare. The urgency, the excitement, only added to the wonder.

Marius glanced over his shoulder. The first of the machines was rising into the air, dozens of ferrymen latching chains to the chest pieces of their harnesses. Their small, stubby wings flared with light, and steadily the platform left ground. More platforms carried soldiers overhead. They would secure landing zones before the war machines followed, while the knights would ensure no Seraphim bombarded from above or below. Last came a platform full of Marius's specters, eager for their chance to bypass the front lines for a chance to strike at the royalty who would be hiding deeper within the island.

More and more platforms rose, a dizzying display flying at many varying heights to reduce the likelihood of a collision. The sky filled with wings, all the world humming with their pleasant thrum. Glorious. Just glorious.

Once half the soldiers were ahead, a ferryman supervisor hovered near, shouting an order to the others. The chains tightened, the ferrymen lifted, and then Marius's platform lifted off the island and began making its way toward Weshern. Marius settled into his throne while Jaina kept herself steady by holding the throne's side.

The gathered force of Center's might flew through the air. They had no need for the element of surprise. What did it matter? They had the power to destroy worlds. Marius did his best to relax. They moved at a steady, easy pace. The knights ahead hovered more than flew, their legs dangling as they drifted southeast. The floating green-and-brown sphere that was Weshern steadily neared. Occasionally, the island vanished behind a cloud, reemerging that much closer. If Marius squinted his eyes, he thought he could see the tiniest of specks swarming the island's outer edge. Weshern's Seraphim preparing for battle. What trick might they attempt? What hope did they have against such might? No doubt desperate messengers were flying to Candren, Sothren, and Elern. The other islands would see Center's invasion on their travel. Marius hoped the incredible display would dissuade them from joining in.

"It seems Weshern still plans to fight," Jaina said, the island now dominating the foreground. "Fools. I truly believed they would surrender."

"I wouldn't have accepted it," Marius said. "The sheer cost of coming here was tremendous. We will not leave without offering an example to the other islands."

"And what example is that?" she asked.

"All of Weshern burned to the ground."

Even Jaina looked taken aback.

"But what of their rivers?" she asked. "Their forests and towns? It will take years to replace, rebuild..."

"Perhaps decades, even," Marius said. "But it can be done. A total collapse and submersion beneath the Endless Ocean? That cannot be rebuilt. There is no undoing such a catastrophe. I want the very thought of rebellion crushed this day, Jaina. No more illusions of being separate nations. No more Archons and lords and Seraphim. They will be extensions of Center, obedient and powerless."

The Er'el did a remarkable job keeping her voice calm.

"Why were we not told this beforehand?" she asked. "You said you only wished to crush Weshern's military."

"And we will," he said. "But there was no reason to risk doubt among the theotechs as to the necessary level of destruction. As we progress city by city, continue giving orders to attack. The rage of battle will quell any potential doubts. I have already informed Allison of the full extent of the destruction we must unleash. The fire and stone of her Seraphim will scorch the earth raw. Only select fields will remain unscathed, for our people must be fed. When we resettle Weshern, it will be with loyal citizens of Center."

Jaina waited a long while before answering.

"So be it," she said. "The angels have ordered the destruction of sinful civilizations many times before. I will ensure everyone knows that this was their punishment for sending Galen crashing to the ocean floor. But what of the other islands? Will they submit to a dismantling of their hierarchies?"

Marius looked upon the beautiful lakes of Weshern, the thin, sprawling forests surrounding them, and he felt a pang of sorrow for the impending loss.

"After they see the price of rebelling, not a soul will dare resist our power."

Jaina's hand clutched the side of Marius's chair hard enough to whiten her knuckles.

"We do this for the future of our race," she said. "I understand. In time, our people may view this day as one of triumph, but I will not preach it as such. Not while I live. Is that acceptable, my Speaker?"

"Ours is a heavy burden to bear," Marius said. "And yes, I accept. I would be a cruel man if I demanded your heart rejoice in slaughter."

Weshern was so close now, the southern edge of the island looming before them. Marius saw little spots of silver hovering about the island, no doubt the Weshern Seraphim scrambling together to form a defense. It would not be at the island's edge, he saw. Neither soldiers nor Seraphim awaited their landfall. The villagers fled in thick streams northward like panicked little ants.

"Give the order," Marius told Jaina.

The Er'el slipped her hand into her pocket and pulled out a small light elemental prism. Set into the back of Marius's throne was a golden gauntlet, and she pulled it free and slid it on, powering it with her element. Aiming upward, she activated the gauntlet. Instead of destructive ice or fire, the gauntlet shone a thick white beam heavenward, signaling the other theotechs manning the war machines. Jaina cut it off momentarily, then shone it two more times, the signal for beginning the invasion. The knights scattered in all directions, creating a firing window. The thrum of wings magnified tenfold, bone-chilling in its volume as the ancient machines drew power from their prisms. Marius caught himself clutching the arms of his chair and he forced his fingers to relax.

For our future, he told himself as the first of the cannons erupted. *For our children.*

Balls of flame the size of houses lobbed through the air, their destination the closest of the villages that would be their landing zone. The projectiles detonated upon contact with the ground, exploding outward with a roaring inferno. The grass instantly charred, stone buildings blackening from the heat, their wooden roofs suddenly ablaze. The last stragglers at the northern half of the city vanished amid the smoke and ash, never to be seen again. More cannons fired, the second volley of ice and stone. Boulders blasted through homes, crushing fountains and trees alike as they rolled to a stop. Last came the lightning, concentrated beams that widened over time. Their light was blinding, their power so great that buildings crumbled against it. The beams raked the city, ripping it apart. Deep grooves in the earth marked their passage.

Within minutes, the village was decimated.

"The day is already won," Marius whispered. "Who could dare challenge such might?"

Jaina flashed a single beam of light, ending the barrage. The angelic knights swarmed the rubble in search of potential resistance. None awaited. Marius's platform settled into the heart of the destroyed city. The ferrymen hovered a few dozen yards away to afford the Speaker privacy until he beckoned them back. The ground rumbled. The first of the siege weapons settled to the blackened earth and rolled from their platforms. Smoke belched from pipes of those fueled by fire, others crackled and whirred, their enormous weight counteracted by light elements or their wheels turned by inner machinations powered by electricity sparking through wires from lightning prisms.

"So little remains," Jaina said, absorbing the destruction. Hardly a building stood untouched.

"Lowville," Marius said. "Home of the Skyborn twins. I felt it an appropriate landing."

Jaina shook her head.

"It is, indeed. A shame none will live to appreciate the connection."

"Think to the future," Marius said. "To the retellings. A simple decision now will appear a prophetic justice in the tales of our grandchildren."

Time passed as the numerous engines formed an ever-widening front line across Weshern's southern edge. Next came the soldiers, their platforms ahead of the front line, preparing to advance. Their number stretched for several miles, a brilliant gold line to mark the inevitable. Angelic knights circled above all the while, ensuring no Seraphim dared attack the vulnerable ground troops. Normally those knights would have been the leading edge, bombarding defenses with their elements, but not this day. Not when they had the cannons and siege engines.

Garnett arrived from the front, riding one of Center's finest rare breed of horses.

"We've encountered no resistance as of yet," he said, bowing quickly to Marius in the saddle. "It seems they're all pulling back toward their holy mansion. I expect they're hoping to clump together while our own front lines expand so they stand a chance. It won't matter. We'll surround them from all sides. They'll fall in time, I guarantee it."

"There will be no need," Marius said. "Wherever they gather, we will crush them with our engines. Have your men wait until the bombardments are finished before marching forward. Your duty is to ensure no survivors."

"None at all?" Garnett asked. He kept his voice remarkably steady, but the lift of his bushy eyebrows gave him away.

"None," Marius said. "Weshern is awash in weeds, General. When this is over, we will plant anew."

"Lovely way of describing a slaughter," Garnett said. "But hell, they brought this on themselves. I'll make sure the men get the job done."

He turned the horse about and galloped down the blackened dirt road, careful to slow when he encountered one of the many deep grooves carved by the cannons. Marius settled in his chair, telling himself to relax. This would be a long, long day, and he planned the excursion to continue into nightfall. He mustn't be impatient.

Knights circled above him trading orders and signals, escorts planned to track the gradually spreading army. Marius saw one knight descend toward him, and he had a feeling he knew who it was before the man even landed.

"Yes, Liam?" the Speaker asked the kneeling knight.

"So far there has been no sign of the Phoenix or her brother," he said. "But Weshern is yet to mount any real resistance, so it will likely be a matter of time."

"I trust you know what must be done?" Marius said.

"The Skyborn twins are to be captured and brought before you so you may decree their fate."

"A heavy burden," Marius said, and he put a hand on Liam's shoulder. "But one I know you can bear. Fly on, knight, and may the angels watch over you. Stay low to the ground, and stay forever watchful. You will find your moment."

"Thank you, my Speaker."

"What will you do with them?" Jaina asked once the knight had flown away.

"Execute them, of course, as a fine example to all for the cost of rebellion."

"Will you not reconsider?" Jaina asked, frowning at him. "There is so much we might learn from their blood."

"I've prayed on this a great deal," Marius said. "Er'el Tesdon's plan was doomed from the start. To mix our blood with the blood of demons is a heresy that never should have been allowed. We blinded ourselves to this by dreaming of a future we will never have. I won't entertain the thought any longer. We spat in the face of God, and in return, we suffer the damage the children of such experiments have wrought. To continue on only risks even greater destruction."

The cannons rolled past, theotechs pulling out cracked prisms and tossing them to the ground before replacing them with fresh ones kept in ornate chests built right into the machines. One of the knight giants lumbered past, each footfall shaking the ground. Its grand sword swept side to side, knocking down the occasional wall with ease. The rumble of wheels became a constant quake. Marius rose from his chair and looked upon the mightiest of the war machines. It was an immense cannon named the Spear of God, and the theotechs had not dared test it prior to battle. Not out of arrogance or inability, but simple fear of what damage they might do upon Center soil. The Spear of God was considered one of the true world destroyers, and Weshern would be the first to feel its wrath in five centuries.

"Summon the ferrymen," Marius ordered Jaina. "I want to be there when that one fires."

Jaina shouted to the waiting men as Marius sat back down

in his throne. The chains rattled, the platform rising up to follow the goliath cannon. The marble cannon at the front was short in length but wider than a house. It rolled on ten wheels, each wheel crafted of heavy stone and its axle bathed in oil. Golden images covered its side, all showing a furious angel striking the ground with its spear, the contact causing the gilded land to shatter and break. The back end was stubby and square, with multiple braces pulled upward like the dead legs of a spider.

The soldiers kept in tight formations at the edge of Lowville and the surrounding fields, still waiting for the next barrage. The Spear of God rolled to a halt and the braces dropped, theotechs locking them in place as the machine prepared to fire.

"Higher!" Marius shouted to the ferrymen. "I wish to see the countryside."

The ferrymen obliged, slowly lifting the platform so Marius could witness the next town several miles to the north. Swaying fields filled the space between, marred by only a single road cutting its way through. They were too far away for him to tell how much had been evacuated, but he could see trails of people on the roads between. Marius swallowed down his guilt. They were afraid and seeking safety. But there would be no safety. Had he not warned them of this time and time again? The people should have spoken out against the actions of their leaders. They should have raged for peace instead of cheering for the lies of Johan and the deaths of Center's soldiers and knights.

"Supports ready!" one of the theotechs shouted to the others up front. The six side braces were set, their sharpened ends jabbed deep into the dirt. The seventh and largest bracer clamped down from the back, looking like a great spear piercing the land to keep the cannon in place. The theotech driver put his hands upon the controls, setting the entire thing to vibrating. The golden rivulets brightened as the elements within powered up. The marble itself shone as if every inch were covered with light prisms. Marius understood only a fraction of the technology involved, but he knew one hundred elemental prisms of all types were required to power the weapon. The theotechs had found old scrolls detailing its operation, as well as the distances the cannon would fire, but as for the damage itself, they had only the golden drawings.

A soft glow built at the Spear of God's barrel. It started small, as if a fire had been lit in its belly, but grew stronger and brighter with each passing moment. The braces began to shake as the vehicle rocked back and forth, testing the supports. The golden images flashed, then drained black. Lightning crackled from the barrel's edges. A piercing cry, like that of a furious eagle, rang louder and louder as the Spear of God gathered its power. It released with a sudden, tremendous roar, its shock wave scattering smoke and ash in all directions. The huge cannon rocked backward a dozen feet, dirt spraying to either side as the back spear dug into the earth like a plow. Marius felt his heart stop and his jaw fall slack.

The Spear of God, flashed his feverish thoughts. *Heaven's wrath made manifest. Lord forgive us.*

The beam that blasted out of the cannon's barrel grew wider with time as the energy poured forth. It swirled in a multitude of colors, the heart of it angry and black, the outer portions golden lightning. Leading the way like a true spearhead was a triangular piece of molten earth. The spear thrust through the air and descended upon the nearest town, Glensbee. The sky shrieked from the projectile's passing. The miles between the Spear of God and its target vanished in mere moments. Marius stood locked in place, waiting for the detonation. The drawings showed the spear breaking the earth. The drawings did not lie.

A blinding flash marked the spear's eruption, and seconds later Center's army felt the rumbling shockwave. Gusting wind followed, hot and foul. When the flash subsided, Marius watched the village sink into the earth, collapsing as if Weshern itself had opened its maw to swallow it whole. A black storm cloud swirled overhead, tornadoes of red lightning crackling and dancing through the carnage. He watched buildings rip and twist, pieces flying heavenward as if the ground itself rejected them. The sky between cloud and ground turned red, and an ashen rain fell upon the devastation. The buildings continued to sink. The land itself turned to melted stone and fire. Still the hot wind blew.

It lasted perhaps ten seconds, but to Marius, it felt a lifetime.

The storm abated, vanishing into pale smoke like all other creations of the prisms. The tornadoes fizzled into nothing, the red sky became blue once more. Only the roiled earth remained of Glensbee. The angelic knights hovered in place. Every soldier and theotech stood and watched in heavy silence. Marius tried to speak but could not. A stone had lodged itself into his throat and refused to give.

"We can leave," Jaina said, her voice quavering. "Right now, we can just go. Who will challenge us? Who would dare resist after such a horror?"

Marius felt tears travel down his face, sticky against his skin from the hot wind.

"The way is set," he said. "And you're wrong. We are beyond retreat. Weshern's Seraphim will fight to their very last, and they will welcome death over living through the loss."

He looked to the Spear of God. Smoke wafted from the mouth of the cannon. Frost covered its front half, but quickly melted to water and steam. Theotechs opened multiple compartments, tossing out depleted prisms while others rushed to the companion wagon nearby fully stocked with hundreds more for the cannon's use.

"Must we use it again?" Jaina asked.

"Only once more," Marius said, and he felt relief upon saying it. "Let the holy mansion suffer its wrath. Let Weshern consider that my mercy."

The braces lifted from the goliath cannon. The stone wheels turned with a groan, dragging the Spear of God toward the crater of its own creation.

CHAPTER 11

Kael soared through the skies alongside the rest of the Seraphim, the eastern half of Weshern rapidly approaching. The second they'd spotted the invading armies on their return trip home, they'd left the platforms and ferrymen behind, with Rebecca carried in Argus's arms. Center's forces blotted out the southern sky, a storm of gold and crimson. The barrage of cannons had left a black mole on the otherwise beautiful green-and-blue expanse of Weshern.

Clara flew beside him, and Kael spared a glance her way. Her face was pale, her eyes wide open despite the wind's resistance. He could only guess what she felt. They had all been part of the resistance that pushed for war, but Clara's family had made it official with their declaration upon capturing the Crystal Cathedral. At that moment there'd been no turning back. Kael prayed they would not be forever haunted by the costs of that decision.

The grasslands flashed below them, and Kael felt a moment of relief. At least they were over Weshern soil now. They could be part of the frantic defense.

"Kael!" Clara shouted, pulling up to a stop. Her eyes were wide, her body visibly trembling. Confused, Kael followed her gaze past him to the south as a deep tremor rumbled through his ears. The sight shocked him to a hover, many of those accompanying him doing the same.

A hell cloud swirled above Weshern soil, crackling with red lightning. Chaos raged beneath it. Despite the distance, there was no questioning the destruction happening beneath that cloud. The ground churned. The buildings crumbled. Somehow the Speaker had unleashed pure devastation.

"How dare they?" Clara said. She lifted a shaking fist, clenching and unclenching on reflex. "How… how dare they?"

Kael reached out for her.

"We need to fly," he said. She hovered up and down, eyes glazed, her mind lost in a private horror. He shifted closer and took her hand. She startled, and when she first looked his way she stared as if he were a stranger.

"Clara," he said, struggling to remain calm himself.

"I know," she said. The sudden change was marked only by the growing light of her wings. "Let's go."

They raced across the Weshern fields and rivers, making their way to the holy mansion. Kael saw the roads flooded with people, men and women fleeing toward the island's center with only the clothes on their backs. Center's grim tide rolled onward from the south, cannons thundering another stretch of beautiful land to ash.

Seraphim gathered at the holy mansion, awaiting orders. Argus flew their group past them to land before the front gates and storm inside. Kael followed, trusting him to know where they were going. They passed frightened servants and scrambling soldiers as they sprinted the halls. Near the back of the mansion were two double doors marked with blue swords painted into the black wood. Argus flung them open and the rest followed.

Within was the war room of Weshern. Seven light elements lit the many maps and lists hanging from the walls. Isaac and Avila stood with General Cutter and Olivia West overlooking a grand table in the room's center, its surface carved into a facsimile of Weshern's topography.

"Mom! Dad!"

Clara sprinted past Argus and flung her arms around her mother. Isaac stepped away from the map of Weshern to greet her, kissing the top of her blond head.

"I'm glad you're safe," the Archon said as Clara pulled free. "We feared your group had been intercepted along the way."

"The invasion started when we were halfway home from Candren," Rebecca said, completely ignoring him. Thin red blocks marked the advancing front line of Center's soldiers. Rebecca adjusted several, then tapped her finger on Glensbee. "I observed best I could during our flight. Center has some sort of new weapon, though God knows what. It destroyed the town in a single blast."

"We heard," Olivia said. Her arms were crossed over her chest, and she glared at the map as if she could break all of Center's forces with her mind. "I'm sure we could destroy it from above if we ever had the chance, but that's the problem." She gestured to yellow triangles positioned all about the red line. "From what we can tell, Marius has his knights keeping tight and close to the army's advancement. We won't be able to hit the ground troops without first taking out the aerial support."

"Varl's preparing his soldiers to form the first line of defense," Isaac said. "But it's going to take time, and every minute we wait lets Center conquer another piece of our land uncontested."

"What of the other islands?" Rebecca asked.

"No word yet," Isaac said. "I can only hope they send their Seraphim in time. We have no hope of holding without them."

"And Johan's disciples?" Bree asked, unbothered by the glares from Rebecca and Isaac for interrupting.

"I spoke with Johan only briefly when we first spotted Center's army on the approach," Isaac said. "He promised aid, though I know neither when nor where. For now, we move forward without him and treat any help he offers as a welcome bonus."

Argus leaned over the map, staring at the locations of the many gold triangles.

"If Rebecca is right on their placements, then the soldiers are fanning outward in an expanding circle instead of marching in a straight line toward the mansion," he said. "Marius must believe any resistance we offer will be useless against him. He's spreading his forces out to be the most time efficient in conquering our lands. That means there won't be enough knights to cover the entire front line."

Argus grabbed five blue circles of wood, each marked with a sword on the top. He positioned two along the far eastern side of Center's forces, the other two the west. The last he put directly between the holy mansion and the landing site.

"Marius won't leave knights alone to guard portions of the front lines, nor will he leave any stretch unguarded," Argus said. "That means he'll have knights flying in patrol groups. We can exploit that. We'll divide our Seraphim into five squads, with two pairs at the outer edges spaced about a mile apart. Both hit simultaneously, and the moment either sees sign of reinforcements they pull back. We'll keep bouncing the patrols back and forth, never letting them engage or set up to defend. If they try to split in half, then we'll attack. Mobility and surprise are our best weapons. If we can chip away at their forces we might be able to thin them enough to have a chance."

"What of the center force?" Isaac asked.

"That will contain the majority of our Seraphim," Argus said. "We'll try to harass and draw knights away from the groups, but the main purpose will be to watch for reinforcements and dive on them before they can join up with the larger mass. The longer we keep the side groups separate from the rest of the knights, the more damage we can inflict."

"A clever, if desperate, gamble," Isaac said. "But we have no other options. I will leave it to you to create the five squads, Argus, and may the angels smile upon you in this dark hour."

Argus snapped a fist against his breast in salute, then hovered off the floor. Clara offered her parents one last embrace, and Kael wished he could convince her to stay behind. If this were their final hour, she should be with her family. Of course there wasn't a chance in hell that Clara would remain. Weshern needed her in the air. Clara pulled free, flicked her own wings on, and then joined Kael's side.

Their wings thrummed as they rushed back outside to meet the greater gathering of Seraphim. Chests of elements lay open in the grass nearby. Kael and the others replaced their prisms with fresh ones and grabbed several more for backup.

"Gather here!" Argus shouted to the Seraphim. They immediately obeyed. Kael watched the faces of the men and women. They appeared calm and composed despite their fear, and eager for Argus's instructions so they might finally enter the fight. It seemed silly, but that made Kael feel better. If others were calm in the face of this storm, then he could be, too.

Argus relayed the plan before dividing the Seraphim into five squads. As the names reeled off, Kael realized his name wasn't called, nor was Clara's, Bree's, or Saul's. When the other groups broke, the four remained standing about Argus, confused.

"You four were a squad during the fireborn invasion," their commander told them. "And by all reports you also performed magnificently assaulting the Crystal Cathedral. Given Bree's importance, and Clara's nobility, I have a different plan in mind for Phoenix Squad."

Kael glanced at his sister, saw her apprehension.

"I hope you're not planning to send us away from the battle," she said.

"Quite the opposite," Argus said. "I want you four to fly underneath Weshern, travel along the far southeastern side, and then ambush the outermost edge of Center's forces. After that, move from east to west raking the front line. You have complete freedom to choose your engagements. Flee deeper into unconquered territory if the numbers are too overwhelming. My hope is that when you encounter one of our five other squads, the surprise of your arrival, coupled with its ferocity, will tilt the scales in our favor."

He turned to Clara, and he spoke with surprising bluntness.

"Should we somehow endure, and yet you die, I will stand before your parents and tell them in all honesty I gave you four the safest of tasks, to hit and run at your own discretion. If you wish to be more aggressive, that is on your head. Is that understood?"

Clara stood up straighter, and she did not wither beneath that gaze.

"Understood," she said.

"Good." He turned the knob of his right gauntlet, arming the ice prism within. "I will be commanding the center force. I look forward to your joining us, should you survive that long."

His wings flared and up he went, taking lead of the other dozen Seraphs waiting patiently for their commander. Kael glanced among the four, excitement battling dread in his heart.

"Well," Bree said, and she cracked a grin. "Who's ready to follow me to certain death?"

"I'm sure as shit not," Saul said. "But I'll be right there if you change your mind and lead us to victory instead."

"To victory, then," Kael said, and he raised an imaginary glass. "It's better than the alternative."

The others smiled and raised their own imaginary glasses. It felt stupid and immature but they were a group now, alone and facing a war unheard-of since the time of Ascension. Bad jokes were better than tears.

"All right, then," Bree said. "Let's go kill some knights."

Bree took the lead, Kael and Clara trailing just to her sides and Saul flying middle to form a wedge. They kept parallel to the distant forces of Center, their wings pushed to their maximum. The minutes dragged long and painful. Kael watched the conflict as best he could but they were too far away to see much except for when the cannons fired another salvo. The destruction looked like a plague slowly sickening and eating away at Weshern's healthy surface. Within a day or two, nothing would remain.

Marius would have us all dead than free of his rule, thought Kael. He would have preferred the Speaker sent Weshern crashing to the ocean instead like L'adim did with Galen. At least then Marius couldn't pretend to be the righteous one.

At last they dove over the edge, looped around, and flew toward the Fount while brown earth passed overhead. The white spray and twisting funnel would hide them should any patrols be keeping an eye belowground. Kael found it highly unlikely. If the knights were stretched thin trying to provide cover to all of their ground troops and war engines, Marius wouldn't be able to spare more to patrol underneath the edges of the island.

Closing the distance between them and the edge passed achingly slow, and yet still too fast for Kael's taste. He kept his shield tight across his chest, taking whatever meager comfort he could from its presence. He might not be the lethal killer his sister was, but between his newfound speed and his shield's protection he could keep her safe as she performed her skillful work.

Bree banked upward, the dark brown earth above their heads hovering closer and closer. Kael armed his ice element and clenched his fists. There was no telling what awaited them when they curled up and around to the surface; they had to be ready for anything.

Fly aggressive, Bree's hand signals ordered the other three. Kael grinned. She wanted aggressive? Then that's what she'd get. No one could fly faster than him.

They made their way back over the lip of the island and were once again topside. Blackened grass flashed beneath them. Keeping low, they surveyed the surroundings, Kael spotting groups of knights dotting the sky far off to the west, forming an outer flank for the ground troops marching behind. Bree led them over a burning field, pushing through the heavy smoke. Kael held his breath and squinted his eyes, relying on practiced control to keep himself level and straight. A row of cannons manned by theotechs and soldiers rolled past on the other side of the fire. With their wings bathed in smoke, the soldiers would never see them coming.

Clear sky greeted them on the other side of the burning field. Kael saw the cannons below him, the soldiers panicking at their arrival. He gave them no chance to react. Ice exploded from Kael's, Clara's, and Saul's gauntlets, vicious shards ripping through the unarmed theotechs. Bree dove closer, twirling once before unleashing her flame. A roaring inferno washed over the first cannon, setting its wood frame alight and melting the thinner sections of metal. Kael broke from formation, his shield leading as the first frantic barrage of arrows cut the air. This time he imagined spheres of ice the size of his fist instead of lances. He curled his fingers to help shape the focal prism and then released his attack. They slammed down on the soldiers, the force of their projection plus the added speed of their fall giving them incredible power. The soldiers' armor meant nothing, bones shattering and necks breaking as the ice struck.

Saul and Clara brought down the second and third cannon, boulders of ice smashing them to pieces. Kael curled back toward formation, becoming Bree's shadow as she bathed a large swath of soldiers in flame, her subtle shifts in direction keeping her safe from the few arrows launched in retaliation. As they rose back into the air, Kael lobbed a single boulder of ice. It smashed the final cannon, breaking its wheels and toppling it onto its side.

"Let's go!" Bree shouted over the wind. Saul and Clara resumed their positions, the four racing above Weshern like an arrow. This time they flew on a collision course for the nearest patrol group of knights, their wings glowing a brilliant gold as they rushed to protect their eastern flank.

Three knights, four of us, Kael thought. *We're fucked.*

Not that Kael could feel sorry for himself. All of Weshern was in trouble, and the other squads faced off against far worse odds. Clenching his right hand into a fist, Kael steeled himself. He was a Seraphim of Weshern, brother of the Phoenix, and goddamnit he was going to make that mean something. A burst of silver light pushed him alongside Bree.

Follow my lead, he signaled.

Her confusion was evident on her face, but there was no time to explain. The knights were too close. Swallowing down his fear, Kael closed his eyes to focus on the light prisms inside his left gauntlet. He felt the three of them, two keeping his shield nearly weightless, the third pouring power into his wings. His mind clicked, the connection made, and then all three surged with energy far exceeding the original limitations of the mechanical designs.

His shield led the way, brilliant silver light swirling behind him no different from Bree's twin trails of fire when she wielded her swords. His wings were blinding, his speed incredible. The other three formed a line behind him, unable to keep formation and still follow. Kael focused on the middle knight, careful to keep his aim absolutely steady. At such speeds the tiniest deviations could send him careening wildly. Wind roared against his face and ears despite the protection of the harness. Light flooded his vision.

Stay on target, he ordered himself. *Trust your shield.*

The knights were clearly baffled by his speed and they attempted to scatter while firing. Their aim was true, lightning and fire striking his shield only to vanish within the swirling light. Kael never felt the tiniest of impacts. Backs to him, they retreated three different directions. Kael's center target still underestimated his speed. And why wouldn't they? Knights wore the fastest wings of all the islands. No one could outrace them. No one but him.

The middle knight curled upward, trying to gain distance so he could spin about and fire. Kael gave him no chance. He maneuvered his back and shoulders to shift upward, not chasing but intersecting. The knight glanced behind and saw his doom far too late to react. Kael shifted his thumb down and killed all elemental power to his shield right before impact. Its weight returned, every pound of it. Kael braced his arm and slammed into the knight, breaking the man's body upon impact with the shield. Kael immediately reactivated the light elements and kicked away the corpse. It fell, accompanied by shattered pieces of golden wings.

With the knights' formation broken and the remaining two scattering, Bree's arrival was that much safer. She raced after the knight on the left, her swords drawn and dripping with flame. Saul and Clara chased the other, weaving side to side while flinging shards of ice. They weren't trying to kill him, only corral him away from Bree so she might engage one-to-one. Trusting his sister, Kael looped left and hurried after the other three. The hum of his wings was a roar in his ears, deep and satisfying. Kael found he barely touched the throttle, able to dull or flare the elements of his wings with but a thought.

Is this what it's like to be Bree? he wondered. *Is this what it's like to fly as natural as breathing?*

Saul and Clara fell farther and farther behind the knight, their wings unable to keep pace. Their foe knew this as well, and at last he looped through the air with incredible grace, setting himself on a direct course for the two Seraphim. Kael felt his heart skip a beat. He wouldn't get there in time. His friends would have to endure on their own.

Saul immediately formed an opaque wall of ice a dozen feet long, using it to screen their maneuvers. Clara broke left, Saul right, each releasing a wide spray of shards. They didn't expect to hit him, only keep the knight dodging and to disrupt his aim. He did so, but with only the mildest of corrections. Kael held his breath as the knight broke after Clara and retaliated with small balls of flame.

Clara shifted and spun, keeping her path unpredictable. Fire and smoke passed all around her, far too close for comfort. Kael urged himself faster, demanding even more speed from his wings, more than he thought he could control. The distance between them vanished at a heart-pounding rate. Clara's dodging grew more desperate. The knight was close. Too close.

Clara turned sharply, beginning a wide turn toward Kael. He shifted himself onto a collision course and raced through the air like a comet, streams of light trailing his path. Clara's curl ended, she and the knight directly facing Kael. His approach surprised the knight, immediately sending him banking away. It wouldn't be enough, and they both knew it. As Kael neared, the knight reversed course. They charged head-to-head, the deadliest of scenarios any Seraphim could find themselves in.

The knight released a gigantic plume of flame, expertly placed so that Kael would have no way to avoid it. So he didn't. Shield up, he pushed right on through, not feeling a lick of heat. The distance between them vanished in an instant. Kael didn't try to hit him with a spear of ice, knowing his aim would be too poor and the knight's reflexes too great. Instead he spread his palm and formed a wide wall of ice directly between their paths. They were so close, and flying so fast, neither would have time to avoid collision. It was a suicide tactic, a way to take a Seraph with him into the afterlife during a head-to-head battle... but Kael had no intention of dying. He lifted his shield and trusted it with his life. Light blazed around it. Powerful. Unstoppable. A chunk of the wall shattered into an explosion of shards upon contact, granting Kael his passage through.

The knight had no such protection.

Kael slowed his speed to a hover and turned. Gold wings guided the knight in a slow death spiral toward the ocean, the crushed body hanging limp in the harness. Saul flew to Kael's side while shaking his head.

"Holy shit, Kael," he said. "Since when could you do all that?"

"I think I always could," Kael said. He patted his shield. "I think I just needed this thing to help."

Kael searched for his sister, remembering that battle wasn't necessarily over. He found her flying his way, the fire gone from her blades. She must have dispatched the knight during his confrontation.

Clara joined their group first, and Kael grinned to hide his lingering fear for her safety.

"Nice dodging," he said. Clara smiled only briefly.

"I thought I was dead," she said.

It wasn't meant in jest or humor. Kael didn't want to imagine her fright as the knight had steadily closed in for the kill. Kael put an arm around her waist. No overconfident grin this time, only sincerity.

"You flew well," he said. "And you'll keep flying well all day, you and me. We'll survive this together, I promise."

She leaned her head against his shoulder, a singular moment of weakness before she pulled away.

"We're Seraphim of Weshern," she said. "We're not just going to survive. We're going to bring hell to Center, won't we, Bree?"

Bree hovered up to join them, still in the process of sheathing her swords.

"That we will," she said, turning to Kael. She didn't compliment him for his maneuvers. Didn't even crack a smile. "Two to my one." Her eyes twinkled. "I'll have to try harder."

Exhaustion threatened Kael's limbs, a headache lingered at the edges of his mind, and he wanted nothing more than to lie down and cry. He laughed instead.

"It's about time you had some competition," he said.

Kael froze. There, in the distance, faint but unmistakable. The others followed his gaze. Clara was the first to speak, and she didn't try to hide the tears rolling down her cheeks.

"The other islands," she said. "They've come to our aid."

Clusters of green, yellow, and white dots speckled with gold. They'd arrive together from the south, striking the vulnerable back line of Center's troops. Weshern's seemingly hopeless task now had a chance of success.

Kael nudged Bree's side, and he gestured farther east, to where other battles still raged.

"Lead on, sis," he said. "We have a war to fight."

CHAPTER 12

The four Seraphs raced over the Weshern wheat field with Bree leading the way. Elements lit the sky before them, a battle already begun between a squad of Weshern Seraphs and a trio of angelic knights. Rows of Center's soldiers formed protective lines in front of their cannons, dozens of bows at ready should the knights fall.

Follow my lead, Bree signaled to the other three. They flew low over the ground, an eye on the aerial battle at all times. So far neither side had scored a kill. The Weshern Seraphim outnumbered the knights two to one, but they kept on the cautious side, lobbing shots from afar and swarming any knight who tried to push forward instead of retreating. Bree doubted that stalemate would last. Both sides were too skilled to avert bloodshed for long. But the ground army was vulnerable while the knights were distracted and, if luck was with them, also completely unaware of their approach.

Bree's fingers danced, relaying another message.

Ground first.

Bows were the most dangerous defense against the Seraphim's attack. The archers were set up facing the aerial battle raging to the north, whereas Bree led their small squad in from the west. She shifted their path southward, trying to remain unseen by keeping in the soldiers' rear arc. All it would take was one man to spot their arrival. The difference between scattered arrows, and a prepared volley, was tremendous, and potentially lethal.

Bree dropped even lower. Her gauntleted fingers brushed the tips of the wheat, using them to track her height and tilt upward if she ever dipped. She couldn't see the army that low, but she didn't need to. The cannons had devastated half the field with their barrage of elements before advancing during their steady march deeper into Weshern territory. The moment Bree entered the empty ash land they'd be arriving right on top of the army.

Burned pockmarks passed beneath her, momentary gaps of nothing touching her fingers before the wheat resumed. Streaks of earth gashed by long spikes of ice and spears of stone. They should be just behind the army. So close, so very close.

Bree glanced over her shoulder, eyeing Kael as an idea came to her. He was capable of tremendous speeds, no doubt in part due to the lightborn blood flowing in his veins. His shield also gave him protection unmatched in the history of Seraphim combat.

Kael, she signaled. *Take lead. We follow.*

Her brother never hesitated. Kael shifted higher, his shield shimmering white. His wings flared momentarily, and then he shot ahead, a trail of liquid silver light sparkling in his wake. Bree drew her swords as she pushed her own wings to their limits. The wheat field ended, becoming a black scar upon the land. Center's army was positioned in the heart of the damage, advancing upon the nearby village of Angburg. Kael's brilliant shield led the way. Bree felt immediate justification for her change of roles, for their approach had indeed been spotted. A volley of one hundred arrows soared into the air, carefully spaced apart to leave no room to dodge. But there was no need to dodge. Kael's shield somehow seemed to grow larger, wider, a wall of protection for the other three to follow behind. Arrows shattered to splinters upon contact, accompanied by a bright flash of light.

Phoenix Squad gave them no time for a second volley.

Ice plummeted into the archers, thin shards from Kael, larger boulders from the trailing Clara and Saul. Bree clenched her fists around her sword hilts, dipping closer while the other three moved higher into the sky for safety. Her blood was fire. The element was a part of her, and more and more she realized how great a gift she and her brother carried. What limits had they not tested? What depths did their power possess that they were yet to discover?

I am the fire, Bree thought as she raced overhead Center's invading army. *Now obey.*

She slashed with her swords, shaping the fire in her mind exactly as Instructor Kime had taught her. Her blades gave her focus; her confidence gave her power. The fire about her swords leapt from the metal as Bree felt her elemental prism drain. The projectiles took shape, an enormous X made of two long streaks of flame more than one hundred yards of length hitting the ground with a roar. It looked like the finger of God burning two lines across the dead land. Any archer caught in its wake collapsed amid the smoke, more ash to fill the battle-scarred field.

Bree arced into the air, breathing heavily as her vertigo rapidly came and went. The maneuver wasn't as exhausting as releasing all her fire in a great prism-draining explosion, but it still carried a heavy toll. She scanned the archers and saw the few that remained fleeing south.

Good riddance, she thought.

"Bree!" she heard someone scream. She looked about, realized she'd been staring off into nowhere. Saul was beside her, his hand on her wrist to keep them steady. His face was a perfect mixture of worry and annoyance. "We need you!"

Kael and Clara were already barreling toward the chaotic fight with the knights. Bree felt a pang of guilt, and she nodded to Saul.

"I'm here," she reassured him. "Let's go."

The two trailed a half minute behind Kael and Clara, giving Bree a chance to assess the aerial battle. The Weshern Seraphim looked ready to retreat, their defensive retaliations all the more desperate. Despite having a two-to-one numbers advantage they'd failed to score a single kill on the knights. The superior skill of their foes was weighing on them. Any moment they might break completely, one fall leading rapidly to another. Bree knew Argus had ordered the other Seraphim to perform hit-and-run tactics, but with the knights' superior wings, they'd be hard-pressed to do so without sustaining significant casualties. It seemed the Phoenix Squad's arrival could not happen at a more fortuitous time.

Kael's shield led the way, a reckless charge straight at the nearest knight. Clara followed in his silver path, taking steady, careful shots with ice lances. The two Weshern Seraphs who'd been fleeing immediately spun about, unleashing their own assault of lightning and stone. Under attack from all sides, the knight had no chance. Lightning struck him down, freeing

Clara, Kael, and the other two Seraphs to shift focus to two other knights.

The knights knew the battle was hopeless and immediately turned to retreat. One went east, the other west, both leaving the ground troops to fend for themselves. Bree directed Saul to join her in pursuing the westward knight. They came in at an angle from the southwest, cutting off his retreat. Kael chased the other, able to outrun even the fastest of knight harnesses.

Farther, Bree signaled to Saul, gesturing for him to fly an even sharper, westward angle. The two separated, Bree watching the knight with an unblinking gaze. He'd see her soon, which would leave him two options. One would be to engage her directly, allowing the others in chase to catch up. The other would be curl northwest, adjusting his retreat so she could not cut him off, nor could the others catch up. That move would put him directly into Saul's new path.

A warning spike in her heart forced her into a dodge as she realized the skilled knight had chosen to do both. He curled northwest, flying backward as he shifted his body so he could fire with his gauntlet at his pursuers. A burst of lightning crackled through the air, streaking so close above Bree's head she could feel the hairs of her neck stand on end. Bree immediately shifted left, then rolled to the right. You couldn't dodge lightning the same way you dodged ice or fire. You had to fly erratic, never letting your foe predict your path. Lightning tended to shoot in very thin beams, requiring pinpoint accuracy, whereas wide plumes of flame or tremendous boulders of stone covered a far larger area.

Bree purposely kept her dodges shifting her to the west. If she kept him focused on her, and not the blind path he traveled...

Two more blasts ripped within feet of Bree's body, and then Saul arrived. He streaked in from below, clutching his gauntlet with his free hand and blasting a single, lengthy lance of ice. The sharpened projectile struck the knight in the abdomen and sank in deep. His golden wings flickered, then ceased completely, the body beginning a lengthy, curving death spiral to the ground below.

Bree shifted to watch for Kael and Clara, and she smiled at the sight of a sky free of knightly wings. Had her brother caught up with the other knight, or had Clara brought him down with her ice? Perhaps if by some miracle they all survived, Bree could ask them one day. The other Seraphs seized the moment to attack the cannons along the back row and send the remaining soldiers scattering like rats from a burning building.

The leader of the other four Seraphim flew to Bree, gathering the others around her.

"Commander Argus is calling for us to regroup over Owl Creek Crossing," she said. Blood trickled down her lips, her face was covered with bruises, but the older woman looked overwhelmed with excitement. "Aid flies in from our allies, and we must capitalize."

"Very well," Bree said. "Lead the way, and we'll follow."

The nine of them zoomed across Weshern, leaving the initial battle line behind. Bree hated the thought of letting the conquering forces destroy land and homes unimpeded, but her worries appeared unfounded. She looked to the east and west, and saw the distant golden stars that were knights pulled back.

They need to protect all sides now, Bree thought. *We'll never get a better chance than this.*

Bree saw more than a dozen Seraphim hovering over Owl Creek. Even more heartening, still several miles away from the wide red bridge that traversed the creek, the massed ground troops of Weshern's army marched, finally ready to clash with Center's.

The nine landed near the stream, guided by a waiting Seraph. The others in the sky dropped low, joining the meeting. Bree kept to the outside, arms crossed as she listened. Commander Argus stood in the center of their circle, silently counting numbers. Bree managed eye contact with him only a moment. His relief was palpable.

"Seraphim of Weshern!" Argus shouted. His silver wings hummed as he raised himself a foot off the ground so all would see and hear. "For once, Center faces a foe greater than herself. We have made their soldiers pay. We have brought low knights spread far too thin across our lands. And now, in this hour, the Seraphim of Sothren, Elern, and Candren fly to join us in our stand. From all sides, we will rip them apart. From every angle, they will find our fire and ice. We picked at them like a swarm of insects, but now we fly together, a singular blow to break them completely."

A chorus of tired cheers met his speech. Argus refused to let emotion touch his face, his lips never budging from his firm, focused frown.

"There will be no surrender," he said. "This is it. This is our moment to shatter the bones in the Speaker's fist as he fails to hold us in his grip. Make your nation proud."

The various squads took to the air, gathering in groups for the upcoming charge. Argus gestured for Bree to wait, and so she did. When the others were airborne the commander shut off his wings to land beside her.

"There will be no second chances," he told her. "No more battles if we lose this one. I'm having the rest of your squad join Chernor's. As for yourself, I'd like you to be among what is left of my wolves. We must use every advantage we can muster, and that includes your flames. Will you lead the way, Phoenix?"

Bree glanced to her brother, hovering alongside Clara in the sky.

"I will," she said. "But only if Kael flies with me."

Argus seemed surprised but did not argue the matter.

"If that is required," he said. "So be it."

Bree smiled.

"Thank you."

She joined the rest of her squad of four. They eyed her warily, having seen her brief discussion with Argus.

"I'm to lead the assault," Bree told them. "Kael, I want you there with me when I do."

"You sure that's a good idea?" he asked. The eagerness in his eyes belied his hesitation.

"I'm sure," she said. "Saul, Clara, you're to join Chernor's squad."

"Special treatment as usual," Saul said, but he sounded more amused than annoyed. "Stay safe, you two."

"Thank you," Bree said. Clara hovered close, her arms wrapping her in a brief embrace.

"Keep Kael safe for me, will you?" she asked softly.

"Quite the opposite," Bree said, forcing a grin in an attempt for comfort. "It's Kael that'll be keeping *me* safe."

Clara smiled as she pulled away.

"Of course," she said. "What was I thinking?"

She turned to Kael, embracing him as well. Saul thudded a fist against his breast, and Bree responded in kind.

"Bree! Kael!"

Olivia hovered close, gesturing for them to hurry. A mild press of the throttle and Bree drifted away. Only three original members of Wolf Squad remained alongside Argus, now that Chernor was to lead his own squad. Bree took point, Kael beside her, the two pushing the Wolf Squad up to six.

The rest of Weshern's Seraphim rose up around her. Bree felt a deep ache, for they were a pale number compared to their force that had assaulted Galen in her first ever battle. So devastating, the cost of the past few months.

Kael flew to her right, Argus her left, and the commander hovered close to relay an order.

"I believe the other islands are waiting for us to start the battle, so do not hesitate. Aim for the heart of Center's forces. When knights gather to defend against us, fly straight toward their number."

Such a bold gambit, but if it succeeded they might overwhelm the angelic knights before the battle had a chance to begin.

"Understood," she said.

Bree pushed her throttle steadily higher, feeling the wind whip against her body as she increased in speed. The remaining Seraphim followed in unison, giving her an undeniable thrill. The hum of their wings sang a deep chorus, fifty pairs blazing a silver trail across the blue sky. Bree did as commanded, leading them straight into the heart of the blasted ash and ruin wrought by Center's cannons. She kept her swords sheathed. She had a time planned for their reveal, but it was not yet.

The army of Center's knights slowly came into view, two dozen golden wings merging together from all parts of Weshern. Bree spotted dozens more to the southeast and southwest, forming lines to engage the armies of the other islands. With the knights separated, this was their best chance to crush the superiorly skilled and equipped enemy.

Bree slowed slightly, allowing Kael to catch up. She grabbed his wrist with her right hand, steadying them in flight as she drifted closer.

"Take lead," she shouted.

He looked at her as if she were insane.

"That's your job," he shouted back.

Bree grinned, her excitement growing.

"Lead with your shield, and I'll follow. It's time they feared *both* Skyborn twins."

A tiny part of her had feared her brother would back down from the challenge. That tiny part of her was dead wrong.

"Fine," he shouted. "Try to keep up."

Kael readied his shield, the light about it growing brighter as his wings flashed a brilliant silver. Bree knew his salvaged knight wings were already faster than the rest worn by Weshern. When combined with his innate connection to the light prism, he'd be a soaring comet ahead of their forces, and Bree would be its fiery tail.

The distance closed between them. The knights spread out into pockets of three, the trios hovering in tight triangle formations. Bree jammed her wrist hooks onto the top of her hilts and then pulled the weapons free. Fire bathed her blades. She twirled, wrapping the silver light about her and mixing it with her flame into a glorious spiral. All eyes would be upon their approach. All of Center would learn to fear that mixture of light and flame.

The knights burst into motion, charging headfirst into the fray. Kael's wings blazed in kind, pulling him farther and farther ahead. Bree jammed her throttle to the max, her heart pounding with adrenaline as she tried to keep up.

Knights launched their initial salvo. Walls of ice and stone formed barriers against Weshern's return fire, as well as screens to disguise movement. Bree spotted fireballs racing their way, coupled with a massive slab of stone formed by the combined effort of three knights. At their speed, dodging was impossible, but they needn't dodge at all. Bree clutched her swords tightly and trusted her brother.

The silver light about Kael's shield magnified in size like an exploding star. The balls of flame vanished into smoke the moment they made contact. The stone wall shattered at its touch, blasting apart as if God himself had smote it with his fist. Bree kept in her brother's wake, determined to follow his lead to the very end. A wide spread of knights baffled by their survival hovered before them. Kael zoomed for their center, showing no fear of their numbers, and then broke suddenly for the nearest knight. The woman, having slowed to help create the stone wall, had no chance to escape. Her body shattered against the silver wall of light.

Kael curled back toward the rest of the forces. He didn't release his ice. He didn't try to hide his path. He just flew. Bree spotted another knight trying, and failing, to pierce Kael's shield with his lightning. She zipped out of the path of light, her blazing swords hungry. The knight cut skyward, but Bree had the better angle. She twirled just before impact, lashing his body with both swords to the chest, severing him from his harness. His body plummeted, his wings continuing on a moment longer before shutting off. Bree arced back into Kael's silver path as quick as she exited, following him through the knights' formation and out the other side.

When they emerged and turned about, they saw a world of chaos. Elements filled the air like a sudden storm. Wolf Squad led the way, Argus showing no desire to conserve his element. Thin shards of ice splashed out in tremendous waves, dozens of the projectiles intercepting the paths of his targets. Knights scattered in all directions, some in chase, most in retreat from Weshern's superior barrage. The tide of elements had been too much for the knights to challenge, but Bree knew the momentum would soon shift. Superior numbers gave the Weshern forces tremendous advantage on the initial head-to-head assault. Once the pockets of battle spread out and the enemy could engage in closer combat, the knights' skill would quickly equalize the situation.

Kael's speed lessened, his wings losing a bit of their brilliant sheen. Bree caught up with her brother, and he leaned in close.

"Your turn," he shouted.

Bree grinned.

"If you insist."

He fell a few feet behind her and to the side as she raced back into the battle. None of the knights had given chase, unable to amid the explosive arrival of Weshern's Seraphim. Bree looked for the nearest enemy. Two knights kept to the outer edge of the battle, providing support for the others nearby. Bree saw them strike down a Seraph chasing after an injured knight, twin blasts of lightning ripping through his chest. Target decided, Bree sent her wings to thrumming. She'd hoped to surprise them, but to her horror she realized she'd been baited. The two spun immediately, gauntlets up to fire as she barreled headfirst toward them. Golden light gathered from their focal points, the prelude to a staggering amount of electricity.

Shit, Bree thought, unsure of where to dodge. That hesitation should have cost her her life, but once again she'd underestimated her brother. Kael burst ahead with such tremendous acceleration she could hardly believe his body able to withstand it. He rolled left to right, cutting across her path with shield at the ready. Lightning blasted from the knights' gauntlets, the raw power beyond anything Bree had witnessed. Instead of thin and sharp, the bolts that pierced the air were the size of tree trunks. Even that power meant nothing to Kael's shield, the lightning swirling into its silver light and vanishing in a crackling flash of smoke.

Kael dropped back, once more giving Bree the lead. The distance closed, the knights foolishly remained in a steady hover to improve their aim. Bree could not have had an easier target. She flew between them, sword out to either side. One died instantly, the burning edge cutting across his throat. The other lost an arm, but a quick shot of ice from Kael ended his suffering.

Bree curled toward the outside upper edge of combat, wishing to gain some space so they might dive in again in ambush. She spared a glance to the distant battles, the skies alight with fire and lightning. Center had more combined knights than the minor islands had Seraphim, but the reinforcements were hitting all sides, and the knights could not pull back lest they leave the ground troops helpless against the destruction that would rain down on them from the sky. It was a tenuous situation, and a single bad exchange for one of the minor islands could tip the scales hard against them, but so far they all held strong.

Kael flew beside her as they reached the top of the loose spherical area that had become the battlefield.

Ready? he signaled.

Ready.

They dove together, Kael leading, she following in his silver light. Her brother led her straight into the thick of it, showing him equal to her bravery. Lightning scarred the air, stone and ice falling wildly about them, but they never slowed or panicked. Bree watched for vulnerabilities, unwilling to engage any knight directly. The others would dance the careful dance. Bree and Kael would be the brutal finishers.

Kael spotted the first, intercepting the path of a knight who flew backward so he might shoot bolt after bolt of lightning after his chasers. Kael's wings blazed with light, crossing the distance faster than anyone might dream. The knight dropped low to flee. Losing none of his momentum, Kael curled low in chase. The light on his shield vanished, the tremendous weight coupled with the powerful wings blessed by his blood slamming him into the knight from above. The wings twisted and broke, no match for the steel shield. Kael continued his dive, pushing the knight toward ground. Right before banking back up to safety he reactivated the light of his shield, effortlessly gliding while the frantic, helpless knight plummeted the last few feet, his body rolling and snapping across the grass.

Bree spotted another knight swooping in to ambush Kael and she shifted her path while raising her gauntlet. A tremendous plume blasted out from her focal prism, washing over him. He continued downward, limp, the ground his new destination. Bree gasped as she felt her blood flooding the prism with power. She had to be careful. Too many more times of that and she'd barely be able to lift her swords.

Wolf Squad flashed underneath them, flying mere feet above the field below. A trio of knights chased after, their elements unleashing a steady stream with frightening accuracy. Bree didn't even think, only dove on reflex. Kael followed at a gentler angle. He arrived first, falling into the rear of Wolf Squad before spinning about. His shield flared with light, the barrage of attacks halting before his power. Argus sensed the change immediately and turned, momentarily hovering in place before racing headlong toward the knights. Kael's shield protected Wolf Squad assault, but the knights had no such aid.

Suddenly under attack, the knights' attention focused solely on the battle before them. It couldn't have been more perfect. Bree dropped through the heart of them, cutting down one knight who tried to break free to the side. Argus's lances of ice brought down another, and when the final knight flung up a wall of stone to protect herself, Bree arched her back and tore at her from underneath. The knight burst away from her, avoiding the steel of her blades. Bree swung her right blade on instinct, flinging the fire off as a projectile. The slash of flame ripped through the air, catching the fleeing knight across her wings. Gold melted, sending her crashing to the ground.

The knights were in full retreat now. Argus led the chase, his Wolf Squad fanning out to relay orders to the other squads. Bree fell back and hovered in place, relaxing the muscles in her shoulders and back for a brief moment as she caught her breath. The day was far from over, and she could not risk her energy or body being spent from the initial conflicts. Off in the distance, the other battles fared similarly, the knights retreating to form a tighter defense above Center's cannons and ground troops.

Kael flew to join her, the tired smile on his face rapidly vanishing as he pointed past her.

"Bree, the road!"

She turned to follow his finger. It took a moment of searching, but there, in the distance, a flood of black filled one of the streets. Bree recognized their uniforms, as well as the glint of silver on their backs.

"Specters," she said.

"An army of them," Kael added. "We can't let them through!"

They must have passed unseen during the chaotic battle. There was no doubt where they traveled. The holy mansion was up ahead, and the specters were dashing full speed for its distant gates. It seemed Marius would not leave Weshern without claiming at least some form of victory.

"Go get help," she said, pointing to the fleeting figures of Weshern Seraphim. "I'll follow the specters!"

Only Kael could catch up to the rest of Weshern's forces using his knight wings and light affinity. Her brother waved, then blasted power into his wings to soar off in a trail of light. Bree flew higher into the air to safely watch the wave of specters travel.

"I've waited for this," Bree said, flexing and closing the focal point of her gauntlet. The last time she faced specters was during the slaughter at Camp Aquila. Dozens of Weshern's best and brightest, many her friends, had fallen that day.

Not this time.

This time, she would have her vengeance.

CHAPTER 13

Kael's wings didn't hum. They roared. Wind blasted across his body, a futile protest against his speed as he flew for the nearest group of Weshern Seraphim. No time for patience. He'd seen that look in his sister's eye. At any moment she might decide she didn't need reinforcements.

"Chernor!" he screamed as he flung his legs forward and cut power to his wings. The giant Seraph cocked his head as he slowed his own wings and ordered the rest with him to halt.

"What is it, kid?" he asked, gesturing to the rest of the Seraphs racing to engage in the next major battle over the ground troops and war machines. "We'll fall behind and miss out on all the good stuff."

Kael flung his arm back to the north.

"The holy mansion's under attack!"

Chernor frowned as he looked to the distance. Four others

in Chernor's group, including Saul and Clara, pulled back from the chase to join their flight leader in hovering.

"The sky is clear from what I see," Chernor said.

"Not the sky," Kael insisted. "On the ground. An army of specters is almost to the mansion. We need to hold them off."

That got his attention.

"Is your sister following them?" he asked.

"She is."

"Then let's join her and rain hell down from the goddamn sky."

Chernor took lead, Kael falling to the back of their V-shape formation to fly beside Clara. She reached out to take his hand and squeeze it once, but that was it before they both focused back to the battle at hand. They crossed the short mile, rejoining Bree. His sister beckoned them on, impatiently waiting for their arrival.

"Keep high!" Chernor screamed to them as Bree fell back to the other tail end of the V-formation. "Speed and height are our advantages."

The paved road wound below, flanked by rows of homes on the way to the holy mansion. The specters raced ahead of them, at least forty in number. Chernor angled higher, his hand signaling to hold their elements until his order. Kael clenched and unclenched his gauntleted fist, eager yet nervous for the attack. They would not be helpless like most ground troops, reliant on meager arrows to cross the distance. The specters wielded their own gauntlets and prisms; this battle would be far from even, and Kael had a feeling they were not on the favored side.

Chernor gave the order to attack. Chunks of ice and stone dropped in a steady barrage, punctuated by Chernor's lightning bolts. It was more than enough to crush the men and women below, but the specters had their own defenses. Two jagged cliffs of stone merged from the concerted effort of multiple specters, rising up from the ground to ram together as a shield. Another wall of ice quickly followed underneath, absorbing the blast of lightning and dispersing it harmlessly. Chernor's squad's barrage rained down on the stone, cracking pieces off but unable to pierce through. That which did manage to make it through the cracks in the stone shield had to break the ice next, and often the attack would halt completely.

Distance kept Kael's group safe from the specters' stone and fire, but it meant little to the bolts of lightning ripping through their numbers. The Seraph nearest Chernor cried out as a trio of lightning bolts tore through his neck and chest. His convulsions tilted him downward on a collision course with the rows of homes. More bolts passed frighteningly close, filling Kael's vision with painful flashes and dots. All pretense of continuing the barrage vanished as Chernor twisted and lifted their formation higher and away from danger. Kael followed, his body tense and his eyes wide as the air around him crackled with yellow and white energy. Only Bree refused to flee, instead diving lower with her wings ablaze with light. Kael fought the instinct to follow. She'd be too far away by the time he turned about. He'd have to trust her.

Bree's dive was steep and erratic, her right arm reaching out as if she were attempting to touch the ground. Preparing for a furious blast of fire, no doubt. Kael doubted any defense the specters summoned would withstand her fury, but they gave him no chance to find out. Lightning lashed the air, a sudden storm unleashed upon the clear blue skies. Bree's speed, coupled with the dive, gave her tremendous maneuverability, but it mattered not when more than a dozen specters greeted her with lightning and flame. Kael's breath caught in his throat as his sister ducked and weaved, all thought of attack abandoned. She was a fly weaving through a spider's web. The slightest error would be fatal.

"Quick!" Chernor shouted as he pulled them up and around to a stop. "Buy the Phoenix time!"

Their leader braced his arm and let loose a tremendous beam of lightning, balls of flame and ice trailing soon after. The specters summoned another set of walls, and the barrage of attacks ceased as Bree fled. She changed directions to fly several hundred feet higher, then joined the waiting group.

"There's too many," Bree said. "And they're too accurate."

"We can't just let them go untouched," Chernor said. "That's our Archon they're after. Risking our lives for him is part of the job."

"But we don't need to risk it yet," Kael said. "We can outrace them to the mansion. One of us can fly the royal family out of danger while the others prepare the defenses."

"You can fly my father and mother out," Clara corrected. "But I'm not going anywhere. If Center wants to send her specters to my home, I'm going to be there to give them a proper greeting."

"Then let's not waste time we don't have," Chernor said.

They flew to the holy mansion, giving the sprinting group of specters a wide berth. Kael glanced over his shoulder, trying to catch sight of the larger engagement of armies. They were but distant colors and dots. Center's troops were spread out across dozens of miles, and the minor islands likely attacked from multiple locations. The battles he could see were certainly not the only ones. It might take days to fully realize the cost in lives on all sides.

Chernor's squad crossed over the outer fence to land directly upon the steps of the holy mansion. Soldiers standing before the heavy doors hurried to open them. Kael let his shield sink into the dirt, its heavy weight returning as he shut off the light elements attached to it.

"You four stay out here on watch," Chernor ordered. "Me and Brett will get the Archon and his wife ready for flight somewhere safe. I'd say we have about ten minutes before the specters get here, so don't get too comfortable."

Chernor and Brett didn't even wait for a salute in response before rushing into the mansion. Kael rubbed at his eyes, and then, with a moment of panic, looked through the thick glass in his left gauntlet. His light prism was pale, much of it cracked and gray. Less than a fifth, by Kael's estimate. When he checked the additional prisms powering his shield, he found them similarly dull. On the plus side, at least half his ice remained.

"This shield and these wings are doing a number on my light prisms," Kael said.

"Mine's not in too great a shape, either," Bree said, popping open the compartment for her light prism. She slid it out and then offered it to Kael. He stared at it for a moment, confused as to her request, until the obvious connection clicked. His blood. He'd used it to repower their prism when they flew far beyond Weshern's shores to the edges of the dome. With the battle far from over, it made no sense letting their momentary rest go to waste.

"Oh, right," Kael said as he removed his gauntlet. "It's been a long day."

"I'd expect it to keep getting longer," Saul said.

Kael offered a hand to Bree, trusting her more than himself. She put her prism into his palm, then used the tip of her sword to open a small cut along the bottom of his wrist. He lowered his hand, letting the blood run to his palm and into contact with the first of several light prisms.

"Mine as well, please," Clara said, retrieving her own. Kael felt the energy flowing out of him and into the prism, banishing the gray and sealing over the cracks. His blood dried and peeled from the prism's touch, which turned flawlessly white. He handed it back to Bree, then held up a hand to Clara.

"Give me a moment," he said. "Doing that feels a bit like a crazy sprint."

She kissed his cheek and did just that. Kael put a bit more of his weight on his shield, staring to the dirt as he waited for his momentary vertigo to pass. A sprint, yes, but not just a sprint. It felt as if something he didn't understand was siphoning out of him.

"All right," he said. "Hand me another."

Kael watched the far distant battle as he filled the fourth. The sun was on its downward descent, the red sky highlighting the silver and gold of their wings. Keeping his mind distracted helped with the sudden exhaustion associated with refilling another prism. They were much too far to have any idea what was going on, the wings like little flittering stars, but he did see that four such golden wings had pulled away from the rest. They hovered in place for a long minute, their light steadily growing brighter.

"They're on their way here," Kael said, realizing what was going on. He wanted to run but the dizziness kept him still, so he clutched his shield and pushed his worried sister away.

"Find Chernor," he said. "Isaac and Avila need to leave this instant!"

Bree vanished through the doors. Kael tossed Saul his recharged light element and then began wrapping a cut piece of his pants around his palm as a bandage.

"It's only four," Saul said. "We can take them. There's no need to panic."

Kael flicked power back onto his shield, allowing him to easily lift it from the dirt.

"We'll see," he said. "But I've a feeling they know what they're doing."

By the time Chernor and Brett arrived with the royal couple, the specters were closing in on them, as well as the four knights approaching in the sky.

"I see we have company," Chernor said, squinting at the knights. "Four's not too bad. If we're careful we can take them."

"We don't have time to be careful," Bree said. "The specters will be with them. If we fly now, they'll catch us carrying the royal family. If we engage them in the air, the specters will attack the mansion uncontested. If we focus on bringing down the specters, the knights will bring the whole mansion down."

"There's no good options left," Kael agreed. "We'll have to lure the specters and the knights inside the mansion and defend it while Isaac and Avila flee."

"Flee where?" Saul asked.

"The tunnels," Clara said. She hugged both her parents, and accepted their kisses in turn. "Please stay safe, you two."

"Make us proud," Isaac said, saluting them all. "And improper or not for me to ask, please, keep my daughter safe."

"We'll do what we can," Kael said, forcing a smile.

The two hurried back inside, soldiers slamming the doors shut behind them. The secret door to the nearby escape home wasn't too far from the entrance, but it would take them a long while to crawl the tunnel. If the specters flooded the mansion too quickly they might discover the tunnel and pen in the royal family before they could escape. Kael could only hope that, live or die, their group provided enough time.

"Well, I'm glad you two are done doing all the planning,"

Chernor said, lightly punching Kael on the shoulder. "That'll leave me the easy stuff, like taking out several knights and a few dozen specters."

"We need to take positions inside the mansion," Brett said. Of the five, he looked the most displeased with the change in plans. "Near windows, I'd say. We must whittle at their numbers if we're to have any chance of survival."

"We're vastly outmatched," Chernor said, his eyes never leaving the army of specters. "Forget defending doors and windows. It'll just be a losing battle. I say we let them in uncontested."

"You'd not fight back?" Kael asked, baffled.

"I never said that," Chernor snapped. "The far battle looks like it's going our way, so those specters and knights are on a strict time limit before reinforcements arrive. If we fight, they'll collapse the whole building down on top of us and hope for the best. But if we sucker them into coming inside, we might have a shot in close quarters."

"If they come inside to search, they may not have enough time to retreat safely back to Center," Clara said.

"They're not planning on leaving this island," Chernor said. "They're here to kill our Archon and Archoness. Between safe holes, tunnels, and our own elements, there's too much chance the royal family survives an outside barrage. They won't risk that failure, not if they have the chance to get up close and personal."

"Are you willing to bet your life on it?" Kael asked.

The big man grinned.

"Well. Yeah. I wouldn't be in charge if I wasn't."

It made sense, though the idea of letting Center's specters walk right into the holy mansion was most unpleasant. If only the specters had been without aerial support. No matter how fast they ran they'd never have kept up with a pair of Seraphim wings.

"Then let's do it," Kael said. He dropped to one knee, pressed his gauntlet to the stone walkway, and then yanked it back. A wall of ice rose from the ground, hiding their movements from the approaching forces of Center. They were not yet through the front doors when the first specter attack plinked against the ice.

"We won't win anything close to a fair fight," Chernor said as they gathered in a circle beside the doors. "Our jobs are to hit and run while retreating farther into the house. Brett and I will take the east wing, Bree and Kael, the west. Saul, Clara, you two will stay deep with the soldiers."

"No," Clara said. "Kael stays with me."

Chernor didn't bother arguing.

"Fuck it. Fine. Saul, Bree, you two take the east instead. Everyone meet in the middle of the mansion, and if not there, then meet in the heavens so we can stand together before God and tell him he did a piss-poor job protecting us fools down below."

They all scattered. Kael reinforced the front door with ice, then followed Clara down the hall, his wings softly humming to keep his body near weightless. A window shattered somewhere near, then another. A stone boulder smashed in the front door, twisting ice and metal into ruin. Clara grabbed his arm and pulled him through a door. Once he was inside, she pushed him out of the way so she could close and lock it.

The two were inside an oval room meant for entertaining guests. Gaming tables covered with little playing pieces sat between the many chairs, and on the northern wall several dozen books rested on a shelf. Clara stepped behind one chair and aimed her gauntlet at the door.

"Wait for noise," she whispered. "We need the surprise."

Kael braced his shield beside her while arming his own

gauntlet. Whatever retaliation the specters offered, he would be there to protect her.

They listened for the passing of the specters, holding their breath to hear better. Detecting them would be no small feat. The specters moved silent as their namesake, the mansion eerily quiet but for the odd, distant wail or cry. Kael flexed and unflexed his gauntlet, nerves fraying. The search was too organized, too methodical. Where was the needed overextension?

Wait, Clara signaled when Kael started for the door. He frowned to show his impatience, but she shook her head and remained behind the chair.

They come to us, was her response.

Before he could signal back, he heard the tiniest of clicks from the door. Instinct poured power into his shield as he braced his legs. The door exploded inward with a burst of flame and smoke, a scorching fireball ripping through the debris to slam against Kael's raised shield. It detonated impotently, the heat and flame dissipating into the shield's glowing aura.

Clara retaliated immediately. Three jagged spikes of ice shot from her gauntlet through the doorway, two finding their mark. A specter dropped dead, chest and abdomen completely punctured. Two more stood beside him, gauntlets sparking with electricity and frost. The first charged in, using his lightning to blind and disorient. Kael fell back, his shield up to protect him and Clara from any attacks. Shield still up, he pushed his flat palm to the floor and focused his mind on the desired shape. Ice crawled across the carpet for several feet before bursting upward inside the doorway, separating the two specters from each other.

With no room to run, the specter released his lightning in a powerful attack. Kael trusted his shield, his eyes closed as the strain pulled against both mind and element. Clara dropped to her knees and formed a second ice wall, trapping the specter between the two. With a savage cry she stood and flung both arms forward, sending her ice wall crashing backward to smash against the other. The two walls crumbled together, gore and mangled metal all that remained of the first specter.

Both walls now crumbled, the second specter had a clear shot and tried to blind Kael and Clara with a wide spray of frost, the cold sticking to the tables and furniture and clouding the air with white. Kael shrugged off the cold while squinting against the sudden flurry. Their foe dashed aside, rolling below a spike of ice from Clara's gauntlet before coming up with a blast of his own. Even through the frost, Kael could see that the specter's aim was slightly off and he would strike the side of Kael's shield, so he stayed put. Ice piled against a bookshelf to their left, sealing it over. Clara retaliated with smaller orbs of ice from her own gauntlet. The specter dropped to one knee and curled a half sphere of ice about himself for protection. The sound of steel rang through the room as the specter drew a sword in his left hand.

"Your Seraphim training betrays you," the specter said. "You lack understanding. You lack *imagination.*"

The specter clenched his fist. The ice across the bookshelf exploded in a spray of razors, bypassing the protection of Kael's shield. He dropped to the side, crying out in pain as the thin shards struck. They were sharp but frail; their Seraphim jackets and uniforms provided adequate protection. Their exposed faces and necks were a different matter. Thin, stinging cuts opened across the both of them, the damage superficial but the distraction the attack caused deadly. Both their guards down, the specter lunged with his sword. The tip passed by Kael's shield and would have pierced his heart if not for Clara's quick reaction.

Clara shot a beam of ice directly into the back of the chair she stood behind, flinging it forward to slam into Kael's back. The force rammed him into the specter, closing the distance and plunging the thrust harmlessly into the air behind him. The two tumbled together, one over the other. Kael reacted without thinking, shutting off the light elements to his shield the second he was atop the specter. The shield's tremendous weight returned at once, to gruesome results. The specter screamed, the bones in his right arm and shoulder pinned beneath and snapping like twigs. Kael grabbed for the specter's throat, closed his fingers about it, and let loose his ice. It spread from his palm, encasing the specter's head and neck in a frozen coffin.

"Holy shit," Kael said, rolling onto his back. Blood trickled down his face and neck. "I feel like I've been clawed by a dozen cats."

"The scars will give you character," Clara said, offering him a hand.

He took it and stood, sparing only a glance at the specter he'd crushed. The macabre image was more than enough to force his eyes away.

"Where to now?" he asked.

"We follow the sounds of battle."

Such sounds had grown numerous since the start of their fight. The specters must have reached the first line of defense set up by the house guards. Kael sealed off the broken doorway to protect their flank and then exited the other side. The carpet in the hall was slightly charred. Farther ahead he saw two bodies lying facedown, their corpses blackened to the bone. They lacked any armor or weaponry. Servants, then, or perhaps one of many nobles trapped inside when the battle began.

"No time," Kael said, powering up his wings. "Fly with me."

The hallway was tight but he could manage to fly if he kept

his wings steady. His silver wings hummed, and Kael burst down the short hall. When it split into a T, Kael barely slowed. He twisted the upper half of his body while crouching his legs. He slid in the air to the left side of the hall, and the moment before he hit the T he kicked out against the wall, shoving him into the right hallway.

A lone specter stood guarding a doorway, her back to Kael. The woman spun upon hearing his wings, and fire swelled in her palm for a brief moment before she dove to the ground. Kael shot overhead and twisted his body around, enduring the awful pain in his back and sides to reverse his direction. He floated a half second, momentum equalizing, and then he shot back to the specter. She rolled onto her back, gauntlet up to release her flame. He gave her no target, just his shield. Judging the distance, Kael cut off power to both his wings and shield. Immediately he felt the heavy pull against his limbs. Like a stone he dropped, the lower edge of his shield leading. The specter pushed off with her hands and legs, trying to dodge, but she misjudged his path.

He landed directly from above, the immense weight of his shield slamming the hard ground with its bottom edge, decapitating the specter where she lay.

Kael rose to his feet, his shield at guard, the light upon it reigniting. Two specters rushed out from the bedroom upon hearing the noise to avenge their fallen comrade. They unleashed a swirling mix of lightning and stone, a powerful barrage that would have crushed any other Seraph. Light flared about his shield, surging with power. Kael gasped at the strain, feeling it tearing at his mind and sucking the air from his lungs. The lightning fizzled, the stone cracking to dust the moment it made contact with the brilliant blue sword emblazoned across the center of the metal.

Clearly the two specters hadn't expected him to endure the attack, either, and they hesitated for a moment to work through what they'd witnessed. It was in that moment of hesitance that Clara turned the corner, gauntlet up and ready. Two long spears, one for each specter, pierced their backs. One died instantly, his rib cage ruptured. The other rolled across the ground, the spear glancing off his silver wingless harness. He came out of the roll before Kael could ready his own ice, the furious specter flinging his open palm up to fire. Nothing emerged from the dead focal point but a soft burst of sparks from the damaged unit. Kael ended him with a lance of ice to the skull.

"This is awful," Clara muttered. Kael turned to find her standing before the open door the two specters had exited. Her arms were crossed over her chest as if she were cold.

"Don't let it in," Kael said, coming to her side. He didn't need to look into the room to see the innocent dead within. He didn't need to confirm the pain and sorrow he knew she felt. "We can break later, but not now, all right? Not now."

"I know," she said, turning away. "But knowing changes nothing."

The end of the hall was a grand dancing room, not quite the extravagant ballroom where they'd hosted the solstice celebration but large enough to fit the six house soldiers who were standing side by side in the center. Their shields were linked together, that wall of steel the only protection against the elements of the two specters darting before them, the bodies of four dead guards at their feet. The specters alternated hits, one thrusting the moment another retreated away from a spear. Their gauntlets flashed with elements, either fire or lightning to bathe the shields. The guards screamed every time, but they fought through the pain to hold their ground.

"I'll take left; you take right," Kael told Clara behind him, the hall not wide enough for the two to stand side to side. "Fire on three."

Any missed shot risked harming one of the guards, but the longer the battle lasted the more their lives were at risk anyway. Together they raised their right hands, Clara steadying hers with her left hand, Kael positioning his shield below his arm as a brace. The two specters still had their backs to them, too focused on their vicious dance to realize they were flanked. Kael led the countdown, not tracking a specific specter since they too often switched locations but instead keeping it focused on the left half of the doorway.

"One, two, three."

Kael unleashed three thin lances of ice, not trusting his aim but trusting the shields of the guard to withstand should any of Kael's attacks miss. Two did, and as he'd hoped, their long, sharp tips broke against the steel. The third lance struck the specter through the shoulder and pierced out the front. The hit knocked him closer to the guards, and off balance; he was easy prey for their spears. The other specter fared even worse. Clara's lone shot cracked against the back of his skull and knocked him out instantly.

Kael felt no elation at the hits, too drained for anything other than relief. A flick of his thumb shut off the element to his shield, and he leaned against it to take in a quick breath.

"How fare the others?" Clara asked the soldiers as she joined them in the room.

"We do not know, Miss Willer," their leader said after bowing low. "We are the last of us in this wing."

"Start patrolling the east then," Clara ordered. "Push the invaders from our home."

"As you wish," the leader said. "For Weshern!"

"For freedom!" the others shouted in unison.

Kael rubbed at his eyes and pulled his shield up from the ground as Clara returned.

"Are you going to make it?" she asked.

"It's not like I have a choice," he said, grinning to hide how tired he was. "What next?"

"Next we find Saul and Bree," she said. "And we make sure not a single damn specter escapes death."

"You're scary when you're bloodthirsty—you know that, right?"

"And you're surprisingly handsome while cut up and bleeding."

"I do what I can."

Despite their flippant words Clara took his hand in hers and squeezed it tightly.

"Thanks for being here when I need you," she said softly.

"Nowhere else I'd rather be," he said, squeezing back. "So let's find some unwanted guests and show them how scary we both can be."

CHAPTER 14

The specter advanced upon Bree with his wide grin still visible upon his masked face. Bree stood wing to wing with Saul, the two trapped on either side by Center's elite assassins in one of the holy mansion's numerous hallways. Their serrated swords swam through the air, ice and stone hovering above their gauntleted hands.

"Come now, Phoenix," her foe said. "Let me see those blades you are so famous for."

Bree lifted her burning swords, her knees bending as she posed for a pounce.

"Are you sure?" she asked. "No one has survived them yet."

In answer, the specter slid his gauntlet across the smooth edge of his blade. Ice sheathed the weapon, thin and sharp.

"You have your fire, and I have my ice," he said. "Let us see which is stronger."

"Stay on task!" the other specter called, his gauntlet up and ready to counter the moment Saul made a move to use his ice. "The Archon is our goal."

"It's the damn Phoenix," the first specter shot back. "I will not turn down such a chance at glory."

"You want a shot at glory?" Saul asked. "Take it. I'll make sure the playing field stays even."

Ice poured from his gauntlet, forming a solid sheet across the hallway. The specter on the other side smashed it with boulders from his gauntlet, shaking the ice wall and shooting deep cracks throughout. Saul's gauntlet never stopped spraying, banishing the cracks and thickening the wall with each passing moment so it might withstand the opposing barrage. It was a test of elements. Bree didn't know who would win, but she could not spare a moment in aid.

The specter ripped off his mask, revealing himself as a dark-skinned man with even darker hair cut close to the scalp.

"A private duel," he said. "I could not ask for more. See the face of your better, Phoenix. It's come time to pay the price for your blasphemy."

"Shut up and fight me already."

She flicked her wings with a momentary surge, gaining speed as she lunged toward the specter. Her burning blades hammered against his sword. It should have melted right through the metal but instead the ice held strong.

"Did you think you were special, Phoenix?" the specter said, laughing. "We've been watching your tricks, and we've been learning. You are not the only one who can bless their blades with elements."

He shoved her back, then spun while ducking low. His gauntlet passed over his sword, refreshing the icy sheath so that a fully covered blade cut for her knees. Bree barely blocked, the contact between their weapons releasing the hiss and crack of fire on ice instead of the sharp ringing of metal on metal. She chopped with her other hand, not surprised in the slightest that the specter easily blocked. He batted his weapon back and forth, ice crumbling off it as every single attack she made found a waiting answer.

"Where is the skill?" he asked. "Or have you relied on your fire to hide your flaws, Phoenix?"

Bree parried twice, staggered backward to avoid a thrust she missed, and then had to cross both her swords together in an X to stop a vicious chop toward her neck. Three blades screeched, fire dwindling, ice melting. Bree felt the strain in her mind, an exhausting pull similar to the one she'd felt when she had been forced to release her flame back in the dungeon. If the specter felt a similar strain, he hid it well.

"Your lack of skill will make the honor of killing you a falsehood," the specter said, his sword a blue blur as he weaved it through the air. "Not that it matters. You will be dead, and only the worms will know how terribly lacking you were in all things."

Bree leapt onto the offensive, hoping to surprise him while he boasted and blustered. Her swords rained down on him with all her might channeled into the blow. The fire roared, her mind equally focused on overwhelming him with power. Her swords were blazing infernos slamming against a spinning, dancing beam of ice. Every hit showered the ground with frost. Every hit, that ice returned to withstand another blow. She kept going, no finesse, no feints, just savage rage.

This time the specter did not laugh and mock.

Bree sensed him weakening, sensed her control over the battle becoming singular and total. Her world swam red, all her fury unleashed on the boastful, unbearable specter in the form of two, simultaneous downward slashes. She bellowed out a mindless, formless battle cry. The specter clutched his sword with both hands and blocked, but his strength was not enough. Nothing could possibly match it. The flame across her blades' fine edges sparked a blinding yellow, the entire hallway between them flooding with a sudden eruption of fire. No dodging. No avoiding. The prism in her gauntlet cracked and drained, but the power continued to flow out from her through the blood washing over it. The ice about the specter's sword vanished into white mist. The metal melted as if it were warm butter. The eruption surged on, swarming over the specter's body, blackening his flesh and reducing his clothing to cinders. When Bree's swords cut through him, they scattered only ash and bone.

"Holy shit," Bree said as she dropped to her knees and gasped for air. She'd lashed flame out from her swords, and she'd released greater infernos before, but never had her swords themselves blazed with such heat and fury. Even Center itself would have split in half at her strike.

"Bree!" Saul screamed.

Bree spun to help her friend. Ice roared from Saul's gauntlet, fighting back against an advancing wall of stone. Spikes lined its front, and like a battering ram, they were beginning to punch through Saul's ice barricade. It was only a matter of time before Saul's wall shattered completely.

"Back away," Bree shouted, a plan forming in her mind. "Strike when I give you an opening."

Her confidence was a mask. Bree felt exhausted, and though the elemental prism in her gauntlet shone vibrant red once more, the toll of refueling it was wearing on her. Could she pull off what she needed for her plan to work?

Not that she had a choice. Saul gave her one last doubtful look before ending his stream of ice. The specter's spiked stone wall shattered it to pieces with the sudden lapse in reinforcement, then continued scraping forward, carving deep grooves into the carpet and walls. Bree braced her legs, lifted her gauntlet, and closed her eyes. What approached appeared stone, but it wasn't truly stone. In mere minutes it would begin fading into mist. It was merely a magical creation of a prism, no different from her flame, and its power would reflect its master. The specters were skilled wielders of demonic power, but Bree did not wield it as they did. She carried that power in her blood. It pulsed within her veins.

A scream escaped her throat as she braced her arms and legs. A burning sphere swelled before her gauntlet, then erupted like a volcano. A thick beam of fire flowed into the wall, the pressure of its release jarring Bree's shoulder back so hard she feared it broken. The roar of it deafened her ears. The heat of it warmed the metal of her gauntlet. She felt its contact burning her flesh, but flesh would heal. Her foe would not.

The jagged stone wall lost all momentum. It hardened and cracked, its earthy brown turning black. Bree took a step forward, still screaming, her every muscle locked tight. Unconsciousness flitted at the edges of her mind. The fire pushed deeper, sinking into the wall, crumbling away its form, until it broke through with a thunderous clamor. Bree immediately clenched her fist, ceased the fire, and collapsed to her knees. She could only watch through blurred vision as Saul dove through the smoldering crack in the stone wall, his gauntlet a shimmering beacon of blue ice.

Someone's hand touched her arm. Not Saul's. She tried to cry out but lacked the strength. Another hand, lifting her up by the armpit. Her view turned. Her heart warmed.

"Hey, Kael," she said, her words slurred as if she were intoxicated. "You missed the fun."

Her brother shifted her arm over his shoulder, taking on

more of her weight. Clara stood next to him, concern painted across her bloody face.

"I saw the end of it," he said. "Goddamn, you're terrifying."

Bree laughed.

"Fear me," she said. "The girl who can barely stand."

Saul stepped through the cooling opening in the wall. Blood trickled down his face from a gash above his brow, but he otherwise appeared unharmed.

"Kael, Clara," he said, nodding to them both. "You two look like shit."

"I think what you meant to say was, 'Hey, Kael, glad you survived this awful nightmarish day,'" Kael said. "But don't worry. Bree's alive, so I'll forgive you."

Clara knelt before Bree, her hands carefully touching Bree's gauntlet. Both winced.

"That's what I thought," Clara said. She loosened the buckles on her gauntlet one after another. Bree stifled a cry when she pulled it free, the tiny needle in her skin hurting more coming out than it had going in. She had to admit she felt immensely better with it removed. Clara set the gauntlet aside and took her hand to examine it. Deep burn marks covered her skin from her fingertips to her wrist.

"You're supposed to heal wounds from your own element unnaturally fast," she said. "But even then, I think you'll have these for a few days. You have to be careful, Bree. You wield your fire with far more power than these wings and gauntlets were originally devised to control. Give yourself a chance to rest. I think we've cleared out the last of the specters in this area."

"Make that the whole mansion," a deep voice called from down the hall. Bree followed it to see Chernor calmly approaching, his maul slung casually over his shoulder. Blood dripped from cuts along his waist and left leg. "Nice to see you four survived. I shouldn't be surprised by now; you're all tougher than cockroaches."

"Where is Brett?" Bree asked.

"It's only me." Chernor stepped to one of the windows and peered outside. "Have you checked for the patrolling knights?"

"Still there," Kael said. "Still watching for any escapees. They'll suspect something's amiss soon enough, I think."

"Which is why we should attack them before they realize their precious specters are dead," Chernor said. "Five on six isn't the best odds for us, but if we catch them with their pants down we might take out a few to make it manageable."

"They've got the high ground," Saul said. "How could we be the ones on the surprise?"

"We won't with that shitty attitude," Chernor said, waving him off. "The knights are waiting for fleeing royalty, right? I say we give them exactly that."

All eyes turned to Clara, who stared back with an icy glare.

"Bait," she said. "You want me to be bait."

"It's either you or the Phoenix," Chernor said. "And I know which one they'll underestimate more. Plus, she looks a little on the woozy side if you ask me."

Kael took her hand in reassurance.

"No one's going to make you," he said.

"Like hell," Chernor said, pulling his maul off his back. "Our whole island's in danger, so no special treatment for Archon's daughters. I'm still your superior, so consider this an order, Seraph. Either abandon your harness or join us in ambushing Center's knights currently laying siege to your home."

Clara stood up straighter, all emotion drained from her face.

"I will not abandon my home, my island, or my friends," she said. "Tell me what to do."

CHAPTER 15

Kael wished he felt as calm as Clara looked. Despite Chernor's assurances, he knew their plan was both drastic and dangerous, especially for Clara.

"You better not let anything happen to you," he said as they stood in the center of the garden, hidden from the knights' view by the thick gathering of trees.

"Or what?" she asked.

"Or I'll die avenging you, and then when we meet in the afterlife I'll be really, really mad for at least a whole day."

Clara kissed his lips, her left hand gently settling atop his shoulder.

"The angels spare me such a fate," she said.

"You two lovebirds ready to start?" Chernor asked.

They nodded in answer.

"What about you?" Kael asked his sister.

Bree pulled her gauntlet over her burned hand, wincing as it clamped tight.

"I feel much better," she said. "I promise."

"That's good to hear," Chernor said. "Saul, ready?"

He saluted in answer.

"All right then." Chernor turned back to Clara. "It's all up to you now. Go when you're ready, little Archoness."

Kael separated from her, and he prayed to every angel who might listen that it not be for the last time. Clara steeled herself, her emotions vanishing beneath a careful mask of concentration.

"I'm ready," she said. "Don't let me down."

Clara soared skyward over the garden. Their hope was that she appeared to be fleeing from the specters inside the mansion. The garden put her in the center of all four knights, with no apparent escape. Kael readied his wings, his left thumb flicking back and forth atop the throttle. This was the most dangerous part of the entire plan for Clara. She raced eastward, drawing the knights after her. The two on either side of her steadily closed in, while the one ahead of her stayed where he was, waiting as the other two corralled her toward him. The fourth shifted so he could hover over the center of the mansion, keeping watch on all exits. The position put him directly above the garden within easy reach of ambush.

"Turn around," Kael whispered. "Come on, Clara, that's far enough . . ."

She was leaving the mansion behind while drawing in the other three knights with her. Little distance separated them from Clara, yet still they kept their elements in check. Kael chewed on his tongue, horror clawing at his heart. He repeated the same thought over and over in his mind as if he could deny it from becoming reality.

You are not about to watch her die. You are not about to watch her die. You are not about to watch her die.

Clara finally completed the plan. With a knight ahead of her there was no way she could outrace the other two. Instead she dove sharply, spinning into the dive so when she pulled back up she faced back toward the mansion. The two chasing knights veered outward, mimicking her maneuver. Now they unleashed their elements, ice and lightning tearing through the air. Every blast was a needle to Kael's heart. He couldn't breathe. Couldn't move. She weaved and shifted, every bit of speed pouring into her wings as she returned to the holy mansion.

"Trust your girl," Chernor said, settling a hand atop Kael's shoulder. "She's got a bit of fire in her as well."

The knights would catch up to her in time, of that Kael had no doubt. But she only needed to survive for a few seconds more. Back and forth, constant dips and turns. Lightning flashed so close to her he nearly cried out. Her path lowered, drawing them into the ambush. The knight above them was completely distracted by Clara's approach, no doubt readying for an intercept path.

"It's time," Chernor said. "Fuck 'em up."

The four tore into the air, a barrage of elements marking their arrival. Chernor shot for the closest knight, his bolt of lightning perfectly aimed, while Kael and Saul sent sharp lances of ice flying toward the other three. Chernor's bolt ripped through the knight's chest. The knight convulsed, his wings keeping him in a hovering pattern. Chernor flew closer and swung, his maul striking the killing blow.

Clara remained perfectly still as attacks passed by on either side. Knights saw the incoming elements with barely any time to react. Two scattered while the third formed a squat wall of stone in protection. Saul's ice connected, the spear cutting through a knight's leg, separating it at the knee. The knight bathed the wound in flame from his gauntlet before resuming the attack, a feat of concentration Kael would have found admirable if it weren't so frightening.

Bree, however, cared not for distance attacks. Her wings blazed silver, twin trails of fire dripping off her flaming swords as she streaked in for close combat. Kael separated from Chernor and Saul, connecting with his light element to push his wings beyond their normal limits. His shield was ready. Their ambush may have begun, but Clara was still closer to the knights than the others, and the brunt of their retaliation would be aimed at her.

The stone wielder raced over his protective wall while the two others curled in from either side. Shot after shot of stone lobbed through the air, arcing with perfect accuracy at Clara. She kept watch over her shoulder even as she fled, waiting for the projectiles and adjusting as best she could. Kael tracked them as well, saw they were too numerous for her to consistently predict. Wind screamed against his body. His wings thundered. Shield up, he curled slightly higher and maneuvered himself directly into a barrage of four human-size boulders.

Kael braced his body for the worst. Charging headlong into such boulders at his speed should shatter his bones and leave his wings in tatters, but he trusted his shield.

Fire, lightning, stone, it's all the same, a voice spoke in Kael's mind, one he wasn't sure was his own. *All of it will break.*

Light exploded about his shield, flaring just before the first of the stones made contact. Instead of hearing the hard clang of collision, he heard a deep hum coupled with a loud crack. The boulders broke apart in an explosion of smoke and mist. The outer halves fractured and separated, spiraling wildly with only a trace of their former speed.

Kael never felt the slightest hit against his shield, instead feeling the strain on his mind as the light element drained.

"More!" Kael taunted, two other boulders careening straight for him. "Give me more!"

His mind ached, the connection growing stronger, his shield growing brighter. The stone blasted to pieces, whatever magic holding it together failing against his own. His greater speed sent him past Clara and alongside his sister. The two chased the nearest knight together, Kael keeping slightly ahead. Their foe readied to attack, realized Kael's shield led the way, and instead drew his weapon. It was a long metallic staff wrapped in red leather. A trio of flails hung from chains on each end, spinning together as the knight twirled his staff in a flourish.

Kael slowed his wings, giving himself space and time to fire. Four shards launched from his palm, each one slightly higher than the last. The knight's wings momentarily flared, pulling him higher as he twisted his body to one side. The flails spun, smashing two of the shards out of the air, the other two passing harmlessly by. Kael led with his shield, hoping to ram the knight out of the sky. Again the knight dashed away, avoiding the charge while attacking with his flails. They struck his shield with a deep thud, the impact jarring his shoulder. Kael didn't know if his mind was too exhausted to withstand the attack, or if the nonmagical nature of the flails minimized the protection of his shield. Either way, it hurt like hell.

Bree followed after, unafraid to engage the knight in close quarters. She swung with her left hand, had it blocked by the staff. Kael whirled around, and he saw bits of stone crumble on contact. Had the knights learned some trick to protect themselves from her flame? His sister shifted her body sideways, thrusting into yet another parry. The two circled each other, a revolving dance as they alternated blows, their bodies never still, their eyes never leaving the other's. The knight spun the staff a full circle, building power into his flails, and then swept one end toward her face. Bree killed her wings and dropped beneath the strike. The flails swooshed the air, hitting nothing. Bree's wings immediately surged back to life, carrying her upward as she slashed with both her blades against her foe's weapon. The staff, reinforced as it was, could not endure the sudden blaze of flame and split in the middle. The light elements that had been reducing the staff's tremendous weight immediately ceased to function. Both halves ripped from the knight's hands and plummeted downward.

The entire exchange lasted no longer than a few seconds, but the sheer number of attacks and parries made it feel like it had been a lifetime. An opening revealed, Bree burst forward, right arm slicing across the knight's chest, who was then exposed and distracted by the pain. Kael buried him in ice, ending his life.

Opponent defeated, the two turned their attention to the rest of the battle. Saul and Chernor had brought down another knight, and now with Clara at their side the three chased after the injured knight with the severed leg. He must have fled east the moment the battle started, for he had a good mile lead over the others.

"I can't catch up," Bree shouted to him as she drew near. "But you can!"

Kael tilted his body, squared his shoulders, and flooded light into his wings. His speed increased at a dramatic rate, pulling on his limbs and straining the buckles of his harness. Kael kept his eyes on the fleeing knight, hoping to intersect his path. The ground below was a blur, the protection for his face against the wind straining. A small voice in his mind dared wonder a question he partly feared to answer.

Do I even need the throttle?

The throttle sent power from the light element in his gauntlet to his wings through the connecting wires, but what if he ignored the throttle completely? The light element was under his control, pulsing so clearly in his mind he could see every little blemish and crack in its slowly draining prism.

Kael envisioned himself slowing down as he curled slightly to cut the knight off. He imagined the wind reducing, the hum in his ears lessening. And it happened. His turn was perfectly smooth. Curving back around, Kael clenched his jaw tight and demanded speed. All of it. Every bit his prism could give him. The throttle was a suggestion, its maximum setting a feeble limiter. He angled his shield before him and let it part the wind while buoying him higher. Faster. Faster. Not just the ground a blur but the sky as well, his friends, all of Weshern. His eyes narrowed on his prey as the trio of Saul, Chernor, and Clara receded in a blink.

Second by second, Kael closed the gap. Every muscle in his body tightened, every bit of his concentration focused on keeping his body perfectly straight and still. One slip up, one twist of his shoulders, and he might spin to his death before even realizing he'd lost control. The knight looked behind him and spotted Kael's approach. Still he tried to flee, the greater battle between Center's forces and the outer islands just ahead. Kael doubted the knight understood how much speed Kael harnessed in his wings.

He crept his right hand around the shield, his fingers curled into his palm while his knuckles pulled back to stretch open the focal point. Blue mist swirled about his palm, building with power. Kael shifted again, racing directly toward the knight. He kept the imagined projectile in mind, but he didn't release. Not yet. Not until the gap was all but nothing.

The knight saw him and panicked at his sudden proximity. A ball of flame shot from his gauntlet, badly underestimating his speed. It burned in Kael's wake, accomplishing nothing. Kael never changed his direction and blasted straight past the knight. His arm swung back, the pent-up power releasing in the form of a giant square wall directly in the knight's path. The knight's body slammed into the wall with a scream of bone and metal. His body careened wildly to the ground on dying wings.

Kael pulled himself erect and slowly eased back his speed. The pulsing of his light element grew less vibrant in his mind, more drawn out. Kael gazed upon the battle as he fought to regain his breath.

"Impossible," he whispered.

Varl Cutter's army pushed through the barren wasteland that had once been a beautiful field. Center's soldiers formed uneven lines, a paltry defense to stop Cutter's onslaught. Seraphim of all islands hovered over the battlefield, raining down destruction. Dozens of cannons lay broken across the battlefield, and dozens more broke as he watched. Kael couldn't contain his excitement. The battle... they'd won it. They'd achieved aerial superiority over Center's troops. The knights were already pulling back, keeping tightly together, making any attempt at chasing them extremely dangerous. Platforms hovered in their midst, the few soldiers and machines who'd managed to flee.

Still the war machines fought on. Kael watched one gilded machine in humanoid form raise two arms that ended in focal prisms the size of a man's fist. Fire sprayed from them in tremendous streams, matching those of the cannons. Two Candren Seraphs flew through the inferno, coming out the other side with blackened clothes and melted wings. Stone and ice boulders rained down from Candren's furious Seraphim, smashing into the mechanics. The giant knight collapsed. A storm of lightning bathed its center, ensuring the death of the controller inside.

"We did it," Kael said, in shock that such a miracle had come to pass. Then louder, with a whoop, "We won!"

He swung about to look for his friends. They were farther away than he expected, and he waved to them in greeting. Bree let loose two quick jets of flame beneath her in response, tiny little specks of red in the distance. Kael frowned. A warning, but for what?

Kael looked down to see a plume of flame rising upward. Ice flashed out his gauntlet in a panic, forming a thin wall against the heat. It quickly melted away but sapped the power of the blast so that only a painful jet of steam washed over him, blistering his skin and stinging his eyes. Kael pushed his throttle, disoriented and not trusting his ability to manipulate the elemental prism with his concentration so broken. A knight was below him, just one, it appeared, but what was he doing alone and so far from the battle?

With his vision blurred he could only send back a few haphazard lances of ice as he climbed higher. Squinting, he saw that the knight was flying at him at full speed. Kacl pushed his throttle to the maximum, jarring his body as he shot higher. Not good enough. The knight overtook him, and for the first time Kael saw the strange gauntlet on the man's right arm, four slender cannons where there should have been a fist. Kael brought his shield up the moment they crossed paths. The size of the blast shocked him with its power. This wasn't normal fire. This was akin to Bree's most vicious rage. He cried out as the attack broke against his shield. His head pounded from the sudden strain, and more blinding steam splashed across his body. His skin tightened and peeled as if he'd spent hours beneath the sun.

Kael moved his shield aside to retaliate with his ice. A prolonged fight meant death. Had to end it now. The knight dashed closer before he could release, left hand grabbing his wrist and shoving aside his gauntlet so the ice sprayed harmlessly past his attacker. The strange cannon jammed Kael's throat, the end pressing up against his chin. There would be no dodging this one. He tensed for the killing blow that never came. Confused, he blinked the tears away to stare into the face of his captor.

To stare into the face of his father.

"Dad?" Kael asked. He felt too stunned to move. Too stunned to even breathe.

Liam's eyes narrowed. His face was a mask revealing only deep concentration.

"If you move, I will kill you."

The hand on his wrist released, instead grabbing Kael by the neck and holding him still. A blade extended from the strange gauntlet, its razor-sharp edge cutting through the leather loops of his harness one by one. His wings fell free, yanking the gauntlets with them on their drop. Kael gasped for air as the hand tightened. Liam pulled him closer, chest to chest. The blade sank back into the gauntlet so Liam could wrap the arm around Kael's body and keep him still. Liam's hand yanked two of his own harness buckles free.

"Tie them around both our shoulders," he ordered.

Kael didn't think he could form coherent sentences, let alone tighten the buckles, but his hands moved of their own accord. That finished, they together turned to see the other Seraphs approach. Bree led the way, her swords bathed in so much flame it was a wonder her element was not already dry. Liam's blade extended from the strange gauntlet when Bree neared, the sharp edge pressing against Kael's neck. The message was clear, and Bree immediately pulled back.

"Struggle, you die," Liam said, his lips pressed near Kael's ear. "Try to slow my flight, you die. Say anything, you die. Do not doubt my words, son."

Kael didn't just doubt his words. He doubted everything. He doubted his ears, his eyes, and his very mind. This wasn't possible. His father was dead. Everyone knew it. He died with his mother battling Galen. He wasn't here. He wasn't carrying him to Center like a goddamn trophy. They drifted eastward while facing Bree. Kael wanted more than anything to speak, to ask if he knew those burning swords belonged to his daughter. Did he know? If he did, surely he wouldn't be doing this. Why take them away? He wasn't at Center. He was home. Weshern was *home.*

"Father—" Kael started to say.

Thick metal slammed against the back of his head before the first syllable exited his tongue, ending his confusion and misery with blessed darkness.

CHAPTER 16

Johan stood before the crater's edge amid deafening silence. His eyes swept the starlit ruin of stone and earth. Buried beneath it were the blood and bones of all who'd lived there. What had once been their home was now their grave. Hundreds of innocent souls snuffed out in an instant, and for what? A desperate attempt to retain illusory power? Or had the day's lengthy battle been an extension of their fear? Fear of change should a new power structure emerge. Fear of being seen as weak. Fear of discovering that those who once served would now rule.

"You were always such frightened creatures," Johan whispered to the blasted heath. "Our very visage sent you to your knees. It wasn't the strangeness of our bodies, either. You have always thought yourselves the greatest of beings. To see before you proof of your inferiority... how else could you cope but to worship us? To think us your heavenly guardians?"

The eternal-born shook his head, and he kicked loose dirt into the sunken crater that had been Glensbee.

"You labeled us, put us on a pedestal, and then safely went back to your ways. You didn't want a savior. You wanted a crutch to rest your sins upon."

Center's army had shattered homes and lives alike throughout the long day, thousands dead while the murderers' chests thudded with divine confidence. Johan held no doubt that every minor island's Seraphim would unleash similar destruction upon Center's civilians in retaliation. They too would feel righteous in their slaughter. They didn't need God and angels to justify the blood. It just made things easier.

Johan heard the soft thrum of wings behind him, then the sound of landing feet. He smiled and turned to greet his visitor.

"Welcome, Bree," he said. "It is good to see you survived the carnage."

"Your disciples said I'd find you here," she said. She brushed a bit of dark hair away from her face. The girl had trouble meeting his gaze, Johan noticed. Was it because of the nature of her visit? Or had she begun to mistrust his human persona?

"I needed to look upon this for myself," Johan said, and he gestured to the ruins. "I would see the terrible destruction Center is capable of with my own eyes."

Bree stepped beside him, toes hanging over the lip of the crater. It was so peaceful there, so quiet without the bustle of life. Both beautiful and terrible to Johan's ears.

"You have spies everywhere," Bree said. It wasn't a question.

"I do," Johan said.

"Even on Center?"

Interesting. Johan glanced her way, found her still avoiding his gaze.

"Yes, even on Center," he said. "The people there are not

as blindly faithful as Marius would believe. Many wonder at the source of their wealth and power, and at the source of the prisms their entire economy relies upon."

Bree tapped her fingers against the side of her leg. Johan's curiosity heightened. What could Weshern's appointed Phoenix need from him at such a late hour?

"My brother's been captured," she said, finally blurting it out. "Taken by one of Marius's knights during their retreat. I need to know where he is, and what they'll do to him."

"You're hoping to rescue him," he said. "A fool's errand, I assure you, but I have doubted you before and been proven wrong. I'm surprised Argus has signed off on such a plan, though."

Bree started to answer, hesitated, then sighed.

"He didn't," she said. "Argus said the Archon would send a formal political inquiry, and that maybe we could do a prisoner transfer."

Just as Johan suspected. Ideas started whirling in his head, ways to take advantage of the situation.

"And I assume you don't feel like waiting?" he said.

"The theotechs have taken an... interest in me and my brother," she said. "I don't think they'll ever give him up. They may lie and swear he's been killed while they hide him deep below Heavenstone. I have to know the truth for myself."

"And I have devoted my life to spreading the truth," Johan said. "I will send word to my spies immediately. Meet me here tomorrow, just before nightfall. If you have others you trust to come with you on your rescue, bring them as well. Tell no one else."

Bree stared at the heart of Glensbee's crater. It hadn't been simply crushed inward. The ground itself had lifted and swirled, stone melting from the heat. Upon settling, and the rock cooling, it had left a bewildering array of twisted, mangled structures, like art pieces of a grim madman. Johan felt it appropriate, for this was Marius's artwork, the culmination of his egotistical reign.

"Despite all the death, there is beauty in the remains," Johan said softly. "Even amid destruction so terrible. When Galen fell, others banded together to save whom they could. Battle ceased, enemies forgiven so all might work together in the rescue. I have always felt that is humanity's greatest, and most often wasted, trait. Peel away the anger, hatred, and pride of men's souls and you'll find an innate desire to protect others. Such a shame it requires a terrible catastrophe to jostle this selflessness free."

"Silver linings," Bree said, and she turned her back to the crater. "I know many seek silver linings, but I'm not one of them, Johan. Galen fell, and there was no beauty in its fall. Glensbee broke beneath Marius's wrath, and the beauty of those twisted structures is nothing compared to the dead. If Kael died, my aunt would tell me I'd still have my memories of our times together. I don't want memories. I don't want petty reassurances. I want my brother back."

Johan smiled at the young woman.

If only all of humanity were that honest with itself, he thought. *Perhaps then it would have been harder for them to justify devouring one another.*

"With such determination, I hold no doubt you will bring him back to Weshern," he said. "Now go, take rest. It has been a long day for all of us."

Bree looked so exhausted Johan thought her capable of sleeping for days, but she wouldn't take the opportunity. Lives were in danger. Such dedication was a sorely lacking feature of far too many humans.

"I'll meet you here tomorrow," she said. "And I'll bring those I trust with me."

Her wings shimmered silver and began to thrum. Johan dipped his head low in respect. He sadly shook his head as she shot into the night.

"I sense the fire in your blood," he said to her vanishing silver star. "The rage and dedication. How many of the redeeming qualities I find in you are stolen from the fireborn your kind enslaved for centuries?"

It was an interesting thought. Johan had sensed lightborn essence flowing in Kael's veins during his brief time with him. Perhaps that was why he'd been so timid compared to Bree's rage, so weak compared to her strength. Had the eternal-born blood in them molded their personalities, or was Johan seeing only biased confirmation of his personal theories? Curious, but there'd likely be no chance to investigate it further. Come tomorrow night, he expected both Bree and Kael to die, broken upon Center's soil.

Johan turned southeast, skirting the edge of the crater as he traveled toward Weshern's edge. It would be several miles' walk, but the distance meant nothing to him, nor did the time required to travel it. Night was a refuge of peace and privacy. The frail human bodies lay down to recover from a mere day's strain, blessing the floating island with a rare quiet. Johan drank it in as he walked through the devastation wrought by Center's cannons. Bree had brushed him off, but Johan had spoken the truth about finding beauty amid ruin. Deep grooves marred the land, great burned patches and forests consumed to ash, but among these scars Johan still sensed the natural.

A little copse of trees grew in the center of the fields separating Lowville from Glensbee. Fire had slowly consumed the fields, spreading outward from the devastated town like burning ripples, but those three trees seemed mostly spared, the fire having licked the grass below them but not climbed the bark.

Johan shifted directions, approaching the trees as ash crumpled beneath his footfalls.

Behold the consequence of humanity, thought Johan as he gazed upon the burned fields. *Behold nature struggling mightily to survive their reckless anger.*

Johan stopped before the trees and smiled up at the many high branches. Deep among them scurried frightened squirrels and birds, shining like little lanterns in Johan's mind. He sensed their worry, their rapidly beating hearts. What could the day have meant to such little creatures? The weaponry and machinery was far beyond their understanding. The world erupted in fire, and yet they clung to life. Such wonderful creatures.

One of the little lanterns was worrisomely dim, huddled on one of the lowest branches. Johan closed his eyes and expanded his false body, rising upward as his legs extended into poles of shadow. Huddled on its side atop that branch was a small sparrow. Its eyes were glassy, its breathing slow and uneven. Too much smoke, Johan was certain. Perhaps the sparrow would live. Perhaps not.

Johan reached a hand toward it, just a momentary forgetfulness before he yanked it away. Even that brief proximity to his hand had caused the bird to tremble violently.

"Forgive me," he said. "It was not my intent to cause you harm."

As much as he tried to be calm, Johan could not stop the growing anger in his center. There was a time when his touch would have healed away every illness from the little thing's body. Just being near him, awash in his aura of life, would have ceased its pain. But those days were long past. His light had ceased the moment he slew one of his fellow lightborn. Now his shadow granted sickness and death.

Johan shook his head and tried to smile for the sparrow.

"Fight on, and live," he said. "The world needs more of your song."

He lowered himself back to the ground, shadow receding and molding itself into a visage of legs, feet, and robes. His trip toward Weshern's edge turned somber.

Whose fault was it that he could not heal the sparrow? Was it his own for succumbing to anger and extinguishing the light of his brethren centuries before? Or was it God himself, cursing him like men of old in the religious fables? He didn't know, and no amount of debate had drawn him closer to a solution as the decades steadily rolled on.

I cleansed humanity from the world but for these wretched islands, Johan thought. *All is grasslands and forests and river lands, awash with life where stone and steel once proudly mocked the natural. As billions died, God never intervened. My cause is righteous. My shadow is my own manifested guilt, and nothing more.*

It might be a self-serving lie, but it was an easy one to believe.

Johan's strides grew longer the farther from civilization he traveled, until he no longer walked at all, instead floating along like a cloud upon the wind. Another city passed beneath him, the childhood home of the Skyborn twins, if he remembered correctly. Another poignant loss. The twins were pawns in many people's games, and the cost of playing along was suffering, capture, and likely death. Johan floated until he reached the soft earth at the island's edge. Even there, the land bore the scar of the invasion, the deep green grass churned and trampled by the wheels of Marius's great engines.

Johan knelt beside the island edge and looked to the ocean below. The rest of his shadow bathed the surface, and even from such a distance, Johan could feel every dip and swirl of the water. It was painful being separated from his essence in this way, but such was the cost of finally bringing down the protective dome the last of the lightborn erected to keep him at bay. Soon he would be whole again. So very soon.

A wave of Johan's finger and the shadow roiled, giving the signal for his allies below. Johan crossed his legs and sat as he patiently gazed over the edge. Several minutes later he saw the first hint of the iceborn rising into the sky. The tiny creature was no bigger than his fist, and it swirled in a circle atop a steadily growing cylinder of ice. When it reached Weshern's surface, it hopped off the butte of ice, dropped to its hands and knees, and lowered its tail in respect.

"What are my orders?" it asked.

"Kael Skyborn was captured by Marius's knights during today's battle," Johan said. "I want my disciples searching for him on Center. This is of vital importance, so no risk is too great. I must know where he is being held."

"If the Speaker has him, then he is dead," the iceborn said, its pale blue eyes sparkling with intelligence. "Why risk searching?"

"Because his sister would rescue him," Johan said. "If she succeeds, Marius is humiliated yet again, and the other islands emboldened. If she dies she becomes another martyr to keep Weshern's royalty dedicated to war instead of accepting peace."

The iceborn's tail flicked side to side, revealing its excitement.

"Still we play the games," it said. "Is there a need? We are ready to make the climb, L'adim. Give us the order. They will never survive our wrath."

"Not yet," Johan said. "They have willfully forgotten the crimes they committed upon you and your brethren, and buried in ignorance the threat we once possessed. Let them devour one another. I would not lose more of you to their blades and prisms. Too many fireborn perished already."

The iceborn clicked its tiny little tongue.

"Very well," it said. "I shall spread your message. When shall I return?"

"Tomorrow night," Johan said. "And bring word of whatever information my spies have found."

The iceborn bowed low again, then turned and leapt atop the long, thin icicle. Its tail wrapped around it twice, and then the creature slid downward, the ice melting after him.

Johan rose to his feet with a sigh.

"So many games," he said, understanding the iceborn's impatience. "But we are almost there."

Five centuries he had pounded at the dome, weakening it enough for him to slip this small, diminutive version of himself through. Five centuries, and after that it had been a mere thirty years of adopting names and faces, exploring the remaining world and sensing its weaknesses before he brought Galen crashing down. Soon Center itself would be no more. What was once a matter of centuries had become a matter of days.

Johan looked to the stars and grinned at the impotent God he imagined staring down from behind their glittering curtain.

"Humanity feared your wrath before we ever set foot on this world," he whispered. "But you are nothing, only a dream, a hope, a vision, a mirage. I am what they should have feared."

He left Weshern's edge, crossing miles with ease to the holy mansion, to once more whisper truths into the ears of the doomed island's Archon.

CHAPTER 17

Kael found himself in the unenviable position of comparing the dungeon cells of Candren with those of Center. They were equally dark and hidden away from sunlight, and Kael could only guess how deep into the bowels of the enormous island he was stashed. Unlike Candren's, though, there were no bars or distant lights of guards. Instead he'd awakened in a small cube, every wall and ceiling made up of smooth stone. The only crack he'd found was a straight line embedded into one of the walls, which he guessed to be where the door was. He had no food, no light, and nothing but his Seraphim uniform to keep warm in the oppressive chill. His many cuts itched, and they lacked any sort of bandage or wrapping.

Where's Bree when you need her? Kael thought, and he smiled to combat the growing loneliness. *At least we could swap bad jokes about how hopeless our situation was.*

Kael sat in a corner, positioned so he faced the hidden door.

He huddled his arms and legs to his chest, closed his eyes, and did his best to sleep the time away. His feet softly tapped the floor, the rhythmic sound necessary to keep himself sane. If not for that, all there'd be to hear would be the sound of his heartbeat and the shallow inhalations and exhalations of his breathing. Even worse, he might dare focus on his thoughts. He might focus on the man who had betrayed him: his father.

Hours passed. How many, he could only guess. Time was but a crawl in this emptiness. How much he slept was equally a mystery. Based on his hunger, though, it couldn't have been too long. A day maybe?

At once, a thunderous crack filled the room, followed by blinding light. Kael squinted against it, fighting to see through the tears in his adjusting eyes. He saw the silhouette of a man holding a small lantern. Even that tiny flickering of flame was more than Kael could bear. A deep scraping sound, of stone against stone, marked the closing of the door behind his visitor.

"I pray you have used this time to humble yourself to the wisdom I come to offer."

Kael's breath froze in his lungs. His heart thundered in his chest. That voice, that painfully familiar voice... the voice of his father, addressing him without greeting, without love. It was a tender knife, a wonderful familiarity and a terrible realization of the gulf now between them.

"Not really," Kael said. "Mostly I've just slept."

Liam set the lantern down as he sat opposite him in the other corner. Neither spoke for a long while, each soaking in the changes of the other. Kael looked upon the face of his father, now bald and marked by seemingly countless swirling tattoos. He saw wrinkles where there'd been none before. He saw the eyes that had once looked upon him with love, and he searched for that same affection. It was there, it had to be. No matter what his father had endured, surely the memories remained?

"It is... it is good to see you again, Kael," Liam said. Every word hung with hesitance. "You've grown strong in my absence."

"Seraphim training will do that to you," Kael said. He tried to keep the hurt out of his speech. It did not help him, not now. He tried to think on what to ask. So many questions he needed answered, but one in particular stood out above all the others.

"Why did you abandon us?" he asked. "We thought you were dead."

Liam rested his head against the wall. His eyes looked to the ceiling, unable to meet Kael's gaze.

"In many ways, I was dead," he said. "With my new position as a knight, I had to cleanse away the weaknesses and distractions of my old life. A painful sacrifice, I assure you, and not a day went by without wishing to look upon your faces."

"So that's all we were to you?" Kael asked. "Distractions?"

"Don't belittle yourselves," Liam snapped. "You're a Seraph now. You know you've had to make your own sacrifices. Devoting a life to God is the noblest of goals, above serving a nation or a ruler. I laid my love of you and your sister upon an altar so that nothing lay between me and the God I serve. I trusted you to live on, to follow in my stead as worthy Seraphim of Weshern." He looked to Kael. "Instead you turned your back upon all I taught you."

"What parts did you teach that we dishonor?" Kael asked. "To worship madmen? To believe lies and accept abuse? Can't say I remember those lessons."

"You think yourself wrapped in the truth?" Liam asked. "You'd say that while following the heretical words of Johan?"

The conversation was spiraling out of control. Kael wanted nothing more than to scream and cry. Here he was, meeting his long-lost father, and all he could do was argue and spew bitterness and venom? Where was the comforting embrace? Where was the shared remembrance of all their times together?

"Why are you here?" he asked, fighting to remove his anger and speak honestly. "Are you here to berate me? Tell me I disappointed you? If so, then you've done it. Leave me alone, unless you just want to hurt me worse."

Liam sat down across from Kael, crossing his legs beneath him and leaning against one of the walls. He stared intently, and Kael could see the intense debate raging inside. Did he have anything left to say? Or would it just be more regurgitated propaganda of the Speaker?

"I've never forgotten the day I lost your mother," he said. A hitch immediately hit Kael's lungs. His father's words had suddenly grown soft. This wasn't belligerent. This wasn't more theological convincing. This was a confession. "We thought Galen's Seraphs would be chased away by our show of strength. We'd had small skirmishes before, petty duels and such, but never a meeting of our full Seraphim forces. When they issued their nighttime challenge, we thought it was all bluster. Until the elements began to fly."

"We watched the battle," Kael said when his father fell silent for a moment. "Me and Bree, we snuck out to the island's edge. It was . . . overwhelming."

He didn't mention the fear he'd felt. Didn't mention how badly he'd begged God to spare his parents during the chaos.

"Yes, it was overwhelming," Liam said. "Few of us had experienced anything like it. But Commander Argus led us through. That man . . . it's such a shame, the role he's taken on now. I'd have laid my life down a hundred times to save his back then. We won the initial exchange, and it should have been a slaughter afterward. But then the bastards . . ." He sighed and shook his head. "Galen fled, not to their own island, but above ours. Hesitance in battle is a killer, Kael. That's what they did to us, flying over homes so we knew that if our shots missed we might take an innocent life. It was a cowardly move, and one that shows why it's so important Center oversee our conflicts. Marius banned the maneuver the very next day, did you know that? He's a wise man, a holy man, and he knew that we'd destroy ourselves trying to find the slightest advantage."

Kael remembered cowering in an alleyway as fire and lightning rained down upon Lowville. It was hard to argue with the cruelty of the strategy.

"Did you see how Mom died?" he asked. He'd long desired the answer but always been too afraid to ask the surviving Seraphim who'd flown with them.

Liam wiped at his eyes and nodded.

"Our elements were running low, yet neither side had signaled surrender. Your mother and I resorted to our blades." His entire body shuddered with his deep breath. "She closed in to melee with another Seraph and missed her first block. His blade cut across her stomach. I knew it was lethal, Kael. I saw it and just knew. She fled the battle immediately, making her way toward home."

Liam closed his eyes and leaned his head against the cold stone. He took in several long, slow breaths, his lips murmuring a quiet mantra or prayer. Kael didn't mind the break. He'd seen his mother's body before they'd taken her away, seen the gash across her stomach and the pool of blood building beneath her. It was an image he'd struggled to banish from his mind ever since.

"Cassandra was everything to me," Liam said, eyes still closed. "When I watched her cut down, my mind went blank. All I saw was blood. Understand I mean no insult when I say I didn't want to live through the battle. My beloved Cassandra, opened like a pig at a butcher's shop. I'd rather perish in combat than endure the sorrow I knew would follow when the fight ended. To be alone with my thoughts?" He chuckled bitterly. "No, I'd have rather died, so that's what I tried to do. I crashed into the man who killed Cassandra. No swords. No element. I just slammed us together and took us both to the ground."

Liam's eyes opened, and he stared at his hands.

"I don't know how I survived. I shouldn't have. When we hit ground I blacked out from the pain. The vultures were hovering over me when I came to, and I think they were as surprised as I was that I was still alive. Theotechs bundled me into a sling and carried me to the surgeons in Heavenstone. I remember all of it, every second of that hellish trip. I'd broken four fingers, my left arm, my left clavicle, and three ribs. I kept coughing blood. Even the slightest sway of their sling increased the pain tenfold. They thought I'd still die. I heard them talk among themselves. I was a dead man, they said. My body just didn't know it yet."

Kael shifted in his seat, growing increasingly uncomfortable.

"Marius came to me as I recovered," Liam said. "He told me there was a reason I had survived, and it was to grant me a new life with a higher purpose. I could cleanse my heart and become one of his most trusted knights, ensuring that the carnage of the battle we fought would never be repeated. So I accepted. I wanted the hurt to go away. That's all I wanted, but he granted me far more. In Heavenstone I found my place, and it felt like home more than Weshern ever did."

"A shame you couldn't come to your old home," Kael said. "I'm glad the Speaker managed to replace us as well."

"You were never replaced," Liam said, his eyes starting to swell with tears. "You were ever a source of pride. And I did want to say good-bye, but the theotechs told me that you and Bree believed I was dead. I...I thought in some ways that was better. Why not let you grieve and move on? And I *was* dead, Kael. Deep down, I was broken, and I thought I couldn't be fixed. But Marius brought me back to life. He never let me wallow in pity. He never coddled me, never let me pretend I was better or worse than I was. Day after day he took time from his schedule to sit down and speak to me. Sometimes he'd listen to my grief, other times he'd lecture me on the need to harden my heart lest it bleed forever. And in time, I did heal. I had a purpose, a life, a blessing."

"Yet you never came back to us," Kael said. "You hid here and made yourself feel better while we grew up without you. I'm sorry, father, but you're not going to earn my pity because of that."

"I don't want your pity," Liam snapped. "I want your understanding. Marius is a good man, a *holy* man. He cares for the lives of all his citizens, not just those on Center. None grieved worse for Galen's fall than he. All we've done, we've done to save Weshern from itself. And yet you've rebelled against wisdom. You've swallowed the words of the heretical Johan in a bid to elevate yourselves, thereby denying the very order God created when he spared us from oblivion during the Ascension."

Kael laughed. He couldn't help it. What had become of his father? That calm, quiet dignity he'd possessed had been warped into a sick version of faithfulness and loyalty. Liam saw his laugh and misinterpreted it as mockery.

"Do you not understand the situation you're in?" Liam asked. "A death sentence hangs over your head, but there is still a chance for your survival. Like me, you can find a second life and a new purpose. Repent your deeds. Acknowledge the divine nature of the Speaker, and vow to fight against heretics of his holy word. This war is ending, and I believe Marius will soon offer peace. Put the conflict behind you, and open your heart to the one true way." He offered his hand. "You can be at my side, Kael. No more hiding. No more secrets."

Kael's body shivered while his mind froze. His stomach twisted and looped knot into knot into knot. For years he'd dreamed his father had survived and they could be a family again. With his every accomplishment he'd wondered if his father watched him from afar, proud of all he'd done. But to betray his island, his own sister, to achieve that dream?

"No," he said. "I will never abandon Bree. I will never acknowledge the Speaker as holy. He's a liar speaking only for himself."

"You're wrong," Liam said, voice rising. "Listen to me, Kael. Listen, and repent! I know he speaks for the angels, for I have seen them with my own two eyes!"

Kael had to fight to keep down his bitter laugh.

"I've seen them, too," he said, taking mild pleasure in his father's surprise. "I spoke with L'fae in the heart of Weshern and with A'resh hidden below Candren's Clay Cathedral. I've listened to their words. I've witnessed the Ascension through their eyes. I know the truth, and I know the truth is not what Marius delivered to us. He's lied, time and time again, to hide the angels' existence. He's locked away their wisdom to keep it in his hands alone. He's not a holy man, father. Not even close. And now his pride threatens us all with extinction at the hands of the shadowborn."

The reference to the shadowborn shook Liam's composure. Kael sensed his father's wavering resolve. It was so close to breaking. Deciding his father had had enough time on the offensive, Kael rose to his feet. His turn.

"Don't you see what you've become?" he asked. "What

they've taken away from you? You lost your son and daughter, and for what? To become a killer in the Speaker's name? Marius labeled us heretics and ordered our deaths, yet our only challenge was the divine nature of his words. If you've seen the angels, then you know where they are. You know the suffering they're enduring. The theotechs have buried them in secrets and lies below their cathedrals, locking away their words. They did it for *power*, father. When the shadowborn comes we should be united in our stand. Instead Marius has left us fractured. The dome protecting us was cracking. What warning did Marius give us? The Speaker forced our ignorance to what it might mean. Fireborn fell from the sky, yet Marius had the knights that were sworn to protect us instead abandon us to our fate. His secrets are ripping us apart. His lies are destroying the unity we desperately need. We must be fighting the shadowborn, not each other!"

The statement shocked Liam into silence. He stared at Kael as if they were suddenly strangers. Perhaps they were.

"For a very long time I wondered why the Speaker was so insistent I never make contact with you and your sister," he said. His voice sounded dull, almost dead. "And now I understand. Your rebellion is key to the shadowborn's return. Why else would you be so blessed by the blood of demons?"

Nothing could disguise Kael's hurt.

"Blessed by demons?" he said. "Is that what you believe?"

"You don't deny it?"

Kael shook his head.

"No. There is no point. Leave me be. I'd rather sit in darkness than be reminded of all I lost."

Liam rose to his feet, and he brushed dust off his uniform.

"Consider your wish granted. You're to be dropped into a well tomorrow morning during a small military ceremony. I'm sorry, Kael, but I did my best to save you. This is the only fate you deserve."

Hardly surprising, but Kael felt slapped by the news anyway.

"Will you be there?" he asked. "Or will you turn your back on me again?"

Liam opened the door to the cell, and he blew out the light of his lantern, blanketing them both in darkness.

"You never understood the strength and dignity of the faithful," he said. "I won't just be there for your execution, Kael. I'll be the one holding your rope."

CHAPTER 18

"I guess I should not be surprised by the number of friends you convinced to rush headlong into danger," Johan said as Bree landed. Her four companions fanned out behind her as if attempting to maintain a safe distance from the man. They quickly shut off their wings, for in the early night their glow would be visible for miles.

"They're here because they're Kael's friends, not mine," Bree said. She left out the part where she'd been in tears upon asking Chernor and Amanda.

"Is that so?" Johan looked past her to the four. Chernor stood in their middle, arms crossed and looking openly cautious of Johan. Saul and Amanda kept to his left, the two fidgeting nervously. It was the last of the four that pulled a reaction out of Johan.

"Clara Willer," he said, softly laughing. "Imagine the fervor if it were discovered you snuck off Weshern for a desperate gambit on Center."

"I imagine it'll be even worse if I die," Clara said. "I've left a note beneath my pillow. My parents will know of your involvement come morning, so pray your advice is accurate."

"Such unearned coldness," Johan said. "Before the first knight set foot on your island I warned of the dangers Center presented. Yesterday's destruction shows I have spoken truth, and only truth, since the day I began anointing disciples. If you think I am pleased by what has come to pass, you're wrong. I warned against danger, and then the danger came. All the world would be a better place if I were wrong, and Marius were a far better man than he is."

Clara took a step back, accepting the rebuke. Bree positioned herself in the way, trying to draw the discussion back to the matters at hand.

"I have my group as you requested," she said. "Do you know of my brother's location?"

"I do," Johan said. "Well, to be more precise, I know where he *will* be come tomorrow morning. He is scheduled for a quiet execution at sunrise before an audience of military and wealthy elite. I believe Marius wants to keep it a small affair to avoid additional ire from Archon Willer. Both sides have their prisoners, and I anticipate Kael will be one who they claim died before any possible negotiations could take place."

"Can you get us there?" Bree asked.

"Myself, no," Johan said. "But I have spies on all islands, little Phoenix, and that includes Center. I will tell you where to meet one of them, and he will provide a safe house until morning. Then he will point you toward the execution. Beyond that, Kael's life will be in your hands."

"How will we make it to your spy safely?" Chernor asked. Despite Johan's arguments, he appeared no happier to be in the man's presence. "Center is sure to be crawling with knights watching for our retaliation."

"Indeed," Johan said. "But retaliation from an entire army, not a small squad. Their numbers are far too diminished to fully patrol Center's perimeter. Fly fast, and fly low, and I believe you have a good chance to make it unnoticed."

Johan pulled out a small piece of cloth and handed it to Bree. A flick of her wrist lit a spark of flame to dance atop her gauntlet, granting light to see. The pale cloth was marked with ink, revealing a map of sorts indicating a dock with five piers, a lake, and two burning fires.

"Center will be difficult to navigate in the dark," Johan said. "But there are a few landmarks that are still easily locatable. Fly low above the ocean and keep close to the crawling darkness. Come up along Center's eastern side, searching for the proper dock. It'll be one of the smaller ones, used solely for transporting the wealthy between the islands. From there, follow the map until you see the final signal ten miles inland. My disciple, Dunneg, will be waiting for you there. Please, show caution, and if you are spotted, do not attempt to find him. If you come unseen, he will grant you shelter. If you come with knights on your heels, he will be there to watch you die."

"A cheery scenario," Saul said. "How do we get off Weshern unseen?"

Johan gave him a wry smile.

"Weshern is your home," he said. "I trust you will be able to manage that on your own."

"Thank you," Bree said, interrupting a potential response from Saul. "We won't forget the risks you and your disciples took to help us save Kael."

"I am eyes and ears for the truth," Johan said. "It will be you five who extend your necks before Center's executioner and dare him to swing. But I'm sure you will be fine. The angels, after all, most certainly watch over you."

Johan bowed low and then left smiling.

"I still think he's a creepy little shit stain," Chernor said once he was gone. "I hope you're right to trust him, Bree."

She chuckled.

"So do I."

The midnight shadow flowed beneath them atop the angry waters of the Endless Ocean. If Bree stretched, she might touch it with her fingertips, but she didn't dare. Merely being close to it left her feeling terribly uneasy. To some extent, she now knew what it was: a part of the shadowborn. Did it watch them? Could it rise up at will, a formless blob of rot and evil to grab her body and drag it below the water?

Bree tilted her back and rose a few feet higher. Hell if she knew, but better safe than sorry.

Chernor let a brief crackle of electricity light up his hand so they might see his signal.

Almost here.

One of Center's three tremendous Beams was close to their right, the Fount about it dwarfing those raised by the outer islands. They were deep in Center's shadow, hidden from the stars, but still the crawling darkness was shades blacker than the night itself. She saw it gathered around the Fount, remaining still instead of being sucked up with the rest of the water. Bree thought of it crawling up the Fount and shivered. So much they didn't know about their foe. So many possibilities that sounded like nightmares.

Chernor angled them toward the curved shadow rimmed with stars that was Center's eastern edge. Johan's prediction had been correct so far. The few knights they'd spotted patrolled several miles inward from the island edge. Even if one of them spotted their group during the approach there was little the knight could do. Seraphim from Candren, Sothren, and Elern also flew the airspace between the islands, keeping tabs on Center's movements. So long as they weren't noticed curling up and over Center's landmass, they would remain safe.

The black ring grew in detail the closer they flew, revealing uneven edges, trickles of waterfalls, and long piers. Bree searched for their intended landmark: five piers closely linked together at a dock. She saw several larger docks, but nothing matching the drawing on the map. Chernor guided them northward at a fast clip, keeping the island several hundred yards above. The longer they lurked below Center, the higher the chance a random knight discovered their presence.

Saul was the first to spot their destination, and he flew equal to Chernor to point it out. Their squadron angled to the west and emerged on the other side. There it was, five squat piers hanging over the edge of the island. Starlight shone upon them, leaving Chernor's hand symbols easily visible.

I'll scout.

The four fell into a hover while Chernor slowly glided toward the pier, his wings dull and barely humming. Bree drew her swords, just in case. A minute crawled by before Chernor reached the island edge. The man took hold of one of the piers and shut off his wings, hung there for another minute, and then pulled himself up. Bree held her breath, her thumbs drumming atop the hilt of her swords. Chernor was up there for less than a minute but still it felt like an eternity.

Safe, he signaled.

Bree took lead, carefully rising to join Chernor on the pier. One by one they landed on the creaking wood and shut off their wings.

"Quieter than I expected," Saul whispered. A lone path led inward from the pier, cutting through the brief stretch of grass before entering a towering pine forest.

"And much appreciated," Chernor said. "Where to next, Bree?"

She unrolled the small cloth map Johan had given her. An arrow pointed away from the dock, leading to an uneven circle she assumed was a lake.

"Northwest," she said. "Look for water."

Chernor took lead, the five passing over the tips of the pines. Bree let them brush against her hands, their hard caress soothing. In mere moments the trees ceased, replaced by a wide swath of blackened trunks and ash-covered ground.

The fireborn, thought Bree. *They ruined even the beauty here.*

At least half the forest was burned away in long, uneven patches. The shadow of it increased Bree's discomfort. Despite all the terrible destruction Marius had unleashed with his assault on Weshern, he still was not their true enemy. Their true enemy would bring Center crashing down as readily as he did Galen.

Dim lights of a sleepy town lay ahead of them. Chernor started to shift to avoid the town, but seemed to think better of it. Did it matter if any townsfolk spotted them? They'd be long gone before any might summon a knight to chase. Bree swallowed down a shiver and raced overhead. Despite the town's quaint size, the buildings themselves were several stories tall and massive compared to those on Weshern. Bree wished for a world where she could walk among them, seeing the sights and meeting the people.

The pleasant thoughts vanished in another wave of burned

and crumpled buildings. It struck Bree how similar it felt to flying over Weshern after Center had retreated from their invasion. So much death. So much loss. They all suffered. Why could they not see the common thread of humanity they shared? Why not face the frightful enemy seeking their total annihilation?

Lower, Chernor signaled, immediately diving. The others followed, dropping below the rooftops of the homes as they flew along one of the streets. Bree spared quick glances in both directions, searching for what spooked Chernor. If there was a knight, they were distant and blocked by the homes. Chernor kept them low, their wings rattling windows with their passing. They cut through another burned part of town, following it all the way out. Green hills awaited them, and Chernor followed their bumps and dips, mere feet above the ground. Tense minutes passed, the empty sky above their only reassurance.

They didn't spot the lake until they flew right above it. The hills dropped suddenly into cliffs, and far below was a grand lake with houses nestled against every inch of its shoreline. Chernor immediately looped back around and landed atop the cliffs overlooking the lake.

"Where now?" he asked.

Bree checked her map.

"Straight west," she said. "We're supposed to look for two fires side by side."

"Guess that shouldn't be too hard to find," Chernor said. "Are they in a field somewhere, or a town . . . ?"

"Hey, we've got company," Saul said, turning their attention the way they came. A single golden speck pierced the night sky like a comet.

"Do you think we were spotted?" Amanda asked.

"Doesn't look like it's chasing after us," Chernor said, squinting at the distant shimmer. "No time to wait for them to leave. We'll use the cliffs to hide our wings."

Chernor leapt off the cliff with his hands forward in a dive. Bree followed, free-falling against the wind. When they were halfway down they flooded life into their wings, curling upward while banking to the west. Rippling reflections of their wings chased them across the lake. The sprawling town was terribly dense against the water but, once beyond, it opened into another field of green pockmarked with burns. Bree glanced over her shoulder, unable to fight the paranoia. If they'd been seen before landing on the cliff for even an instant…

They were two miles from the lake when the golden image shimmered over the cliffs. Bree swore as she dove to the town below. She scanned for a secluded spot, found several storage barns on the town's edge, and then landed between them. The others followed her lead, and they one by one landed and turned off their wings.

"That knight followed us," Bree said. "We must have been seen."

"We can kill one knight," Saul insisted.

"But it won't be just one knight," Chernor said, shaking his head. "We start throwing fire and lightning and we'll attract knights for miles in all directions. We can't afford the risk."

"Are you sure we were spotted?" Amanda asked. "What if it's just a coincidence?"

A fair enough point. Bree hugged the edge of the barn and stepped around. The gold-winged knight shone like a distant star. No matter how long she waited, it never changed course.

"Shit," she said, stepping back. "Whoever it is may not be certain, but they're definitely looking."

"We don't have time to wait," Chernor said. "Daylight's

getting closer. Once the people wake we won't make it ten feet without being spotted."

"I say we at least wait and see," Bree said. "Maybe this is just their patrol path. Our destination's close. We can afford the delay."

Chernor shrugged but didn't argue. They could easily hide between the barns during the knight's pass overhead. The five didn't speak, only hugged the sides of the barns and waited. The golden wings grew more defined, shining on a dark form with a white tunic. For a long, tense moment he pierced the sky above them, cutting through the middle of the town. Bree breathed a sigh of relief. They weren't spotted. The knight was leaving town.

Except he wasn't. The moment he reached the edge of town he curled back around, following the town's edge. He circled it over and over as the minutes dragged on. Slowly, steadily. Like a vulture. Like a bird of prey on the hunt.

"What do we do?" Amanda whispered.

"He saw us land near the town," Chernor whispered back. "Maybe not all of us, though. He might not even be certain there's anyone here. I can use that to my advantage. I'll fly east to distract him. The rest of you, get your butts to Johan's contact."

Saul stepped forward, adamantly shaking his head.

"No, not you," he said. "I'll do it."

"You forget your place, boy," Chernor said. His glare alone sent Saul back against the barn. "I outrank all of you combined. I'm doing this. It's the only way I can know for certain it gets done right."

Bree thought of watching Aisha and Loramere soar into the sky in opposite directions, flying to their deaths to protect her and her brother during the Academy's evacuation. It was happening again. She couldn't allow this. She couldn't bear the guilt a second time.

"He'll give up soon," she said, grabbing Chernor's arm. "He'll search elsewhere while we move on foot."

"That knight's not leaving," Chernor said, shoving her away. His eyes were wide, his face more terrifying than she'd ever seen before. "If we do nothing, we all die. I'll guide him away. Me, just me."

"There's got to be something else we can try," Bree insisted. "We . . . we'll stay together, we'll fight. We'll win. That's what we do."

Chernor removed the maul from his back and tossed it to the ground.

"Bree, please," he said. "This is hard enough."

Bree bit her tongue and stepped away. What few tears trickled down her cheeks she quickly wiped away.

"Fly fast," she said. "Fly well."

Chernor let out a soft chuckle and smiled at the whole lot of them.

"You better save Kael's sorry ass," he said. "I'll be very, very pissed off if you don't."

The others saluted with fists against their breasts. Bree joined in late, the thud of her fingers against her jacket a dull stake into her heart. Her friend turned his back to them, ignited his wings, and streaked east. Bree watched him fly, the knight immediately curling after. They quickly became two glowing orbs among the stars. Bree waited. None of them said a word. A second golden star rose from the north, joining the chase. A third from the south. Still Chernor flew on, his silver orb becoming a star, a dot, a speck, a nothing.

"Let's go," Bree said. She spoke the words like a death sentence.

They flew over the rooftops, no other patrolling knights in sight. The town below ended, replaced with the ruins of a great forest burned down to blackened husks that were once tree trunks. Beyond that came another town, and along its eastern edge burned two small campfires side by side, a shadow of a man waiting between them with his hands in his pockets. Bree landed first, her wings quieting as she drifted to the ground.

Their contact was a man in plain brown pants, a faded shirt, and a woven grass hat atop his bald head. He spat out a wad of something he'd been chewing and welcomed them all with a nod.

"Shut off your wings and follow me," Dunneg said, extinguishing the fires.

Dunneg's home wasn't large but he had two rooms to spare for the night. Saul and Clara shared one, Amanda and Bree the other.

"It'll be just like at the Academy," Amanda said. "And you'll likely spend all night staring out the window like you used to as well."

"Except I won't be watching for boys," Bree said, smiling. "Well, not good ones, anyway."

"Dean was never a good boy. You'd not have been so in love with him if he had."

Bree laughed as she took off her jacket. Their harnesses were all stored in a shed behind the house along with their gauntlets and prisms. Though she felt naked without her wings, she still had her swords, and Bree laid them carefully beside the thick blanket on the floor that would be her bed.

"Dean was the first to push me toward what I could do instead of condemning me for what I couldn't," Bree said, the melancholy falling not unwelcome across her heart. For such a long time she'd been thoroughly worthless at her flame element, a mockery at the very bottom of her class. Dean had never once belittled her for it. They'd trained with swords day after day despite knowing she would likely never make it past the six-month evaluation. Swordplay had been her love, as it had been his, and he had invited her to share it without judgment or hesitation.

"I only met him a few times," Amanda said. She settled atop her own blanket, her jacket bunched up to be a pillow. "He seemed nice."

"He was," Bree said, as if that could cover it all. "He really was."

Someone knocked on the door twice, then waited.

"Come in," Amanda called.

The door slid open. Saul peeked around the corner. He was dressed down to his pants and white shirt, his arms crossed over his chest.

"Hey, Amanda, it all right if I speak to Bree for a few minutes, alone?"

"It's fine," Amanda said, hopping to her feet. "I won't mind keeping Clara company."

She paused to pat Saul on the shoulder as she left. He stepped inside, shut the door behind him, and then leaned against it.

"I want to make sure you're ready to do this," Saul said. "It's not too late to turn back."

"Turn back?" Bree asked. "Chernor already died getting us here, and my brother will die tomorrow if we do nothing."

"We don't know that he's dead yet. And besides, Chernor dying doesn't force us to our own deaths," Saul argued. "We can turn back. We can *always* turn back, so long as we are willing to bear the consequences. You're here to save Kael's life. I'm here to tell you that you can make a decision that might save Clara's, Amanda's, yours, and mine. And yes, Bree, it is a choice you'll be making, no matter how hard you try to pretend otherwise."

"Fine," she said. "You want me to make a choice? Then I will. While Weshern was under Center's control, Kael broke into their cathedral to rescue me from a prison cell. He risked everything to save my life despite knowing it would likely cost him his. Our places are switched, but nothing else has changed. I will risk everything to save him. He's earned that from me. And if you don't agree with that choice, then, well..." She gestured to the door. "Like you said. We all have a choice. I'll fly alone to his execution if I must."

Saul refused to back down.

"I lost my parents saving your lives," he said. "I lost my social standing and the land our family had owned for decades. But I gave up it all up because I knew I was doing what was right. For the longest time, I hated you and your brother for it. You know why? Because I thought neither of you would ever do the same. All I saw in you was a selfish desire to prove you were the best at everything. You didn't fly well in a team, you couldn't master your fire, and by hanging on like you did I thought you were only putting our lives at risk when battle finally arrived."

He let out a soft chuckle.

"But then you became the Phoenix. Everyone's beloved little figurehead. Trust me, I thought that would make you even more insufferable, but when Galen fell..." He shrugged. "I don't know if I saw you for the first time after that, or if its fall changed you, but I saw it then. If you believed it was right, you'd give everything for it. You'd risk your life to save others. You wouldn't just die for your brother; you'd die for strangers at night at risk of demon fire. All of Center could rise up to crush our little army, but there you'd be, right in the heart of battle fighting anyway."

Bree felt taken aback. She kept still on her blanket, hands knit together, her tongue at a loss for words.

"That's when I decided," Saul said. "I decided long before we ever flew for this run-down little hideaway. You *did* mean something special to Weshern, not because of what you could do, but for who you are. With what meager skills I have I will do my best to keep you safe. If you fly home for Weshern, I will follow. If you head into an execution to save your brother, I will follow. Either way, I'll know I do the right thing."

Tears trickled down Bree's cheeks.

"Thank you," she said. "It really does mean a lot."

The left half of Saul's face pulled up into a halfhearted smirk.

"Don't let it get to your head, though," he said. "I still think you're an insufferable girl trying to be the best at everything."

Bree sniffled and laughed and wiped at her tears.

"Go to bed," she said. "We've an early morning, and a dangerous flight ahead."

"Back to Weshern?" Saul asked, despite clearly knowing she meant otherwise.

"Like hell," Bree said. "Tomorrow morning, we're saving my brother's life."

CHAPTER 19

The night was late when Johan approached the newly built Weshern encampment. Multiple camps had been merged into a single noisy, bleeding sleeping ground after the failed invasion. Johan recognized the scene well. Blood, fear, and pain were intermixed with joy and relief, a camp-wide feeling of a hard sacrifice given for a worthy cause.

It was the stink of victory, and Johan hated it.

Celebrate the dying, thought Johan as he stepped into the darkened shadow of a home. *Feel pride in your murder. I expect nothing less from your pitiful race.*

Johan held still, safely hidden from any prying eyes. The shadow of his essence swirled around what remained of his corporeal body, malleable, changeable. His face melded and shrank, his height lessening as his legs shortened. Tendrils of shadow curled off the back of his head, firming into strands of hair. His false eyes came into shape, followed by an outer layer of shadow that formed into a Weshern Seraphim uniform. Johan focused on various memories of his new body, analyzing speech patterns, accents, even the tiniest little tics humans rarely noticed of others. And then he opened his mouth.

"This is how I sound," spoke Bree's voice from his false lips.

Satisfied, Johan adopted a wearied look of relief and strolled into the encampment. Bree would join in their sorrow, but she'd also feel hope for a peaceful resolution. Like countless humans before, she believed war led to peace in the way dawn inevitably led to dusk. But war wasn't a sunrise. It was a fire, consuming as it spread, caring not for its destruction. Either you stamped it out, or it spread until there was nothing left to burn.

Johan wound through the seemingly haphazard array of tents. They'd set up the camp earlier that day. He'd been there, in Johan persona, when Argus Summers made the request of Archon Isaac. Argus wished to hide the extent of the wounded and dead from the populace, wanting them to only focus on their grand victory. It had burned Johan's heart, but he'd kept silent, with no reason for his persona to question the decision.

"Of course you'd hide your casualties," he whispered, amused by hearing Bree speak the words. "Diminish the loss, exaggerate the gains. It makes it that much easier for the populace to swallow."

"Saw you fighting over Angburg, Phoenix," a nearby Seraph called to her from his seat beside a fire. "You flew like a goddamn lunatic."

"Thanks," Johan said, tilting his head slightly away and mimicking embarrassment coupled with a tiny smile. Johan knew the girl took pride in her skill but disliked the attention it gained her. She liked the fame, yet wanted it distant, nonintrusive.

"How many knights did you bring down?" a friend of the first asked.

Johan didn't turn, only held up his hand with five fingers spread wide. He didn't know if he over- or underestimated, but it seemed close enough to earn him another whoop from the two Seraphs. A wry smile stretched across Johan's feminine lips.

Keep praising my murders, he thought. *All while condemning Center for theirs.*

When Johan had visited the camp earlier in the daylight, he'd expected to find his target occupying an extravagant abode, but Argus Summers had taken a small standard-issue camp tent. The only difference was that his was separated from the others by a wider stretch of grass, giving his tent a feeling of solitude the rest lacked.

Johan could have taken a more direct path but he didn't want stealth or secrecy. He wanted multiple campfires to see Bree's presence, and at least several to see her approaching Argus's tent. The campfire outside it was dull and smoking, but the flicker of a candle lit the interior of the tent.

"Argus?" Johan asked, pausing by the entrance. "Is it all right if I come in?"

Perhaps not as direct as Bree would ask, but Johan wanted to add a bit of hesitance to his aura. Self-indulgent as it was, he wished to toy with his prey like a cat with an injured mouse. His opportunities for pleasure had been fleeting the past five centuries, after all.

"Come in, Bree."

Johan ducked through the tent flap. Argus sat on a wooden chair that looked out of place atop the blanket-covered grass. A slender table was before him, lit with a half-melted candle. Several papers lay scattered atop it, and his eyes never left them.

"Are you writing something?" he asked.

"No," Argus said. "Looking over the latest reports of the dead."

Johan felt a pang of sorrow for his initial desire to toy with him. As despicable as the human race might be, there were always shining examples of their true potential. Men like Argus had given his fellow lightborn hope over the centuries, but they were too far and few between. While others celebrated, Argus would read over the dead. He'd focus on the loss. He'd remember the cost come time to battle again. Peace often came not from glorious conquerors but from men and women like him. If only he'd dedicated his skills and time to an art separate from war. What paintings might his brush have created if he'd given it the same dedication? What sculptures could those careful, dexterous hands have created if not locked in a Seraphim gauntlet to slay men with ice?

"Such a shame, isn't it?" Johan asked. Not entirely a Bree response, but Johan was more interested in Argus's reaction.

"A loss that never should have needed paid," Argus said, and he leaned back in his chair and finally looked up. "And one I pray will not need paid again. Is there something you need, Bree?"

All that Johan really needed was to put the commander at ease, but his curiosity was still there. He sat atop the commander's bunk and stared at his own thin, pale hands.

"We... we can win now, right?" he asked. "This war isn't so desperate as we first thought."

"It would appear so," Argus said. "We chased Center off, and the other islands didn't suffer near as terribly as we did."

"Do you think the Speaker will surrender? Or maybe offer some measure of peace?"

This was Johan's true worry. He wanted humanity to eat itself. The weaker it became, the fewer of his eternal-born that would suffer and die during the final extermination.

Argus's chair gently rocked back and forth, easing his gaze into nothingness as his mind raced. Johan could sense the uncertainty whirling within.

"The other islands are surely preparing for an offensive as we speak," he said. "Combined with Center's losses today with the damage they suffered during the fireborn attack, and it's possible we could achieve another victory. If Marius likewise believes this, he might finally request some sort of treaty. Whether or not we'd accept, or he'd be able to swallow his pride and give us all we've demanded, is another thing entirely. I don't know the man well enough to say for certain."

He looked at her, a strange emotion passing over his face that Johan failed to read.

"Bree...I'm sorry about Kael. I really am. If we're to have any peace, I swear his safe return will be part of the conditions."

Johan thought a moment on how to respond. This was one of the trickier aspects of humanity, the moments when logic and emotion directly contradicted. Would her national loyalty outweigh her bond to her brother? Would the assurance of a commander she respected soothe her fear enough to remain rational? With Bree currently flying to Center in preparation for a likely suicide mission, Johan knew well enough that answer, but his Bree was not that Bree.

"I understand," he said. "I hate it, but I understand."

Argus looked much relieved.

"We're sending messengers to the other islands," he said. "Hopefully we'll know their plans by the morrow. I hope we see peace, Bree, but if we must continue to fight, then we will. The cost we've paid is far too high for us to surrender now."

He nodded but said nothing. Best to pretend to sulk and let the commander talk. The man's nerves were easing, and it seemed he'd been rather bothered by a fear that Bree hated him for his decision. Johan knew that not the case. He could have lied and feigned anger, but Johan could not deny in his heart that the man did not deserve such deception.

"You did well today," Argus said, gathering up the papers and setting them facedown in a pile. "Weshern owes a great debt to you for protecting the royal family. Your mastery over your fire is also noteworthy in its improvement."

Johan mimicked another pleased, embarrassed smile. Ah yes, Bree's fascinating skill of flame and blade. Stolen power from fireborn blood, yet the ignorant people cheered her for it.

"I'm just doing my best," he said. "Trying to live up to your reputation, after all."

"Live up to it? I'm certain you've surpassed it, Bree. Years from now, people will tell stories of your deeds while I'll have been long forgotten."

Johan decided he'd had enough carrying on with the ruse. It just wasn't enjoyable. Argus was a man Johan would have loved to visit with in ancient times, when he was still a lightborn.

"You're right," Johan said. "I'm an excellent killer. My fire makes me stand out among those risking their lives alongside me, achieving equally great accomplishments with their lesser talent and gifts. People will brag as if I single-handedly ended the war and brought Center to her knees, while those like you, General Cutter, and Miss Waller, the vital pieces who engineered the entire war in the background, will go unnoticed."

Argus frowned at him.

"I've never heard you so cynical before, Bree," he said. "We're not fighting to be remembered. We're fighting to free ourselves from Center's tyranny and ensure the safety of our people."

Johan shook his head.

"No," he said. "You're fighting because I wished you to, and your race knows no other way."

He lunged from the bed, his arm elongating in shadow as he reached for Argus's throat. The commander's eyes widened, his bafflement and surprise overriding his finely honed Seraphim reflexes. Johan's strength was so great the wooden chair shattered as Johan slammed Argus to the ground. He kept his grip tight to prevent any sort of warning cry from escaping. Argus frantically kicked with his lower body as his hands wrapped around Johan's, desperately trying to pry them loose. His face flushed red from his exertion.

Johan abandoned the ruse, letting his visage return to one Argus recognized. At first the man recoiled in horror, and then anger flooded into his frightened eyes.

"It should not be so surprising," Johan whispered. "Have I not demanded war with my every breath?"

Johan shifted so his right leg pressed down on Argus's chest, easily pinning him to the ground. He released his one hand, using his other to keep Argus quiet. The weaker grip allowed Argus a bit of air, and he gasped out his final words.

"They won't believe it's Bree."

"I don't need them to believe," Johan said. "I only need doubt and confusion. The war must continue, Argus. Your death will help ensure that happens."

His right hand elongated, wisps of black curling as it shaped, peeling back layers as it thinned into a long, curled Seraphim blade. His shadow hardened, becoming steel.

"You were a fine man," he whispered. "But a flower among a field of rot must still burn with all the rest."

He slowly pierced the blade through Argus's chest, stopping only when it reached the heart. Argus convulsed, his internal mechanisms failing. Johan leaned closer, careful to keep the sword still. He did not wish to increase the man's pain. He felt no joy in it.

"You are too rare," he whispered. "Beyond these islands is a world of beauty, wild with animals and awash with the song of birds. I salvaged it from humanity's grasp. I saved it from good men like you and evil men seeking war and death. If I could, I would give it to humanity's best. But even the best of you may become the worst. Your will is free. Your choices are your own. It is the curse an impotent God placed upon you. Please, die knowing you die to achieve a peace humanity could never reach on its own."

Argus's shudders ceased. Johan rose to his feet, pulling his sword free and returning it to the shape of a young girl's arm. Bree's face replaced his, and he shook it sadly.

"Your extinction cannot come soon enough," he said.

Johan exited the tent and walked back through the camp, ensuring many saw her tired expression, her dead eyes, and her swords swinging loose at her hips.

Most of all, he wanted them to see the faint spray of blood across her clothes.

CHAPTER 20

Kael awoke to a pillar of blinding light invading his prison cell. He couldn't see who entered but heard their footfalls, heavy and armored.

"Stand up," a gruff voice commanded. "It's time."

Kael rose to his feet while leaning against the wall to keep steady. No food. No drink. He felt like a drained, weaker version of himself.

"A pardon from the Speaker?" he asked the knight who pulled him from the wall and slapped manacles on his wrists.

"Shut your mouth, prisoner."

"Is that a yes?"

A mailed gauntlet backhanded him across the mouth. Blood trickled from Kael's lip and down his neck. Two men held him by either arm, guiding him into the light, a third walking just ahead. Kael squinted, impatiently waiting for his eyes to adjust. Were any of the three his father? They walked down a wide corridor with a low ceiling; the wings of the two knights who held him nearly scraped the walls. Kael kept his eyes on the third knight while he more stumbled than walked forward. The knights lifted him higher, their hands digging deep into his armpits. His feet barely touched the floor after that.

The corridor ended at a thick iron door locked with three separate bars. Soldiers blocked the way. An older man with a massive tome on a pedestal waited beside them.

"Kael Skyborn," the first knight said.

The old man closed one eye to peer through a monocle on the other.

"Properly scheduled," the man said, scribbling a few quick marks with a quill. "Let them out."

It took four men to lift each bar from the rungs. Kael listened to their grunts with dire humor. It appeared there would be more effort spent removing him from the prison than actually executing him. A trio of escorts, a record keeper, and a squad of soldiers for his release compared to a single knight, a dropped rope, and an empty well for his death.

"Something amusing, prisoner?" asked the knight on his left.

"Nothing," Kael said. "My mouth is shut, remember?"

Kael dared a glance at the knight now that his eyes were adjusted. He was a shorter man but thick with muscle. His dark skin stood in stark contrast to the glimmering gold of his armor. The knight grabbed Kael's face, and he leaned down close to stare eye to eye with him.

"One more word like that and I will break your jaw."

It was stupid. So stupid. But Kael said it anyway.

"I'm about to die. Why the hell do I care about a broken jaw?"

This time it wasn't a backhand that struck his mouth but a clenched fist. The impact sucked the air from Kael's lungs. His knees buckled, and he slumped awkwardly, the other knight still holding his right side erect from underneath his arm. Pain radiated out from his jaw, and when he spat blood, he felt a cracked part of a tooth go with the glob.

The knight leading them turned to glare.

"Control yourself, Dorian," he said. "Kael is to arrive unharmed."

Dorian pulled Kael back up to his feet as the iron door swung open with a loud, grating rumble.

"Understood," he said to his superior. Kael looked beyond the door, surprised to see lush green grass and a nearby row of trees. The three knights led him through, setting him down on a tightly packed dirt path. The prison behind him didn't look like a prison at all, only a wide iron door built into the side of a low-rising mountain. Trees dotted the path sloping downward, statues of angels evenly spaced between them. Each one was bowed low in some form of humility or supplication.

The lead knight turned to the other two.

"I think it wise Vicar carry the boy instead," he said. "I would hate for there to be an incident on the way to the site."

Dorian was left to hold him as Vicar accepted straps from the lead knight and began connecting them to various hooks on his modified harness. Kael leaned closer to his captor, dropping his voice low.

"My jaw's not broken, Dorian," he said, giving the knight a bloodied grin. "Try to keep your word next time."

The knight's brown eyes promised murder but his stance remained professionally rigid.

"Stand still," Vicar said, harness ready. The knight stood behind him and began looping the various straps into place. One went about his waist, two his chest. Dorian helped with the buckling, and Kael felt the man pulling the leather tighter than necessary. The worst was the final strap about his neck.

Kael's head locked against the knight's chest, his throat struggling against the bond to perform the simple act of swallowing.

"Avoid flying over cities," the lead knight ordered when they were ready. "Make no stops until arriving at the site. Marius gave strict orders for the prisoner's execution to be a low-key affair. No parading him before crowds, no bloodletting, and no public humiliations."

"No special treatment?" Kael asked. "Such a shame."

The knight stepped closer, his seriousness turning into something frightening.

"Dorian, the neck restraint is not tight enough," he said. "Please fix it."

Dorian was all too happy to oblige. The leather loop crushed into his larynx, prompting a gag reflex from Kael. When he sucked in air, it came in thin, weak gasps. Even the slightest movement worsened his pain.

"Much better," the knight said. "Dismissed."

Dorian and Vicar took to the air, Kael hanging beneath by the straps. The added pressure amplified his discomfort. Every breath required him to tilt his head as high as his neck allowed to gain another thin, cold slice of air.

So stupid, he thought. *When will you learn, Kael? I'd rather have a broken jaw.*

Kael rolled his eyes and forced the thought away. No use berating himself now. Sure, lesson learned, right before all lessons forever ended.

The rolling landscape below was Kael's only distraction from his impending fate. The sheer size of it was still awe-inspiring. No matter where you flew on Weshern, if you rose into the air and turned, you'd see at least one of the island's edges. Not so here. They flew westward, to whatever site they'd planned for his execution. The green lands rolled along, but as Kael focused, he began to find the signs of the fireborn invasion. Patches of black marked long yellow fields. Forests that should have been green now looked as if a colorless fall had stripped clean their branches. Everywhere they flew, the destruction snaked and spread. It was akin to Weshern's damage, only here it was . . . greater. Less controlled. With so many fireborn falling upon the massive island, and too few knights to contain them, they'd gone unchecked for far longer than they had in Weshern.

Kael clenched his eyes and smashed the back of his head against Vicar's chest to suck in another gasp of air. Sure, their destination meant his death, but he couldn't wait to arrive anyway. He'd rather get it out of the way than endure another ten minutes of constantly feeling his lungs ready to burst.

Kael was surprised by just how few waited for their arrival at the execution spot. He counted maybe twenty civilians quietly milling about in the patch of grass before the forest. Their clothing looked as expensive as the jewels and rings they wore. Several theotechs walked among their number, their red robes startlingly plain compared to the extravagance around them. A dozen soldiers stood at attention between the civilians and the stone well, separating them. Kael counted only a single knight among their number, and he felt his stomach twist. The spool of rope at his feet was enough to reveal the knight's identity. Behind them was a dark forest of pines, their shadows deep and inviting.

Dorian and Vicar settled down beside the well. Liam greeted them with a respectful bow.

"I see he did not arrive unharmed," Liam said. He yanked the buckle free from Kael's neck, eliciting a long, gasping series of coughs. Liam's fingers gently traced the raw line left by the leather, then touched Kael's bleeding mouth. "The Speaker's orders were explicit on this."

"The prisoner's tongue is as reckless as the rest of him," Dorian said. "But leave the matter be. His injuries are superficial. No one will notice nor care."

"I have noticed, and I care," Liam said. Kael was startled by the anger in his voice. "Next time follow orders, knight, or I will speak with Marius of your contempt toward his demands."

Dorian reacted as if he'd been slapped, and he quickly apologized.

No idle threat, thought Kael at Dorian's rapid act of humility. *Father must speak with Marius often.*

The remaining straps loosened. Kael dropped to his knees and fought off a wave of dizziness. Air flowed in and out of his lungs, reawakening the rest of his body. Liam stood over him, showing no worry of Kael attempting to flee.

"Take your positions beside the well," Liam ordered. "I will handle the remainder of the execution."

The two dipped their heads low and obeyed. Now alone, Liam knelt beside Kael and grabbed an end of the spool of rope at his feet.

"Stay still, and do not fight me," Liam said. "Let me work undistracted if you wish for a clean death."

"I'd rather not have a death at all," Kael said.

"And I'd rather not execute my son. This world is not made of our wishes, Kael, but of our actions. Yours have led us both to this moment."

It hurt listening to his father speak so callously, as if Kael's impending death was nothing more than an inconvenience. What had happened to the man who'd told him stories of his visits to the other islands, of the wonderful caves of Candren and the sprawling glass gardens of Elern? The man who'd always been there to pick him up from the ground after a fall?

Kael looked to the crowd, and he used his humor to hide the growing hurt. A bitter smile hid his tears. "Why such a small ceremony?" he asked. "I'm the brother of the Phoenix. Surely I'm worth a little bit of a grandeur."

"Your Archon requested your safe return," Liam said. He looped the rope twice about Kael's waist. "To deny him would endanger the negotiations we have begun, but to give in risks the wrath of our people. This little ceremony is our compromise. You will die a quiet, unheralded death. When asked, we will say your passing preluded any negotiations."

"Such unfortunate timing," Kael muttered. "Isn't it funny how things work out sometimes?"

"You waged war against Center while spreading heresy," Liam said. "You should be glad you will not suffer torture and humiliation before our citizens for your crimes."

Kael shook his head as he laughed.

"You're to drop me into a well, shatter my bones, and make a mess of my insides, yet you think I should *thank* you?" Tears trickled unwanted down his face. "I'm such a fool. I still thought my father was in there somewhere, but he's not. You're not even him. You're just an ugly-hearted theotech wearing his skin."

Liam knelt closer. His hands paused, his knuckles white as he clutched the rope.

"Do you still not understand?" he asked. "I *am* your father. I am the man who raised you, loved you, and sought only the best for your future. Why do you think I came to you in your cell? Why do you think I reached out with the Speaker's mercy? I want you to live, Kael, but it must be on the path of righteousness. I would save your soul and sacrifice your body if I must, for it is far better than to salvage your body yet lose your soul forever."

Liam tied a knot along Kael's waist, then looped the rope around the manacles holding his wrists together. Then came another knot.

"That's what you think this is?" Kael asked. He tried to hear his father, to find the heart beneath the awful words the Speaker had grafted onto his father's mind. "You think this will save my soul?"

"I don't know," Liam said. Three loops around the shoulders and chest. "But the presence of death can change a man. I know this well. The drop will feel like an eternity, my son. Reach out to God. Ask for his forgiveness, and I promise you, angels will be there to carry you into the golden eternity."

Kael struggled to control himself as his father tied another knot. There was too much sincerity there, and it made him hate Marius all the more. Liam loved him, and that love was now twisted and confused. Execution led to mercy. Death led to forgiveness. He truly believed it.

"I'm not reaching out to God," Kael said. His voice trembled. "I'm reaching out to you."

Liam shivered, and he refused to meet Kael's gaze as he looped the rope into a cast from Kael's elbows to his wrists, locking the arms together.

"Do not reach for me," he said. "I am imperfect and sinful. Listen instead to the Speaker's words. Acknowledge his truths so you may find redemption."

"And what? You'll let me live?"

Finally, his father turned his way. Tears twinkled in the corners of his eyes, unfallen.

"Your earthly fate is sealed, my son. Only your spiritual fate remains undecided."

Kael refused to break contact. His father was looking at him, really looking at him, for the first time. The crowd and soldiers seemed miles away. Just the two of them stood there upon the grass. Kael's voice dropped to a whisper. No pretense at being tough. No mockery of the Speaker or his damned theotechs. Just honesty.

"You're right, father," Kael said. "We must acknowledge the truth. Think back to who you were. Remember your pride as a Seraphim. As a father. Do you remember holding me and Bree as children? Do you remember all you did to raise us well? There was no sin there. You were a good man. You were a good father. I remember how mother looked at you. She loved you. We all did. We all still do. But what Marius says you are, what he's carved into your skin, it isn't you. It isn't righteousness. It's slavery."

Liam's body trembled. At last the tears fell from his eyes unhindered. Kael sensed the raging turmoil within, a buried corpse struggling to free itself from the dirt.

"It's not too late," Kael said, seizing the moment. "You have your wings. Fly us back to Weshern. You'd rather lose the body to save the soul? That's how you do it, father. Fly us home, and fight against all who'd try to stop us, even if it means our deaths. There's no salvation here, no righteousness, only damnation for dropping your own flesh and blood into a *fucking well*."

Liam was broken. Kael saw it so clearly. A broken, weeping semblance of the proud father who'd raised him. But his heart was there. It was beating. It was begging for a return to a happier past. Kael's own tears poured forth, for at last he'd reached him, reviving his hope, reigniting that chance to be a family again.

"Kael," Liam said. He spoke the words as if it weighed a thousand pounds on his tongue. "I am the blade of the angels.

I am the flesh on their bones. I am the blood on their feathers. What is holy must never break."

The prayer put the pieces of the man before him back together, and its form was nothing recognizable.

"My mother and father died years ago together," Kael said as Liam's gold wings began to shimmer. "Dry your tears, knight of Center. I am not your son. I'm just an enemy about to die at the bottom of a well."

The length of rope went taut, lifting Kael's bound arms up and over his head. The interconnected bonds tightened across his body, keeping him properly aligned and centered beneath his rising father. They hovered slightly to the east, to where the stone well awaited. The construction was more ornamental than the ones on Weshern. Built of white stone, its sides were wrapped with golden supports and gilded chains. Five silver angels stood around the well's edge, their arms raised high in praise yet their heads bowed low in sorrow. In their center, swallowing all light and returning none, was the deep, hungry pit.

Kael stared at the crowd, preferring their disgust over the cold alien being above him. He thought they might cheer, hurl insults, and mock his death. Instead they kept quiet, only whispering a few murmurs among themselves. They looked tired, Kael decided. Perhaps as drained as he was. Center had suffered under the fireborn's arrival, and they'd lost thousands of men and women in the assault on Weshern. Their very way of life was threatened by the minor islands' rebellion. Why wouldn't they be exhausted by the last few weeks? Why wouldn't they, like he, wish for it to be over?

The haunting eyes of the nobles and soldiers rose with him, and Kael almost felt like their gaze propelled him upward instead of the scratchy, constricting rope.

"People of Center!" Liam shouted when they reached the

designated distance above the stone well. "I present you a traitor to God's heavenly order, a spreader of war, a speaker of heresy, and a heart most stubborn to humility and redemption. For his crimes, I carry him here before you. For his sins, the Speaker has decreed he suffer the greatest fate suffered by traitors to heaven since before the very first days of man. From the arms of an angel, I drop him, and into the abyss below, he shall fall, to where not a ray of light shall touch his bones, nor his soul forever after."

The crowd cheered, and with surprising boisterousness. Perhaps Kael was wrong, and they weren't quite defeated yet. They'd enjoy his suffering. Perhaps it would even give them a little respite from the sorrows of war. The rope lifted higher, Liam drawing in the slack so they might stare eye to eye. Kael noticed his father never spoke his name. Kael had a feeling his execution would be an open secret in Center, the kill denied in public yet celebrated in private.

He's wrong, Kael told himself. No dark hell awaited him. The Speaker did not voice the word of God. The blood of angels flowed through him, and he'd been blessed by L'fae to speak their word. Rage bubbled in his stomach, fueled by his pain and sorrow into a rapid boil.

"Do his lies comfort you?" Kael shouted over his shoulder to the gathered crowd. Despite the pain in his throat, he was stunned by how loudly his words echoed across the plain. "Does condemning my soul make it easier to swallow my murder? Does my drop elevate your own meager lives? No angel holds me aloft, but angels will be there to catch my fall. I go not into the abyss, you damn fools, but your Speaker leads you to one by the throat. Listen! Demand truth, not comfort! Demand deliverance, not safety! Or can you not already hear the demons' laughter as they come to feast?"

Kael's words shocked the crowd silent. No more cheers. No more claps or whistles. They stared at him as if he were a fiend of hell come to tear their lives asunder. It, unfortunately, reminded Kael of when the disciple of Johan had been improperly dropped to a well while he and his sister watched, his head splitting open like a melon against the well's stone lip. The disciple had yelled and screamed, yet none had changed their minds. At least Kael knew why the man had still railed to the very end. Watching those happy faces ready to cheer his death was beyond maddening.

Liam lifted him higher, then turned him to face the crowd, his hands releasing the top of the rope to instead hold him by the chest. Kael thought him too cowardly to look him in the eye the moment he let go.

"Threats and lies," Liam said with trembling tongue. "They do not sway the faithful."

"This is your last chance," Kael whispered, ignoring the vapid rhetoric. He had to cling to hope. He had to save his father. "You can still come back to us. Don't let go, father. Please. Don't let go."

"I . . . I am the blade," Liam stammered. "I am the blade. I am the blade."

Kael could no longer listen to his father's words. Instead he looked out over the forest. To the distant glint of silver.

"I am faithful," Liam continued. "I am loyal. And I will suffer all I must on this world so I might meet your mother again in the next."

Another shimmer of silver, then another. A thin streak of fire trailed after the lead, closing in at tremendous speed. Fresh tears wet Kael's eyes. He was not abandoned. His sister had come to save him. Even if they would be too late, he could take solace in knowing they'd made such a sacrifice.

"May you find peace in the hereafter," Liam said. "May the angels carry you to your final resting place. Your life, and death, are no longer in my hands. I give them over to God's."

His father let him go. The moment passed in startling clarity. The hollow look in Liam's eyes. The vibrant blue of the sky painted with random strokes of white. The faintest moment of weightlessness before gravity's pull dragged him down with ever-increasing greed.

The fall will feel like eternity, Liam had said, and he spoke true. Kael felt his world slow as he looked to the circle of black surrounded by uplifted arms of silver angels. Would Bree even see his body? Would she have the strength? They couldn't reach him in time. The well would swallow him before they caught his fall.

That they would risk so much for nothing awakened Kael from his numb descent. Even now, he would fight. He would survive. That was his sister out there racing across the forest, all consequences be damned. That was her fire streaking across the blue sky. The wild, roaring essence of the fireborn blazed within her. But what of him?

I am the blood on their feathers, his father had spoken as part of his mantra. But it wasn't true. Only one man carried that title. The blood, the light, it all ran in his veins. Kael closed his eyes and clenched his fists within their bonds. Bree was fireborn. Bree was unstoppable destruction and rage. Kael was lightborn. He bore their gifts, and not just their ability to share memories. He wielded something more. Something he'd only scratched the surface of. He'd sensed it when he first formed his memories into a gift to give others. A lurking power. A complete manifestation of his blood inheritance.

The wings of an angel.

Kael dared not think of how close he was to the ground, to the well, dared not think what might happen if knights had spotted his sister on the way to his rescue. He only focused on his blood and the connection therein. He sensed it immediately, and power flowed out from him with a terrifying eagerness. A sound like thunder accompanied a sudden brilliant warmth across his shoulder blades. His fall halted. Ringing filled his ears. Kael opened his eyes. The silver hands of the angel statues reached up for his hovering toes. The crowd recoiled in awe. He turned his neck, saw what they saw, and he mirrored their awe.

Brilliant ethereal wings spread from his back, their light flowing from his spine like water. The wings didn't flap or push. They only shimmered in place, a heavenly version of the harnesses their earthly Seraphim wore. Their overwhelming brilliance should have burned his eyes, but despite the incredible light, it soothed instead. Kael gasped, the tremendous strain of keeping the connection to the light in his blood active steadily eating at his strength.

Move, he thought. His mind imagined his travel, and the wings tilted in response. Kael slowly hovered from over the well to the soft green grass. It took only a moment, but it felt as if Kael had run multiple miles. His mind blanked, and in that momentary darkness, the wings vanished. He fell to his back. Air escaped his lips, followed by a laugh. He saw his father above him, staring with mouth agape and body rigid. Kael couldn't imagine his confusion.

Fire and ice preceded his sister's arrival. The elements ravaged the crowd. The few knights present died before they could even retaliate. A single bolt of lightning ripped into Liam's chest, knocking him aside. He flew toward the forest upon recovering, weaving around a barrage of lances from Kael and Clara. The fact that he survived filled Kael with guilty relief.

Saul dropped to the ground before him while the others continued to attack the few remaining soldiers.

"I highly doubt you're worth all this," Saul said with a grin. He wrapped his arms underneath Kael's armpits and lifted off.

The four raced away from the execution, on a path straight for Weshern. Kael peered around Saul's shoulder. His father did not give chase. Kael closed his eyes, relaxed against the leather straps, and thanked God for small favors.

CHAPTER 21

They landed before the gates of the holy mansion, an additional escort of two Seraphs accompanying them from since their arrival over Weshern soil. Bree powered off her wings, relieved to set foot on solid ground. They were home. They were safe. Saul unbuckled his harness to free Kael from his perch. Her brother stumbled a bit before dropping to his knees.

"I'm fine," he said when Clara moved to help him. "Been a rough few days, that's all."

"Wait here," one of their escorts said. "Commander West has been demanding your presence all morning."

"Of course," Bree said. It took a moment before she realized what the Seraph had said. "Wait—Commander West? What happened to Argus?"

The Seraph glared at her, the viciousness in his eyes enough to send her back a step.

"Just wait."

He crossed the stones and into the holy mansion. The four waited under the watchful eye of the other Seraph and several soldiers who were standing beside the gates. Bree didn't like the way they watched her group. She knew she'd gone into Center without permission, but why would so many think ill of her? And why was Argus no longer commander?

The strength in Kael's legs returned soon enough. He whispered something to Clara, then separated from her and Saul while gesturing Bree closer.

"Bree, there's something you should know," he said with lowered voice.

First Argus, now this. Bree frowned and crossed her arms. "What is it?" she asked.

Kael kicked at the grass, eyes downcast. Bree knew this reaction well. Whatever news he had to share, he hadn't a clue how to tell her.

"Kael, whatever's wrong, I'll understand," she said, trying to reassure him.

"It's Dad," he blurted.

The word laced ice around Bree's spine.

"What about him?" she asked.

"I met him," he said. "In the prison, we talked. He . . . he was even at the execution."

It couldn't be true. Anger flushed her chest. She didn't even know why, only that she couldn't believe such a ridiculous idea.

"Kael, he's dead. It can't have been him. They fooled you, that's all."

"No," Kael said, grabbing her arm. The look in his eye frightened her. "I talked to him. He survived the battle against Galen, and the theotechs brought him to Center to become a knight under orders that he never reveal himself to us."

Bree glanced at the doors to the holy mansion. So far no sign of Olivia. A shame. She'd have given anything for a distraction.

"How...I...Kael, this is incredible," she said. "What did you talk about? Does he know of all we've done? Will he visit once this war is over?"

"He's been brainwashed. We're enemies now, don't you get it?" he said, a bit of his own anger bubbling forth. "The only thing he told me was how we were traitors to him and Center."

"Only because we're at war," Bree said, not sure if she believed it but *needing* to believe it nonetheless. "Once things calm down and we find some semblance of peace, then I'm sure he will return to us. He has to, right?"

Kael snapped completely.

"Bree, he wasn't just at my execution. He was the one holding the rope."

She couldn't believe his words. Surely it was a lie. The world couldn't be that cruel.

"That can't have been him," she said. "He would never. That's not who he is. He couldn't do that. He wouldn't."

"He's our father," Kael said, "but you're right, it's not him. It's not the man who raised us. Marius owns him now."

Bree was at a loss for words. She stood there, hands shaking, fighting back tears. Out of everything Center had taken from them, of all the death and destruction, must he take that from her too? Not only must he return her father from the dead, but as a foreign, hateful thing? Couldn't he have stayed dead? Couldn't her memory of him remain untainted?

"I'm sorry," Kael said. "I almost didn't tell you. I thought maybe I'd just keep it to myself, you know?"

She flung her arms around him and held him close.

"And it would have been unfair to you," she said.

"Don't worry about that," Kael said. "We can handle everything, even this."

A metallic hum pulled their attention upward. Olivia landed in the middle of the four and shut off her wings with a flourish.

"Where have you been?" she asked.

Not addressing all of them, just Bree.

"Getting my brother safely home and out of his imprisonment in Center," she said none too kindly. "Is that a problem?"

"That will depend," she said. "Come with me. The Archon has questions for you." Olivia looked her over, then snapped her fingers at one of the escorting Seraphs. "And remove her harness and swords."

Bree reluctantly let them take her equipment. The lump in her throat insisted this went beyond simple questioning. They'd never before demanded that she disarm in the presence of the Archon. Why do so now?

"Clara, your parents requested you return to your room and await their summons. The rest of you, return to camp. A Seraph will come to question you shortly."

Olivia took her into the mansion, guiding her to a private library near the heart of the building. The small room was quiet and empty but for three people. Archon Isaac and Avila sat in padded chairs softly talking. Johan waited a respectful distance away, calmly standing with his arms crossed behind his back as he glanced over rows of pre-Ascension books. When the doors opened to allow Bree and Olivia entrance, the scarred man turned to face them and dipped his head low in greeting. The two joined Johan in standing before the royal family.

"Thank you for coming," Isaac said. The coldness in his greeting worried Bree greatly. What was going on? Would the consequences for rescuing Kael be worse than she anticipated?

"Leave us, Commander," he ordered Olivia. The Seraph bowed low and left. Bree waited with her arms crossed behind her back, hands clutching her wrists to minimize her fidgeting amid the unbearable silence.

"Is something the matter?" she asked the second the doors echoed shut.

"There is," Isaac said. "I have listened to multiple testimonies regarding Argus Summers's assassination, and all appear to lead in a direction I would never have anticipated."

A combination of shock, denial, and horror slapped across Bree's mind.

"Argus's assassination?" she asked. "This . . . no, that can't be. When? How?"

"That's why we have summoned you," Avila said. "Multiple soldiers have confirmed to me that you were the last to visit with the commander prior to the discovery of his body this morning."

"Not only that," Isaac said, "but that you left with blood on your clothes."

It was too much. First her father miraculously returned from the dead, then Argus Summers was murdered in his sleep, and now witnesses claimed she left Argus's tent covered with blood? She felt tears building in her eyes, the stress of it all scraping away any sense of her composure.

"I don't understand," she said. "I wasn't there. I haven't spoken to Argus since the day of Center's invasion."

"So the men lied to us?" Rebecca asked. Bree sensed the accusation lingering behind every word.

"No, I . . ." Bree shook her head. "I wasn't even on Weshern soil last night. I was hidden on Center preparing for Kael's rescue."

"And that in and of itself is another matter," Isaac said.

"Seraphim of Weshern represent *all* of Weshern, including myself. Assaulting Center without orders undermines my authority and sends a message I did not authorize to give. You acted behind my back, disobeyed my orders, and now you would tell me to trust you over the eyes of my own soldiers? Then what illusion did they see? How do you explain it, other than that more than eight of my men are either fools or liars?"

Bree shook her head, her jaw locked open. Was she even hearing this? Or was she lost in some terrible nightmare?

"This . . . this is insane," she said. "Listen to what you're saying, my Archon. You would call me a traitor, a murderer of my commander, to—to what end exactly?"

"Did you inform Argus of your desire to rescue your brother?"

Bree's face flushed.

"Well, yes, but—"

"And did he approve?"

He certainly hadn't. He'd pushed for her to keep pressuring Rebecca and the Archon to resolve the matter.

"No," Bree said, standing up straight and swallowing. "He did not."

The Archon looked equal measures depressed and frustrated.

"Then this tells a simple tale," he said. "You requested aid in rescuing your brother and Argus denied you. When you persisted, he tried to stop you. Perhaps you didn't mean to hurt him. Perhaps you were surprised and your combat instincts took over. Tell me the truth, and I shall give you every inch of leniency you deserve given your deeds as our Phoenix."

It was too much. Bree felt betrayed by their mistrust and confused by the statements of their witnesses. She'd left Argus's tent covered with blood? How was that possible? Could someone have disguised themselves as her, perhaps an agent of Center to assassinate Argus and sow discord throughout Weshern?

Bree started to speak up but Johan cut her off.

"Archon, might I offer up words in defense of our dear Phoenix?" he asked.

Isaac leaned back into his chair and gestured for him to continue.

"First, I must ask, when did your soldiers witness Breanna entering the tent to speak with the commander?"

Rebecca didn't even have to glance at her notes.

"Sometime after midnight," she said.

Johan smiled.

"Breanna has not yet told you, but her plan to rescue her brother was plotted with me over the course of two nights. She conveyed clearly to me that Argus was unaware of her plans, and that if he was, he would object. Not only that, I was there when she and her friends departed together for Center. Our meeting was just before dark, and unless they turned an about-face for her to sneak into the camp, execute Argus without reason, and then depart, well . . ."

The robed man shrugged.

"I suggest questioning those who flew with her to see if she attempted any such thing."

Isaac's eyes narrowed as he frowned.

"Yet again I am asked to take your word over the word of my soldiers."

"Perhaps," Johan said, a hard edge entering his voice. "But which of us would be the wisest to believe?"

The implied threat was there in the open. Johan was staking his reputation, as well as his aid in Weshern's rebellion, on Bree's innocence. Rebecca looked disgusted, while Isaac appeared simply tired.

"You have spoken truth after truth to the people of the islands, even if they were truths no one wished to hear," the Archon said. "For that alone I will give your insistence a heavy weight. For now I must think on this, as well as wonder what it means if Bree is indeed innocent of the murder. Rebecca will be talking with everyone who joined you on your reckless mission, and I pray your testimonies do not contradict. One of the most important citizens of our island was brutally murdered. No one is above suspicion, not even you, Phoenix."

"I understand," Bree said, trying to control her emotions. The last thing she needed was to be perceived as reacting guiltily.

"Arresting you, or even declaring you a suspect in the murder, will only further damage our people's fragile morale. While we continue the investigation you will be confined to the mansion grounds and denied access to any elements or Seraphim harnesses. I will issue no official decree. I will not even relay this order to my guards. This command is between us only, do you understand? However, if you leave the mansion for *any* reason I will publicly declare you a traitor to Weshern and demand your arrest, morale be damned. Have I made myself clear?"

"Perfectly," Bree said. "And I promise to cooperate in any way you would ask of me. I am a Seraph of Weshern, my Archon, and I always will be."

Isaac nodded.

"You are dismissed. Servants are already preparing you a permanent room on the grounds. Ask any one of them for directions and they will lead you there."

Bree didn't have the heart to say thank you. She hesitated to leave. A hope had been building in her since Center retreated from Weshern soil: peace. And now, knowing of her father's survival as a knight, that hope had only grown in her mind.

If their nations reached peace, she could meet with him. They might talk, hear stories, fill in the many missing years in both halves of their lives…

"My Archon, if I may make one request?" she asked.

Isaac rubbed his chin.

"For all the good you've done our nation, I will allow you at least this. Speak it."

Bree knew she walked on thin ice, but she'd seen more than enough devastation across both Weshern and Center soil. What could she say that would put her in any worse position than the one she was already in?

"We've both suffered greatly," she said slowly and carefully. "Friend and foe alike. Center's fields and homes are scorched and our Seraphim numbers dwindle. Surely now is the time to sue for peace? What demands could we make that Marius would not at least consider?"

Johan cleared his throat behind her.

"Rare is it when pursuing peace is an ignoble goal," he said. "But this is one such time. Center's defenses are at their weakest, and our alliance with the other islands has never been stronger."

"All of which implies our bargaining position has never been higher," Avila interjected.

"Indeed," Johan said. "But think carefully on what we may ask. Peace is not enough. Marius's execution is not enough. Not even freedom from Center's control will grant your children and their children everlasting peace. Only one thing, Archon Willer. The secrets of the elements."

"We can continue to trade for our needed elements," Bree argued. "Impose restrictions on the theotechs, trade agreements and the like. We can do that, can't we?"

"Agreements can be revoked," Johan said. "Trade can diminish. Perhaps it will take years, maybe even decades, but so long as Center holds all the secrets to the creation of elemental prisms, the outer islands will never be safe from reconquering by an enemy bearing limitless weapons of war. I do not reject the idea of peace, I assure you. I reject a peace that is merely a trap set to ensnare our future generations into the same prison we revolt against now. Do not accept a fleeting victory that will only lead to a slow, painful defeat."

Bree felt frustrated and helpless. Deep down she knew there had to be a way for their nations to find peace, but neither could she refute Johan's iron logic.

"I sympathize with both of your desires," Isaac said. "And I will be sending another offer to the Speaker requesting his surrender and acceptance of all our desired terms. If the angels are kind, their pride will not prevent them from seeing the better way for all our people. If Marius refuses, or offers anything less than full compliance with our terms, I will think on our next course of action. For now, let me grieve for the dead we have already lost."

Bree and Johan bowed in unison at the dismissal. They exited the library, nodding perfunctorily to the soldiers protecting the entrance.

"Do not lose your fire," Johan said to her as they left the guards behind. "Do not forget your rage. Peace is not our final goal."

"Then what is?" she asked. Johan smiled down at her, something troubling about the eagerness in his voice.

"Victory."

CHAPTER 22

Isaac Willer stood on thc balcony of his bedroom and gazed over the island he was born to protect. What had once been a beautiful green lawn dotted with carefully trimmed trees was now a burned and ruined mess, the surrounding stone wall blasted with holes from the attack by Marius's specters. Much of the surrounding homes were smoldering piles of ash and rubble. Farther in the distance, the green and blue beauty of Weshern was pocked with black stretches, as if infected with a burning disease.

"This was but one attack," he asked. "Can we endure another?"

He did not hear his wife's soft footsteps behind him, only knew she was there when her arms wrapped about his waist. She kept careful with her embrace, not wishing to agitate his injuries.

"We will always endure," Avila said. "The wiser question is if Center can also endure?"

Isaac leaned his head back so he might press his cheek against hers.

"Their weapons are endless, while ours shrink with each battle," he said. "But we have a smaller populace, and enough food to last through the cold season."

"Are you suggesting we lay siege upon Center?"

"It was a thought," Isaac said. "With their crops heavily damaged, and our trade cut off, we could focus on hit-and-run tactics against their surviving animal stock and farms."

"A lot of innocent people will starve," Avila said. "And the common folk will starve long before the soldiers, knights, and theotechs. You know that."

Indeed, Isaac did. It was why he had not proposed the idea during the discussion the day before. Someone as bloodthirsty as Johan would shrug off the innocent dead as a casualty of war, but Isaac could not bring himself to such ruthlessness. He wanted freedom for his own people. He had no desire for the people of Center to suffer for the actions of their military and religious leaders.

"I want to do what is right," Isaac said, turning to embrace his wife. His fingers rustled through her blond hair. His eyes closed, and he breathed in the lilac scent of her hair. "I just don't know what that is. So many have died. I must find a peace that does not leave that loss in vain."

Avila pulled back, and he opened his eyes to find hers locking him into her gaze.

"Then embrace war with all your heart," she said. "Center reels at the precipice of an abyss. Push them over, and free ourselves from their theotechs forever."

"If they will not reveal the secrets of the elemental prisms, then war must follow," Isaac said. "It pains me knowing Johan is correct. But I will not embrace that war with my whole heart, not in private. Not when alone, or with you."

Avila smiled a sad smile.

"We have always lived two lives," she said. "This is no different."

Isaac kissed her tenderly, without force or passion. He wanted comfort from her, and she offered it with the gentle caress of a hand on his face and another at his breast.

"Thank you," he whispered when she pulled away.

She started to reply but a knock on the door interrupted her. Isaac pulled free and slowly passed through the thick curtains at the balcony entrance. Beyond was their extravagant bedroom, the bed, dressers, and mirrors all coated with silver. His bare feet sank into the absurdly thick and soft blue carpet. Isaac pulled back a chain lock, followed by the slender dead bolt beneath, and opened the door a crack.

"Yes?" he asked.

An older soldier stood outside, his eyes long circles of exhaustion. He wore no helmet, revealing much of his gray hair had recently been burned away.

"My Archon," he said. "I come bearing an urgent message."

"Then speak it."

"A messenger from Center stands at the entrance of the mansion. He says he brings a written request for peace from Marius's own hand, to be read by your eyes only."

Isaac's heart skipped a beat. A request for peace? The grand weight on his shoulders trembled ever so slightly. If the terms were acceptable, then the bloodshed, the war, it might all end with the stroke of a pen . . .

"I will need to dress," he said. "Assign the messenger an escort, and do not let him leave the mansion grounds."

The soldier bowed low.

"Yes, my Archon," he said.

Isaac shut the door and turned to find his wife standing beside the bed, a hand nervously twirling the sapphire amulet hanging from her neck.

"Center seeks peace?" she asked. None of Isaac's hope mirrored itself in her tone.

"It seems that way," Isaac said. "We'll need to know their exact terms, as well as discuss the matter with the other three Archons."

"It might be a trick."

Isaac thought for a moment, then shook his head.

"Center may offer us too little," he said, "but I do not believe Marius one to play frivolous games that may tarnish his virtuous image. The dead mount on both sides. My gut says this offer is sincere."

"But if it *is* a trick?"

Isaac sighed.

"If it is, I'll have my guards rip the messenger into a dozen pieces and have my Seraphim scatter the pieces from miles above Center."

Avila said nothing, but he saw the lurking doubt in her eyes. Isaac knew he was risking much, raising his hopes in this way, but he could not help it. This war was hell, consuming both their worlds. It needed to end.

Isaac and Avila dressed in their separate wardrobes. They would greet any messenger of Center in their finest. Despite all of Center's cruelty and recklessness, the messenger was still an official envoy, and deserved all the treatments of such. Isaac finished first, his black suit tight and proper, and he helped his wife lace the deep blue corset of her dress. When done he offered her his arm. She took it, and they exited the room.

Two soldiers waited on either side, their arms crossed behind their backs.

"To the throne room?" one asked.

"Indeed."

They walked, the soldiers two steps ahead.

"Did the messenger come alone?" Isaac asked.

"It appears so."

"Why was I not informed when he first arrived on Weshern soil?"

The soldier glanced over his shoulder ever so slightly.

"Because we did not scout his arrival until he was several miles from the mansion."

Isaac frowned. They had multiple patrols watching the airspace between the various islands. For one to slip by so easily reminded him of how much territory they needed to protect, and how few Seraphim were left to protect it.

"Very well," he said. "I will speak with Commander West about tighter patrols. We cannot afford to slacken our defenses."

The throne room bore the name of the seats of power of old, but hardly resembled a true castle throne. The wide hall was designed to greet diplomats and civilian representatives. Long tables on either side of the room were covered with glasses and plates. Comfortable chairs formed semicircles around four fireplaces. At the far end were two chairs, by far the most ornate decoration in the room. The legs and back were stained silver, the cushions a flawless blue.

Isaac and Avila took their seats, Avila sinking into hers, Isaac at the edge of his. His fingers tapped the armchair, a habit he ceased the moment he noticed. This messenger would be reporting back to Marius, and Isaac could not afford to weaken his negotiating position by appearing overeager for peace.

"Bring him in," Isaac said.

The nearest soldier opened the wide door, allowing in the messenger and his two escorts. The man was on the shorter side, and he wore the deep red robes of the theotechs. That detail did not go unnoticed by Isaac. Messengers were normally trusted knights. To send a theotech added importance to the carried message. The man's head was covered in a soft coat of white that appeared more like down than hair. He approached the two thrones with a limp, his face covered with wrinkles, his curled hands cradling a rolled scroll sealed with wax.

"Welcome, theotech of Center," Isaac said. His voice echoed in the heavy silence. It seemed even soldiers were holding their breath. "Might I have a name for my guest?"

"Titus Cenborn," the older man said. "A loyal servant of our holy Speaker, Marius Prakt, and have been from the very first day he ascended to his position. I come with his words in hand, and a message to deliver if your ears are open to hearing it."

Nothing revealed yet, but it intrigued Isaac that it would be delivered verbally first, before the scroll was handed over. Most Archons preferred to rely on their written words instead of a messenger adding inflection and emphasis where there might be none. Most often the verbal deliveries were of good news, good wishes, and congratulations.

"Our ears are open," Isaac said, settling a little bit farther into his chair and forcing himself to relax. "Speak, and I pray you come with tidings of peace and humility instead of further warmongering."

Titus controlled his emotions masterfully, but Isaac caught the tiniest of twitches at the corners of the man's mouth. The hints of a smile?

"In such times, we all pray for tidings of peace," the older theotech said. His voice was aged yet firm, with not a hint of wavering. "But peace is an agreement, and I can only bring an offer."

"Is that what you bring?" Isaac interrupted. His wife chastised him with a glare, but he didn't care. Men and women were dying. He didn't feel like enduring a long slew of flowery words prior to hearing what really mattered.

"An offer of peace?" Titus straightened himself, and he slowly nodded his head. "Yes, Archon, I come seeking peace between Center and Weshern, if you must be so hasty."

That flicker of hope and light strengthened in Isaac's heart.

"Under what conditions?" he asked, knowing that any peace he reached must secure safety for the future of his island, and not just a temporary cease-fire that would one day leave them vulnerable.

The theotech cleared his throat.

"Our Speaker believes that this conflict has arisen out of misunderstanding and confusion, and not of true animosity between our nations. We kill and burn over differences of rights and privileges. These things we must resolve peacefully, and without needless death. Marius says this not out of fear of defeat or of the rise in power of the minor islands. We face a greater threat than we can imagine. Living fire fell from the sky. We see the stars, and the stars shine on our vulnerability. The eternal-born come for us, Archon Isaac. They come, and we must be united in our defense against them. Nothing will quell their anger. Nothing will sate their fury. Only blood."

Isaac could feel the awkward discomfort spreading through the room. Achieving peace and freedom was absolutely the desired goal, but the chilling threat of a new conflict dampened that relief.

"Weshern will stand against any foe, supernatural or otherwise," he said. "But we will not stand in unity with Center as if the atrocities you committed against us never happened. Entire towns burned beneath your invasion's fire."

"And we offer repayment for our transgressions," Titus said. He motioned with the scroll held in his tightly curled fingers. "Nothing will return the dead, not for either side. Mutual trust is the only step Marius believes will matter. The angels ask for reconciliation, and they have revealed the path to our holy Speaker. Here, in my hands, I hold the truth of the elemental prisms that we have, until now, strictly controlled."

"Center will reveal the secrets of their creation?" Isaac asked. He could hardly believe it. That information represented complete freedom from Center. No more reliance on their trade, no more duels with other islands for the thinly spread supply.

"If you will accept peace," Titus said. "For we gain nothing without that."

Isaac beckoned for one of his guards to fetch the scroll for him to read.

"Let me see for myself," he said. "If what you say is true, I will gladly accept peace."

The old man let out a hacking cough.

"It is for your eyes only," he said, glaring at the guard. "We are entrusting very much to your hands with this offer, and we expect discretion while terms are negotiated."

The nearby guard looked his way for confirmation. Isaac waved him off and ordered the theotech to hand over the scroll. Titus shuffled closer and extended an arm. The scroll hovered unsteadily in offering. Isaac took the scroll and broke the wax. His shaking hands unrolled it. On the yellow parchment there was but a single sentence at its very center, carefully written in a tight, flourishing script.

Demons shall never ascend above angels.

Isaac looked to Titus, to question the deceit, to demand an explanation, but he had barely opened his mouth before the old theotech closed the gap between them with the speed of a young man. Titus's arm wrapped around his neck, locking him in place. Isaac's instinctual attempt to pull back meant nothing, for it felt like immovable stone held him. His mind baffled as to how a scrawny, elderly man could possess such strength.

Sharp pain sliced across his throat. Warm blood ran down his neck. Isaac tried to speak, to scream and curse, but his body betrayed him with only gurgles and coughs. Titus's face shifted ever so slightly as he leaned in closer, cheek to cheek, an intimate embrace. His eyes shifted from brown to blue. The features of his face smoothed ever so slightly, shrouded by a hood that would reveal this horror, this betrayal, this disease with a nightmarish grin, only to him.

"You damn fool," Johan whispered.

The face became Titus's once more. The iron grip released. Isaac collapsed to the floor. His mind could barely process it. A mere few seconds ago he'd read words on a scroll. Now he lay dying. He saw the ceiling, only dark and clouded. His ears heard screams, the shouts of guards. Fighting, and far away. Johan must have immediately fled. Isaac tried to sit up but his body weighed a strange ton more. His head barely lifted off the blood-soaked floor.

A loving hand touched his. His wife. Her face overtook his vision.

"Isaac," he heard her whisper. "I love you, Isaac. I love you."

He would have whispered it back but he had no air in his lungs to voice it with. He kept his gaze upon Avila, hoping she could read the message in his eyes, hoping she'd know his appreciation for all their years together.

Kept it as the world turned to shadow.

Kept it as his wife's face vanished beneath the black.

CHAPTER 23

Bree sat in the holy mansion's walled garden, hands scraping through the soft earth. Flowers surrounded her, dark red and purple shades of bellflowers, an appropriate somberness to their blooms. Even the birds seemed quieter, and why shouldn't they be? Surely they sensed the destruction around them. Bree had been given temporary stay in one of the holy mansion's many rooms. On her way to the garden she'd passed burned and broken walls. She'd walked over vast stretches of charred carpet. Worst of all had been the hidden tears and quiet crying of the soldiers and the staff.

Weshern's heart had been ripped out of its chest yesterday, and somehow the world had to go on.

"Miss Skyborn?"

She glanced over her shoulder to see a guard standing awkwardly on the path.

"Yes?"

"The Archoness has requested your audience."

Bree rose to her feet while brushing at her uniform in an attempt to clean it. Off came the dirt, but no amount of brushing would remove the many bloodstains.

"Lead the way, if you'd please," she said. "I'm still learning the layout of the mansion."

The soldier nodded respectfully.

"As you wish."

They left the garden. A starling's voice burst to life as she stepped through the glass doors. Bree tried her best to take comfort in the song. They passed through the halls, but instead of traveling to the throne room they entered Avila's bedroom. Two more guards stood at attention on either side of the door. Bree was surprised there weren't more.

"Lift your arms," one ordered. Bree frowned at him.

"I'm sorry, miss," the other said, stepping closer. "But at this point not even the Phoenix is free from caution."

"I understand."

They thoroughly patted her down, ensuring she had no hidden weapons. When finished, they allowed her access to the door. She knocked twice, then stepped back a pace. Her throat felt raw and dry, and no amount of swallowing seemed to help. What might the Archoness wish from her?

"Come in," Avila's voice called from the other side.

Bree obeyed.

The window to the Archoness's balcony was the only source of light. Avila sat in a chair before a tall oval mirror, staring blankly at her own reflection. She wore a black dress with silver buttons. Her face was covered with a blue shroud. Even with its covering Bree could see the smeared lines of tears.

"Thank you for coming," Avila said. The eyes in the mirror glanced her way. "There are important matters we must discuss."

Bree stood up straight, her hands locked behind her back. It took all her focus to remain emotionless and professional in spite of the palpable sadness rolling through the air. Though Avila's voice remained strong, her grief was a spiritual force. The room itself seemed to quiver when she spoke.

"I am your loyal Seraph," Bree said. "Whatever you need of me, ask."

Avila turned her way, and Bree quickly bowed in respect. She couldn't meet the woman's eye. Her personality had always been forceful yet controlled, a guiding hand for her husband's actions. That was gone. The Archoness had inherited the Archon's title, and now there was no need to keep her strength in check. When she spoke, her words were iron, and the only thing that matched her sorrow was her smoldering rage.

"The people are furious," she said. "And they have every right to be. Thousands are dead on both sides, and yet it is not enough for the bloodthirsty monster that rules on Center. To be so petty, so cruel..." Avila took in a deep breath, let it out. "I will accept no treaty offered by the theotechs, no matter how generous. I don't care what direction the winds of battle turn. I don't care if Marius threatens to bury us below the ocean waves like he did Galen. We shall have no peace until the Speaker drops in a Weshern well, and we bury his corpse with the bones of the dead his war machines wrought upon our land."

Bree found herself unable to argue against the sentiment. Everyone felt betrayed. The joy they'd felt at their victory against Center's invasion had lasted but a moment before being tainted by an assassin's blade. Such a vile deed demanded punishment.

"We Seraphim are ready to lay down our lives for you," Bree said. "Give your orders, and know we shall carry them out to the best of our abilities."

"Indeed, you risked your life many times this past week,"

Avila said. "Both you and your brother were vital in our defense, which means I'm a fool to continue to sequester you here for Argus's murder."

"So you believe my innocence?"

"What I believe doesn't matter anymore. Weshern's fate is all that does."

Avila put a hand on her shoulder, bidding her to rise. Bree obeyed, and dared meet the woman's gaze, inwardly berating herself. She had faced Center's wrath. She could face a widow's grief, no matter how uncomfortable it made her feel.

"I still remember the first day I met you," Avila said. "It was at the solstice ball. You were just a skinny little thing, shy to hold the hand of her date. I could hardly believe you were the child of two skilled, vicious Seraphim." Avila smiled at her. "Then I heard of your reckless attack on the Seraph who slew your lover, and I knew I'd been wrong. You had the spirit of your father, his same fire. He'd have been proud of you, Bree. Very proud."

The words were meant to give comfort, but they only reminded Bree of how much her father had changed in Center's clutches. No, he wasn't proud of her. Instead he viewed her as a betrayal to his teachings. She debated telling Avila of her father's survival but decided against it. The last thing the Archoness needed was more conflicting feelings.

"Isaac saw the same fire," she said. "He believed, just as Argus Summers believed, that you represented something magical. You were a powerful symbol the people could understand. You were untamed. Uncontrolled. Unbeatable." Both of Avila's hands held Bree by the shoulders. She felt the fingers tremble. She heard her words turn desperate and tired. "We need that symbol again, Bree. Too many have died, and I fear the rage will suffocate beneath the anguish. We need hope in this dark hour. We need something to cling to among the loss."

Bree stammered for an answer.

"Give the order," she said. "I am still a loyal servant of Weshern."

"Thank you," Avila said. The Archoness released her iron grip, took a step back, and composed herself. "I've ordered messengers to spread word throughout Weshern that we will be continuing our battle for freedom against Center. I would like you to accompany them, in a sense. For many citizens, our rebellion truly began when your swords lit the darkened sky. Will you do so again? Will you let the people know the Phoenix still flies?"

Bree's dry throat had progressed from sand to a coat of razors.

"And my imprisonment here?" she asked.

"Do this for me, and I will end it. Investigation into your guilt will halt until the war is over. For the sake of our island, we need this from you, and we need it now."

There was no rejecting this request. Bree stood up straighter and thudded her fist against her breast in salute.

"I will," she said, surprised the words even exited her mouth.

"Good. You are dismissed, Seraph."

She bowed low and then fled the room as if a thousand fireborn nipped at her heels.

Bree stared up at the dark night sky, trying to remember that initial awe and wonder at seeing the stars for the very first time. The whole world felt new after the removal of the suffocating midnight fire. The stars felt tranquil in comparison to the constant, moving chaos. Against that crawling midnight fire her flaming swords had been a protest, a signal of rebellion. What would it mean now when it carved through a sky of diamonds?

For some, it'll mean the world, she thought.

Bree adjusted one of the belts on her harness, tightening it. The wind was cool, nature itself mourning the fallen Archon. She stood in the mansion garden, one of the few places of solace in the entire building.

Nothing to this, she told herself. *Just a simple flight like before.*

Except it wasn't the same. Before, when she unleashed her flame over Weshern, it had been in celebration as well as warning to the occupying forces of Center. This was neither. This time she was offering the people a promise. She was asking them to trust her despite everything, and deep down, Bree didn't believe herself worthy of such trust.

Waiting would only make it worse. Bree flicked power to her wings, felt the thrum travel down her spine. Her feet drifted off the ground, weightlessness taking her. Before she flew away, she closed her eyes and offered a rare prayer.

Make this mean something.

Bree flew straight up, knowing she'd need significant height to ensure her flame burned visible for miles in all directions. The mansion receded, just a blur among the rest of the dark land. Bree turned her eyes upward. *Stop fearing the ground. Start watching the sky.*

You fly among the stars, Bree told herself. *You fly where you belong.*

Bree ceased her ascent and put her left hand across the right gauntlet. With gritted teeth she jammed in the needle, drawing blood into the fire prism's chamber. The pain quickly faded, her awareness of the prism growing in her mind. Another flick of a switch armed the gauntlet. Last, she drew her swords.

"Let's go," she breathed into the silence.

Bree tilted forward and flooded life into her wings. As her momentum increased, she made the mental connection in her mind, channeling the flame. It swirled out from her focal prism, danced across the hilt without burning, and then bathed the blade. A clack of her two swords spread the flame to the other. Their heat washed across Bree's skin with a pleasant warmth. The fire streaked behind her, trailing off her swords. Bree felt the drain on her mind, just a minor thing as her blood easily kept the fire prism full.

Not enough, thought Bree. *Avila wants a message, so I'll give them one.*

She focused on her swords, building her rage. The fire built, growing hotter and brighter than she was used to. She kept her swords far out to either side to minimize the discomfort. There was nothing she could do for her hands, so close to the heat she felt her skin turning raw. Randy Kime had insisted her skin would heal quickly from wounds caused by her element. She prayed that was the case.

Her flame streaked across the night sky. The greater fire wore at her mind, and she found herself breathing rapidly, as if in the middle of a sprint. She pressed on. The twin trails were enormous now, vicious and blazing. Bree found herself sensing it for the first time. She could shape it, in a way, envisioning it spreading out flatter and wider. The flame obeyed. It would always obey.

Weshern passed beneath her like the hours, quiet and dark. Bree bounced her gaze from the stars to the ground, needing the heavenly light above to chase away her sorrow. The closer she neared southern Weshern, the more destruction littered the landscape. She saw craters where there should have been houses. She saw flickering orange embers where there should have been tightly packed fields. She saw black spaces of abandoned towns where there should have been lanterns, candles, cook fires. Docks were closed. Stalls vacant.

Bree let her fire roar above it all. Perhaps the Phoenix moniker had been more prophetic than anyone realized. With her fire, she would do all she could to bring her beloved home back to life.

Glensbee and Lowville approached. Bree hadn't realized she flew that direction, but there was no doubt. Center's cannons had blasted it all away, nothing but painful scars to remind Weshern of what had once been. Bree felt guilt claw at her throat. She had helped start this conflict. She'd pushed and pushed so that a small rebellion turned into a grand war.

Her feelings only worsened as she flew over the complete ruination of Glensbee. What had once been a town was now a crater. Bree stared at it in horror, unable to believe the power laid witness before her. How could Marius unleash such a terrible weapon and still claim to be God's voice? Hundreds of lives, snuffed out in an instant. Not warriors. Not rulers and rebels. Men, women, and children, running from a war they could not outrace. It should have fueled her rage, but it only added to the weight on her shoulders. There below, another cost of their rebellion. One of many. Worst of all, it was a cost they might pay again and again, for there'd been no sign of the weapon responsible amid the abandoned and destroyed war machines left on Weshern soil.

Lowville, at least what remained of it, was just past the tremendous crater. Bree looked for familiar sights and found depressingly few. Everything was burned and flattened. She pieced the ruin together in her mind, seeking their old home. She spotted one of the town's wells still intact and flew down to it, shutting off her flame and putting an end to her lengthy flight across the island. Bree walked the street, or at least, the winding gap between the two long stretches of broken stone and burned wood. And then she found it.

"Aunt Bethy?" Bree whispered aloud. "I'm home."

The wood roof had collapsed in on itself, and based on the impact, she guessed a large blast of lightning had slammed through it. The walls had crumbled on three sides. Stone, perhaps? Or ice? No evidence remained, the elements long since faded away into mist. Bree stepped through one of the broken walls. Little parts of their old life littered the floor. Broken dishes. The ashes of the fire pit. The wooden chair Aunt Bethy had rocked in beside the fire. It was broken in half, clipped by a large chunk of stone wall. With the upper floor collapsed, it was that much harder to decipher what had belonged where. Feathers from the ripped mattresses covered the eastern wall, gathered there by the wind.

"I hope you're fine, Bethy," Bree said. She didn't even know if her aunt had survived the attack. So far as Bree knew, Center's advance had neared, but not reached, the surrounding farmlands of Selby. Bree prayed the fury of the cannons had passed over the farmstead. She also prayed her aunt never had to come back to see what was left of her home.

Bree sat in the center of it all, her knees curled to her chest. The tips of her wings dipped into the clutter, holding her in place. Her strength was gone. It had drained away in the flight, and the energy it had taken to refill the fire prism and keep her swords alight was only partly to blame. Her life had been a dull chore for so very long, working in fields and preparing meals for their little family of three. The months of training in the Academy were a blur, each day ending with her collapsing exhausted onto her bed.

Yet when the Academy burned to the ground, everything that followed had happened so fast. The discovery of the power in her blood. The assault at Camp Aquila. Her imprisonment and experimentation upon by Er'el Jaina. The collapse of the dome, and the fall of the fireborn. All of it, one after another, mixed with memories of the dead and dying. Center's defense of the Crystal Cathedral, and then the invasion of their war machines. Kael's near execution. The return of their father. It was too much, too much. Each day a trial. Each week a lifetime.

Her tears fell, and she didn't stop them. She brushed away debris to reveal a part of the wooden floor covered with dust. Bree put a finger upon it and began writing. Cassandra. Dean. Brad. The names of the dead. The names of those dear to her forever lost. Argus. Isaac. There were so many, so very many. Chernor. Randy. Aisha. Loramere. Some had no names. The mother, reaching up to her as Galen fell. The child in her arms. The tens of thousands free-falling in that brief moment of twilight horror before the island struck the water and sank into the ocean.

Out here, without soldiers, Seraphim, and teachers, without theotechs, without the Mariuses and Johans of the world, Bree settled into her dark private place and finally broke down. She sobbed for it all, the dead, the living, a mother who died in her arms, a father who returned to only offer condemnation. For the responsibilities she was terrified of failing. For the promises she'd already broken. She stopped pretending the weight on her back didn't exist. In one glorious space of time, the Phoenix ceased to be. Only Breanna Skyborn remained.

The tears slowed in time. Bree dried her face with her hands, and she looked about the home in a new light. No, she didn't want to remember it burned to ash. The memories remained, and one day, they would be built anew.

A soft shimmer of silver flew overhead. Bree didn't need to look to know who it was. The hum of wings replaced the silence, but only until Kael landed beside her and shut them off. He looked her over, at the mess she surely was. His lip twitched. His guarded brown eyes gave away nothing.

"Hey," he said, plopping down next to her. "Need a hug?"

She burst out with a tearful laugh.

"Yes," she said. "Yes, I do."

He wrapped his arm about her, and she leaned into him, sniffling but already feeling infinitely better than when she first took flight.

"Figured you'd be here," Kael said as the silence dragged on. "I mean, it wasn't exactly an amazing guess since I just followed your trail of fire. I wanted to fly with you, by the way, but you never told me what you were up to." He winked at her. "Weshern could have used a bit of my shield's light as well, you know."

She leaned harder against him.

"Sorry, but I think I'll hog it all for myself for now."

"If you insist." He looked about what was left of their home. "Well. This place got wrecked, didn't it?"

Another laugh. Bree elbowed his side.

"Show proper respect, Kael. Can't you see I'm having a moment?"

Kael pulled away and grinned at her.

"And can't you see that I'm doing my job? No sulking when Kael's around. If I have to act like an idiot to cheer you up, then that's what I'll be doing. So, please stop making that job difficult by oh, say, flying off to be a symbol of the revolution the night after our Archon's death."

Bree sniffed as she wiped at her eyes.

"If I ever have to do that again, I promise I'll invite you along with me."

"Damn straight," Kael said, rising to his feet. "You're already famous. Give me a chance to get a little bit of that glory. I'm still playing catch-up."

Bree stood and flung her arms around him, clenching him tightly. She felt his body tense, then relax as he embraced her back.

"Thank you, Kael," she whispered. "Thank you so much."

"I'm here for you, Bree," he said, his joking tone vanished. "And I always will be."

She pulled away and fluttered her wings back to life.

"Let's return to the mansion," she said. "I'm pretty sure Clara needs you more than I do."

Kael's smile cracked the briefest second.

"She's stronger than anyone gives her credit for," he said. "But you're right. Let's go."

His wings hummed along with hers, silver light flooding the debris. Bree gave it one last look, refusing to dwell on the rubble but instead the memories it brought forth. To keep hopeful instead of buried by the loss.

The Skyborn twins soared into the air, little silver dots among a star-filled sky. They left behind the loss, the old life, and the painful names of the dead.

CHAPTER 24

A furious Liam passed the line of wagons full of tributes leading back to Heavenstone's entrance. His chest twisted into knots and his hand clenched into a fist despite his attempts to remain calm. The news rattled inside his brain, banging against his skull. Along with the frightening memory of the execution, it all created a cacophony the knight desperately wished for the Speaker to silence.

It can't be true, he thought. *It can't mean what I think it means.*

The people were devastated by the recent series of defeats, and the once unthinkable was becoming a reality: Center herself might soon face invasion. Rumors and fear spread like wildfire. Marius was performing an emergency tour of major cities throughout Center in an attempt to keep the public's support, a task Liam didn't envy in the slightest. That morning the Speaker would be in the nearest village, Seralworth, before continuing on. Liam knew he should fly there but he kept the wings on his back dark. His steady jog lit a pleasant fire in his muscles. More important, it gave him time to grasp the latest in what had been a long string of shocking and terrible news: Weshern's Archon, Isaac Willer, had been killed by Marius's agents.

The distant walls faded, the grass turning to fields of grain worked by Seralworth villagers. Liam did his best to ignore the blackened gaps the soft wind revealed with the bending of the stalks. There was enough on his mind. He didn't need to add in the fireborn assault and the possibilities of future attacks.

Seralworth was the final town all traders passed through on the way to Heavenstone, and it had been hit harder than most by the cessation of trade, hence Marius's visit. He'd come to assure them the trade would resume, the minor islands would fall in linc, and all would return to as it was. An impossible promise, Liam knew.

Center or the minor islands, it doesn't matter who wins, Liam thought. *Our world will never be the same.*

Liam jogged down Seralworth's streets. It bore more warehouses than homes, and those warehouses were impressive structures several stories tall with curved brown roofs. Their long stone walls were all painted with images of fields and mountains, a nod to the proximity of the theotechs' main fortress. The marble homes were carefully arranged around straight, wide roads, which allowed Liam to easily spot the gathering at the town center.

Liam slipped through the enormous crowd, heading not for the wood stage Marius spoke upon but instead the gilded platform bearing Marius's throne. Two knights stood guard, and they nodded upon recognizing him.

"I'd have a word with the Speaker when he is finished," Liam said to the first.

"If the Speaker allows it."

"Alone," Liam added.

The two knights exchanged a glance.

"Again," the knight said. "If the Speaker allows it."

Liam paced as he half-paid attention to Marius's plea for bravery and patience. A scowl crossed his face, and his heart raced. His fingers drummed the golden cannon of his arm. What he planned was dangerous. Marius might have shown him special attention the past few years, but that did not mean Liam was immune to punishment. To criticize the Speaker invited risk. To propose blasphemy to his face required the will of a madman.

Your heart is true, Liam told himself as Marius stepped down from the stage, four angelic knights forming a protective barrier between him and the crowd. *Marius knows that.*

The crowd parted, allowing the Speaker access to his carrier platform. Liam kept where he was, carefully watching Marius's reactions. One of the knights joined the holy man's side and whispered something. Marius looked over and saw Liam waiting beside the transport. His practiced smile slipped momentarily, further agitating the vipers wrestling in Liam's gut. The Speaker waved the knight off, and the smile was in full bloom when he greeted Liam beside the platform.

"Is there something amiss?" he asked as he stepped onto his platform.

"I seek a private audience," Liam said. "It is of great importance."

"Stand beside me," Marius said. "We will talk while traveling to our next destination."

The Speaker settled into his golden chair, and Liam accepted the offer. Men took up the chains and lifted into the air. It never rocked, the platform masterfully controlled to prevent the slightest upset. The townsfolk gathered around as they lifted off the ground, waving and cheering. Liam wasn't surprised. No matter how dire a situation, Marius had the power of personality to reassure.

"So," Marius said, slumping deeper into the chair now that he was out of sight of the crowd. "Given your homeland, I assume you wish to question me on Isaac's death?"

It had been a question of his, yes, but not the most important one.

"It has made me wonder," Liam admitted. "Some people think it is a cowardly act beneath you."

"That's because it *is* beneath me," Marius said. He glared at Liam. "What do I gain by executing Isaac in such a way? No matter how brave my words to the people down there, our army has been decimated and our victory no longer certain. Any further losses and we may need to barter for peace, but any attempt I make will carry the inevitable paranoia of another betrayal. Archoness Willer most assuredly wants my head, another stumbling block on any road toward a rational cease-fire. No, Liam, I did not send the assassin who took Isaac's life, and if that is what you've come to ask me, then fly back to Heavenstone and stop wasting my time."

Liam was taken aback by the sudden anger. The Speaker was always careful to present himself as calm and in control even when discussing things in private. Had the recent trials started to affect him greater than anyone realized? Or was his patience growing thinner every time his decisions were questioned? What Liam did know was that he believed him. That raw anger, that overwhelming frustration, could be born of nothing else.

"Forgive me, my Speaker," Liam said, and he dropped to one knee and bowed his head. "I met Archon Willer several times when I served as their Seraph, and I believed him a good man deserving a better fate."

"Stand up, knight," Marius said. "All of Center is below us. I don't need acts of piety here. Just speak your truth." He sighed. "And yes, Isaac was a good man. He ruled with a sincere desire to help his people, an attribute rarer than one might hope. But you delude yourself if you believe him deserving a better fate. It was his nation that sparked this rebellion. It was his decree that officially began the minor islands' war against our rule. Only Johan deserves greater blame for our current chaos."

"Forgive me," Liam said. "A well-deserved rebuke. I should never let my memories interfere with my judgment. A good man committing treason loses his right to call himself a good man."

Marius hardly looked ready to continue the discussion. He pointed ahead, to a gray cluster of buildings wrapped around a sparkling lake. Clearholm, if Liam remembered correctly, and the second destination for Marius's tour about Center.

"Down there are a thousand people ready to pass judgment on a decision I never made," he said. "When we land, I will assure them the cowardly act was not done by my hand, but they won't believe that. They'll think me saving face, or saying only the politically appropriate response for a Speaker. Some will loudly praise me. Others will quietly denounce me. All will have an opinion to share, and all will feel certain theirs is the correct one. Think of how mad this world has become, knight. A thousand praises and condemnations heaped upon my head like hot coals, regardless of my words, and over something I have not done. Such a sad land we rule, where the truth is decided by the ignorant mob."

"The truth will rise above the lies in time," Liam said, trying not to let the cynicism win. It was painful hearing such world-weariness in the Speaker's voice. Frightening, even. "Stand tall, and the storm will pass."

Marius stood from his chair and walked to the edge of the platform. He crossed his hands behind his back and gazed over the lands under his rule. "The truth *doesn't* always win out. Sometimes it's the easy lies that take hold. Have not even we theotechs told our fair share? We denied the survival of the demons. We pretended ignorance to the reason of the protective dome and the dangers lurking beyond. We told comforting lies, and now that they've been exposed, the people no longer trust us. We never should have hidden this from them, I see that now. How do we convince them we are in control of a situation we denied even existed? When the eternal-born attack again, how do we promise safety when we spent the past centuries insisting those eternal-born were dead?"

Liam could hardly believe what he was hearing. He'd come fearing to speak blasphemy, but here he was listening to blasphemy from the Speaker's own lips.

"My Speaker," Liam said, struggling to find the proper words. "If you need privacy, I will gladly leave and come back later."

Marius shook his head.

"No, out with it, knight. I know there's something else you wish to ask, and I don't want that weighing on your mind until the next time we speak."

Liam joined the Speaker on the platform's edge, letting his eyes drift out of focus as he watched Clearholm's approach.

"Do you know of what happened during Kael Skyborn's execution?" he asked.

A frown crept at the edge of Marius's tanned face.

"I received the report, yes."

"Then you know the feat my son performed?"

"This changes nothing, Liam. Your son was a heretic then and he is a heretic now."

Liam flung up his arms, both real and mechanical.

"How does it not?" he asked. "I saw it, Marius. I saw the wings emerge from his back with my own eyes, and they were beautiful. Our harnesses, our mechanical approximations, they are nothing but earthly attempts to re-create what I witnessed. It has to mean *something.*"

Marius pulled his attention away from Clearholm. His blue eyes narrowed, and Liam watched dormant rage spark back to life within the irises. When he spoke, Marius's doubt and confusion were miles away.

"Do you not remember?" he asked. "The great betrayer L'adim was once a lightborn like his brethren. He bore such wings when he committed the greatest act of treason imaginable against God and his creations. That your son bore them for even a moment means nothing. Deceit is how the shadowborn operates. It is how the sinful sway the hearts of the just. The weak stab their foe in the back, not the chest."

The Speaker pointed to Liam's golden arm.

"I wonder if I was wrong to grant you such a gift. Twice now your son has lived when death should have claimed him. Is your love of your treacherous family overwhelming your loyalty to God and his angels?"

"My loyalty was true," Liam said, unable to keep the anger off his tongue. "By my hand, Kael dropped to his death. If he was spared, then it was by God."

"Then you are no different from the people who believe I was involved with Isaac's death," Marius snapped. "You attribute the work of the devil to God's hand and then demand an explanation from God as to why. You are wrong, Liam.

It is that simple. From the words of angels, and the voice of God himself, I declare you deceived. Cast aside these heretical thoughts or I shall be forced to take action against you."

Liam trembled. The fate of a heretic was clear. The Speaker threatened death.

"So be it," he said, stepping back and dipping his head. "My pride is not so great as to think me above the wisdom of God's appointed. Forgive me, Speaker."

"And you will be forgiven, in time," Marius said. "Now go prepare at Heavenstone. Weshern will retaliate soon, I feel it, and the other islands will join them when they do. We must erase our initial failure with a crushing victory."

"Of course." Another bow. Before he left, he had one last request. He tried to present it carefully, each word a footfall upon breaking glass.

"My Speaker...might I speak to the three angels in the heart of Heavenstone? Perhaps they might know the source of the wings and ease my troubled mind?"

"Do you not trust me to speak to them myself?" Marius asked. His look jammed a stake of ice into Liam's heart. This wasn't a question. This was a threat.

"I trust you above all," Liam said. "I was unsure if you would have the time, given the state of the war."

The Speaker didn't buy it for a second. Liam stood there, arms crossed behind him, waiting for the ax to fall. He'd crossed a line. Damn idiot. Must his faith be so weak he would question the Speaker to his very face?

"The next time I speak with them, I will ask about your son's wings," Marius said. "But I assure you, they will give me the same answer I gave you: the shadowborn is a deceiver. Sometimes you don't need darkness to disguise the truth. You only need a light most blinding."

The platform started its descent. Marius settled into the gilded chair, his head resting back against the cushions.

"Leave me," he ordered. "Tend to your prayers, knight. I have no more patience for your weak heart. With war at hand we can only survive by the strength of the faithful. All else must be cast aside."

Liam bowed low. His golden wings flared with light, and like a shot he soared east. He left exactly as he came, with heart troubled, mind doubting, and certain of but one thing: the Speaker hid too many truths behind those sapphire eyes.

CHAPTER 25

Kael paced before the door inside Clara's room. The young woman lay on her bed, hands underneath her head as she watched him. She wore the black pants of their Seraphim uniform, her blouse a dark blue. It was still the brightest color he'd seen her wear since her father's death.

"You don't have to be so nervous," she said. "The meeting with my mother will go fine."

"And if it doesn't?" Kael asked. "I could make a complete fool of myself. Probably will. What if she thinks I'm insane and bans me from ever seeing you again?" He shook his head. "Forget it. It's not worth it."

Clara rolled her eyes as she rocked to a sit and then hopped off the bed.

"Kael. Stop. Nervousness is making you stupid. The Archoness will listen, and she won't mock or banish you, all right? This is what L'fae asked for you to do, and this won't even be the first time. You convinced Archon Evereth, right? I assure you, his mind was far more closed than my mother's will be."

She grabbed his hand and tugged as she opened the door with the other.

"Now come on," she said. "Stalling will only make you worse."

The two walked the hall to the throne room. Avila was inside, surrounded with advisors. A long line of people waited to meet her. Kael recognized the more fanciful outfits of the traders. In some ways they'd done well; the increased scarcity had raised prices, but at the same time, bringing in new goods from the other islands had grown all but impossible. If trade didn't reopen soon, their brief boon would end and the people would have to do without. He guessed several others to be mayors of smaller towns, and at least one to be a representative of the small population of Galen refugees, once again forced to relocate after New Galen's complete destruction by Center's cannons. The only face he recognized for certain was of Rebecca Waller, calmly jotting down notes on a board a half step behind the Archoness.

"I guess we should get in line?" Kael whispered.

Clara looked at him like he was insane.

"I'm the Archoness's daughter," she said. "We aren't waiting in line."

Clara took his hand and led the two of them to the front of the line. Kael's neck blushed as he caught several of the traders glaring and muttering to themselves. Avila was discussing something with one of the advisors, the older man writing down occasional marks on a scratchboard. The next petitioner was about to step forward and receive attention. Clara stepped ahead of her, and she gave the elderly woman a cursory nod.

"Forgive me, but this is of great importance," Clara said.

"Of course," the woman said, words polite but tone icier

than anything Kael could produce from his gauntlet. "We'd never interfere with the lovely young Willer's daughter."

Avila finished her discussion. A curious look overcame her as she realized who waited next. The Archoness beckoned them closer.

"Is something the matter, daughter?" she asked.

Clara jammed an unseen elbow into his side. Kael cleared his throat and took another step forward.

"Actually, this is a matter I wish to speak with you about," he said. "Privately. It involves the theotechs."

A bit of her curiosity faded into caution. The Archoness beckoned to the other petitioners.

"Please give your names to the soldiers so they may mark your place in line. I need a moment to rest and prepare before addressing more needs."

Not a soul looked happy about it but none dared voice their displeasure too loudly. Kael guessed they'd do that when safely away from the mansion's soldiers. One by one they filed out, until it was just Kael and Clara standing before her throne. Avila politely ordered the other advisors away, out various doors on either side.

"Well, we are alone now," Avila said. She stood from her chair and smoothed out the wrinkles in her gray dress. "What is so important that you must interrupt state matters?"

Kael took in a deep breath. He had to be confident. He had to sound like he knew what he was doing. Too much was at stake.

"I know you're prepping our Seraphim for an attack on Center," Kael blurted out. He took a moment to compose himself, slow down his speech. "I've come to argue against it."

"Is there something the matter with the invasion plans?" Avila asked.

"Not with the plans," Kael said. "Just the concept. We need to end this war, now, or we'll all be dead."

Beside her throne was a small silver table covered with a blue cloth. Three glasses rest atop it, two with water, one with wine. Avila took the wine and sipped at it as she dragged out the time between the question and her response.

"Center's soldiers and machines killed thousands of our civilians. If Marius is not our true threat, pray tell me, who is?"

Kael took Clara's hand, and he squeezed it for comfort.

"L'adim is," he said.

Avila tilted her head.

"Who?"

Good start.

"The shadowborn," Kael said. "The great betrayer that led the demons against the old world. He is the one who broke the dome that protected us and sent the fireborn raining down from the skies."

Another long sip of wine.

"Even if this were true, we are safe in the skies. No demon may reach us, and should any try, we'll crush them like we've crushed all our other foes."

"Not if we're too busy killing each other," Kael insisted. "L'adim is yet to show himself. Our armies are all weakened, and an invasion against Center will drain even more of our elements and diminish our numbers further. We've got to stop this, Archoness. Center's been bruised and humiliated. Now is the perfect time for peace so we may prepare ourselves for the real danger."

Avila returned to her chair, and it seemed her spine was more rigid, her expression colder as she took her seat.

"I have heard of you making similar claims during your visit to Candren," she said. "We have already suffered greatly under Center's religious zealotry. It disappoints me to see you prone to similar doomsaying."

"I speak the truth," Kael said, feeling his opportunity slipping away.

"As do I," Avila said. "Weshern shall have both freedom and vengeance. I will not bow the knee to my husband's murderer and ask for peace. Marius will bow to me, and when he does, I will be holding a sword."

Her mind appeared set, which meant only one option remained. Clara squeezed his hand again, understanding the same.

"Do it, Kael," she said.

Kael let her go and approached the Archoness.

"You do not know the absolute horror we face," he said. "But I can show you, if you will trust me."

Avila looked to her daughter.

"Please," Clara said. "He's earned this at least."

"So be it. What would you have me do?"

"Summon a guard."

Beside her chair were multiple hanging ropes, and the Archoness pulled the one on the left. Immediately a door on the same side opened, two guards marching in with shields and spears. Avila gestured to Kael, turning their attention his way.

"I need one of you to cut my hand," he said.

Likely not what the guards expected, but they neither hesitated nor questioned it. One approached, his grip on the spear shifting so he could hold it steady.

"Just a tiny bit," Kael added, worried the guard would show a little too much enthusiasm. He held up his palm. The guard put the spear's tip into the center of the palm and then dragged it across the skin.

"Will that suffice?"

Kael clenched his teeth against the pain. Blood pooled on his skin.

"Yes."

The guards turned to Avila, bowed low when dismissed, and then left the room.

"Now what is it we gain by having you bleed upon my carpet?" Avila asked when they were gone.

"You'll see," Kael said. He offered her his hand. "Touch the blood with your fingers and do not let go."

Avila frowned, and she cast another glance at her daughter. Clara stood perfectly still, arms crossed behind her, as if Kael's request were the most natural thing in the world. Kael could imagine the thoughts going through the Archoness's mind. *Maybe that Skyborn boy you like isn't quite right in the head.*

Letting out the softest of sighs, Avila removed one of her long gloves and set it on the arm of her chair. She stepped closer, eyeing the blood, the fingers of her bare hand rubbing together. Kael said nothing, only waited. Hesitation past, Avila gently dipped a single finger into Kael's bloody palm. Kael closed his eyes, his heart racing despite his best attempts to remain confident. He was growing stronger, he knew that. His control increased with every attempt. Just like his sister, Kael was learning the true power lurking within his eternal-born heritage.

"Close your eyes," Kael told her. "Try to keep your mind blank. Look at only darkness. Focus on nothing but my words."

As he spoke, Kael conjured up images of his own. They weren't naturally his, which was the biggest reason for his hesitance. This was a vision granted by L'fae. Kael remembered the moment of Ascension, the armies of demons crashing against humanity's final refuge. Most of all, he conjured the memory of the shadowborn's arrival.

And then he gave it to her.

"Open your eyes."

Kael saw as she saw. He no longer felt her finger touching his palm. The sounds of battle overwhelmed him. He and Avila were one, together experiencing L'fae's sadness and terror as she watched the crawling shadow swarm through the legions. Lives ended by the thousands, flesh ripped apart, bodies burned and shattered. Fear pounded in their breasts. Sorrow weakened their minds. Pain pulsed from the many tubes piercing flesh to drain away the needed blood for the great Ascension. Kael felt the image starting to distort and weaken, the toll even greater on his body than revealing his own memories. He kept strong, focusing on the terrible rage of the shadowborn and his tremendous power. Even as the islands rose, they heard his sickening voice echo in their minds.

You suffer for nothing, my brethren. Humanity will reach its end, even if I must wait centuries...

Kael pulled away his hand, ending the vision. Avila gasped in air as if she'd been holding her breath all the while. Her balance teetered, Clara rushing to her side to hold her steady. Kael hardly felt any better.

"That monster at the end," Avila asked. "The one commanding the demons. Was that L'adim?"

"It was."

The Archoness straightened herself and pulled away from her daughter. She stammered a moment, trying to find a way to properly phrase her next question.

"And who... whose body were we? Whose eyes did we look out from? It was surely not human."

"That was L'fae," Kael said. "The lightborn whose power keeps our island afloat."

Avila looked overwhelmed by the information but she took it in admirable stride. Her gaze was frighteningly focused. The anger in her eyes had no equal.

"Is there more you can show me?" she asked. "I would know what this L'fae knows."

"I don't have the strength," Kael said. "But you can meet her for yourself. Come with me to the Crystal Cathedral. Not even Johan Lumens can refuse you entrance."

It looked like nothing in the world could stop Avila from accomplishing exactly that. She returned to her chair and pulled the center rope, sounding a deep, resonating bell.

"Fetch me a Seraphim escort," she said as the doors opened and soldiers flooded in. She addressed one in particular who bore the mark of a guard captain. "And send a squad of soldiers immediately to the Crystal Cathedral. I would have them arrive shortly after we do."

The guard bowed low and then rushed off to deliver the orders. The Archoness turned back to the duo, a bit of life sparkling in her tired green eyes.

"Go don your wings," she told them. "We leave at once. If what you showed me was true, then you may have spared our entire island from a tragic mistake."

Avila refused a platform, instead opting to be carried by a Seraphim. Clara and Kael led the way, an older Seraph carrying Avila in his arms, Olivia at his side. The town came and went beneath them, turning to grasslands as the Crystal Cathedral neared. The stone road was barren, all worship and visitation canceled since the theotech's expulsion. All for the best. A dozen soldiers marched down the road a mile behind them, ready should the Archoness need them after meeting with L'fae. No need for prying eyes that might alert Johan to their plan.

The hairs on Kael's neck stood on end as the cathedral came into view. The glass ceiling was broken, and Kael winced with remembered pain. He'd been the one to help break it, barreling through wings-first. The wide wooden doors, smashed open during the siege, were now blocked by three men dressed in Johan's brown disciple robes.

Kael felt a tap on his arm. He turned, saw Clara gesturing behind her, and stretched his neck further. Olivia was signaling for them to slow. Kael pulled the throttle back by a third. The new Seraphim leader left the Archoness behind and joined the two of them, taking hold of Kael's wrist to keep them both steady.

"Ignore the doors!" she shouted. "Land inside."

Kael returned his attention to the disciples, a grin cracking across his face as he imagined their sudden panic. There'd be no arguing, no posturing, no questioning of authority here. Four Seraphim and the Archoness of Weshern. Let them try to stop them.

Olivia fell back, Clara taking lead. One by one they flew through the broken ceiling and to the carpeted floor strewn with broken pews and thick shards of glass. Disciples of Johan rushed in from the doors crying out for them to wait or halt, as if they'd listen. Kael landed in front of the door leading down into the sublevels of the cathedral, between it and the disciples, blocking access. The younger men fumed with impotent anger.

"This area is restricted," one had the courage to yell. "For the safety of Weshern, all access—"

"*I* decide what is best for the safety of my island," Avila interrupted. "Or would you dare tell me that Johan commands greater authority than the Archoness?"

Kael joined the others in arming the prism of his right gauntlet. Soft blue lights shone on the disciples. They looked to one another, sweat glistening on their foreheads.

"Of course not," the protester said. "But below are the machines that keep us afloat. Should you damage something through carelessness we may all plummet to the Endless Ocean."

"Don't you worry," Kael told them with a mischievous grin. "I've been down there before."

He checked the door and found it locked.

"Entrance is barred from the inside," the disciples informed them. "We open only for Johan."

Olivia looked ready to strike the three of them down with her lightning, practically begging the Archoness for permission with her eyes.

"Can you get us inside?" Avila asked.

"Don't worry," Kael said, smiling despite the sudden pang of loss. "Chernor showed me how to knock."

He spread his palm and braced his wrist with his other hand. The ends of his fingers curled inward slightly as he imagined the anticipated attack. A thick boulder of ice blasted out with tremendous force. The door crumpled without offering resistance and the boulder rolled on to the far end of the hallway before stopping.

The older Seraph stepped close to Avila and dropped his voice to a whisper.

"I'll keep an eye on them," he said, nodding his head toward the three disciples.

"Do we have reason to worry?" the Archoness asked.

"I'm not sure, but I'd rather not risk it. They give me bad feelings every time I look at them."

Avila acquiesced. Matter settled, Kael led the way into the halls below the cathedral. They were lit by the soft glow of light elemental prisms wedged into the ceiling in evenly spaced sockets. Clara and her mother followed, with Olivia taking up the rear. The older Seraph stayed back, arms crossed as he guarded the doors down.

The four slipped around the corner past Kael's boulder of ice. Kael's pulse increased with every step. He'd met two lightborn in his life, and both had been awe-inspiring. Part of him felt more nervous than the others with him. They didn't understand what they were to meet, not really. Not until the light fell upon you and the psychic emanations washed over your body with naked emotion could you truly grasp the comforting, yet alien, presence.

They passed the rooms that had been used to house knights when the theotechs still controlled the cathedral. Most doors were open, the insides tossed and looted. Kael slowed as he approached the next turn. His pulse pounding in his neck, coupled with a sudden certainty he'd made a mistake. If the secret doors were to open only for Johan . . . then where were the disciples guarding the halls?

Kael turned, meaning only to warn Olivia to keep an eye out behind them, but then felt his heart halt as the doors to two rooms silently swung open.

"Behind!" Kael shouted, gauntlet snapping up. Olivia dove, dragging Avila with her to the ground. Clara whirled, legs braced as she brought her gauntlet to bear. Four disciples rushed from the opened doors, the front two wielding swords, the back two holding bows. Arrows loosed, one sailing down the hallway, the other plinking off the wings of Olivia's harness.

Kael retaliated with arrows of his own, razor-sharp projectiles of ice tearing into the chest of the leftmost archer. He turned his aim to the other, trusting Clara to handle the nearer two.

Clara dropped to one knee, her right palm pressing to the ground. A wave of ice rolled out, coating the floor. The disciples slipped on their approach but kept charging forward. Even as they stumbled and slid, they lashed out at Clara with their swords. Kael took the opening to fire a single ball of ice down the hall and into the other archer's face. The bow dropped, the strung arrow springing harmlessly against the wall.

Clara slid back another foot and then rolled as the archer fell. Her hand touched ground, blue light flared, and then a solid wall of ice rose up from ground to floor, sealing the disciples away on the other side. Metal plinked against the other side, then quieted.

"They'll escape," Olivia said, jumping to her feet. Lightning shimmered across her palm. "Clara, drop it, now!"

Clara rolled to her ice wall and pushed her hand against it so the firing prism made contact. The ice broke on her command, shattering into a fine mist to reveal the other two disciples sprinting down the hall toward the broken door. Electricity swirled into a beam from Olivia's gauntlet. It thundered down the hall with a deafening clap, striking both of them down.

Ringing filled Kael's ears in the ensuing silence. Avila accepted Clara's hand, and together they stood over the bodies of the disciples.

"Johan has much to answer for," the Archoness said. "Did he plan to hold the cathedral as a blade above my neck?"

"We won't know until we ask him," Kael said.

"Trust me," Avila said, taking lead. "We will. About a great many things."

They crossed the final stretch to L'fae's chamber. The grand double doors loomed above them. Golden writing danced across the doors, pulling Kael back in time to when he first laid eyes on their design during his frantic rescue of his sister. He never could have guessed the wonders waiting within, nor the connection to his blood that L'fae had sensed the moment he stepped inside.

"Ready?" he asked.

Avila stood with shoulders back and head held high. She'd seen the vision, and she looked ready to meet L'fae as if she were a diplomat of another island. Clara looked far more eager, having heard Kael's tales but not seen a lightborn for herself. Only Olivia appeared afraid.

"Whatever lies beyond that door is not of our world but of heaven and hell," she said. "I can feel it. Must we enter?"

Her hands were trembling. Kael could hardly believe it. The woman was unflappable during battle, so why was she frightened now? He turned back to the door, frowning as he put a hand upon it. L'fae's presence dripped through, faint waves like light fading from a distant campfire. It reeked of sorrow and despair.

"Something's wrong," Kael said. He grabbed the handle and pulled it with all his might. The right door cracked open and shuddered as it moved wider. Kael ran inside, the other three following with slow, worshipful steps.

L'fae hovered in the center of the room, her light dimmer than he'd ever seen. Her golden eyes were downcast, her hands limp above her in their chains. Liquid light pulsed out of her through the tubes, and it seemed to move slower than Kael remembered. His footfalls prompted her eyes to meet his, and he felt her shock reverberate through his every bone.

"L'adim!" the lightborn cried. She flung her body toward Kael, towering over him as the chains rattled and groaned. Whatever fading of her color ended with a sudden flourish of blinding white light across her skin. Her cry was a desperate shriek contained within his skull. "Where is L'adim?"

Kael glanced to the others, baffled. Clara and Avila stood with mouths agape. Olivia knelt beside them, head bowed low in respect.

"L'adim?" he asked. "I don't understand."

L'fae stretched her hand as far as the chained allowed.

"The shadowborn is here, Skyborn. See his face."

The lightborn's memory entered his mind, but this was not comfortable like the other times. This felt like an assault, the image hurriedly slammed over his eyes and consciousness. The others let out similar gasps, all four sharing the same sight.

He hung from the ceiling, chains supporting his weight as blood poured out of him at a steady rate. The grand doors cracked open and a man entered. No fear filled his chest, not yet. Just curiosity.

"Another stranger come to visit?" he asked.

"Not a stranger," this newcomer said as the light fell across his face. "Hello, L'fae."

Kael felt his body lean closer. He knew that face. He knew that voice. Johan pulled back his hood as he smiled. The shimmering lightborn essence washed over him, but instead of illuminating it burned away flesh, peeling it like the skin of a fruit to reveal swirling shadow of rottenness beneath.

"L'adim?" Kael heard himself cry without lips and lungs but instead with a psychic shriek of horror. That horror remained as the memory tore back out of him, returning him to the chamber deep beneath the Crystal Cathedral.

"Johan," he gasped as he fell to his knees. "Johan is the shadowborn."

"That is but one name and face of many," L'fae said. "He came to gloat of his success. Ch'thon . . . he slew Ch'thon to kill everyone on Galen. And he's not done. He will not be done until the last human soul is extinguished. Please, if you come to me, then tell me you have defeated him."

"No," Avila said, the first to recover her strength. "We have not defeated him, but we know his face. My army will put an end to him and his disciples." She spread her arms wide and bowed in respect. "Please forgive me, angel of the heavens. I must start at once, before the fiend does any more damage. I will return, though, I promise. I am Archoness Willer, and I will not rule without hearing the words of the one who suffers in our stead."

Kael had to scramble to catch up with Avila. The other two stayed behind, and he heard Clara asking the lightborn a question.

"Wait," he cried to the Archoness. "What will you do?"

"I will put a bounty on Johan's head," Avila said. "Every soldier and Seraph at my disposal will scour Weshern until he's found."

"But you heard L'fae," Kael insisted. "Johan's just one of his faces. If he finds out we're searching for him, he'll take the appearance of another, one we've never seen. There will be no capturing him then."

Avila stopped, and he heard her sigh.

"You are correct," she said. "We must bring him in unsuspecting."

"Arrest the three disciples here and request a meeting with Johan from one of the disciples back at the mansion," Kael said. "Put him right where we want him for an ambush."

"The threat of the shadowborn, the threat you showed me... might we stop it then and there?"

"I don't know," Kael said. "But I pray it does."

"Then fetch the others," she said. "We'll end that monstrous shadow forever, bleeding and burning him out on my mansion floor."

CHAPTER 26

Bree lurked behind the long red curtain, her hands on the hilts of her swords. Fire raged within both blood and breast as her mind worked around the sudden revelation. Her brother crouched next to her, their silver Seraphim wings touching.

I spoke with L'fae, he'd told her. *Johan is the shadowborn. He came to her, and she showed me. L'adim. He's right here.*

Every memory of Johan, every word spoken between them flushed her mind. She remembered her unease about him, the fervor in his eyes as he spoke of his hatred for Center. Was she really so blind? Could they all have been so foolish?

He fooled the old world, she told herself in a futile attempt to comfort herself. *Don't be surprised he fooled you.*

The doors creaked open. Terror stabbed Bree in the stomach. Was he here? Was this it? She clutched her hilts and closed her eyes, fighting to keep her hands still. She couldn't make a sound. Couldn't risk being heard in hiding…

Kael's hand settled atop hers. His smile eased her calm.

We got this, he mouthed, then gave her a smug grin.

I hope so, she mouthed back.

Johan was a shadow, an unknown demigod from a time long lost to the living. She didn't know what to expect, only knew that an entire world had collapsed failing to defeat him. Perhaps foolish pride allowed her to think they might defeat him now, but what other choice did they have?

More creaking came from the main entrance. Bree glanced to either side. A dozen Seraphim hid among the curtains or behind doors, all waiting for Avila's signal. Some looked frightened, others eager, most furious. What little respect Johan had earned for his aid against Center had been washed away by utter betrayal.

"My Archoness," a voice spoke from the entrance. Bree tightened her muscles, sensing the soldier's nervousness. "Johan is here."

Avila sat on her throne, Rebecca Waller at her side. Bree could see a small portion of the raised dais if she peered from around the curtain. Nothing of the Archoness, but Rebecca restlessly shifted her weight from foot to foot.

"Send him in," Avila said. Bree's pride in their ruler increased. Avila's order sounded perfectly normal, if not a bit bored.

"As you wish."

The door shut. Bree flexed her fingers. They'd been waiting for what felt like an hour, and her muscles had started to tighten. She needed to be ready. Whenever the battle started, it would be sudden.

The door reopened, and it felt like it sucked all the air out of the room. Bree couldn't see him past the curtain, but she could imagine Johan strolling in through those doors with a little smile on his face. His robes would be immaculate, his hood pulled over his scarred face. Always walking as if he owned the place he inhabited.

"My dear Archoness, I am honored as always," he said. The proximity nearly made Bree jump. They were positioned near the middle of the room, and what seemed like plenty of distance during setup now seemed a painfully small gap between hunter and prey. "Your messenger spoke of preparing plans for Center's invasion, and I would gladly offer any assistance you require."

The doors shut again. Unknown to Johan, they would be locked and barred from the outside. The trap was almost set.

"You have been a valuable asset in our fight for freedom," Avila said. "Though I would question how much has been to serve your own goals."

"My goal is a free people," Johan said, nonplussed by the mild accusation. "Though my anger at Center does contain some measure of personal revenge. I assure you it will not cloud my judgment, nor affect my advice as we prepare for the coming siege."

Such soothing words. Denying nothing, yet promising any stated fear as unfounded. How many times had he fooled them in such a way? How many of his disciples knew the truth of their prophet? And even if they knew, would they care, or would the desire to punish Center override their disgust?

"And what would you have me accomplish during our invasion?" she asked. "What measures would you suggest I take?"

"You ask how far I think you should go for victory?"

Avila did not answer verbally, but Bree expected she nodded, allowing Johan to continue.

"In this conflict we are the righteous," he continued. "Which means the unrighteous must be fought to the very bitter end. Accept no surrender until that surrender is complete. No power must remain in the theotechs' hands. To ensure our freedom we must break the hands of the slave master and cast away his chains so they may never be used again."

"Even if it sends Center to the Ocean?"

A soft chuckle from Johan.

"A dark thought, Archoness, but there would be a dire irony to the act. They sent Galen crashing beneath the waves. Perhaps letting her people experience the same terror would be poetic justice."

Bree heard Avila rise from her chair. When she next spoke, her voice was hard, all semblance of politeness vanished in an instant.

"I'm sure you'd like that," she said. "Wouldn't you, L'adim?"

That was the signal. Kael and Bree armed their gauntlets, drew their swords, and stepped from behind the curtain.

Johan stood at a respectful distance from Avila, halfway down the hall. His hands rested at his sides, and he showed no care or fear as Seraphim emerged from curtains with their wings shimmering. More entered from doors behind the throne. Four Seraphs rose into the air and positioned themselves in a square above Johan's head. No one said a word through it all, not even Johan or Avila. Bree thought he'd be angry, dismissive, or even deny the accusation.

Instead, Johan laughed.

"I see one of you was finally smart enough to visit L'fae," he said. "Truth be told, this ruse went on far longer than I anticipated, and certainly far longer than I needed. I have already achieved victory, Archoness. This cute little ambush changes nothing."

"Your influence is at an end," Avila said as Olivia stepped protectively before her. "After centuries of ruin, you will finally pay for your sins."

That removed the smile from Johan's face. His head lowered, his eyes narrowed.

"My sins?" he said. "What is sin, but an act against God? I tell you, I have committed no sins, for there is no God to sin against. No, it is you who will pay for the crimes committed, of your ancestors, and your priests, and your gods. All of your race but you wretched few are bones and ash hidden beneath fields and stone. You are the last splinter of a tree I burned down centuries ago, a tiny bit of grit I have not yet swallowed. Stand tall and proud, but you are a lone piece of fruit on a dead tree loudly proclaiming greatness to the ravens."

"Enough," Avila said. "Seraphim . . ."

Bree tensed for the order to attack given, but the Archoness froze as Johan looked up. His robes were gone, folded into his body to become a sharp blue vest. Hair tumbled into existence. He sneered, an ugly look on a handsome face.

"I watched you cry as I died," this phantom resemblance of Isaac Willer said. "You were right to cry. The meat of my body broke down. My blood spilled out and my breath ended. I'm nowhere now. No heaven. No soul. Empty nothingness. Your memories are all that's left of me, did you know that, Avila? Your faded, jumbled memories are all I am, and they too will die. Do you know why, my precious wife?"

Tears trickled down Avila's face. She looked mesmerized by Johan's words despite recoiling against each one as if it were a lash across her back.

"Why?" she asked softly.

Isaac reshaped back into Johan, who seethed with pleasant rage.

"Because despite your every insistence, from the very first moment you draw in a wailing breath to the very last death rattle, you are not special. You are not elevated above all creation.

You are animals among animals, only unlike the snake and the rat and the pig, you have convinced yourself of a far greater purpose."

He spun, this time addressing the gathered Seraphim under the guise of Argus Summers.

"The prisms that allow you to wield fire, ice, storm, and stone come from the blood of my fellow eternal-born," he told them. "Daily you chain them to steel tables and bleed them of their power to make yourself weapons and tools and trinkets. Would you submit a human to such a torture? Would you look upon your children bound in chains and bleeding from slit wrists and declare it a mere requirement of civilization? Or would you *rage*?"

He turned to Bree and Kael, his face shifting again, a liquid shadow reassuming new form. Bree felt her heart ache as her own mother now stood before her.

"I once tried for peace," the living lie said. "I begged humanity to reconsider. Let us free these creatures and elevate humanity not through their blood, but through their uniqueness and wisdom, through the building of a new society here on this earth between the eternal-born and the mortal. I said this with tears in my eyes. I said this to my fellow lightborn, who claimed to speak the very heart of God. And do you know what they said?"

Now he was Marius Prakt, only his teeth, nails, and eyes were made of gold.

"We are their angels!" he roared, his sudden thunderous voice startling many. "We are their protectors! They compared our own brethren to deer and cattle, and you as their masters. You, you mortal fools stealing from your betters to pretend to be equals. You selfish wretches, who would destroy the world before giving up a feather's weight of power to your neighbor.

Despite all evidence proving you flawed, destructive, hateful beings, we pretended you were something holy."

Bree felt unease prickling at her spine. Something was wrong. Johan appeared to be almost... glowing. No, not glowing. The rest of the room was darkening. A sensation swept across her akin to being in the presence of the lightborn, only this wasn't comforting or healing. This was sickness. This was horror. Her stomach recoiled, and she was but one of many who suddenly vomited upon the carpet. Johan returned to his original form and stood with his head high and his hands spread wide, his smile one of purest calm and satisfaction.

"I will slaughter humanity down to the very last child," he said. "And when that final life dies in my hand, I will know that you were animals. If you were creations of God, he cared not for your existence, nor your survival. You weren't special. You weren't blessed. You weren't beloved. You were meat and blood and bone, and all of it will rot."

A thin shadow, like a wisp of smoke, floated out from him in all directions. It passed across Bree like an illness, sapping strength from her limbs and flooding her mind with revolting thoughts. Avila staggered away, clutching her chest as if she'd been stabbed.

"Kill him," she said. It wasn't the triumphant order she'd no doubt envisioned. It wasn't even angry or disgusted. The Archoness was terrified.

Johan exploded into action before the first element shot his way. Ice broke against the floor, thick shards chasing a half second behind him as he dashed toward the nearest Seraph. Bree summoned fire across her swords, fearing the damage she might do if she unleashed a spray inside the cramped quarters. The Seraph flung his arm up and flooded the air before him with lightning. It crackled and sparked like a spider's web, not moving, only waiting to entrap.

But Johan had no desire to reach the terrified Seraph. He stopped just shy of the lightning, spun on his heels, and then lashed his hand in a wave at the four Seraphs flying overhead. Shadow rolled off his fingers, becoming a thin blade of darkness. The Seraphs could only rely on their elements to defend with such little room to maneuver, summoning small walls of flame and ice.

The shadow ripped through them like cloth. Men and women screamed. Bodies fell. The Seraph before Johan abandoned his lightning wall as he pulled back his arm for another blast. It soared just shy of Johan's dodge and elicited a cry of shock from Bree as the bolt sundered the wall directly above her head.

"We have to get in closer," Kael said, lifting up his shield. Bree nodding in agreement.

"I'll lead."

Johan leapt upon the closest Seraph, tearing into him with hands that now resembled bladed claws. Pale smoke built at his feet, like the first smoldering hints of a wildfire. The other Seraphs blanketed the area with ice, lightning, and flame as the dying man screamed. Johan used the body of his victim to block the initial attacks. The rest he dodged, moving with speed far beyond human capabilities. The carpet ripped and burned, the walls cracking with each errant shot.

"Get the Archoness out of here!" Olivia shouted, putting herself between Avila and the suddenly charging Johan.

Bree crossed the blistering madhouse of chaos that was the holy mansion's throne room. It seemed no Seraph could draw a bead on Johan, his dodges too erratic, his speed inhuman. Kael used his ice to form a wall separating Johan from Avila, hoping to give her time as a Seraph rushed her to one of the hidden exits. Johan paused before the wall as the Seraphim penned him in.

"Which of you is brave enough to seek the kill?" Johan asked. "Will it be you, Phoenix?"

"It's over, Johan," Olivia said, standing atop the ice wall Kael had formed. "At least die with dignity."

"The only thing over is this game," Johan said, the cloud of shadow at his feet sucking in momentarily before exploding outward in a wide sphere that swept across the entire room. Bree braced herself at its approach, too surprised and confused to react. Not so her brother. Kael dashed in front of her, his shield raised up and shining bright against the incoming darkness. The haze parted around them, but the others were not so lucky.

Olivia moaned as she collapsed atop the ice wall. Several others stumbled away, their bodies ramming walls as their wings flew them unguided. Others shivered and screamed with unrestrained terror, their eyes glazed over with a white fog. Only Kael and Bree remained standing as the cloud rolled back, dripping into Johan's feet like a stream flowing into a lake.

"You Skyborn twins are such stubborn survivors," he said. He walked to the nearest crippled Seraph. Bree's heart skipped a beat when she realized who it was. Johan seemed unbothered by Kael's shield or Bree's fiery swords, his attention focused on poor Amanda. "I know not whether to commend you or mock you for it."

"I don't care for either," Kael said, ice flashing from his palm. Johan dodged the shards of ice, ducking beneath one, sidestepping a second, and rolling his shoulder beneath a third. Each time it seemed the bones of his body moved faster than his skin, the liquid facsimile of flesh and hair and robes flowing after. His smile, however, always remained in place.

"You have no idea the talent I faced when I ripped apart the old world," he said. A spear grew from his palm. Kael shouted, a larger sphere of ice flying from his palm for Johan's center mass. Johan batted it aside with one hand. Frost and smoke exploded around him, causing no harm. The other plunged the spear downward, straight into Amanda's heart.

Bree screamed. She blasted her fire at Johan, setting the wall and ceiling aflame. Johan dropped into a roll, dodging the initial burst and then cutting through the fire to emerge on the other side. Her lungs burned as she gasped for air, her prism temporarily drained. Despite a few black marks upon his skin, marks that quickly healed away, Johan appeared unharmed.

"I fought Seraphim of such skill that your best and brightest are mere children compared to them," he said. "The world warred without ceasing back then, allowing the gifted in slaughter to rise up and be named heroes. Even those broke before me, as will you."

He was close now, so close. Bree contemplated releasing a second burst of flame but decided against it. She was already tired. A second release would leave her drained, and she feared how Johan might take advantage of her weakened state. Kael sprayed another wave of ice shards, more to slow Johan than anything, and then lifted his shield. The light shone across Johan's face, peeled back skin to reveal undulating shadow.

"Do you think you've found yourself a weapon?" the monster asked. "Come then. Try to use it."

Kael's shield shone its brightest as he charged the shadowborn. Bree followed without hesitation. Her brother would not fight alone, not now, not ever. Johan crossed his arms before his face, his robes fluttering away, the whites of his eyes thickening to bury the irises. It seemed he would meet Kael strength to strength. The shield crackled.

Johan smiled.

Shadow rose up from the floor the moment Kael passed over it, faint, ethereal ghost hands latching on to her brother's limbs. He halted in place mere inches away. The light seared into Johan, banishing any hint of his disguise. Bree swung at them with her swords in hopes of freeing Kael, but her weapons did nothing to the formless creations performing the shadowborn's bidding.

"The gift of your blood is incredible," Johan said. A single finger pressed against the top of the shield, pushing it down. "And wasted."

His other hand struck Kael square in the chest. He let out a garbled cry as he flew through the air, the light of his shield fading out as it left his grasp. Bree screamed his name, but she could not dare look to see how he fared. Johan was far too close, his smile far too pleased as his flesh and robes returned.

"Little Phoenix, I did not lie when I spoke admirably of all you have done," he said. His fingers extended from his hands, thinning into bone-white claws when the pale flesh receded. "But the pebbles of the noble few are nothing compared to the mountain of evils that is your race. I will mourn your passing, but I will not spare you."

He slashed for her face. Bree blocked, her swords nearly wrenching out of her hands at the shocking power of the impact. Despite Johan's thin frame, he wielded strength more akin to a man like Chernor. Fire licked his boney claws, darkening them. He cut twice more, and this time Bree dared not attempt to block. She parried what she could not dodge and fell back with nearly every step. Each parry felt like she was forcing a falling tree to veer along a different path. Twice she attempted a counter, but his speed dwarfed her own.

"Mighty Phoenix," Johan said. Wisps of shadow rolled off

him, his aura growing stronger. Bree's mind twisted and fought against the despair seeping into her. "Hope of Weshern. Will you not defend your people?"

He was mocking her. Playing with her. Their entire ambush was nothing more than an amusement to the vile being. His every sentence was punctuated with another slash she would keep away by the slimmest of margins.

"Where is your rage?" he asked, hammering both claws down at her. Bree had no choice but to block. Her knees and elbows shook at the impact.

"Where is your *fire*?"

Three claws sliced across her arm, easily parting the fabric of her coat to cut the flesh beneath. Blood sprayed across the floor as Bree screamed in pain. Johan immediately followed up with another cut, this one across her chest. The buckle to her harness cut loose, her wings collapsed to one side, her shirt ripped open. Blood flowed from a trio of cuts from her collarbone to her waist. Bree dropped to one knee, gasping in hurried breaths as she fought against the shock. More blood spilled with every heartbeat, staining the carpet crimson.

A sharp edge pressed underneath Bree's chin, gently guiding her upward. She moved slowly, meeting Johan eye to eye as she rose to her feet. The shadowborn was toying with her. His smile relished her vulnerability. She dropped both of her swords to the floor. A mouse in a cat's paw. A dangling piece of meat before a hungry lion. Johan soaked in every bit of her fear, feeding on it like the demon of hell he was. The edge cut in deeper, a fresh stream of blood trickling down her neck.

"You want my fire?" Bree asked through the pain and tears. "Then take it."

He stood in a pool of her own blood. Scarlet drops covered

his claws. Little rivulets trickled down his wrists. With but a thought, she set it all aflame.

Johan cried out, whether from surprise or pain, she didn't know. The great gout of flame billowed up from his feet, setting his entire lower body aflame. Bree swung her right hand forward and spread her fingers wide. All she had within her, she released. Regardless of how much blood she had already lost, she would drain the prism dry. Her fire washed over Johan's upper body, eliciting a monstrous scream. He turned away from her, clutching at his seared face. His body trembled, and his robes became something not quite solid. Bree grabbed one of her swords off the floor and rushed for the kill.

He spun just before she thrust.

"Please, don't!"

Kael's face, tears in his eyes. Bree hesitated, not long, not even for a full heartbeat, but it was enough. He pointed toward her, his eyes vibrant orbs of white. The entire room darkened. Invisible claws pulled at Bree's arms and legs. Johan's aura was absolute, a pool of emptiness and abandonment drowning her, suffocating her. She couldn't move. She couldn't breathe. Johan stepped closer. The skin on his hand peeled back to reveal shadow, which peeled back again to reveal another hand, this one small and frail and paler than marble. Bree tried to move but could not. She tried to scream but could not.

The thin, shriveled fingertip, like a bone covered with thin burlap cloth, brushed her cheek in a loving gesture. Only her paralysis held in her scream. Her skin crackled and blackened, dying at his very touch.

"Again you impress," he whispered. "Perhaps I will let a few of you live on, nurtured under my care. The blood of the eternal-born might yet elevate your existence. What might you become without your gods and scriptures, and instead my touch to guide you?"

Tears trickled down Bree's paralyzed face. She sensed the rest of Johan's image loosening. The shadow was peeling back from his hand, his arm, and his face, the enveloping darkness giving way to the truth that lay beneath. Never before had she so desperately wished to leave her body and fly far, far away. That singular stroke of bone-flesh across her cheek left her blood chilled and her innards twisted into knots.

"Get away from her, you goddamn lunatic!"

Kael barreled in, his shield a shining white missile. Bree felt the light pass across her, banishing the invisible hands that held her. She dropped to her side and rolled, making way for Kael's charge. Johan cried out, shadow lashing from his hand. The attack crumbled against the brilliance of his shield, flaring away into mist and air. Kael's shield never connected with Johan's body, for the shine of its light alone flung him against the wall as his illusion of flesh roiled like a disturbed lake surface. Bree craned her neck to see, praying against all hope that the hit had been lethal.

No. Not lethal. Johan shoved Kael away with strength far beyond human. Her brother slammed to the ground and then rolled onto his shield. The disturbed shadow hardened around Johan's body, but it didn't look quite correct. His clothing appeared faded, his skin burned. Many parts were missing entirely, little swirling swaths of shadow where there should be flesh and cloth.

"You think you can hurt me?" he said. His voice rumbled, deep like stone, far deeper than his Johan persona had used before. Darkness pooled at his feet, seemingly made up of his own essence. "You think you can endure what I possess?"

The shadowborn's entire being exploded outward in a rolling

wave of materialized hate and anguish. Bree gasped against it, her eyes slamming shut against their will. Foreign thoughts and desires assailed her. The wrongness of it, the violation, sickened her to her core. She felt hatred toward those she loved most. She saw faces of family, friends, and wished them mutilated and dead. All of it at a distance. All of it falling away from her, leaving her in a solitary pit of abandonment and isolation.

Bree clutched for anything that was separate from the invasive foulness. Something to anchor her to reality. The cold steel of her swords. She could feel it against her fingers. It would have to be enough. She remembered its touch. She envisioned the fire burning, and she let that fire encase her mind. Flames hid the images of death and despair. A roaring inferno drowned out the words of hatred and ugliness. She pushed away the horror. She denied the disease eating at her mind. Warmth flowed across her skin. The image was no longer merely mental. Her sword blazed before her, pulling her back into the throne room, carrying her mind into her body and unifying it under her own control.

Eyes opened, sword aflame, Bree stood alone and faced the shadowborn.

"I'm still standing," she said with labored breath.

Johan knelt before her, hands holding himself up. The shadow retreated into his body, swirling back into him and forming into pieces of cloth, hair, and flesh. All of it looked hazy, as if he were hidden behind a faint fog. The blue of his eyes had turned black, the whites rippling with a gray liquid like smoke.

"You fight a mere pittance of what I am," he said, rising to his feet. His upper body sagged. His left arm clutched at his chest where the light of Kael's shield had seared a permanent black scar across the illusionary form. "I am the shadow that swallowed the world. You fight but an echo. Your frail defenses mean nothing to my combined might."

Bree refused to break his gaze. No one else had endured the explosion of shadow. The rest of the Seraphim lay upon the floor or against the walls, still writhing, incomprehensible mutters and denials escaping their lips. If she broke now, all of them would die.

"Come prove it, then," she said, lifting a flaming sword and pointing it toward him. "Break me if our defenses are so frail."

Bree tried to read the furious expression across Johan's face. So much of it was rage, but she saw, or at least hoped she saw, an inkling of fear hidden behind it.

Johan let out a guttural scream. Bree braced for battle, but he charged for the door instead, smashing it open with a strike of his hand. Bree watched him go, the fire about her swords rippling in great waves. The moment he was gone she banished the flame, unlocked her joints, and collapsed.

I am the shadow that swallowed the world, his voice taunted inside her exhausted mind as she lay there on the carpet. *You fight but an echo.*

The rest of the Seraphim and soldiers stirred, distant conversations starting up as Bree's mind and body finally relented to the damage Johan's shadow had dealt to her.

Perhaps, Bree thought, and she closed her eyes to the inevitable sleep. *But your echo fled, you bastard. You fled, not us. Not us…*

CHAPTER 27

Kael slowly weaved back and forth through the perfect row of trees lining the exterior of the mansion, enjoying the fresh air, when Clara found him.

"You have a hard time relaxing, don't you?" Clara asked, her black dress a somber contrast to the pleasant weather.

"It's felt like time hasn't paused to take a breath since the day Marius burned down the Academy," Kael said, accepting Clara's offered kiss on his cheek. "Two days of quiet? This is just weird."

"Well, maybe we can put an end to that," Clara said. "My mother wishes to speak with you."

"Am I in trouble?" he asked.

Clara offered him her hand.

"I don't know," she said. "Let's find out together."

It seemed her mother had similar ideas about relaxing, for she was not in her throne room but instead in the larger garden at the far rear of the holy mansion. She lay barefoot on a long white chair, two servants on either side of her ready with a platter of drinks and fruits. Unlike the formal wear Kael was accustomed to seeing her in, she wore a simple pair of pants with a short-sleeved blouse, their colors muted in mourning for her slain husband. She kept her eyes closed as she rubbed her temples with her thumbs. A pile of documents lay beside her on a small table. Kael snuck a glance at a few and saw a mixture of troop reports, supply tallies, and communications with the Archons of the other minor islands.

"We're here, mother," Clara said.

The Archoness sat up and retrieved a full glass from the servant beside her.

"Give us a moment of privacy," she ordered. The servants bowed stiffly and left. Avila slowly rose to her feet, the pink liquid in her crystalline glass gently swirling.

"How is your sister?" she asked Kael.

"Fairly well, all things considered," he said. "She has some nasty stitches, but her strength is returning, and Bree insists she's already strong enough to fly again."

"Good, good." Avila gestured to the rows of flowers intermixed with fountains of angels flowing with water. "Among tragedy there is always beauty. When the demons fell we lost forests and fields, but this garden, a jewel of our island since the first days of Ascension, survived." She took a drink from her glass and frowned. "But among beauty there is also tragedy. I'm beginning to see that now. What I thought were times of peace negotiated by my husband and I were only smoke screens against the building fire."

"No one predicted this," Kael said. "The only one who did was the one behind it all."

"Johan," Avila said. The Archoness spoke the word as if it

stabbed her tongue upon leaving her mouth. "I've begun arresting members of his cult, mostly those too proud to hide or too stubborn to flee. I sent word to the other islands of Johan's betrayal. Hopefully they will believe me and act accordingly instead of waiting to investigate on their own."

"What about Johan himself?" Kael asked.

Avila took another sip and shook her head.

"Given his . . . abilities, I doubt we will ever find him, assuming he's even still on this island. No, the best we can do is minimize the damage he's done and ensure he can't make things worse."

The Archoness walked the long, winding stone path through the garden. Kael and Clara followed, still holding each other's hand.

"I've spoken with L'fae twice since our first meeting," Avila continued. "With her help I've begun piecing together Johan's influence, which is vast. He slew the angel inside Galen during our attack, sending it to the ground and leading to our occupation. The collapse of the dome protecting us from the fireborn was certainly Johan's doing as well. His constant warnings of war and invasion only prepared our people to accept that exact outcome. There is no doubt he is guilty of killing Isaac and Argus. I suspect even my son's death upon liberating the Crystal Cathedral was by his order. Always keeping us angry. Always convincing us peace could never be reached."

Avila stopped before a sculptured bush of white roses shaped like a long, feathery wing.

"Can it?" Kael asked. "Everything's been quiet at Center. Will we finally seek peace?"

The Archoness took in a long breath. Whatever her answer would be, he could tell it pained her.

"Though Marius's crimes are many, I will not pursue war

against Center. I've attempted to convince the other islands, but it has been no easy task. I fear it may already be too late."

"We'll convince them," Clara encouraged. "Give it time. No one wants to see this bloodshed continue."

"I hope not," Kael said. "Is there anything you wish from me, my Archoness? Or did you just want to check up on Bree's health?"

Clara squeezed his hand painfully tight to show her disapproval of such a blunt request, but Kael couldn't take the waiting. Avila chuckled, thankfully unoffended. Her smile quickly vanished, replaced with earnest gratitude.

"Kael, the only reason I discovered any of this was because you forced me to face the truth. Despite my best efforts otherwise, you brought me before L'fae. Our island is indebted to you, as am I."

Kael felt his cheeks flushing.

"I, uh, it was nothing," he said. "Just doing what I thought was right."

"Then may we all do better at doing what is right," she said, smiling warmly.

One of the dismissed servants hustled down the path, head bowing the moment he caught sight of Avila's glare.

"My Archoness, Commander West brings a message she insists is most urgent," he said.

"Send her in."

The servant vanished, replaced by a frowning Olivia with a curled scroll in her left hand.

"Reports are coming in from our men keeping eyes on Center," she said. "The retaliatory strike has finally begun."

"Which islands?" Avila asked.

"All three. It appears to be a coordinated attack on Center."

"Then my missives for peace were too late," Avila said. "The other islands think only of revenge."

"Archoness, our Seraphim are eager for your orders."

"Whether we're joining in, you mean," Clara said. She looked to her mother. "Are we?"

The Archoness looked away, her small mouth locked into a frown. Kael shifted his weight from foot to foot. He would accept whatever answer she gave, despite the dread that filled his heart at the thought of facing off against more knights of Center.

"Any Seraph who wishes to watch the battle may do so, but I forbid them from entering. Weshern seeks peace, whether with the theotechs of Center or the new government that replaces it. Our island is done with war."

Oliva bowed low.

"As you wish."

Was that disappointment in her voice, or relief? Kael didn't know. No doubt a large number of Seraphim wanted vengeance for Center's invasion. Hopefully the number tired of the death and loss would be greater.

"I'd like to watch as well," Clara said once Olivia left.

"I understand," her mother said. "Stay safe."

They hugged, and to Kael's surprise, Avila turned to him for one as well. He accepted it graciously, for once feeling like he was part of their family. Not that much remained. Avila's husband was dead, her two sons lost during the occupation. No wonder she was tired of war.

"Don't you worry," Kael said, unable to keep quiet as he felt the sorrow draping on him. "If she tries to fly into battle I'll lock her in a block of ice and float her back to Weshern safe and sound."

The Archoness smiled.

"My daughter would murder you if you tried."

He glanced at Clara, who nodded in agreement.

"I would."

"Well then," he said. "For my sake, let's hope she behaves."

The mood was somber and tense at the armory. Few Seraphs talked to one another as they put on their wings and inserted their elemental prisms into their respective compartments. A few nodded or saluted in respect to Clara before leaving. Kael eyed their reactions carefully, wondering how many were second-guessing their Archoness.

"Are you ready?" Clara asked.

"Ready," Kael said, tightening the last of the buckles.

They stepped outside, gently powered their wings, and flew northeast for Center. Weshern rolled beneath them. Kael wished it were nightfall. In the painful light of day, nothing hid the ruined cities and scarred fields. How many years would it take to rebuild? Would it ever be the same? It was hard to imagine a restored Weshern, but Kael knew time was the most powerful healer. He prayed he saw it blossom again in his lifetime.

Weshern vanished, the Endless Ocean now visible below. Silver wings clustered ahead of them, Weshern Seraphim flying as groups of friends instead of tight formations. Clara led them through slices of clouds, their wings a pleasant hum. Slowly the dot of green and brown that was Center grew closer, more distinguished. It took another ten minutes before they closed enough distance to see hints of battle. There wasn't much to them that they could see, not yet, just tiny specks occasionally punctured by a blip of flame or flash of lightning. Up ahead, and far closer, more than thirty Weshern Seraphim hovered together. By the time Kael and Clara joined them they'd closed enough distance to watch the battle unfold.

The invasion had split into three major engagements, the forces of each outer island battling a portion of Center's angelic knights. The regal white outfits of Center helped distinguish them from the outer island's jackets, giving some semblance of organization to the engagements. They were still too far away to make out individual fights, but the spheres of battle ebbed and flowed in a visible pattern. Amid the flashes of elements they could see combatants fall, see which formations pulled back in retreat and which pushed their advantage. After a few minutes of watching, Kael felt a real sense of who was winning which battle.

"Elern has the advantage," he told Clara. "Same with Candren. Only Sothren appears to be losing."

"It's only the beginning," Clara responded. "Things can change in a heartbeat."

It didn't seem to be swinging in Center's favor, though. The two battles over the eastern and western edges crumpled, the knights retreating inward. The third quickly followed. To their surprise, the outer islands didn't chase with their Seraphim. It seemed they were grouping together, perhaps to ensure Center couldn't suddenly retaliate while they were scattered. That didn't explain the flashes of elements they saw dot the formations, though.

"We need to get closer," Clara said.

"What if it gives the impression we're joining in?" Kael asked.

"I don't care. I must know."

She tilted her body parallel to the ocean and pushed her wings out of a hover and into a soar. Kael followed, and a glance over his shoulder showed that the other thirty Seraphs followed. They passed several more miles, Center filling their vision. Clara slowed back into a hover. Kael did the same, his throat locking tight and his eyes watering.

The Seraphim weren't chasing the knights because they were bombarding the many towns across Center's edge. Fires spread throughout fields and homes. Docks shattered beneath concentrated blasts of lightning. Roof after roof smashed inward under the weight of ice and stone.

"They're daring the knights to come back and fight," Clara said. Her voice was cold, passionless. It was as if she were so shocked, so numb she couldn't afford emotions. "Either fight or watch their people die."

For ten long minutes, that was what they did. They watched people die. The knights grouped up in formations. They too watched. They too must have felt similar horror, for finally they charged back into the fray. The knights split back into three even groups, looking to equally engage the other islands' Seraphim, but the far eastern group suddenly turned and cut west mere minutes before engaging with Sothren's forces to join the fight against Candren. Their wings shone a brilliant gold, outracing their Sothren foes easily. The outer islands had grown too confident. They'd forgotten their wings were still the slower.

While the knights had been heavily outnumbered for much of the battle, this time they had superior numbers to go with their superior skill. Candren's Seraphim attempted to disengage when they saw Center's reinforcements coming in, but they couldn't break away. The knights bore the faster wings. Forced into a battle, the Candren Seraphim took the offensive, furiously blasting away with their elements. The knights kept close and defensive. Time was on their side. The Sothren forces would not catch up for another few minutes. Kael held his breath, eyes peeled as the two groups merged together, and the knights retook the offensive.

Even from their distance, Kael could tell it was a slaughter. The Candren Seraphim took the best course of action, pushing through the reinforcements in a desperate bid to reach the Sothren forces still attempting to catch up. The battle turned into chaos, too much of a blur to follow accurately until the Candren and Sothren merged together. Even then their numbers were now only equal to the knights. It would be a losing battle, and they all knew it.

They couldn't hear the horn, but they saw the reactions when the call to retreat sounded. Both Candren and Sothren flew toward the edge, defensive walls flinging up behind them coupled with blind shots to fill the air and endanger their chasers. Sometimes a few would break off from the rest, sacrificing their lives to buy the others time. Kael winced with every shimmer of gold that blinked out of existence.

With two islands in full retreat, a portion of knights split off from the chase to join the attack in the west. Elern had seen the crumbling of the other two and their Seraphim quickly pulled away while they still had the numbers advantage. Knights gave chase, but it seemed halfhearted.

"Center held," Clara said, breathing out a long sigh. "Just barely, but for good or ill, they held."

The three islands clustered together on their flight home, their numbers painfully diminished from their initial invasion. It seemed they purposely avoided any path that might fly them close to Weshern's watching group.

"What do you think it all means?" Kael asked.

"I don't know," Clara said. "I pray this means we may finally restore peace among us, but..."

She looked to the fleeing forces of the other islands.

"But what?" Kael asked when she hesitated to continue.

"But I fear we made enemies of our allies."

"It still wouldn't have been worth it," Kael said, shaking his head. "Imagine what would have happened if Center lost."

"Our war would be over," Clara said.

"Except it wouldn't. Hundreds of Seraphim can conquer the skies, but what of the miles and miles of land below? Who will occupy the territory? Who would take out the thousands of ground troops? Center's knights would retreat, lick their wounds, and prepare for another defense... and what do you think the Seraphim will do after what Center did to us here?"

Clara's face paled as she realized his point.

"If our combined Seraphim can't conquer and hold Center..."

Kael looked to the distant capital island.

"They'd bombard everything they can from the sky. If we'd joined in, we might have participated in slaughter on the grandest scale since Galen's collapse. Your mother did the right thing. *We* did the right thing, Clara. You know that."

Clara gestured to the diminished number of Candren, Elern, and Sothren Seraphim flying back to their homes.

"And if they don't?"

"Then I'm glad your mother is charge instead of me, because I haven't the slightest idea."

CHAPTER 28

Liam walked the halls of Heavenstone, wishing they felt as comfortable to him now as they had been over the last five years. Other knights milled about, an alarming amount of them sporting fresh cuts and casts for broken bones earned in the battle the day before. Liam shook his head. The combined might of the minor islands had been terrifying to witness, and they'd held on by a razor's edge. If Weshern had also joined in…

If Weshern had joined in, then Center would have fallen, her people slaughtered, the Speaker executed. Liam tried to push away the thought of what that world would be, and how it would feel to no longer have the Speaker to command his life. Blasphemous thoughts. Weak desires for escape and ease over the righteous path. They didn't represent his heart. His heart was pure. He was the blade of the angels. He was the flesh on their bones, the blood on their feathers.

"Are you all right?" a servant asked Liam, stirring him from his thoughts. He started to rebuke the young man for disturbing him, then stopped. Liam hadn't realized that he'd stopped walking. Instead, he stood unmoving before a bare wall. His left hand was balled into a fist, and his forehead rested against the cold stone.

"Yes, I'm fine," he said, stepping away from the wall. "Just needed a moment to think."

The servant didn't look convinced, and that worried look pushed Liam even faster through the halls and up the stairs. His nerves were shot. His doubt was growing. Liam didn't want to reveal this weakness to the Speaker, but there was someone else who might be able to answer his questions. Someone who might have a better answer than the deflection Marius gave him when asked.

The third and highest floor of Heavenstone was also the quietest and most luxurious. Liam's heavy footsteps were muted by the thick red carpet. The stone walls were hidden behind long curtains colored violet, with gaps left for a multitude of paintings. Their beauty was incredible, little glimpses of a long-vanished world of deep forests, sprawling mountains, and moon-frosted lakes. There was no crawling darkness in that world, no midnight fire. Just peace.

The door Liam halted before lacked any obvious markings, but that didn't mean there weren't any. Liam pulled back one of the curtains, revealing a name lightly carved into the stone: Er'el Jaina Cenborn. He knocked twice, then released the curtain. Straightened his uniform. Waited.

"Yes?" Jaina asked, her door cracking open and her head peeking out. "Oh. Hello, Liam. Is there something the matter?"

Liam worked up every nerve in his body, needing the strength. He was already on tenuous ground, having been reprimanded multiple times for his lack of faith, but he felt he must challenge his past and demand the answers they'd avoided giving him for years.

"My daughter wields flame within her blood," Liam said. "And my son sprouted heavenly wings to save himself when falling to his death. I want to know how, and why. The Speaker insists these powerful gifts are from the deceiver, but at risk of committing blasphemy, I refuse to accept that as an answer."

Despite the empty hallway, Jaina glanced in each direction and then sighed.

"Very well," she said. "It seems pointless to keep hiding it. Come in, Liam. We must discuss this in private."

She opened the door wider and stepped aside. Liam entered a posh room flooded with fanciful little decorations. He couldn't help but notice a particularly violent bent to the many paintings on the walls. Like most that hung throughout Center, they were images of the world prior to Ascension, detailing ice-capped mountains, forests spanning hundreds of miles, and deep red rock carved with canyons. Most, however, also contained scenes of battle, be it with swords, spears, or bows and arrows. A few even showed lines of men slaughtering one another with primitive firearms. Others depicted graveyards, disease, or towns aflame. The largest painting was of a dark-skinned man with a noose around his neck hanging from a tree, a crowd of furious people holding torches and rifles above their heads as they hollered silent, permanent rage.

"That's a cheery one," Liam said, nodding toward it.

"Given Center's heavy nostalgia for the pre-Ascension world, I like to remind myself humanity has always been cruel and sinful. It was true then, and it is true now."

"Then why did the angels pull us into the heavens instead of letting us die like we deserved?"

"I don't know," Jaina said. "Perhaps even the angels have a nostalgic heart."

She settled into her leather chair beside a large bookshelf filled with faded tomes predating the Ascension.

"Know that everything I tell you here is not to be repeated," she said. "Not even to other knights or theotechs."

"Understood," Liam said.

Jaina rocked back in her chair, fingers tapping.

"We were hoping to save ourselves," she said, staring at him. "You need to understand that. All we did, right or wrong, we did with the best of intentions. Perhaps that won't save us when we kneel before the creator, but I'd like to believe it so."

Liam crossed his arms and stood before her, impatiently waiting.

"Go on."

Jaina smiled bitterly.

"Er'el Tesdon championed the idea for much of his life, and sadly we only acquiesced in his final days. He swore that our reliance on demons for elements would be our eventual undoing, and that by keeping them enslaved we were repeating the failures of the past that led to the Ascension. Plenty disagreed with him, but we all knew our system wasn't perfect. Worse, every demon that died attempting to escape was forever one less to bleed for prisms. Underneath the dome, we had no means of procuring more demons, and the demons themselves did not procreate. Something had to be done, for no matter how many centuries it took, our supply would eventually run out."

Jaina slumped further into her chair, her slender fingers rubbing her lips in thought.

"Tesdon's idea was simple: could humanity harness in their blood the same power of the demons?"

Shivers spiked Liam's spine.

"Blasphemy," he said in shock.

"Perhaps," Jaina said. "But there was a bit of groundwork already established. Men and women, seemingly at random, were born with varying degrees of affinity toward specific elements. That affinity allowed manipulation of the elemental prisms, albeit with mechanical aid. Tesdon insisted the next step in our own evolution was going beyond affinity into actual manipulation with human blood, removing the need for the demons. Once Marius gave approval we began selecting candidates from the populace for our implantation experiments."

Pieces started tumbling into place, not all of them, but enough to paint a picture that terrified Liam.

"The Ghost Plague," he said. "That wasn't a real illness, was it? Our people were being taken for your experiments."

Jaina nodded.

"We invented symptoms, declared us the only ones able to detect the disease early, and then moved in quickly before anyone knew what was going on. It's easier than you might think, Liam. First you start with the poor and the homeless, the ones who are likely already ill or isolated. Once we took them, everyone feared catching our fraudulent plaguc. Wc weren't proud of this, mind you, but the implantation process was frighteningly lethal, and due to the nature of our quest, and the need to keep the source of the prisms quiet, we had to explain the disappearances to the populace somehow. We tried inserting prisms of various sizes into subjects' bloodstreams, grinding them into powder, sewing them into flesh within body parts, anything we could think of. It never mattered. The fever inevitably came to snuff out the subjects' lives."

Ferrymen had taken dozens of Liam's friends and neighbors across the sky to Center, fearful and seeking a desperate cure for the disease the theotechs claimed they'd contracted. But they hadn't been cured, for there was nothing to cure. They'd been executed. Liam's head swam, and he asked his next question while certain of the answer.

"You experimented upon me as well, didn't you?"

"We did," she said. "Does that bother you?"

"I don't know."

Jaina spun in her chair and opened a drawer. Among some papers and books was a broken piece of a fire elemental prism. She took it out and set it on the table before her.

"This was half of the prism we shattered and inserted into your blood," she said. "We'd reached the end of our trials. Nothing appeared to work. The best we'd concluded was that those with an affinity toward an element survived longer if implanted with that same element. You, among others, had a stronger affinity for your element than the rest of the populace."

"And so I survived," Liam said. "Did that prove your theory?"

Jaina smirked.

"You were an outlier, Liam. Among the thirty we tested with incredibly strong affinity, two managed to survive the coming fever, and only then by us submerging them in ice water and forcing liquid into their veins when they could not eat or drink."

Two survivors. Liam knew the other. They'd discussed it before. A miracle, they'd called it. Their own little miracle, showing how God desired them to meet one another.

"Cassandra was the other," Liam said. "You experimented on her as well."

"We did," she said. "And while you two survived, you were two of hundreds, a pitiful survival rate with no chance of replication among the general populace. Er'el Tesdon's blood modification program was deemed a failure. Not long after, he himself passed away."

Liam tried to take it all in, to understand what this meant. Him and Cassandra, the only two survivors...and set up to meet on a blind date by friends.

"You put us together," he said, trying to keep control of his growing rage. "Why?"

Jaina shrugged.

"I took over what was left of Tesdon's experiments after his passing. Even if the process couldn't be replicated, I wondered at the meaning of yours and Cassandra's survival. Perhaps your blood might be used in further transfusions instead of more prisms? And what of your survival? Did it mean you had inherited the powers we were hoping for? We tested this, of course, draining over a hundred vials of blood from each of you. Every experiment, a failure. No affinity. No elemental manipulation. Nothing."

Liam remembered being drained of blood. They'd told him they were seeking a cure for the Ghost Plague should it ever reemerge. But they weren't seeking a cure. They were seeking a weapon, and they'd killed hundreds injecting demon blood into their bodies to achieve it.

"And me and Cassandra?"

"I was curious how further generations of children might be affected by your implantation, and I didn't want to risk diluting the blood, hence your pairing. A mere final act of the experiment before we sealed away all results completely."

So clinical. So heartless. As if the time they'd spent together, the love they'd felt between them, meant nothing at all. After Cassandra died in battle, they'd taken Liam to Center and anointed him a new knight in service of the Speaker. It had been a great honor, one that would require great sacrifice. His body bore the tattoos, each one chasing away the sin in his mind. His heart bore the greater scars, the separation from his two young children. Now Liam saw that separation, not as an honor, but just one more part of a damn cruel experiment.

"My children," he said. "They finally showed the promise you were looking for."

"At first it appeared nothing more than a slightly stronger affinity to an element," Jaina said. "Kael's was with light, but we pushed him into Weshern's Seraphim Academy instead of becoming a ferryman. I thought his abilities would be better put to the test there. I kept an eye on their training status, not thinking much on them, to be honest. They showed peculiarities but little beyond that. Your daughter even lagged behind other members of her class when it came to elemental manipulation, a quirk that left me puzzled and disappointed. Just another dead end, like everything else involved with the implantation experiments. At least, until your daughter wielded fire on her swords in her battle against Galen."

Liam remembered that day. No one had told him directly, but too much conversation was filled with talk of the unusual skill shown by the Weshern Seraph. His heart had been filled with pride, and he'd asked Marius for a chance to meet with his children. The Speaker had chastised his weakness and warned that even then his children might be succumbing to the words of the heretic, Johan.

"We attempted to take them in quietly," Jaina continued, as if oblivious to the fury growing in Liam's breast. "Sadly our attempt failed, and it was only after Galen's fall that we apprehended one of them for renewed experimentation." She sighed. "Such a shame Breanna escaped. Her blood was everything we had ever hoped for. If only the process were not so fatal, but even if it weren't, I have a feeling the rest of the Erelim would not allow it to continue. The rebellion of the so-called Phoenix of Weshern is a vibrant warning as to what may happen when power is given freely to civilians of the minor islands instead of being tightly controlled."

Jaina stood from her chair and brushed off her robes.

"I understand this is a lot to take in," she said. "Remember—we had the best of intentions for our experiments. Our whole race, freed from reliance on demon blood. Some suffered and died due to those experiments, true, but they died for a noble cause."

Liam touched his shaved head with his fingers, tracing the lines of tattoos he knew by heart. Er'el Iseph had repeated words of repentance and salvation during the tattooing process. Cleansing his soul from the sins he'd developed on Weshern, he'd claimed. Elevating his mind to become more than a lowly Seraph and a father, but instead a true knight of Center. A blade for the angels. Teaching him to revere the Speaker above all, to put his wisdom above family, friends, and country. *You were chosen,* Iseph had claimed. *Your name whispered by the angels themselves to join the holy ranks.*

"Marius... the Speaker swore the angels spoke my name and spared my life," he said. "None of what you say denies that. I survived. My wife survived. Two of thousands, and now our children... our children bear blood blessed by the elements."

"I would hardly call it blessed," Jaina said, frowning at him. "It is still demonic essence that empowers them."

"You would deny the Speaker's interpretation of events?"

The woman looked exasperated.

"I would state the mere facts, knight. I don't need fanciful retellings to cloud my understanding of this world. Your son is not blessed from the heavens. No divine intervention spared his life. The flaming swords your daughter wields are mere tricks used by manipulating fire in a way other Seraphs never thought to attempt. Just like their parents, they're nothing but statistical aberrations, freaks of nature that will never be replicated in our lifetimes. To be quite blunt, they're lucky to even exist."

Freaks of nature, thought Liam. *Statistical aberrations.*

Liam lunged, his left hand closing about Jaina's neck and slamming her against the painting of the hanged man. His right gauntlet jammed into her stomach just below her rib cage, pinning her body to the wall. All his vision turned to red. All his emotions raged within his veins.

"I am not a freak," he hissed into her ear. "My children are not aberrations. We're not failed experiments. We're *human beings,* you fucking monster."

"Human mixed with demon," Jaina said with great effort, her face turning pale. "Which side controls you now?"

The blade sprang from his golden gauntlet, piercing straight through to the heart.

"The father," he told the dying woman.

She tried to scream. His fist tightened, choking out the last futile gasps. Blood dripped across his golden gauntlet. Tears trickled down his face. He pulled the blade free as her body stiffened and let her collapse to the floor. His rage washed away, replaced with a growing panic. He stared at the blood-soaked blade as if it were a traitor.

"What have I done?" he whispered.

Killing a member of the Erelim was one of the greatest sins possible against heaven's design. Only slaying the Speaker was worse. At his feet lay the body. Her blood marked his clothes. There would be an exhaustive investigation; could he hide his guilt under such questioning?

No, he knew he could not. Liam had just ordered his own death sentence.

You gave in to your anger, a soft, mocking voice assured him in his mind. *Accept it. Own it. Perhaps confession will grant you mercy when you hover above Hell's fire.*

Perhaps. Perhaps not. Liam could not concentrate on it now, not with the body collapsed before him. He had to get out. He had to think. Liam used Jaina's robe to clean his sword and gauntlet, then hurried to the door and flung it open. He had to buy time. Had to get away for a moment.

No distance is great enough, that mocking voice insisted. *You know that, Liam. Hiding only compounds your guilt.*

Liam ran down the empty hall anyway, painfully aware of the blood that stained his pristine white uniform. He was halfway down the stairs when he heard the first of many horns.

Have they discovered her body already?

It was nonsense, panic speaking instead of logic. He knew what that signal meant. The angelic knights were being called into battle. Liam stepped onto the lower floor to see knights and servants rushing toward the armories. They paid him little attention despite his halfhearted attempts. Something was wrong. Even when the combined might of Elern, Candren, and Sothren had invaded, the people of Heavenstone had reacted calmly to the threat. What could possibly disturb so many so? He saw knights scrambling half-dressed, others shouting at theotechs for extra elemental prisms.

Determined to get an answer, Liam grabbed a half-dressed knight by the shoulder.

"Do the Seraphim attack again?" he asked.

"I wish," the knight said. "It's not the islands. It's... it's demons. They're swarming all four minor islands."

Liam's dread grew. So this was it then? L'adim's great invasion? They'd battled a taste of it when the fireborn fell, but now after all of Marius's warnings, the true war had arrived.

"What is our task?" Liam asked. "Where shall we fight them?"

"Weshern's the only one who sought peace when the others attacked, so it sounds like we'll be going to Weshern's aid first."

The aid of my children, Liam thought, new purpose flooding into him. *The salvation of their home.*

"To battle then," he said, saluting his fellow knight, hoping to inspire away his fear. "To a noble cause, and a nobler death."

CHAPTER 29

Kael and Clara landed at the edge of Weshern, joining Bree and the dozens of Seraphim peering down. Not thirty minutes ago the first warning had sounded, resulting in the mad scramble that had brought the Weshern Seraphim out to defend.

"What do you see?" Kael asked his sister. She crouched before him on one knee, squinting at the clouds below.

"Not much," Bree said as she stood. "They're too close to the Beam. We won't know what we face until we fly over."

"We know exactly what we face," Clara said. "The shadowborn's army. This is it. Can't you feel it?"

Kael did feel it, a tangible power hovering in the air. Not that anyone wanted to voice that belief. Everyone prepared as if this were just another battle. They spoke as if Center's knights were the ones flying up toward the Beam to engage. An army of demons? Creatures of ancient stories with power similar to the fireborn that had rampaged across Weshern's surface in one hellish night?

No, Kael felt no surprise in seeing so many of his fellow Seraphim lost in shock and denial. If not for his time standing in the presence of the lightborn, he might have joined them. Their entire flight from the holy mansion to the island's edge had shown chaos below, shops closing up, windows and doors boarded shut, and hundreds fleeing toward Weshern's center. The initial reports had only been of demons rising from the ocean and climbing the Beam toward Weshern's surface, but as more scouts arrived, detailing similar assaults on Sothren, Candren, and Elern, the panic had grown. This was it, the large-scale, coordinated attack Kael had warned them about, and hardly anyone believed. The nightmare was coming true.

"If this is his main assault, then consider it a blessing," Bree said, flexing her right gauntlet as if it itched to fire. "We can end L'adim's threat here and now."

"Nice of you to remain optimistic," Kael muttered.

"Someone has to, so I guess it's my turn."

Olivia lifted into the air from the center of the group, signaling for attention. She didn't get it. Everyone was too lost in their own arguments, their own thoughts, so she had to whistle multiple times to finally gather all eyes her way.

"There will be no formations for this battle," Olivia shouted. "We fly as one unified force. The demons are climbing toward our home, Seraphim! Our people are scared, our cities in danger of ruin. Those monsters must not set foot on our blessed lands, do you hear me? Weshern is ours. Bleed and die for it."

The new commander turned around and dropped over the side of the island. The remaining Seraphim of Weshern followed, one long swarm diving over the edge. Kael's chest beat with excitement and nervousness. Olivia was right. A victory here would be immense. A loss, however, meant everything.

Bree led their way, Kael and Clara trailing after as the trio formed the tail end of Weshern's attack force. They pushed through the clouds, their wings solely for control, their speed coming from gravity's pull. Kael shifted the shield on his shoulder so it was before him. Whatever surprise awaited when they broke through the clouds, he'd be ready for it. The sky darkened. Their direction shifted inward, a swarm of silver wings entering the shadow of Weshern. In its shade they saw the demons' ascent.

Nine iceborn climbed a blue-white pillar built from the frozen Fount surrounding the Beam. Their size stole Kael's breath away. They dwarfed the fireborn giant they'd battled in Elan Village. They made mockeries of Center's war machines and cannons. Six hands clawed into the wide spray of water, each finger bigger than Kael's entire body. Their heads were the size of houses, their brow crowned with frosted horns, their hair made of long icicles larger than any waterfall. The Fount shimmered and froze at their touch, hardening into one more piece of the growing tower. They saw the approach of Weshern's defenders and opened their mouths in unison. Their words roared throughout the land, louder than the Beam, louder than the cracking ice of the Fount.

"THE AGE OF MAN ENDS. COME DIE."

Stoneborn giants followed, a third the size of the iceborn but far greater in number. They bore no crowns or hair, but their hands and feet were long, curved hooks like ice axes and crampons that allowed them to climb the iceborn's pillar. Swirling all around them, clinging to both stone and ice, were the stormborn and fireborn. They remained the slender little creatures Kael recognized, flitting rapidly about as they waited for their bridge to be complete. Already they reached halfway up the Beam, and it seemed the iceborns' pace increased the closer they neared the top.

Stay back, Bree signaled, relaying the order all the way from Olivia at the front. *Strike from distance.*

Their commander wished to test the defensive abilities of the giants, a wise enough decision. Kael turned the knob to activate his focal prism. He wasn't sure how useful his ice might be against fellow iceborn, but the giants would feel his sting. Besides, they didn't need to kill the brutes to protect Weshern. Sending them crashing back down to the ocean waters would be enough to buy precious time.

Olivia shifted their path so they gently curled toward the nearest iceborn. The creature continued climbing, each one of its six arms pulling it higher. Ice flowed out from it, extending its tower out at an angle from the Fount. Others were joining it, Kael saw. They didn't need to just follow the Beam, but also extend away from it so they might reach Weshern's edge and then the surface. Under no circumstances could that happen.

On mark, Bree signaled. Kael looked to Clara beside him. She caught his gaze and gave him a wink.

Give them hell, she mouthed.

Their prey paused as the Seraphim closed into range. Two of its arms ripped chunks of ice free from the frozen Fount and flung them through the air. Others nearby did the same, their throws lobbed higher, precisely timed so they'd cross paths with the Seraphim during their projectile's descent. The Weshern Seraphim split, half curving left, the other half right. The first few boulders ripped through the heart of their formation, clipping two unlucky Seraphs and shattering their wings.

Olivia guided their swarm back together, more boulders falling harmlessly to either side. The iceborn giant now in range, the commander let loose with her lightning. The single hit was unimpressive compared to the target's size, but then the rest unleashed their elements.

Stone lances smashed the creature's sides, pounding cracks into its hard body. Fire bathed the weakening form, punctuated by lightning. Kael joined in with the rest of the ice wielders in forming a wall jutting out directly above the giant's head to block its path. The demon roared, deep and pained. Two arms smashed at the ice above, two others throwing chunks in wild, desperate sprays. The barrage continued, breaking it, tearing it apart. The giant fell in pieces to the frozen ocean below. Kael pumped a fist, their swarm of Seraphim immediately speeding toward the next massive eternal-born.

The iceborn giants rushed closer together, merged onto a grand platform built by their combined power. The waters of the Fount splashed weakly nearby, what little that continued to flow up the hollowed center of the frozen tower. Olivia circled it from afar. Kael kept his shield at ready. The next defensive barrage could be devastating with so many gathered together. The eight giants stood perfectly still, a chilling image. Kael knew the lightborn could speak to each other with only a thought, and he wondered if the other eternal-born bore similar powers. The giants then broke apart, whatever plan of theirs officially decided. The stoneborn soon followed, remaining evenly spaced apart with arms raised and boulders ready to throw. No matter where Olivia led their attack, at least one of the stoneborn would be ready. As for the iceborn, they began forming a bridge jutting up and out from the platform, the sides of it curling to form a sort of tunnel. Now walking instead of climbing, their progress came at a frighteningly rapid pace. Only two worked the front, the others constantly reinforcing the bridge as well as watching for attacks.

Olivia led them lower to the base of the frozen tower instead of heading them off. Stormborn swarmed it, climbing up to Weshern. Nothing a second barrage couldn't fix. Ice and flame wreathed the tower, scattering the demons. Olivia landed upon the tower, jamming the sword in her left hand into it like a pick. Fire and lightning blasted the ice in an attempt to break the structure at its root.

By the time the barrage ended they'd cut maybe a foot into the structure's wall. Kael realized why it had taken so long for the iceborn to climb their way up the Fount. They'd layered and braced the bottom in anticipation of just such an attack, its thickness at least fifty feet. Olivia leapt off, the Seraphim following. She continued the barrage against the base, this time from afar. Stormborn scattered, lurking at the outside edge of the concentrated fire. Watching. Waiting.

When the Seraphim settled to a hover with their firepower most heavily concentrated, the stormborn leapt off the ice. They crossed the air like little bolts of lightning, their speed breathtaking. Kael blinked once at the brightness and then the stormborn were among them, clawing at whatever they could get their hands on. One had the misfortune to grab hold of Kael's shield, its hands sizzling into mist as the light flared. Another died with its head lopped off by Bree's sword as it scratched its claws into her wings. Clara flitted about, striking down the falling stormborn with her ice. Dozens of the stormborn fell to the ocean, either unable to take hold or still clinging to a dead Seraph in their grasp, their eyes burned away, their mouths leaking smoke.

Four Seraphs died in total, and many others hovered away

injured. Olivia quickly ordered the retreat. Stormborn gathered in the center of the crater Weshern's army had chipped away, chittering and laughing in mockery of their attempts. All the while, the iceborn giants above steadily advanced toward Weshern's edge.

A double blast of lightning skyward signaled for them to gather about their commander.

"The iceborn are the key," she shouted. "We can't stop the swarm, and we can't break the base. We have to stop the ice's spread. It's our only hope." She glared at the stormborn. "Break apart into smaller formations. We're more vulnerable together than we are apart. Fly strong, fly fast. There is no retreating from this battle. Fight until you fall like soldiers. That is my last order."

Dread spread throughout them, and Kael felt it strong in his heart. He glanced to Bree and Clara, unspoken communication bringing them into a triangle formation.

Olivia rushed back to the sprawling bridge, which reached for Weshern's edge like the long strand of a spider's web. Weshern's forces followed, this time much more spread out. Bree shifted their path toward a length of bridge least defended. Fire bathed her swords. Light shimmered across Kael's shield. Two stone giants waited for them, hands clapping together as if eager for their approach. Bree picked the nearest, her body gently bobbed up and down so her path would be harder to predict.

The stoneborn curled their boulder-fists close to their chests and slammed them together. Their own bodies cracked. They flung their hands, the pieces exploding outward in a massive spray of stone shards. The three refused to pull back. Live or die, they were going to fight. They avoided the first two such attacks, their wings shimmering as they increased the throttle to close the final gap. The stoneborn defended again, this time hastily, without much time to aim.

Bree corkscrewed through the shards, momentum growing, giving strength to her slashes. She curled sharper inward, her swords exploding with fire as they ripped across the stoneborn's pale right eye. It roared and fell back, green blood showering the air. Kael and Clara jammed heavy lances of ice into Bree's newly opened wound, puncturing the eye and digging deep into whatever lay beyond. The stoneborn slid off the side of the bridge, body tumbling for the ocean.

Momentum carried the three beyond the bridge. They curled about for another pass, giving Kael time to assess the battle. With the Seraphim spread so far apart they were better able to pressure all points of the ice tunnel. The problem was the fewer numbers made it that much harder to damage the gigantic iceborn. They couldn't break the ice faster than the giants repaired it, especially now that it was close enough to the island's underside that the iceborn could build long veins of supports to keep their bridge aloft. The lesser demons crawled through the tunnel, safe from harm. Foot by foot, the bridge tunnel reached for Weshern's edge, the stoneborn defending it with barrages of thin, sharp javelins. Bree pulled their little squad away and slowed to a hover, allowing the other two to catch up.

"I can try to use my fire near the base of that tunnel," Bree said, pointing toward the great ice spire. "I'm not sure if it'll be enough, but we have to try before there's too many supports near the top."

"They'll be ready for us," Kael said. "Look at how many stormborn and fireborn are waiting. There's not a chance you make it there safely."

"There is if you lead with your shield."

He shook his head.

"I can block some attacks, but what am I to do when they dive atop us? I'm not a miracle worker here."

"Liar," Clara said. "You both are miracle workers, so act like it. We collapse the tunnel, we end the entire invasion, yes?"

Kael shrugged.

"I believe so," he said.

"Then we go for the base, danger be damned. And you're both wrong. This time, I'll lead. I have a plan."

Clara angled parallel to the ground and fired up her wings. Kael knew he could overtake her with his stronger wings but he kept a safe distance behind. If she wished to lead, then so be it. He'd trust her, just as she'd so often trusted him.

The wide platform with the connected bridge steadily neared. Stoneborn waited ready to defend it, an additional two dozen stormborn cackling and zipping about their feet as well. Clara kept their path directly toward them, with no attempt to weave or dodge to potentially confuse their attack approach. Kael frowned, yet to see Clara's plan.

Clara slowed just outside reach of boulders from the stoneborn. Her gauntlet weaved a magical dance, creating wall after wall of ice before her. They varied in size, height, and closeness to the bridge, a veritable maze of them all high above and starting to fall. Realizing what she was doing, Kael created a few more walls of his own and then fired up his wings. With so many chunks of ice falling, the eternal-born would struggle to see their approach. The stoneborn flung boulders but their power weakened with the contact of each wall. The three of them split for different walls, dropping with them to use them as a screen for their flight. Kael chose the highest of the plummeting walls, flying closer and closer while the sky filled with explosions of ice, stone, and echoes of thunder.

Kael braced his shield and flooded it with light. The ice wall directly before him blasted apart, granting them passage. Desperate stormborn lunged from their perches. Kael batted them aside with his shield, then followed it up with a wall of ice of his own. It fell to the bridge, blocking another salvo from the stormborn. Clara lofted volleys from afar, slamming her own ice boulders against the defending eternal-born on the bridge, forcing them to scatter.

The way clear, Bree shut off her wings and stabbed a sword deep into the ice to grant herself a hold. Her right hand pressed against the surface. Kael formed a circular wall around her, granting her time and protection. Red light swelled beneath her palm, releasing in a tremendous explosion. Bree drained her prism dry, her fire rolling through the center of the bridge. Water flowed in a torrent from cracks that split in all directions. It didn't break, not immediately, but the bridge connecting Weshern with the frozen Fount was severely weakening.

The fire suddenly ceased. Bree's forehead slumped against the thin ice. Stormborn raced to close the distance, their mouths dripping with electricity. Kael's heart seized with horror when Bree didn't flee. She looked too dazed to even move. Desperation overtook him. He grabbed his gauntlet and fired a single lance at the ice directly beneath her. It crashed through, cutting off her chunk with her sword keeping her connected to the bridge. She fell, demons diving after her in chase. They cared not for the fall so long as they might slay the Phoenix. Kael imagined his speed growing, not needing his throttle to propel himself downward at a maniacal clip. He curled at the last second, undercutting the demons and grabbing hold of Bree's waist. The two banked away, the demons' impotent howls their only weapon as they plummeted to the ocean far below.

Kael gradually slowed his speed as he waited for Bree to recover. He felt her body shudder, followed by light trickling into her wings as she turned them back on.

"I'm fine," she said, gently pushing him away. "Did we succeed?"

He gestured to the bridge.

"I'd say we did."

No iceborn were nearby to repair the damage she'd caused with her explosion of flame. The cracks continued to spread, the noise like a thunderstorm. The long arm reaching for Weshern began to crumble chunk by chunk, eternal-born falling with it. Kael let out a whoop, one that turned out to be premature. The collapse ceased halfway, the support beams linking to the island's underside keeping the Weshern half aloft. Even worse, Kael saw that the bridge had finally reached the surface, curling up and around Weshern's edge and onto the lands above. They'd cut off any potential for reinforcements, but a new battle now raged.

"What do we do?" he asked.

"We have to flee to the surface," Clara said, joining them. "The civilians are our new priority."

"Wait," Bree slurred. She pointed. "We're not alone."

Golden wings screamed as knights of Center appeared from above the surface, their approach unseen due to Weshern's sheer size. Their gauntlets flashed with power. Fire and lightning slammed into the lone iceborn in the middle of the tunnel, melting its frozen flesh. Stone and ice boulders broke limbs and shattered fingers. Kael felt hope spring anew in his chest. Had Marius shown a change of heart? Unlike their response during the fireborn invasion, the knights had not left them to suffer and fight on their own.

"Take out the iceborn giants first," Kael said. "End any chance of more demons joining the fray."

The stoneborn joined the stormborn in racing to Weshern's surface. The few fireborn that had accompanied the invasion remained defensive, little globs of fire flying from their hands as they cackled and howled. Two iceborn giants remained, their efforts focused on strengthening the remaining tunnel's connection to Weshern. Center's knights raced toward one while Bree led their group toward the other giant swarming with Seraphim, bathing its body with lightning and flame. It roared as two of its arms flailed, the other four clutching the tunnel. Ice flowed from its grasp in great sheets. It kept its head down, its body curled inward so its back endured the brunt of the blows.

Bree flew a direct collision course. Fire lashed from her swords, traveling in a long line toward the giant. It melted a thin groove into its back, seemingly nothing compared to the iceborn's size. Kael readied his ice, unsure of its effectiveness. They closed in, nearby Seraphim gathering, their gauntlets eager to destroy the beast. Elements bathed its body. The long blue arms shuddered. Cracks spread from its spine in all directions. Kael rushed closer, thinking it ready to die. He thought wrong.

The iceborn reared back onto its hind legs, all six arms flailing outward. Chunks of ice flew in wild directions, overwhelming in number. Seraphim frantically scattered. Bree's formation broke. On instinct, Kael curled and weaved, convinced every second could be his last, until suddenly the creature was in front of him. The giant towered ahead, arms spread wide and grabbing at nearby Seraphim. Silver wings crunched between its fingers. Kael searched, but every direction led into the reach of its hands.

Well, all but one.

This is insane, Kael thought, his arms crossed behind his shield. *You're insane, Kael, you're fucking insane...*

He felt the twin crystals in his shield burning, eager for

release. Kael granted them their wish. No slowing. No hesitation. Kael closed his eyes and released every shred of power into his shield with a frantic scream. The impact struck his shield but far softer than expected. Ice cracked. Armor gave. Mist enveloped his body. He screamed louder, protesting the pain and resistance with all his might. The ringing of the shield broke the demon. The breaking of the demon overwhelmed his cry.

Kael blasted out the iceborn giant's back in an explosion of blue blood and a thousand shards of ice. He spun into a hover, fists at his sides, adrenaline pounding through his veins. The iceborn faltered, a waterfall of blood flowing out the gaping hole in its chest. Its hands slipped off the ice bridge. Its death cry was a pitiful wail.

The knights swarmed the final iceborn giant near the edge with plumes of flames. The stone wielders smashed the bridge again and again, each boulder focused on the exact same spot. The walls of the tunnel collapsed. The nearby supports crumbled. Kael pumped a fist and let out a whoop as large chunks of the bridge broke and fell in huge sheets. No more eternal-born would reach Weshern's surface.

The formation of knights broke away and flew toward Center now that the underneath battle was won. The Weshern Seraphim flew together around the lip of the island to the surface. Kael waited until he spotted his sister flying in to join him.

"Top that, Bree," he said, grinning ear to ear.

"The day's not over yet."

Kael's easy smile faded at the sight of an angelic knight flying their way. Bree noticed his displeasure and turned.

"Is that . . . him?" she asked.

"I think so," he said.

Their father's golden wings easily crossed the distance. Neither sibling spoke. What might they even say? Liam eased into a hover before them. Tears wet his eyes. Hesitation graced his lips. None of that emotion reached his voice.

"It's good to see you again," he said. "My squadron flies to aid Sothren but I will remain here until the Weshern threat is defeated. Might I join you in formation?"

Bree wiped at her face, and she looked to Kael for an answer.

"The last I saw you, you were dropping me to my death," he said. "And now you wish to join us?"

Their father struggled for words, all the while unable to meet their gaze.

"Turn me away if you must. It is your choice, my children, but I offer amends in the only way I know how."

Was that an apology? Kael didn't know, but he clung to that hope nonetheless. Innocents were dying upon the surface. He would not turn away aid to soothe his own wounded pride.

"Welcome to Phoenix Squad," he said. "Consider yourself a temporary member."

He smiled, so briefly, so fleetingly, but it gave them a glimpse of the beloved father they'd lost.

"Very well. Lead the way, Phoenix, and I will follow."

CHAPTER 30

Bree curled up and around the edge of Weshern to discover the battle unfolding. A hastily assembled force of Varl Cutter's soldiers fought against a veritable tide of eternal-born. Lightning crackled across their heavy shields. Chunks of earth slammed through their tightly packed lines. They thrust with their spears and slashed with their swords, killing what they could of the fast stormborn. But nothing stood up to the stoneborn, and their lines quickly broke when one lumbered through.

"Focus on the giants!" she shouted to her formation. "Keep them from the soldiers!"

Bree, Kael, their father, and Clara sailed overhead, weaving occasionally to avoid a thrown boulder. She readied her swords, their grips clutched tightly in her hands. Her angle tightened. Their formation dove in for a strike. Bree ducked underneath its fist, twisted ninety degrees, and slashed across its chest with her swords. Her arms ached from the jarring resistance but her fire bloomed, slicing open the stone. Liam blinded it with fire on the follow-up. Kael and Clara swooped farther away and shifted their legs to reverse their momentum. They blasted lances of ice into the stoneborn's cracked chest from their hovering position, ripping it open. Verdant blood spilled upon Weshern soil.

Stormborn swarmed the corpse, using it for leverage to leap skyward for vengeance. Bree zipped through the air between them, her swords cutting down two or three at a time. Liam followed, an extended blade from his arm ripping into the bodies of the stormborn. The other two followed, taking up the tail as Bree led them to the next giant. The stoneborn stood in a circle of soldiers, swinging wildly as the men tried to keep it penned in. It was only a matter of time before the giant picked a direction and stampeded through.

Bree kept her formation circling until they dove like birds of prey toward the back of the stoneborn. Her eyes widened, her swords dripping fire to her either side. She flew straight between the giant's legs, each sword ripping into a calf. Twisting her body about, she circled the stoneborn, her right blade continuing to slice a curling pattern up its leg, across its side, and up its spine. Ice battered the giant's form. Soldiers buried their swords into the weakened skin at its ankles. Liam took advantage of the distraction and sped straight for the giant's head. His blade punched through the stone, and then caught. Liam screamed. Fire exploded from his cannon at point-blank range, engulfing the stoneborn's entire head.

A wave of stormborn surged toward the group, the last of the soldiers holding them back, massacred. Bree and Liam dipped low, releasing their fire together in a tremendous blast that washed over the crackling army. The monsters shrieked and howled but they could not escape it. Bree fought a momentary blackout as she curled upward. So much of her element drained. So much left to do.

Bree scanned for the rest of the squadrons. Stoneborn continued to fall under the combined attacks of the Weshern Seraphim. The stormborn fared no better, though they made up for it by tearing into the soldiers with gleeful abandon. Bree spotted a group of twenty trying to break for a nearby stretch of homes. If they escaped the battlefield they could take countless lives with them before they were hunted down and destroyed.

Give chase, Bree signaled to the others. She punched her throttle and soared after the group of stormborn. Kael fanned out to the left, Clara the right. Should the demons attempt to split up, both would be ready. Liam flew just shy of Bree, carefully watching for her orders. The sparking group of stormborn ran faster, little bolts of lightning crackling across the ground before fading away, racing headlong through the town.

Pulling us away from the battle, Bree realized. They'd have to deal with this threat immediately. Her eyes traced the stormborns' path. The road gently curved to the east, homes packed tightly on either side. Bree signaled to the others, pointing out a slightly narrower stretch of road ahead.

There, she signaled.

Kael flew lower, gauntlet spreading a steady stream of ice. A wall formed from house to house, sealing off the street. Clara similarly blocked the other side. Trapped in a small square, the demons could not escape the torrent of flame Bree and Liam unleashed during their pass overhead. The beasts burned and broke into ash and crystalline blood. With that threat ended, Bree brought them back around to rejoin the battle proper.

Only three stoneborn remained, surrounded by an army of the stormborn. They ran without attacking, their path now toward the lip of the island. A retreat. Bree guided her squad overhead, ice from Kael and Clara forming walls to prevent their escape. Walls of stone and fire quickly joined theirs, sealing the eternal-born into an elemental prison. Bree readied for another pass, expecting the demons to assault one of the sides. Instead they drew in closer together, and then, without apparent reason, they turned wild.

The stormborn attacked the trio of stoneborn, their power ripping open chunks of their hard flesh. Bree watched with detached horror. Such brutality, and for what? Now that loss appeared inevitable, they would turn on their own? Green blood flowed across the empty street, sparking with electricity. One by one the stoneborn collapsed against each other, their bodies crumbling apart into a singular pile. The blood beneath them became a river. The stormborn sank into it, their bodies turning fluid.

Kael dashed in front of her, panic in his eyes.

"I've seen this!" he shouted. "We have to destroy it now before—"

The ground rumbled as a thunderbolt shook the heavens, striking the center of the eternal-born mixture. Bree's skin tingled and her hair stood on end. The mass of creatures shifted. Still moving. Still alive. Fresh horror awakening in her breast, she gaped at their newly formed enemy.

One single creature rose to its four feet, a swirling mass of stone held aloft by enormous streams of electricity. The stone hovered and shifted, creating a loose body with vague representations of arms, legs, and a head. Simply looking at it hurt Bree's eyes. A constant crackling roar emanated from the hybrid giant. Sparks of lightning flickered off it in all directions as it took its first few steps. Its arms lifted heavenward. The very air swirled into it, building, gathering, breaking.

The eternal-born monstrosity slammed its arms into its

chest, exploding its essence outward in a tremendous eruption of lightning. Seraphim weaved and dodged in a futile attempt to avoid its touch. Bree screamed as a bolt ripped through her right arm. Pain ignited in her nerves. Her mouth locked open in a scream she could not release. Her heart hammered in her chest, her muscles tight, her mind a whirlwind of pain.

It passed as quickly as it came, the lightning retreating into the creature for a moment before swirling around like a shield. Bree gasped in air, relieved beyond all reason. Her arm ached but otherwise functioned normally. She looked to the others, thrilled to see they too endured. The other Seraphim swarmed in a circle above the giant, bombarding from afar.

Bree motioned for Kael to take lead with his shield. She followed, her and Liam on either side, Clara taking up the back point of the diamond formation. The Seraphim's bombardment continued, but they still hadn't made any real damage to show for it. The swirling beams of lightning forming the demon's shield lashed out whenever anyone dared come near. Elemental attacks found themselves intercepted with overwhelming beams. Kael dove right as the creature turned their way. The shield swelled, building into a single bolt of lightning that shot straight into their path.

Kael braced his shield and plowed into the streak of lightning. The thunderous contact was so great, so powerful, Bree feared her brother would break. The light on his shield flared. Smoke enveloped his body, but the shield endured and the bolt did not. Bree banked higher, frustrated. She would be useless unless she was close enough for her swords or uncontrolled bursts of flame to reach. Clara flung lances of ice while Liam shot tightly coiled balls of flame. Neither attack made it far, the swirling shield of electricity battering them to ineffective pieces.

They looped around for a second pass, this one even farther back than before. Their attacks proved ineffective, their strategy unsound. Bree took lead and pulled them away to a hover.

"I know I can crack its stone armor," she shouted. "But I can't get close enough!"

"Then how do we close the distance?" Clara asked.

Bree bit her lower lip as she stared at the swirling monster of electricity and stone.

"Liam, can you distract it while I take position above?" she asked.

Her father saluted his fist against his breast.

"I am a knight of Center. Of course I can."

Bree's heart pounded with nervousness but she feigned confidence.

"You two wait for my attack," she told Kael and Clara. "When I strike, bury the demon in ice."

Liam flew to the ground and then raced along the blackened grass, taking a wide path toward the creature's back. Bree guided the three of them high into the air directly above the giant. Lightning crackled about the demon, lashing at anyone it saw. Seraphim circled around it, firing barrage after barrage. Ice and stone crumbled against counterblasts of lightning. The fire users struggled to close the gap, the few smaller orbs they launched mere nuisances. Whatever lightning sent its way swirled into the various beams, strengthening it further.

"Focus your ice into the gaps between the stones of its body," Bree told the other two. "I think if we can pull its essence apart we have a chance."

Liam kept dangerously close to the ground as he advanced unseen upon the giant. His wings shimmered and then went dull, their father sprinting along the grass. Lightning crackled through the air, all its strikes flaring upward and to the sides. Bree held her breath. He was close, so close, but all it would take was one glance downward to spot his approach, one step for the eternal-born to crush his body.

Liam reached its leg unseen. He leapt into the air, his wings flaring with light. At the height of his jump, Liam flicked off his wings and turned his body upside down as he soared over the head of the creature. The four pieces of his cannon split wide. A massive blanket of flame flowed from the end, engulfing the creature. Lightning streaked through the fire and smoke, attempting to clear it away. Bree unhooked the clips that kept her swords bound to her harness. One shot. She had one shot.

A burst of golden light marked Liam's wings' resurgence. His body righted, he pulled away from the flailing arm of the creature for a second pass. Again flame rolled out in all directions.

Bree looked to Kael and Clara. They nodded.

"At your mark, Phoenix."

Bree extended her swords out to either side. Her eyes closed. She felt the flame swirling about the blades, her comfortable friend. A loose link in her mind connected their power to the prism in her gauntlet, steadily feeding the fire. She boosted that connection. The flames grew hotter, brighter. Bree clenched her teeth, demanding it be greater. The weapons shook in her hands. The fire swelled so bright she could not look upon it. Kael and Clara floated away, unable to endure the heat. Bree screamed at the pain, the pressure, but it was hers, all hers, and she would not be denied.

With a cry of exultation Bree flung her swords to the ground. They shot like twin meteors, the metal hidden by the tremendous flame. The swords struck the creature's head, sank into its center, and exploded. The head ripped away from the rest of the body, the swirling beams of electricity connecting it stretching to their breaking point. The creature broke into spasms. Kael and Clara unleashed their ice before it might recover.

Two great beams struck the center mass of the creature. The ice flowed across it, fighting against the crackling power. Frost gathered along the stone. Ice sealed away paths for the lightning to escape. The creature tried to stand against the weight pressing it to the ground. Bree held her breath as she watched. Other ice Seraphim joined in, their beams merging together to sheathe the creature in a prison of frost. The stone ceased its movement. Electricity flickered and died.

Kael gasped in air as they finally stopped firing. He and Clara both looked like they'd run a marathon beneath the hot summer sun.

"I pray I never have to do that again," he said.

"Amen," Clara agreed.

Bree floated closer, laughing as she did.

"I think my swords are ruined," she said.

"Take mine," Kael said, pulling his free and handing them over one by one. "I never use them anyway."

Bree slid them into her sheaths.

"I'll try to be nice to them," she said.

Her easy smile vanished. Liam flew to join them, the four barrels of his arm locking back together into a singular cannon.

Clara noticed the tension in the air and gave Kael a kiss on the cheek. "I'll give you three a moment," she said. "I should congratulate the rest of our Seraphim."

She flew past Liam, neither acknowledging the presence of the other. He hovered before them, a wide smile across his face.

"You both fly with such skill," he said. "I couldn't be more proud of the people you've grown up to be."

"That's not exactly what you told me in my prison cell," Kael said. Bree winced at the hurt evident in his voice.

"I believed your actions were enabling the disaster we now face," Liam said. "Was I not correct in the danger and suffering all our islands have endured? Would you not also sacrifice everything to prevent this destruction? I was willing, my children. Two Seraphs die so that thousands live? A terrible cost, but my service is to Center, and her protection extends to all. I could not be so selfish as to put my own desires above the safety of humanity."

There was a logic to it, Bree felt, a twisted sense of honor and responsibility. It didn't lessen the hurt. It didn't wipe away the years of betrayal.

"Follow me," Kael said, breaking the awkward silence. "I want to see how the other islands fare."

The three crossed the ocean toward Center, their conversation halted by the wind and travel. Bree used the time to decipher how she felt. Her conclusion was that she didn't have a single goddamn clue.

The faint images of the other islands slowly came into view. Their Founts shared similar frozen archways climbing up them, but to her great relief she saw that each and every one lacked a bridge to connect it to the island's edge. There was no sign of the iceborn giants, or any of the eternal-born scaling to the top.

"We held," Bree said, then louder, "We held!"

Kael hovered closer, grabbing her harm and pumping it in excitement.

"Damn right we did!" He punched a fist toward the ocean and the swirling cloud of darkness that hovered above its surface. "You'll have to try harder, Johan. We're not impressed."

Kael laughed like he'd lost his mind. Bree felt close to tears.

It was too much. The invasion. The victory. The return of her father.

"A fine day," Liam said, and he sounded so relaxed, so at peace.

"So what happens now?" Bree asked.

"I don't know," Liam said. "But surely now the threat of L'adim cannot be ignored. All rebellion must end if humanity is to have a future. I pray you see our coming here in aid as a glimpse of our goodwill. Unite with us. End this destructive conflict."

Bree wished more than anything to embrace her father and shed tears across his breastplate. It felt so cruel to witness him alive yet simultaneously know all the harm he'd done.

"You want us to be together again?" she asked. Was it a fair dream to hope for? Was it selfish of her?

"Yes," Liam said. "Come with me to Center. Fly with my fellow knights. The Phoenix can still be a symbol for the people, but this time one of unity instead of rebellion."

Unity. Peace. It was everything she wanted. Her heart wished to accept, but her mind knew the coming days would decide Center's power over the outer islands. Their secrets and lies had left the islands weak and unprepared for the conflict with L'adim. For her to abandon Weshern now, in its greatest time of need...

"No," she said. "I won't go."

"And neither will I," Kael said.

Liam sighed.

"I hoped this battle would change your mind," he said. "The foe we face is far more important than petty squabbles over independence and autonomy. After all these years, we could have been a family again."

"And we still can," Bree said. She reached out for him. "Stay *here,* with us. Come home. Be a Seraph of Weshern again. Marius doesn't own you. He doesn't control you. Whatever he's told you, whatever's he's convinced you, it isn't true. It isn't right. We're your family. Please. Come home, Dad. Come back to us."

Liam ran his gauntleted hands over his bare scalp, his fingertips tracing the dozens of scars and runes. His lips murmured something she could not hear, and he did not appear to be saying it for her anyway.

"Marius has done nothing but lie and manipulate the minor islands to his benefit," Kael said. "His will is not of the angels. It's not of God's. I don't care how blasphemous you think this is, you need to open your eyes. He's just a man, weak, selfish, and wrong."

Kael extended his hand.

"Reject the Speaker," he said. "Be our father again."

Liam's fingers rattled against his skull. His upper body curled inward as if he had been stabbed in the gut. Still his mouth whispered unheard words. Faster. More desperate. Tears trickled to the ocean below. Bree dared hope.

A change came over him, sudden and heartbreaking to witness. His back straightened. His face hardened.

"I am the blade of the angels," he said. "What is holy must never break. I love you, my children, but I will not betray my faith for you. Everything Marius has ever said and done has been to protect and save humankind."

Bree felt her own tears building. She wanted to protest but had no words. Together the siblings watched their father flee to Center, to his home, the blessed land of his God. Kael waited until his wings were a distant golden dot before he floated to Bree and took her hand.

"It's all right, Bree," he said. "I think some scars run too deep for even family to overcome."

Bree yanked him closer so she could wrap her arms around his neck. The eternal-born had sent all they had up the Founts, but Weshern had beaten them back. Their sanctuary in the sky was safe. Exhaustion weighed heavily on every muscle in her body, and she clung to her brother for strength. Their military had paid a heavy cost, but at least they'd prevented the slaughter of civilians.

"Let's go home," she said.

"A fine idea."

They flew over the ocean to Weshern, Bree eager to feel the soft grass beneath her feet. She saw faint stretches of the ice wrapping around the Beam, a fading reminder of the invasion they'd just survived. Bree tried to feel hope at the sight. They'd won. Despite everything L'adim had thrown at them, they'd manage to preserve their sanctuaries in the sky.

They had not even been given a chance to land before Clara found them, veering off from a crowd of Seraphim soaring toward Center. Bree immediately sensed something amiss. Clara flew at far too great a speed to be rejoining them in celebration.

"It was a feint," she said upon nearing and dropping her wings down to a hover. "All of it. We need to fly to Center, now!"

"What? Why?" Bree asked.

"L'adim's revealed his presence," she said. "The shadow's climbing Center's Founts toward the surface."

"He wants to slay the lightborn keeping it afloat," Kael said. "And if he does..."

"Galen's fall would be nothing compared to Center's," Bree said. The nightmares of that moment danced through her head. To imagine a catastrophe even greater, on a scale ten times the size...

“Nothing’s changed,” Clara said, gesturing for them both to follow. “What did we say? Today we end this once and for all.”

“You’re right,” Bree said, tightening her gauntlet in preparation for yet another battle. “Humanity proves victorious or the eternal-born render us extinct. Either way, one of us has reached our end.”

CHAPTER 31

Seraphim of all islands flew to Center's aid, a frantic surge frighteningly similar to the swarm that had raced toward Galen before its fall. Shadow swarmed about the three Founts in a mammoth upward curve, flowing up through the water toward the surface. Bree could hardly believe the sheer size of the crawling darkness. Miles upon miles of it, a veritable flood. Knights lashed at the great pillar beneath the island with their elements, each attack a paltry blip upon a nightmarish landscape. Already she saw many of the knights retreating back to the surface.

Objective? Bree signaled with her hand to the others.

Neither had an answer.

Scattered groups of Weshern Seraphim flew ahead of them. Bree followed the majority toward one of the many docks at Center's edge. The crawling darkness rolled along the underside of Center, clinging to the earth as if it were made of webbing. Its movements were so controlled; the shadow gave a chilling impression of sentience. Its destination was one of those docks, a squad of nine knights hovering unsure above. Bree joined them in the skies, the men and women of the two islands sharing awkward glances. Clara drifted closer, searching for the highest-ranked member among them.

"Center came to our aid so now we come to yours," she said. "Where is it we are needed?"

"To be honest, little Archoness," said one of the knights, "we haven't a clue."

"We've ordered the townsfolk to abandon their homes and flee toward the holy mountain," another added. "Beyond that, we wait for the shadowborn's presence."

It wouldn't be long; Bree knew that from their approach. She looked to the gathered Seraphim and knights of all nations and knew their forces were a pitiful semblance of the defense they once could have mustered. Johan had achieved his desired war. They had done half the work for him, killing and slaughtering each other, and now he climbed toward the remnants of their civilization to swallow what remained of the world.

Olivia joined Clara's side. Her face was scarred with a long burn across the left half, but despite the amount of pain it surely caused she spoke calmly and controlled.

"When the shadow crawls over the edge, our elements will be ready," she told the knights. "Trust in us, as we shall trust in you."

They saluted one another, a small act of friendship on a cold, exhausting day. Each began issuing orders, scattering defenders into a long line above the edge.

Bree waited with Clara after receiving her orders to spread out along the edge. Kael was rushing from Seraph to Seraph, asking them something, though she could not imagine what.

"What's he doing?" Bree asked.

"He's looking for another light prism," Clara answered.

"Why not use his blood to refresh the ones he has?" Bree asked.

In answer, she shrugged.

Kael obtained a spare from one of the other Weshern Seraphim and jogged back over, the shimmering white prism clutched in his hand.

"We don't have much time," Bree said. "The shadow will curl over the edge soon. Did you get what you need?"

"I think so," Kael said. He popped open the prism in his gauntlet and removed the ice element within, further adding to Bree's confusion.

"What are you doing?" she asked.

"I noticed something during our fight with Johan in the throne room," Kael said as he slid his light element into the gauntlet instead and pocketed the ice prism. "My shield charge injured him terribly, but it wasn't the shield itself. It was the light that did it."

He slammed the compartment shut and then flexed his fingers. Wisps of light trickled from the focal prism. Kael grinned at it, his hope infectious amid the dire atmosphere.

"Do you think it'll work?" Clara asked.

"Bree's blood is fire," Kael said, "but my blood is light, and I'm hoping that's exactly what we need against the shadowborn."

"We're to split up along the edge," Bree said, snapping her fingers in front of Kael to grab his attention. "Keep your ice element ready just in case it doesn't work, all right?"

"It'll work," Kael said, and he winked. "Light's always easier to control than fire."

"Overconfident ass."

The three flew two miles to the south, taking up the position

Olivia had given them. Bree took the middle, with Kael and Clara several hundred yards to either side of her. Seraphim of the other islands fanned out into lines that stretched for dozens more miles. So many defenders, yet Bree knew vast stretches of the edge would go undefended. Center's landmass was just too huge to properly defend when their foe could strike everywhere at once.

The three hovered in the air above the edge, waiting. Watching. Bree kept her head on a swivel, watching to see if L'adim chose to swarm a particular stretch instead of the entirety of the edge. A flash of light caught her attention, Kael testing out his newly weaponized version of his element. It seemed little more than a powerful torch shining light in a thick beam across the grass. Useless in normal combat, she knew, little better than a potential distraction or blinding against other airborne foes. There was a reason those with light affinity usually became ferrymen instead of Seraphim. Except against this foe, whose essence was made of darkness, the light might be a far greater weapon.

The shadow curled over the edge without a sound. Little fingers grasped the dirt. Rivulets trickled like black veins into the earth. The tall grass withered away, all its color draining to an ashen gray. Bree sheathed her swords upon realizing how useless they would be against such a menace. Elemental attacks would carry the day here, severely limiting her usefulness. No signal began the defense, just a scattered few attacks growing into a tremendous barrage of elements that filled the sky for miles.

Stone and ice layered Center's edge into walls several feet high. The shadow pooled against it, building, rising. Long rings of flame proved most effective, the shadow burning like the now-ended midnight fire. Bree strafed the land, one long burst of fire projecting from her gauntlet. When it ended, she pulled up, needing a moment to recover. The crawling darkness twisted and curled, recoiling from the barrier of flame she'd created, then simply flowed to either side, bypassing it entirely. The sign of intelligent control only heightened her already growing terror. Bree moved to extend the barrier and cut off the flow but a brilliant flash of white light pulled her attention away.

Kael streaked along the edge, his wings shining bright even against the sun's glow. His gauntlet hung low, arm braced with the other hand, as its center streamed out a steady beam of light. It shone upon the crawling darkness, and at its mere contact the shadow recoiled and shriveled. Large swaths sparked orange and red like paper curling into ash. Not even the walls of flame performed such damage against L'adim's flood.

Bree pumped a fist into the air as Kael flew overhead, his back arching him into a U-turn. He waved in greeting as he raced in the other direction, another pass of his element searing the shadow and curling it back toward the edge. Bree turned her attention to her own responsibilities, her strength recovered and her prism recharged by her blood.

Walls of ice, flame, and stone lined the landscape, but it seemed only Kael's passes accomplished any real damage. Knights and Seraphim burned through their prisms, but they built minuscule barriers against an unstoppable flood. The shadow kept coming. New paths were always available to it. The best they could do was stall the flow, but to what end? For twenty minutes they slowed its spread, new walls replacing broken ones, the initial barriers rising higher and higher to combat the growing size of the shadowborn's presence. Bree prayed those twenty minutes were enough for the people to evacuate to safety . . . if there was anywhere safe left on Center.

Olivia fired three bolts of lightning straight into the air, signaling for the rest of the Weshern Seraphim to join her. Bree thought to stay, solidifying her section of wall, but it was clearly a hopeless task. No matter how much she burned, more flowed around it, testing the other walls and slipping through the cracks. Bree flew to join their commander, and as she flew over the defenses she could not see a single stretch of grass or rock. Despite all their efforts, the island's edge was overwhelmed with the crawling darkness.

"We can't hold such a wide area," Olivia shouted to the gathered mass of Weshern Seraphs. "We'll have to retreat inward. Save who you can, but do not tarry. We'll form up a second defense along the inner cities. We'll try again with a smaller defense line."

"You're dooming everyone along the edges," Kael protested.

"They're already doomed," Olivia snapped. "I'm saving what lives I can. Now obey your orders, Seraph, or I'll cut you down for insubordination."

She waited to see if Kael would challenge her. He did not.

"Very well," she said. "Stall the shadow if you wish, but do not cease moving toward the center. Our final stand is yet to come."

The rest scattered, joining the other islands in a massive exodus toward Heavenstone. Only Kael, Bree, and Clara hesitated behind.

"You were right about your prism," Bree said, forcing a smile to her face. It didn't last long. No amount of hope or humor could endure the tragedy unfolding below.

"Yeah," Kael said. "Not that it's helped any. The shadow keeps coming. It swallowed the world, remember? What's my little beam going to accomplish?"

Clara jabbed him in the side with her elbow.

"You, of all people, don't get to talk that way," she said. "People are still in danger, and no matter what Olivia says, we should still save who we can as we fly toward Center's inner cities."

Bree looked to the flood of darkness covering the landscape below.

"I'm not sure there's saving anyone from this," she said.

"Maybe," Clara said. "But if we think like that we're already dead."

She waved good-bye to Bree and her brother, taking up a path toward one of the distant villages. Kael popped the prism in his gauntlet free, cut across the top of his hand with his sword, and used his blood to refresh the cloudy gray prism to its full shine.

"See you soon, sis," Kael said as he slid the prism back into the compartment. "And stay safe, all right?"

He flew a similar path to Clara, only steeper to the east, another distant village his goal. Despite her aching back, Bree tilted forward and gently increased the throttle. With numb heart and broken spirit she flew over the sprawling shadow. It was Galen all over again. Men, women, and children ran through the streets toward the heart of Center. The faster among them could outrun the steady flow, but the elderly? The children? Bree saw a woman with a babe trip mere feet ahead of the flood. The crawling darkness washed over them both. Bree prayed their death was quick.

A group of nine rushed farther ahead, two of them carrying little children. An older man lagged behind with a limp. One of the family ahead turned away despite the cries of those with him, running back to the limping man and flinging an arm around his shoulder. Bree knew neither would escape in time, nor would the little group holding the children. She dropped from the sky, refusing to watch them all be buried by the flood. Fire roared from her gauntlet, and a wall of flame stretched dozens of yards to either side, blocking off the road as well as several buildings. The shadow touched the flames and curled away.

"Run!" Bree screamed at nine. "Run, and never stop!"

Two knights flew overhead, ice lashing the ground from their gauntlets to secure other parts of the town. Bree rested a moment. Already that day she'd used more flame than she ever had before. Was her strength growing, or was she merely learning her limits were greater than she believed? It didn't matter, not really. Bree would continue bathing the land in flame no matter how terrible the cost. Breath regained, she took to the air and continued on.

Bree crossed over a deep forest. So far the darkness had only reached the very edge of the tree line. The thin pine needles of the touched trees withered and fell, their green sapped away and replaced with a sickly white. Stories told of the entire world swallowed by that shadow. Bree didn't want to imagine what it looked like.

Beyond the forest was a massive city with population surpassing anything she'd ever seen on Weshern. The roads were thick with people fleeing toward Heavenstone. Bree took up position at the forest's edge and waited. First came the animals, deer and hounds, little squirrels and puffy-chested birds. After them came the people, slower, weighted down by loved ones and the last vestiges of their homes. They were tired despite their panic, the miles they were forced to cover too much for many. The trickle of humans slowed. The dying trees neared.

"God damn you, Johan," Bree hissed.

She flew to the far edge of the forest, drawing one of her swords on the way. She had to control her flame somehow. If not, she'd be exhausted before ever reaching the other side. Fire wreathed the blade. Bree imagined it in her mind, demanded it obey her control. Dropping low, she extended the sword and released her flame. A thin jet dripped off the tip of her sword and lashed the tree line. Bree didn't need to stop it if she could only control it. The prism burned out slowly as the stream flowed from her blade. The strain was terrible on her mind but she endured. Five minutes later the entire tree line burned red and yellow.

The blazing forest delayed the spread for another twenty minutes. Smoke billowed from distant fires to the north and south. It seemed other Seraphs had come up with the same idea. The forest, though, could be bypassed. The first thin rivers of darkness spilled around the sides, rapidly growing in thickness. Bree wished to halt it, but how? She could block a street or two, but what did that compare to a city of a dozen roads? Already the shadow was curling around the buildings on the outer edges of the city, trapping people in like a hunting pack of dogs. Her only hope was that she'd bought the people enough time.

It seemed the theotechs were not content to hope.

The shaking of the land turned Bree to the west. She recognized that terrible explosion. She knew that darkening of the skies. Whatever weapon had leveled Glensbee had now been unleashed upon the very heart of the crawling shadow in the fields beyond the city. Fire enveloped it. Stone smashed it. Lightning struck from hellish clouds. It was like a hammer smashing a puddle. The darkness splashed in all directions, only a small portion of it burned away completely. From such a high vantage point Bree could see the shadow retreating, like the receding tides of an ocean. Fresh waves from the island's edge surged forward to replace it, but at least it offered more time for the fleeing crowds. Bree watched the recession, noting something curious. The darkness moved like water, and when it retreated she saw there was a distinct point it retreated toward.

"Is that you, L'adim?" Bree asked.

A fresh surge of shadow crossed the emptied field, thin and narrow like a spear instead of the wide wave it normally spread. It smashed into a neighborhood near the outer edge of the city. The location of the weapon, Bree surmised. Knights hovered overhead, their frantic work not enough to spare the theotechs below. Fear wormed its way deep into her mind. The greatest weapon she'd ever witnessed had still meant nothing to the shadowborn. Could there be victory? Was it even possible, or would the crawling darkness eventually swallow them all like it had the rest of the world?

Eyes locked on that center point, Bree kicked her wings back to full strength and soared over the graying Center landscape. After those first few waves it seemed like the shadow was completely retreating. Bree didn't dare allow herself to hope. She raced overhead, careful not to lose sight of her goal. The receding waves of shadow seemed to lead toward that same point. Her gut tightened. L'adim. That's where he had to be.

The landscape turned bleaker and darker the closer she neared her objective. No tree survived. No building stood tall and proud. Everything had rotted and broken. The shadowborn did not create. He did not build. He only ruined what was once good.

Not far now. The shadow roared beneath at a terrific pace, making a mockery of even the speed of her wings. It all pooled toward one area, amassing in size with frightening speed. Bree saw a faint ghost light ahead shining in the center of a swirling maelstrom of darkness and shadow. Johan stood in its center, and he smiled up at Bree as if she were a welcome guest.

"Breanna!" he called to her as she slowed to a hover. "How great to see you've made it this far. I'd have been disappointed if you fell before my arrival."

Bree pointed her gauntlet at him. Johan tsked at her as he wagged his finger.

"Do not insult me," he said. "I have endured the wrath of nations. What are you compared to that?"

The shadow pooled beneath him, lifting him higher and higher into the air. The crawling slowed, the substance solidifying. Rivers built about him, encasing him up to the waist. Bree felt her skin crawl at the sight. She wanted to release her flame, but what might she hope for when he was so protected by the shadow? Giant hands rose and fell in the darkness, each one reaching toward her before sinking back down into the murk.

Johan melted into the darkness. His laughter faded to a haunting memory. The rivers rushed together, forming arms, legs, and hands. She could stay and fight. She could die like all the others in a futile gesture to halt the unstoppable.

Bree turned and fled.

CHAPTER 32

Liam flew through one of the grand windows of Heavenstone and landed. The knight didn't give a damn that he was abandoning the battle outside, not that there even was a proper battle. The knights and soldiers were frantic children battling against a tide of shadow beyond all their comprehension. The ancient evil walked upon the holy ground of Center. They didn't need soldiers and knights. They needed the divine intervention of the angels themselves.

Liam went to Marius's private quarters, found them empty. A lone guard stood before the open door of the room.

"Where is the Speaker?" Liam shouted at him.

"He's not to be disturbed," the guard said, taken aback.

"Our island is at stake," Liam said, grabbing him by the front of his armor and yanking him close. "Now where the hell is Marius?"

The guard hesitated. Liam could tell he was terrified. Not

of Liam, but of all that was happening beyond Heavenstone's walls.

"He's gone to speak with the angels," he said.

Liam shoved him away and used his wings to zip down the halls. There was no time. Servants fled this way and that, interspersed with panicked guards and knights. Never before had Liam seen Heavenstone in such chaos. Did it speak to the level of danger they faced, or the lack of control Marius exercised over the people?

His flight took him straight to the unassuming door they'd passed through on his previous visit with the angels. Liam flung open the door, expecting the room to be empty. Instead Marius sat at his desk, head in his hands. Tears trickled down his wrists as he silently prayed.

"My Lord?" Liam said, feeling guilty. "Please, I must speak with you."

Marius looked up with red eyes.

"Liam," he said. "I'm so glad to see you. I prayed to God for the strength to do what must be done, but I fear I am not strong enough. I'm weak, Liam, frightened and weak, but you are here. You'll be my strength."

"I don't understand," Liam said. He had come to urge Marius to save them all. The war against L'adim would not be won by knights and Seraphim. It would be won by the power of the angels deep within Heavenstone, and harnessed by the holy Speaker's hand. "What task do you lack the strength for that I myself possess?"

Marius rose from his seat and wiped at his eyes.

"L'adim has reached our lands," he said. "The shadow that swallowed the world will soon swallow us, too. I have failed the only task that ever mattered. Only one recourse remains, Liam. One last, desperate course."

The Speaker's words were dire, and they carried a prophetic air that frightened Liam greatly.

"What is that?" he asked.

Marius reached out and lovingly placed a hand on Liam's face.

"Come with me to the angels," he said. "Slay them, and let Center be swallowed by the ocean."

Liam's entire body locked tight. It felt like he'd been stabbed in the heart.

"Slay them?" he asked, his mind reeling. "But . . . but they are God's messengers. And what of the people here? Hundreds of thousands will die."

"Hundreds of thousands have already died," Marius said. His lips quivered, and his hands shook at his sides. "The rest are doomed. Don't you see, Liam? The shadowborn is here. There is no defeating him. Even the Spear of God only chased away his shadow for a moment. Great armies of the old world all failed against his might and cunning. Who are we compared to those ancient empires? Little children hiding on a small speck of rock, that is what we are."

"But why slay the angels?" Liam asked. "Why not fight?"

Marius lowered his head, and he stared into his desk as if it were the most important thing in all the world.

"Did you witness Galen's fall?" he asked quietly.

"I did not," Liam said.

"I did," Marius said. "The moment I heard the Beam was faltering I had my knights fly me close enough to watch the rescue attempts. I didn't believe it would happen, Liam. I thought the Beam might weaken but the lightborn within would recover. The people would survive. The island would endure."

He slammed a fist atop the desk, startling the quiet with its thud. "But our world is not one of fairy tales, Liam. We wrap ourselves in the divine as if it means we are invincible, assured of survival no matter the terrors. Even I swallowed that lie, and it was only when I watched Galen crash to the ground that I realized how precarious our lives are. No golden hands of God reached out to stop the island's destruction. The Beam failed, and the island fell. It was that simple. That cruel."

Liam wished he knew what to say, but his faith was profoundly shaken. This was the Speaker for God and his angels, broken down and overwhelmed with doubt and fear. Everything Liam had ever trusted, that he'd ever believed, he'd given over to the man who was meant to save humanity.

"Why do we speak of Galen?" he asked softly.

"When Galen hit the water I felt the impact in the clouds," Marius said. "It was as if the entire world quaked with sorrow and fury. That power... that power is the only thing I believe might have a chance to slay the shadowborn. No matter the cost, we must take it. We must send Center crashing down in an eruption so grand not even the betrayer may survive."

"All to slay the shadowborn?" Liam asked. "What does it matter if there are none left to live in his absence?"

"You forget our place," Marius said, rising up. "We are the protectors of humanity, not just those on Center. The other four islands will endure. Humanity will limp on, bloodied and small but alive. It is the only hope I have left to cling to, Liam. Now will you help me? Will you, with your blade, bring salvation and freedom to the outer islands? To your homeland, Weshern?"

Liam's insides coiled with uncontrolled fury. Confusion and terror lashed his soul with icy whips. What could he say? What was even right? Was this sacrifice truly worth so much?

"Why must you ask this of me?"

"Because I have not the strength," Marius said. "But you do.

You always have. That's why I chose you, Liam. That's what made you special. Now let go of your fear and follow me."

Liam stepped as if in a waking nightmare, his limbs moving of their own accord. They walked to the lift and rode down into the deep, deep heart of Heavenstone. The twelve keepers of the doors waited at attention, alerted by the creaking approach of the lift.

"Open it," Marius said, lacking the sense of fanfare of their last visit.

The men pulled on their ropes, cracking open the doors with a deep, satisfying rumble of stone. Marius waited until they were finished, then gestured to the lift.

"Leave us," he said.

The men glanced to one another, confused.

"I said leave us!"

They hurried past, abandoning their posts to crowd onto the lift. Marius remained locked in place, not moving a single step until the lift was gone and the two of them were alone.

"The lightborn read emotions like you or I read words on a page," Marius said, eyes locked on that glowing slant of light between the two doors. "You must keep yourself calm and controlled at all times. Do not think on your task, Liam. Simply enter, and when I raise my arms, perform the deed. Do not hesitate. Do not doubt. Let your heart be fully committed to the task." He turned to face him. His eyes were wet with tears. "Can I trust you to do this?"

Liam swallowed down the shards of glass lodged in his throat. He steeled his face and locked his body stiff, attempting to do exactly as Marius described.

"I have always been, and always will be, a servant of the Lord and his angels."

Marius beamed with pride.

"If only all the world were filled with faithful such as you," the Speaker said. "Perhaps we'd have never found ourselves in a situation so dire."

Marius walked through the entrance and into the grand chamber of the angels, Liam at his side.

The three lightborn were huddled low to the floor, their chains stretched taught. Waves of fear and sorrow washed over Liam, overwhelming in their power.

"The shadowborn cometh," spoke the feminine one in the center. "We sense his corruption. We feel the dead mounting. Why do you come to us, Marius? Why do you not lead your people?"

Marius shook his head.

"Because matters of terrible importance compel me before you," he said.

The muscles in Liam's right arm tightened. His awareness of his metallic arm grew, and he felt the blade within eager to spring forth. Liam tensed, his mind reeling again and again.

What must be done, he thought, not daring anything more specific than that. *What must be done. What must be done.*

"Then speak them. The shadowborn must be defeated, and we will offer you any wisdom or counsel you desire."

"I have but one desire," Marius said, lifting his arms. "And it is not your wisdom or counsel."

The signal given, Liam lifted his gauntlet. The four cannons split open and to the sides. The long blade ejected to its full length, its sharp point ripping through Marius's back and piercing out the front of his chest.

"I am the blade of the angels," Liam whispered into the Speaker's ear. "Not their executioner."

Fire burst from the four cannons, enveloping Marius's body from head to toe. The flame swarmed over him, consuming him, purifying him. Ash and bone slipped free of the blade, collapsing at Liam's feet. The lightborn looked on all the while, revealing no emotion beyond mild surprise.

Liam stared at the remains, trying to push himself through the shock of what he'd done.

"He would have me kill you," he said, quiet at first, his voice growing louder with his increasing rage. "He would have me slay you to save us from the shadowborn. Is that what you want from me? Do you want to die and kill everyone living on Center's soil just to hope the shadowborn dies with us in the fall?"

They cast glances to one another, and Liam could tell by the shifting emotions and shimmering differences in light across their skin that they were conversing in a way beyond his understanding.

"We have already given our lives for humanity's," the feminine lightborn said. "And we still have faith the shadowborn may be defeated. But no victory is worth the loss of humanity. Yes, let our hearts beat on, and let this jewel remain high in the sky. Now is not the time to give in to fear. We will offer what advice and aid we can."

Liam stared at the flaking black bits of blood drifting off his sword. Deep in his mind he felt a breaking.

"Let others fight on," he echoed. "You wish to offer aid? Then kill me, you lightborn bastards. End my misery now."

They lifted back as if appalled by the very notion.

"Why would we do such a thing?"

Liam laughed. The very way they phrased the question, so focused on themselves, the tone more curiosity than worry, broke him all the further.

"Kill me!" he screamed. "I have slain he who speaks for God. What worth am I? To myself? To you?"

He sliced his own arm and lifted it so they might watch the blood splatter scarlet upon their pristine marble floor.

"The blood of demons flows through my veins," he shouted. "I am an abomination, a botched experiment and nothing more. Kill me. End this. Show you still have the courage to do something besides sitting here hiding from the world!"

Still they recoiled. As if dirtying their hands would be beneath them. As if they hadn't witnessed the deaths of thousands over the centuries of their long lives. Liam felt tears trickling down his face. When he next screamed, his voice was hoarse and tired.

"Is that it? You won't do it? You cowards. You fucking cowards. Tear free of those chains and kill me. You say you have given your lives for humanity, but you will not lift a finger now in our time of need. Slay the shadowborn yourselves instead of relying on us to bleed and die for you. Haven't we given enough?"

Silence was again their answer. Pity swam in their golden eyes.

"I tried to kill my son and daughter," Liam said, lacking the strength to shout. "What worth am I?"

"You are worth the life of a human," said the feminine lightborn. "And that worth always remains unchanged."

"Liars," Liam whispered. "*Liars!* So what we do doesn't matter? All my sins, all my penance, neither changes a thing? Then what's the point? What is the goddamn *point*?"

The feminine lightborn lowered closer to him, outstretching her hand. Her emotions washed over him, full of compassion and hope but also an undeniable sadness.

"To live for those who love you," she said. "From the lowest of the low, to the very divine."

"Those who love you," Liam whispered. "I have none left. I tried to kill them all."

He retracted the blade in his gauntlet and pressed the cannon against the underside of his chin. All his sorrow and rage drained away, leaving him a hollowed numbness.

"The life of a human," Liam said, tears streaming down his face. "Let's see just how much that's worth."

He ignited the fire prisms with the last dying bit of his passion. He felt the heat, felt the pain.

Felt nothing at all.

CHAPTER 33

Kael drained the last of his prism forming a constant line of light protecting a wide, shallow lake. The shadow retreated as if wounded, appearing thin and frail while it slowly regrew in size from the teeming mass of darkness climbing over Center's edge. Kael reopened the wound on his hand, popped the compartment of his gauntlet open, and pressed the light prism against it to refresh it once again.

"How the hell does Bree do this all the time?" Kael wondered aloud as he felt his energy wane, his strength flowing into the prism to banish the cloudy haze and the multitude of cracks. Gasping for air, he pulled it away and then jammed it into the compartment. Turning the knob to activate the gauntlet, he spun to the shadow for another series of blasts only to discover the shadow wasn't there. It receded from the lake surface, swam through the tightly packed homes, and vanished into the dying trees of the forest.

Baffled, Kael lifted into the air in search of a better vantage spot. Had the shadowborn been defeated? So far it appeared that way. He flew higher and higher, the land becoming a vague green-and-blue shape below. There he followed the retreating darkness with his eyes. It flowed from all directions back toward a single focal point, and Kael felt his stomach tighten. He'd seen this before, with both the fireborn giant and the conglomeration of stoneborn and stormborn. Whatever the crawling darkness would become, he feared its form.

Not a sound marked the shadowborn's rise. Kael watched him lift above the forest on two long legs, his humanoid body stretching out his arms to push himself up from the ground. The sheer size baffled him. L'adim had to be four hundred feet tall, if not taller. His form seemed to consist entirely of condensed shadow. He bore no eyes, no mouth, no markings at all to mar the perfect sheen of black. Each step crushed buildings and trees. A lake of darkness swirled beneath his feet, spreading sickness and death wherever he walked.

Kael wondered who could stand against such a thing. Was this it, then? Was this the demon who swallowed the world? He thought of the destruction the cannons waged upon Weshern, each blast now seeming so insignificant compared to swirling legs of shadow carrying L'adim across Center at a terrifying rate. The demon's direction never changed, stepping across lake and grass and city and crushing them all beneath his gait. Kael traced the path to the obvious end: the fortress of Heavenstone.

Seraphim and knights filled Center's skylines, and every one flew to outrace L'adim to his destination. They would mass together before the shadowborn reached it, giving their final stand against the darkness. Kael flicked his throttle and soared over the land, desperately praying that their combined forces would be enough.

Kael remembered his friend Loramere telling him to land a safe distance from Heavenstone lest he be attacked. It'd seemed good advice then, but now he flew right over its twin barrier walls without any fear. There were no nations anymore, no wars and alliances. There was but one enemy, and he marched toward them in a monstrous visage more suited to a nightmare. Kael looked for the familiar black jackets of Weshern and found them grouped together in a hover along the fortress's western side. Their number was painfully smaller than it had been at the start of the day.

"How're we doing?" Kael asked as he hovered to Clara's side. Few others looked ready to chat, and he couldn't deny the relief he felt seeing her still alive and well.

"Like shit," Saul said, dropping down a dozen feet to float even with them. "How's Bree?"

"She was fine last I saw her," Kael said. He looked to the shadowborn's steady passage toward them. "Actually, I think that's her now."

A silver-winged Seraph flew directly ahead of L'adim, a little speck of brightness amid the solid dark. Kael lifted his shield and let it shimmer with light several times to draw her attention. Her direction shifted slightly, her mad speed lessening over the next minute as she pulled up alongside them. Sweat dripped down her face. Her eyes were bloodshot.

"Are you all right?" Kael asked.

"I saw him," Bree said. "I spoke with him. L'adim is in the heart of that monstrosity. He's in there, and that means we can kill him."

"You say as if that'll be easy," Saul said, and he cracked a grin. "But I guess slaying a world destroying demon would just be another notch on your belt."

She appeared in no mood for any attempts at humor. Her

wide eyes looked to the shadowborn, and her body shivered underneath her black jacket.

"God, I hope so."

A tall woman with fiery red hair flew to the center of the gathered Seraphim forces of all islands and loosed several bolts of lightning directly into the air to summon them closer. Their little group of four followed Clara's lead to join in.

"I am Knight Master Allison," she said once they gathered. A twist of her waist set her to gently spinning to face them all. "On behalf of my knights I thank you for coming to join us in this dire hour."

She pointed to L'adim in the distance.

"That fucking thing needs to die. Our theotechs will assemble across Heavenstone's rooftops with the last of our cannons. Our knight giants will be the front line along the ground, backing up our soldiers. I don't know how they'll face against the shadowborn but we must try. As for you all, I ask that you join my knights in protecting the cannons. We need every bit of firepower we can muster if we're to defeat the damned demon. Can you do that for me, Seraphim?"

Scattered calls of agreement from squadron leaders answered her. She nodded as if pleased.

"I don't know the fate of our worlds," she said. "But I know that it is still within our hands. Fight like hell, my brethren. All of humanity depends upon it."

There were no triumphant choruses, no raised fists and boastful shouting, only tired, grim calls of agreement. Bree, Kael, Clara, and Saul broke off into their own formation of four, one squad of dozens hovering in the air before Heavenstone. The knights took up positions between the two long defensive walls, protecting the near one hundred red-robed theotechs readying defenses on the ground. Cannons rumbled among them, each one turning its aim toward L'adim. A flood of soldiers rushed out the open gates of Heavenstone, several hundred taking up positions in lines ten deep. All in all, it was an impressive defensive display, but the final pieces were yet to arrive.

Stone crumbled from the mountain behind Heavenstone to reveal long tunnels dug into the rock. Platforms floated out from them, each one carried by two dozen ferrymen. Kael watched them drift into position in front of Heavenstone, their occupants slowly shimmering to life. They were the knight giants, humanoid in shape but tremendous in size. Kael could not see wherever the pilot was inside it, though most likely they sat in the machine's heavily armored chest. Its armored plates were thick steel grafted with silver. Their heads were shaped like pre-Ascension armored helmets. Long, slanted eyes shimmered with thin pieces of embedded light elements. All nine swung gilded swords longer than any knight was tall. Their left hands ended not in fists but in cannons similar to the one that had been grafted on his father. Kael had seen only one knight giant in battle, but even its brief display had been incredible. Imagining all nine...

He looked to the approaching shadowborn. Yes, all nine might be impressive, but how would they fare against the monstrosity coming for them?

The platforms landed among the ground soldiers. The nine exited their platforms, their footfalls sinking into the earth with each heavy step. They lumbered forward to form the initial line of defense. Their swords swung through the air, a brilliant white light blazing from the four prisms linked together to form their hilts. A myriad of colors shone from the barrels of their cannons and wafted like smoke to the heavens. L'adim marched on, his hunched form taking up the entire sky. He showed no fear of the defenders readied against him.

This is it, Kael thought. *The best we have. If this isn't enough, then only a miracle from God can save us.*

The knight giants raised their arm cannons. The war machines atop the walls readied their elements. Knight Master Allison swept across the battlefield, her golden wings passing mere inches from the giants' raised arms. She screamed the same line again and again, readying them to fire.

"We are the blade! We are the blade! We are the blade!"

As she passed the last mechanical knight, with the great lake of shadow rolling ahead of L'adim's footfalls about to reach their line, Allison pulled into the heavens and screamed at the very top of her lungs, her drawn sword thrusting into the air to give the signal.

"What is holy must never break!"

The arms of the knight giants rocked from the explosions. Cannons fired one after another, singing a great chorus of destruction. Knights and Seraphim added their own elements to the barrage, thin beams among enormous blasts. Kael held back his light, unsure of its strength at such a distance. With bated breath he watched the massive barrage approach L'adim.

The shadowborn welcomed it with open arms. The liquid darkness froze in spools larger than rivers. Stone pounded through the darkness, tearing at L'adim's physical presence. The fire swarmed him, consuming great chunks at its touch before flaming out. Lightning crackled across his form, its golden light fighting the deep dark of the shadowborn's essence. The great lake of shadow at its feet swirled up its legs, reinforcing the parts of L'adim that thinned or burned from the attack. For a brief moment Kael dared believe they stood a chance.

L'adim's retaliation was swift and terrible. His legs crumpled to the ground. Rivers of shadow burst from his knees, flowing with otherworldly speed between the two defensive walls. The knight giants turned their aim to the ground. Elements slammed the approaching waves, hardening it with ice, splashing it back with stone, and setting it alight with flame. The defense left Bree in awe, but the raw amount of shadow dwarfed their incredible display. The shadow hardened, shaping into sharp claws lunging upward. The soldiers lifted their shields and thrust with their spears. It did nothing. It changed nothing. The claws ripped through their lines, tearing men apart like they were made of paper. Only the knight giants withstood. Their swords cleaved the air, smashing the shadow, cracking it like ice.

L'adim's two arms became four, then eight. Each one thrashed a different direction. Each finger elongated, a thousand spears launching at the remaining knights and Seraphs. Kael flung up a wall of ice just to watch it shatter. He kicked his wings into full speed and weaved higher into the air, desperately hoping the other three might follow. Sometimes he dodged, sometimes not, his survival relying more on dumb luck than any skill. His meager beam of light felt worthless compared to the destruction erupting about him. His shield was but a plaything. Saul vanished somewhere amid the chaos, and Kael spared only a moment's concentration to pray for his safety.

The shadowborn lifted its foot and took another lumbering step. Light prisms flared within the mechanical joints of the knight giants as they closed the distance. Their cannons ripped into the shadowborn's knees. Their swords slashed across its shins. The shadow broke, the shadow retreated, the shadow returned. Spikes shot from L'adim's legs without reason or sense. Every inch of the demon was a threat. The pieces twisted and turned like tendrils, wrapping about the knight giants' arms and legs. Metal shrieked and twisted. The ancient machinery broke, just another worthless toy before the swallower of worlds.

Another barrage from the cannons blasted the shadowborn. The Seraphim were joining the knights in another attack run. Kael flew among them, taking bitter satisfaction at the cavern his light carved into L'adim's form. The shadowborn rocked backward, more and more of the sprawling river below him lifting to reinforce the damaged parts of his being. His arms crossed over his blank face, enduring another barrage. His legs churned. He pushed into the space between the two defensive walls, leaving a wide field of death behind. Kael thought he might attack the walls but instead he crouched closer, his entire body sinking deeper into the earth. The shadow's outer layer of skin bubbled, breaking, loosening.

L'adim rose to his full height, and his shadow blasted out of him as a billowing fog. It spread like a dome, widening in all directions, even into the sky. It would retract for a brief moment before pulsing outward hundreds of yards farther. Kael shot heavenward, Bree and Clara at his heels. Knights and Seraphim fled every which way in complete panic. Kael remembered the sickening feeling of L'adim's presence back in the throne room, and he knew what tore at the hundreds in the sky as they weaved and hovered in wild directions. Every pleasant thought corrupted. Every dream and hope filled with sickness. He pushed his wings harder, outracing the fog. Bree and Clara lagged farther and farther behind, unable to keep up with his blood-blessed wings. Kael continually glanced their way, terror clawing at his throat. The fog was near, so near.

One last pulse before the shadow retreated back into L'adim's form. Bree escaped. Clara did not. The shadow washed over her from head to toe. Immediately her wings went dark. She let out a soft cry before pitching forward, her body going limp.

"Clara!" Kael screamed. He turned about and dove for her. His wings easily closed the distance, and he wrapped his arms about her before she could fall. He saw her face, saw her closed eyes, and begged for fate not to make him suffer so. She was alive. She had to be alive. He held her with his right arm, his left taking her wrist and thumbing her throttle back on. Just a gentle glow, enough to slow their descent as Kael guided them to the ground away from the battle. They landed in the field of grass just off the road leading into Heavenstone. Bodies of dead Seraphim lay all about, slaughtered by L'adim's initial assault. Kael hated putting Clara among them, but there wasn't much choice.

Bree landed beside him and shut off her wings.

"Will Clara be all right?" she asked.

Kael knelt over her body, his ear to her chest. Tears ran down his face.

"I think so," he said. Her heart beat weakly in her chest, but her lungs breathed in and out of their own accord. "She just needs time."

The shadowborn's touch was vile and sickening, but Clara had only been overwhelmed for a second. She might still live. Kael wished he could feel more relief, but what did it matter if Clara survived just to fall into the ocean when Center crashed? Already hundreds of miles of Center's landscape withered and rotted. Everything the shadowborn touched turned to dust, and now he reached for the very heart of humanity's greatest sanctuary.

It seemed Bree felt that same doom. She stood facing L'adim as the vile thing brought down a dozen knights with a single swipe of his arms. The cannons were yet to resume, the theotechs no doubt suffering as terribly as Clara, if not worse.

"Maybe L'adim is right," Bree whispered. "Maybe we aren't special. We'll vanish from this world, and no animals or angels will weep for our passing."

Kael rose to a stand. He could barely control his actions. He closed the distance between them with two quick steps and backhanded his sister across the face. Bree clutched her cheek.

"Don't," Kael seethed. "We mean more than that. All of us, our lives, our deaths, our pain and suffering and joy, it fucking *means* something. Maybe to God, maybe to the angels, maybe just to ourselves, but don't you dare try to tell me that murderous monster was *right*. We are better than that. Better than him."

He hated himself for doing it but couldn't see another way. The terror of losing his sister the same way he lost his father was too much to bear.

"You're right," Bree said. A spark of her old fire kindled in her eyes. "So what can we do? It's just us two, Kael, so what can we possibly do?"

Kael bit his lip. His mind scrambled for ideas, running the battle against L'adim through his mind. The way the shadow recoiled against light and fire. The way any damage against his gargantuan form was quickly erased by a flood of shadow curling up from the veritable lake of it at his feet.

"You said L'adim's inside that monster somewhere, right?" Kael asked.

"Somewhere," Bree said. "But we can't get to him. The shadow always reinforces itself."

Kael opened the compartment to his gauntlet and stared at the mostly full prism within. Wincing against the pain, he cut into a different part of his hand and allowed his blood to refuel the prism.

"It does reinforce," Kael said as he popped it back in. "But maybe we just need to attack even harder. I...I'll do what you do. I'll let it all out at once, every bit of my light prism. Maybe...maybe it'll overwhelm him. Maybe we'll push it all back and find the devil deep inside."

"You don't know you can do that," Bree argued. "And what happens if it doesn't work? You'll die."

"Then I die, damn it," he shouted back at her. He felt his words growing harsher, more desperate. "How's that make me different from the thousands of others L'adim has slain today?"

She stared at him, her own mind racing.

"Fine," she said. "Wait for me, though. I have an idea, too."

His sister dashed among the bodies, checking their compartments and removing any fire elements she found. Kael checked on Clara as he waited, listening to her breathing as a reminder of all he would sacrifice his life for.

"What are you doing?" Kael asked when Bree slid a third prism into her left palm.

"You're right," Bree said, finding two more in a pouch on a dead knight's belt. "It's not sustained damage that'll take L'adim down, but one sudden, overwhelming attack."

She hurried back to him. His eyes narrowed as she drew her sword in her free hand.

"That's not your specialty, Kael. It's mine."

Flame wreathed her sword. She sliced through the top half of his right wing, curled her blade about, and then did the same to his left. The heavy pieces of metal thudded to the grass. Kael stared at them, momentarily shocked, but he yanked at the buckles of his disabled harness, flailing to remove it so he might don another.

“You don’t have to do this,” he shouted to her.

“I love you, Kael,” she said, her wings flaring to life.

“No, don’t!” he cried. One of his buckles caught and he desperately yanked it again and again. His sister left him. He knew what she planned. He begged her return. He screamed his frustration. His last protest. His horror manifest in a lone word.

“Bree!”

CHAPTER 34

Bree raced through a sky full of death and shadow, closing in on L'adim her only goal. His back was to her but it seemed the shadowborn needed no eyes to sense her presence. Spears launched upward from the blanket of black spread before Heavenstone's gates, thin little ropes of smoke keeping the spears connected to the shadow below. Bree dodged and weaved through them, her wings at three-fourths power to ensure she could both slow down or burst ahead as the dodge required.

The prisms in her left hand ached, their sharp edges digging into her skin. Fire flickered from their surface, licking the flesh of her bare skin.

Just a little bit longer, she thought.

The spears were merely the outer defenses. The monstrosity that was L'adim raged before her, his arms slamming down upon the walls of Heavenstone. Each strike dwarfed the power of the cannons firing at him, his curled fists blasting apart stone and mortar. It would not be long before all of Heavenstone lay in ruin. Seraphim and knights filled the air around L'adim like little bees buzzing about a raging boar. Their stings did nothing but anger him.

Free of the spears, Bree pushed her wings harder, her gaze locked on the faceless creature. Once the shadowborn turned his attention to her, that speed would be her only hope. She watched the defense of Heavenstone, such as it was. What few cannons remained thundered shooting elements into the shadow, making temporary indents into L'adim's towering humanoid form. Several struck his formless face, coupled with the attacks of a dozen Seraphim. Fire and lightning swirled across the black, consuming the crawling darkness. Bree prayed the concentrated attack would harm him despite having seen L'adim endure worse during the initial defense.

L'adim's head sank into its body and reemerged fully healed. He took another step, his foot sinking into his own shadow as if it were a deep pool. His hand stretched out, those seven fingers slowly spreading wide. With a sudden jerk, the fingers spiked forward like javelins of impossible length. Each finger ripped through a cannon before tearing open a hole across the top of Heavenstone. L'adim stretched his other hand, the number of digits increasing, nine fingers piercing the heavy stone as if it were straw. Cannons fired their elements into his arms, sheeting them over with ice and slamming through with stone. The fingers retracted, L'adim sparing no attention to the futile attacks. Instead he focused on the flying knights and Seraphim, his body bubbling like a volcano about to erupt.

Erupt it did. Shadowy spikes ripped into the air all around him, piercing out of his body in strange angles and unpredictable directions. Center's defenders immediately retreated, attacking from farther out to maintain some measure of safety.

L'adim shifted and moved so that no space remained safe for long, though his overall trajectory continued toward the fortress of Heavenstone.

Despite every reasonable piece of sanity in her screaming that she do otherwise, Bree soared right into that chaos with the rest of them. Her eyes peeled wide, her instincts taking over. A spear of shadow sailed overhead, just barely missing her wings. Bree rolled to her right, dodging two more, and then rolled left. A dark boulder flew through the air where she'd been only a moment ago, puffing into smoke upon missing. The distance shrank, her goal in sight. A dozen spears rose up from L'adim's chest, launching one by one for her. Bree abandoned the attack, all her skill devoted to surviving the next few seconds.

A weave, a dive, up and around, curling and twisting with every screaming muscle in her body. The world was a maze, each wall a danger, every turn potentially her last. Bree kept her fists clenched tight, releasing no flame and drawing neither of her swords. She had to get closer. If she were to have any chance, she needed to be so near she could reach out to touch his vile form.

There was no pretense to formations among the survivors. Seraphim of all islands flew among one another, momentary allies before separating again when the lashes of shadow whipped after them. Knights kept close to Heavenstone, but they too flitted about in a mad fight for survival. Nothing had slowed L'adim's trek across Center's surface. Nothing seemed to cause permanent harm. His essence pulsed with hatred and hopelessness, infecting everyone close enough with feelings of dread.

Bree twisted sideways, a spear of shadow passing inches from her chest. She continued the roll, pulling up at the last second as two more spears skewered her path. Bree lifted higher, needing a momentary pause. Something was wrong. The shadowborn was gathering his essence into himself, drawing in the wide swath of crawling darkness that covered the grass. Cannon fire thudded into his chest. Knights burned his knees and sank ice into his arms. It didn't even slow him. Bree's eyes widened as she realized his next attack. Heavenstone's defenders were but a nuisance, and it was time for L'adim to crush the building itself.

L'adim seemed to grow taller. Such massive size, yet he moved in silence as he rolled forth, transforming himself into a huge wave. That silence ended the moment the shadowborn crashed down on Heavenstone. The air itself shook with the noise, a blast surpassed only by the sound of Galen striking the Endless Ocean. Nothing withstood the shadowborn's weight. The supports cracked, the towers collapsing, the building tumbling in on itself. Scores of theotechs died instantly, their bodies crushed and mangled. The two outer defense walls shuddered, the shadow spreading like roots across the ground to rip into the foundations. L'adim re-formed amid the destruction, a crouched figure on hands and knees. Shadow pooled beneath him like a lake. He did not stand, nor did he respond to the first of many barrages from knights and Seraphs alike.

A sense of wrongness immediately washed over Bree. She had to flee. Now. The air itself darkened about them. Her hairs stood on end as if she were touched by lightning. Sickness grew in her stomach. Bree aimed straight upward and pushed her wings to their limits, yanking her away from the pulsing shadow. Yet Bree was the only one. She watched the others, confused by their stay. How could they not sense it? The gathering energy. The smoldering disgust. Instead it seemed the knights and Seraphs misunderstood the shadowborn's reaction, confusing it for weakness. They pressed harder, bathing his form with their elements. Fire licked across his forehead. Ice encased his entire left leg from the concerted effort of more than a dozen Seraphim. Lightning struck from all sides, swirling into his form.

"Get away," Bree whispered, for shouting would mean nothing to the roar of battle. "See the trap, see it, see it..."

L'adim sank deeper into the ground, a great lake of shadow pooled up to his waist. His head bowed low, his arms sinking into his chest. Elements bombarded his neck and spine, nothing held back by anyone below. The knights and Seraphs gathered together, the combined forces of humanity, for one last barrage. It reeked of desperation. Perhaps they knew the danger they faced. Perhaps they sensed the trap. But they would not pull away.

The shadowborn rose into the air, legs forming beneath him as he stood. His arms swung wide, as did another pair of arms beneath, long fingers sweeping through the air. L'adim spun once, lashing the battlefield around him. Tendrils snapped out from the four arms like vicious snakes, latching on to any knight or Seraph unfortunate enough to fly nearby, which were many. They could not evade fast enough, not with the sheer size and reach L'adim possessed. Bree hovered in place, too shocked to feel anything as wings fell from the sky in droves.

The remaining Seraphim retreated, their numbers thoroughly devastated. The few with prisms still charged lobbed long, arcing orbs of stone, fire, and ice, little pinpricks that did nothing. Knights flew past the rubble. Bree couldn't imagine where they thought to retreat to, but retreat they did. Dust and smoke blew in all directions from Heavenstone's collapsing rubble. L'adim stepped over it, his shadow swallowing the corpses of the dead and smothering any survivors. Bree watched with ice building in her throat. Without the defenses or the other knights and Seraphim to distract him, all of his attention would now be on her. More than a hundred had battled against him and yet he'd slowly crushed them one by one. How could she possibly hope to close the distance she needed?

L'adim stood in the heart of the broken building, the lower pair of arms sinking back into his form. His head tilted to the sky, hands open and raised in celebration. His face bore no eyes but Bree still felt his focus upon her. The shadowborn rose higher. A crease stretched from side to side of his face. It opened with a grating crack, like an unsealing tomb. Thin black mist dripped down like drool from his lips.

"Breanna," he spoke. The sound of his voice was of worlds grinding together, deep and frightening and louder than the battle itself. "Embrace this end. This peace is inevitable."

His arm reached up for her, hand open. Tendrils shot from his wrists and fingers, dozens closing the distance. Seeking her. Beckoning her.

"You need not suffer. Some may be spared. Create a new world. My world."

A world led by the shadowborn? Such a ghastly thought.

"Beyond the ocean the land thrives," L'adim continued. "Life. Tranquility. We will build upon the bones of the old. A new society. A new faith."

"With you as their God," she whispered.

Somehow L'adim heard.

"Yes," he spoke. The pronouncement shook the land. "As it must. Humanity cannot save itself. I am the way."

More tendrils swooping in from his shoulders, curling far to either side of her. Penning her in, she knew. Still came the beckoning hands. Bree saw no escape, but perhaps she didn't need one. Swallowing down her fear, she let the shadow touch her. A tendril wrapped around each of her ankles, the contact filling her with a need to vomit. Another circled her waist twice, then pulled. Bree reduced the power to her wings, allowing herself to drift toward the waiting monster. A single careful cut opened a shallow groove along her wrist, allowing her blood to flow across the five glowing prisms held in her grasp. Fire started to erupt about them but she suppressed it within her mind. She didn't need it, not yet.

L'adim guided her closer, smoothly, gracefully, with care that belied his vicious presence.

"Embrace me," he spoke. His voice was soft now, not the thundering of a demigod for all of Center to hear. A careful whisper, just for her. "Lead my chosen few to paradise."

"Paradise?" Bree asked. She stretched her right hand toward him. His chest was before her, so close to her touch. His aura of disgust and hatred clawed at her mind and sapped strength from her limbs. She used her rage to fight it. "I will give our people paradise."

A guttural scream building in her throat, she spread her palm wide and gave the shadowborn the only embrace he deserved.

The inferno burst from her gauntlet, swirling into the shadow and setting it alight. Bree could sense the steady drain on her prism. It wasn't enough. Screaming wildly, she demanded it give her all its power. Her blood connected to it, and not just that prism but the five additional blood-soaked prisms in her left hand. The power increased, sudden and dramatic. All the stored power of those prisms flooded in, surging through her blood like a bolt of lightning. Bree's arm rocked backward, and to compensate she tilted forward and pushed her wings harder. She bathed the shadowborn with her otherworldly fire as she screamed. The heat washed against her body, cracking her skin and burning away the shadowy tendrils that had held her.

Still not enough.

"All of it!" Bree shrieked.

Again the fire exploded wider, hotter. The jolt pushed Bree back farther, forcing her wings to their limits just to hold her body in a steady position. The fire washed over L'adim's chest, shredding away the crawling shadow. Great swirls of it pulled in from the ground, desperately attempting to replace the thick wall of it burning up beneath Bree's torrent.

The prisms in Bree's left hand shattered one by one, the pieces absorbing into her flesh. She felt them in her bloodstream, for once granting power to her instead of draining it away to replenish. Every shred of her strength channeled fire from her gauntlet as a roaring inferno. She felt her skin burning. Her shoulder broke against the strain. She screamed, but still she let loose her flame. The metal of her gauntlet melted away, charring the skin beneath. The focal prism exploded. No more wires. No more harness, for her wings were dripping boiling liquid silver like rain. What tears Bree cried instantly evaporated.

The fire never ended. It had no need of focal prisms, no need of wires and wings. The explosion of flame and light roared unending from her bare palm. All of humanity's rage set free. A blinding star. A sun unleashed. Words belted out from her throat, a maniacal cry of victory.

"I. AM. YOUR. DEATH!"

More and more shadow withered beneath the fire. The scream of L'adim's pain was a thunderous roar in her ears. That crawling flesh peeled away, and away, with nothing to replace it. As Bree felt her strength wane, she saw a pale shriveled skeleton of a being hovering in the very heart of the shadow. It, too, screamed. Bree no longer felt her arm. Her mind was only pain. The world was a distant, imaginary thing. The frail ghost of a man flailed against her fire, trying to resist, to hold back the blaze.

Death came for her, but Bree refused to go alone. One last burst of flame with every shred of power in her blood coming forth. She watched until her eyes turned blind. She cried until both were consumed. Her last image was of her fire washing over that weak, terrified, ugly wretch of a fallen lightborn, forever cleansing it from their world.

CHAPTER 35

His new wings hummed properly, yet Kael could not pull his feet from the ground. His every muscle locked tight. His jaw hung open, thin tears curling down either side of his face. Bree's full potential was exploding out from her like hell itself. The shadow of L'adim could not withstand her. His ancient evil could not endure the fury washing over him, fueled by Bree's blood and rage. It could sunder cities, this power, yet it came from the hand of a young woman.

The fire was the most beautiful and most horrifying sight Kael had ever beheld.

The shadowborn wilted before it. The crawling darkness retreated into itself, layering before the brunt of Bree's eruption only to peel back in cinders and smoke. The brightness grew too much, and he turned away with an upraised arm to protect his eyes. L'adim's roar shook the ground. His death shook the skies. A shock wave rolled over him, stealing his breath and knocking him to his knees. His wings flickered and dimmed, the light element itself momentarily faltering.

The light dimmed. The fire faded. Kael looked for his sister, eager to see if she were okay.

"No," he whispered. "No, no, no no no..."

Bree fell from the sky on melted wings.

Kael ran as he shoved the throttle all the way to its maximum and leapt into the air. He didn't care that the straps ripped into his sides. It didn't matter the painful jerk to his neck, or the muscle he felt pull in his lower back. He needed to fly. Bree was falling. He needed to catch her. Rescue her. Know that she still breathed. He raced over the bloody battlefield of mutilated corpses. He passed the ruins of Heavenstone's walls, the dead of her theotechs.

It wasn't in time.

Kael dropped to his knees beside her body, striking off the throttle. He reached for his sister but stopped halfway. He didn't know what to do. His mind was empty. Her face was completely burned and scarred. Both gauntlets had melted away, her right hand blackened to the bone.

"Bree," he whispered. "Bree, please, don't..."

As if she had a choice. The shadowborn was dead. So was his sister.

Kael tried to lift her up but her wings hitched into the ground, resisting. Most of the buckles were already warped, the leather burned. The wings had melted into her jacket, and he had to strip it off her so he could finally hold her. He kept her close as he let his tears fall. It didn't feel right. The world, it wasn't supposed to be a place where he walked without his sister. She was supposed to be there. She was *always* supposed to be there.

"I'm sorry," he said. He hadn't a clue as for what, just that it felt right to say it.

He pulled back from the embrace to wipe at his face and sniffle. The hairs on the back of his neck stood on end. People were coming. So many eyes on him. Unspoken questions. Panic escalated in his breast coupled with an intense need to escape.

"Get back!" he shouted. "I said get back!"

More of them. Many also crying. Others staring in muted shock. It was too much. His own emotions were a demon he could not wrestle. Theirs were impossible. Kael undid one of his buckles, wrapped it around Bree's waist, and then soared into the air. He had but one direction: up.

Center slowly shrank beneath him at a maddeningly slow rate. Kael kept his neck craned skyward, caring not for below. He wanted higher. He wanted to leave every bit of his sorrow behind while he flew to the stars. The wind blew away his tears, and he pretended that meant they weren't there. Its roar in his ears drowned out his own sobs, and he pretended that meant he kept silent. Higher. Higher. He must fly higher.

Kael's head grew dizzy, and it wasn't just from exhaustion. The air tasted thin. Every breath felt less satisfying than the last. Wisdom said to stop but his injured heart demanded higher. The wind grew colder and quieter. Kael clutched his sister tightly, wishing their embrace might share warmth. Her stiff body was against him, her chin on his shoulder, her arms curled about his neck in a lifeless hug. What he'd give to feel that embrace tighten, to hear her let out a soft cry as she awakened. A fool's hope. A denial-filled dream.

At last Kael could risk going no higher. The cold bit too deep and his lightheadedness was threatening to shift into unconsciousness. The world below was a great sea of blue, dotted by the green specks that were the four islands. Any other time, he'd have found the view both awe-inspiring and terrifying.

Now it was another sensation his overwhelmed mind could not process.

Kael pulled out his sword and carefully opened up the compartment containing his light element. He didn't remove the prism. Instead he cut the side of his hand and let the blood drip down upon the element. As the drops fell he felt the connection growing in his mind. Its glow grew brighter. The cracks smoothed over. The cloudy gray receded into powerful white.

That done, he shut the compartment and pondered. His plan was obscenely tricky, not that he cared. First he turned Bree about in her buckles, tightening them further before removing two more of his own to wrap about her instead. That done, he removed his left gauntlet and slowly placed it over Bree's charred hand, careful to ensure the throttle didn't shift from their gentle hover. Now the difficult part. Kael undid the straps about his legs, effectively freeing himself from his harness. He kept his left arm wrapped about Bree's waist as he slid down and out from the straps holding Bree's body. Kael's right gauntlet was still attached to the wings, and he used it to hold himself steady while he maneuvered back up face-to-face with his sister.

"Almost there, Bree," he said. He tightened the straps one by one, removing the slack caused by his removal. That done, he positioned her gauntlet so that she held it against her shoulder. Kael gently increased her throttle, flooding new life into her wings. They drifted skyward, Kael's weight still holding them back. His right hand passed over her left, sheeting it with ice so that the throttle was locked in place. There would be no stopping her, not until the element drained. He didn't know how far that would be. He prayed it would be enough as he freed his right hand and let the gauntlet hang loose.

Kael pressed his cheek against his sister's face. His tears wet her hair. His lips whispered into her ear.

"I'll miss you, Bree."

Rage and acceptance danced together in his heart. His eyes felt drained of tears despite the sorrow just beginning. The world below had been devastated, yet it had also been given a new chance. Bree died a hero, yet Bree still died. Inseparable, exactly as he and his sister once were, and never would be again. Not until a time long distant, and in a world glimpsed only by the angels. Just one thing left to do. One final act.

Kael let his body go limp and his arms open wide.

Let his sister rise.

Let himself fall.

The wind carried him down. The silver wings above faded, swallowed by the orange sky. Kael refused to look away, not until the little silver star was gone completely. He wanted the location memorized in his mind so that every single night he would know where to look.

Kael rolled in the air, shifting so he fell feet-first. Center approached, its green tinted by the setting sun. He thought of letting it greet him. It would shatter his bones like those who'd slammed upon Galen's surface the moment it struck the Endless Ocean. Instantaneous. No more hurt. No morc misery. He'd cry no tears for his sister. That pain in his chest would be gone. A selfish desire. A desperate hope against the overwhelming sorrow.

But down there were people he loved. People who needed him. Kael clenched his hands into fists and closed his eyes.

"Take me home," he whispered.

Ethereal wings burst from his back in a wide plume. Silver light shone from each feather. A hum filled Kael's mind, soft and pleasant. His plummet became a float, his descent controlled and gentle. Heavenstone neared. Kael watched his fall, and with but a thought in his mind he shifted his aim.

He didn't care to speak with any of the theotechs from Center, nor the knights and Seraphim who survived. Only one person mattered.

Clara remained where she'd been when they'd brought her out of the battle. His wings fluttered once, pushing him toward her. He felt his strength waning. His careful fall started to accelerate in spurts. Kael clenched both his shaking fists, demanding he endure. The grass was close. Clara waited.

Kael's legs buckled upon landing, and he screamed as he felt bones break. His wings faded away like vanishing fireflies of light. He knelt there, lacking the strength to stand through the pain. His mental numbness battled with the sudden new rush of pain and adrenaline. Kael watched in a stupor as Clara approached, slowly at first, as if trying to remain dignified, and then in a full-blown sprint. She slid down beside him, her entire body locking him in an embrace.

"I didn't think you'd come back," she sobbed. She held him as he'd held his sister, arms tight around his waist, her cheek against his, her tears wetting his hair. He spoke, and as the words came out, he felt the last strong part of him break, his numbness collapsing against an ocean of emotion. An abyss waited beneath him, and he clutched Clara as if she were his wings.

"I'm here," Kael said, the declaration the best he could offer. "I'm here, Clara. I'm home."

EPILOGUE

Kael stood before the statue in the empty square, the soft hum coming from its base pleasant and reassuring. The sun was only starting its descent but already Kael heard the pounding of drums and drawing of strings. Tonight was the grand unveiling of the new cathedral, and more important, the first yearly celebration of the shadowborn's defeat. Given the massive amounts of hard work all the survivors had put in to rebuild from the destruction, the people were eager for a chance to drink and eat and make merry.

"They'll sing songs to your name," Kael told the statue. "I hope that doesn't embarrass you."

A stone replica of Bree hovered in the air before him. Her arms were angled at her sides with swords drawn. Expertly carved flame wreathed the blades. Wings stretched from her back. Not a Seraph's wings, but those of an angel, feathered and beautiful. Her head was tilted upward, forever looking to the heavens. Beneath her was a large square pedestal, a golden plaque across the front.

Our beloved Phoenix.

Child of Weshern.

Daughter of angels.

Hero of all.

The statue hovered an inch above the pedestal, light prisms freely offered by L'fae to keep the monument powered. Even in memorial Bree would not set foot on the ground. That was never where she belonged.

"They want me to give a speech, you know," he said. He knew the statue could not hear him, but it felt like Bree was out there somewhere, listening. It just felt right. "Me, a speech. I tried to say no, but L'fae wouldn't hear a word of it. I should be the one, she said." He chuckled. "That pretty much ended it. You can't argue with a lightborn and win, Bree. But you probably know that now, don't you?"

He wiped at the tears that had started to build. No time for that. He'd spent enough long nights crying for the dead and mourning his own loss. Tonight was for celebration.

A soft click of heels on stone alerted him to someone's arrival. Kael glanced over his shoulder, relieved to see Clara had come to join him. She looked dazzling in a long blue dress, her hair spun up and pinned with diamonds.

"You just had to wear your uniform, didn't you?" she said, a playful smile spreading across her lips.

Kael glanced down at his prim Seraphim uniform, smoothed and steamed by dozens of servants so that not a crease or wrinkle dared survive.

"I'm nervous enough," he told her. "The last thing I need is to be stuffed into some itchy suit while I stammer and make a fool of myself."

Clara scoffed.

"If I can spend four hours arguing with pompous foreign

representatives, you can handle a quick speech in front of an adoring crowd."

She joined him before the statue, falling silent as she looked upon the hovering form. Kael accepted her rebuke without argument. She was right, of course. Her role on the monthly peace council had been a tremendous strain over the year.

"Did you at least accomplish anything this time?" he asked.

"Of sorts," Clara said. "The most important was declaring all forms of prisms a vital necessity. Center will distribute elements freely to all islands, in equal amounts and without need of trading."

"So we keep the demons chained and bled," Kael said. He shook his head. "I'd rather we be done with them for good."

"Few see it as a viable option," she said. "We don't know how many survived the shadowborn's defeat. To dismiss them risks our safety."

"To keep them risks our safety," Kael argued. "Have we learned nothing?"

Clara brushed his face and forced him to look her way.

"We have," she said. "And I'm on your side, remember? Give it time. A lot has changed in a year, and that change shows no sign of slowing. We'll rebuild piece by piece into a better world, and a better people."

Kael leaned down to kiss her lips, inwardly berating himself for letting his nerves get the best of him. His arm wrapped about her shoulder, holding her close. He turned back to the statue.

"What of the theotechs?" he asked. "Did they decide on a Speaker yet?"

"No, but the options continue to narrow. Whoever wins, we expect they will be a unifier. Center's citizens crave peace after the destruction L'adim caused their world. Stubborn as they are, the theotechs realize their time of power is fading. We're stripping away the last of their secrets. They'll have no choice but to listen to the will of the people."

"Good," Kael said. "It's a needed change. They spent enough time ignoring both lightborn and humanity."

He fell silent. His nerves were still shot, but with Clara beside him and the square calm and empty, he felt content. Not quite happiness, not yet, but it was there in the distance, beckoning him on. Clara cleared her throat, and he raised an eyebrow her way.

"There was one other matter," she said. "The talk of a scouting voyage is no longer simply talk. All five islands are offering supplies and volunteers to join a long-term expedition in search of land. They're hoping you'll be its leader."

Kael chuckled.

"My blood would ensure we were never stranded no matter how far we traveled," he said.

"That might have been mentioned," Clara said. She poked his side. "You're also a war hero and the famous brother of the Phoenix. It feels right you should also lead the search for the old world."

"The old world," Kael said. He thought of flying farther than any man or woman had flown in centuries. The call of adventure tugged at his heart. "And what happens if we find it?"

"Truth be told, we don't know," Clara said. "But... but if the land is alive with life, we might direct our islands toward it. We could land, Kael. We could return to the world we fled, of size and scope we could only dream."

"We could free the lightborn from their chains," Kael said. Of all the reasons, that felt the most justified. "I accept the role, with your permission, of course. You might have to go weeks, maybe even months, without my presence. Are you sure it's worth it?"

She kissed his cheek.

"Sure? No. But I'll tell Rebecca to bump up the date of our wedding. For political reasons, of course. Having the future Archon of Weshern lead the expedition will give us decades of bragging rights."

Kael laughed.

"As you wish."

She wrapped her arm around his and pulled him close.

"Are you ready for your big moment?" she asked.

"Not in the slightest," Kael said. "But I don't have much choice in the matter, do I?"

He kissed his fingers, then touched the foot of the statue hovering above the pedestal. His gaze lingered on Bree's stone face a moment longer, and then he sighed long and loud.

"All right, let's go."

They walked the road northward, exiting the town on their way to the rebuilt cathedral. They were still a half mile away when the crowds of people began. Families sat on blankets, children eating fruits shipped in from Elern and Center and adults sampling Sothren's finest wines. Cook fires sprinkled the wide field, the smell of roasting meat and smoke watering Kael's mouth. Here and there wandered minstrels and singers performing for impromptu crowds, soaking in their adulation, and hopefully, their coin. All of it collected into a warm, comforting din of voices, song, and play.

Wood stalls collected closer to the cathedral, merchants peddling treats and toys and slender torches that burned in a variety of colors. Kael remembered the headache of reviewing every application, Clara having dragged him into the celebration committee to approve or deny stalls and limit what could and could not be sold. She'd argued he needed to acclimate himself to governmental types of work. Kael believed she just didn't want to suffer alone.

A woman spun in the center of the road, ribbons covered with gems reflecting the setting sun twirling from her wrists, ankles, and waist. A red-and-yellow mask covered her face, the sides of it sprouting little wings made of bird feathers.

"Where's your wings, Seraph?" she called as they passed.

"I've been grounded," Kael said, smiling at her. The woman laughed and danced to the next couple joining the celebration.

Soldiers stood guard at the edge of the cathedral, not that there appeared much to protect. The Crystal Cathedral had been torn down piece by piece to its very foundations. The theotechs insisted God wished them to worship in open view of the skies, and so they would in the truest sense. There was more to it, of course. It had been Kael's idea, another reason he'd been roped into giving the initial speech. All that currently remained was a raised stone dais several feet above the grass field. The dais contained no decorations, no seats, no thrones, nothing but empty space. Exactly as L'fae requested.

"Rebecca should be waiting for us," Clara said, needing to lean in close to his ear to be heard over the roaring crowd.

A wall of people blocked Kael and Clara off from the cathedral. Kael stopped a moment and tapped the nearest person on the shoulder to turn him about. Realization hit the man quickly, and he stepped away to give space while bowing. Others noticed, only a few at first but then rapidly dozens. They parted for the pair, several shouting their love for Clara. A few cheered for Kael as well, and he blushed. Receiving praise still left him feeling awkward.

The soldiers gave way, allowing them to climb the steps. True to Clara's word, Rebecca Waller waited in one corner of the cathedral, Archoness Willer beside her.

"I hope you've been enjoying the festivities," Avila said, smiling at him. She looked an older, more regal version of Clara, with a similar dress and similar diamonds pinning her hair in place.

"Your speech," Rebecca said, opening up a small box at her feet. She pulled out a single sheet of paper and handed it to him. Kael glanced it over while squinting in the dim light. He'd submitted it for review days ago, and now he saw it came back rewritten in Rebecca's clear, concise handwriting. Many phrases and parts were tweaked and changed.

"You edited my speech?" Kael asked.

"Under my orders," Avila said. "This is an historic moment, one that will be taught in schools for years to come. I only wished for you to be properly prepared."

"Kael's grateful," Clara said, interrupting him from arguing further. "When does he start?"

"Anytime, though the sooner the better," Rebecca said. "The longer you wait the more intoxicated, and therefore the louder, the masses will be."

Kael looked to the sprawling crowd. A shiver ran up and down his spine, filled with every horrible thought of embarrassment and failure.

"There's so many," he said. "How will they hear me?"

Rebecca retrieved a long cone with a handle from her box.

"Shout into that," she said. "They'll hear you."

She gave him an encouraging smile and then retreated down the steps of the dais with the empty box in hand. Kael looked at the cone and wondered for the fiftieth time why someone else who actually knew how to speak in public didn't take over the role.

"You'll do great," Clara said, kissing his cheek. "Just call for their attention. I'll instruct the guards to help if the people don't notice. After that, it's all you. Read the speech and relax."

"You make it sound so easy," Kael said, smiling at her. She

winked and left the dais with her mother. Now alone, Kael looked upon the crowd of dancing, singing, cheering people. They were unaware of the magnitude of tonight's unveiling, thinking it only a celebration. But dozens of workers had toiled in secret, following L'fae's orders to build the brand-new cathedral. Everything was set. All it needed was Kael to give the word.

Kael lifted the cone to his lips. A handful looked his way, their attention quickly fading when he refused to speak. Iron bars gripped at his throat. Kael thought of a million excuses he could use. He could thrust the speech into Rebecca's hand and demand she give it. He could order the cathedral's reveal without any fanfare whatsoever. Maybe he should. This was insane. Thousands of people staring at him simultaneously, listening to his every stumble and stutter...

A soft voice spoke in Kael's ear, no louder than a whisper, yet he heard it crystalline clear over the din of the crowd.

Have faith, little Skyborn. I am here. You need no help. They will hear you.

Kael took in a deep breath and then let it out.

"Thanks, L'fae," he whispered back. He set the cone beside him on the dais. Clara gave him a confused look, and he waved her concern away. People had begun to turn in his direction, a small percentage of the vast gathering. Kael looked to the sheet of paper in his hand, hesitated, and then crumpled it in his fist. If what he spoke would be remembered throughout history, then let it be *his* words, no matter how faulty or imperfect.

"People of Weshern," he said. He didn't shout it. Somehow, he knew that wasn't necessary. "Hear me."

And hear him they did. All eyes turned his way, a frightened quiet settling over the crowd. Kael felt his nerves sparking with fear and he banished them with an ever-increasing focus. He'd flown skies pierced with the shadowborn's darkness. He could handle this.

"One year ago, we defeated the greatest threat humanity has ever faced," he said. "One year ago, we rose up against the demons that would crush us, and we denied their master who would declare us irrelevant in the eyes of our God. We bled. We died. From the Phoenix to the humblest of men and women, we gave our lives in the hope it would allow others to survive. And we didn't just survive. We won."

Cheers sounded throughout the crowd, hesitant and uncertain. They understood something special was going in. Even the soldiers standing guard before the dais had turned to listen with rapt attention. Kael thought of the flowery words of his prepared speech and cast them aside in his mind. The theotechs had thrived on such language for decades.

"You've heard whispers and rumors," he continued. "This night I put them to rest. Center still votes for a new Speaker for the Angels, but the role is an irrelevant one. We will need no one to speak for the angels, for the angels are here, within our islands, keeping them afloat as they power the Beam. They will speak for themselves, and all of humanity shall hear."

The whispers and murmurs increased. Rumors of the angels' presence had grown since L'adim's defeat. The royal family had neither confirmed nor denied the rumors. Until now.

"For centuries the angels have suffered and bled to keep our islands aloft," Kael continued. "Yet for centuries we never even knew their names. Hear me, people of Weshern! They are A'resh of Candren, Fal'Ce of Elern, M'Ra of Sothren, and Ch'thon of Galen, slain by the shadowborn to bring the island to the sea. Three together hold Center above the skies, Rosi'ia, E'lao, and I'lam. Last of all, L'fae, our beloved lightborn of

Weshern. She has held us aloft since before we were born, and it is time you met her. It's time she heard your praise."

Kael closed his eyes and whispered in his mind, trusting L'fae to hear.

The people await you, L'fae. Come greet them.

The dais rumbled beneath Kael's feet. A long crack split the stone center, steadily widening. Machinery carefully constructed to L'fae's orders hummed to life, powered by the blood of the lightborn. Kael descended the steps, his role in the evening completed. The dais shook, the stone rolling away. The crowd fell eerily silent, adding to the religious somberness of the night. Light shone from the newly opened pit as a great beam rising into the heavens. More lifts. More gears turning. Kael walked to Clara's side and took her hand so they might watch together.

"You did it," she said.

Kael didn't answer, only squeezed her hand tight.

The crowd gasped as the tips of the ethereal wings rose out from the pit. L'fae arose atop a solid platform, the sides of it locking into the stone dais with heavy clicks. Tubes coiled out from L'fae's arms, back, and spine, trailing into a wide hole in the center of the dais. L'fae hovered a mere inch above the ground, light pulsing off her in radiant waves. No chains held her aloft, and neither did they hold her down. Her arms spread wide. Her light twinkled with happiness.

My beloved, L'fae spoke into their minds. *My children.*

The people approached this new cathedral, one of little ornament and no walls. It should have been chaotic, but it wasn't. L'fae's presence filled the crowd with soothing calm. Kael felt the peace ebbing into him, settling the last of his fried nerves. There would be so many questions, songs of praise, and crowds simply seeking to be in her presence. As for himself, he was quickly forgotten by his audience, as he preferred.

"I need a moment," he whispered into Clara's ear.

"I'll be with L'fae," Clara replied.

Kael walked away from the cathedral, no real destination in mind. His hands dug into his pockets, his head bowed. The fields behind the cathedral had been kept clear of revelers, and so to the fields he passed. The tall grass tugged at his pants, earning a soft smile from Kael as he imagined the perfectly cleaned cloth being stained green. The sounds of the celebration drifted away. He glanced over his shoulders once. L'fae shone like a tremendous beacon, her wings floating in the air above her like a lighthouse of old. Perhaps when the night came, you could always find L'fae's light no matter where you were on Weshern. He hoped so. He'd like that.

At last not even the murmur of the crowd reached his ears. Kael stopped, his gaze lifting to the stars, his attention focused on one spot in particular. It had been burned into his mind as he'd fallen back to Weshern, the thin gap of darkness between two stars where he'd released his sister into the heavens.

"I've lost everyone again," Kael whispered. "Dad died during the final battle with L'adim. I never got to say good-bye. We... we never once embraced like we should have. All that time robbed from us, and no chance to make up for it because of what Marius did to him."

He sniffled. If only his father had stayed with them. If only he'd rejected the Speaker's lies and returned to Weshern. If only. If only.

"I think things will be better now," he continued. His eyes lingered on that spot. The statue was a comfort, but that point in the sky was where he truly felt his sister heard him. "Tough, but better. It'd be nice if you were here to see it, Bree. You should have been there with me when L'fae rose up before the crowd."

He bowed his head, wiping at his tears.

"Are you proud of me, Bree?" he asked. "I'm trying. I'll always keep trying. You bought us another chance, and by God, I'm going to make sure we use it."

Wind surged across the empty field, flooding the silence with a soft, steady rustle. Kael lifted his hands and let the wind blow across his skin and tease his hair. He imagined himself flying with long feathered wings stretching from his back. Most of all, he imagined he wasn't alone but instead surrounded by those he'd loved and lost, together with them soaring across the sparkling blue ocean.

The wind calmed as quickly as it had arrived. The grass ceased its sway. The silence soothed him. The stars blessed him. A weight gone from his shoulders, Kael returned to L'fae, to the scores of people, and to Weshern's celebration of a better future.

A NOTE FROM THE AUTHOR

I've learned a few things about myself as a writer while finishing up *Shadowborn*. I think the biggest is that low fantasy is just not the fantasy I enjoy writing best. *Skyborn* started out fairly low fantasy (at least compared to the stuff I normally write). Sure, there's people flying around on wings, and there are some elements shooting around killing people, but that is it. Come *Fireborn,* I started straining against the limits I'd imposed upon myself. But with *Shadowborn,* though? I tossed all limitations out the window.

The start really began near the end of *Fireborn,* where I introduced the gigantic namesake monster merged together with the bones of the dead. That was not originally in my outline when I first set up this series, but I had tired of constant cat-and-mouse skirmishes with the quick, tiny fireborn. I wanted to try something else, so then came the giant version. Once I had that behemoth speak, pieces of *Shadowborn* just tumbled into place in my head. These demonic entities became something more versatile, unpredictable, and dangerous. I wrote the first chapter of *Shadowborn* almost immediately after finishing *Fireborn,* to test out my alternate path. I created ancient war machines, cannons, and gun platforms. I merged iceborn into giants and sent them in waves. No limits. Anything goes. And I had a ball.

This is usually how I write, by the way. For good or ill, if I think it would be an awesome image or scene or battle I toss it in and see if it works. Kael's shield is a prime example of that in *Fireborn,* an out-of-nowhere addition while writing the chapter. So with *Shadowborn* I reworked the outline to give myself far more freedom. The Spear of God nuking an entire town out of existence? Let's do it. Cannons laying waste to the islands? All for it. Kael's shield growing in power? Giants the size of towns climbing frozen pillars to reach the islands? Liam getting a *Metroid*-style arm cannon? Let's freaking go.

As usual, the success or failure of this gambit is up to the reader. Obviously I hope you very much enjoyed it. If not, well . . . come on, you have to admit *some* of it was cool.

There are a few common questions I'll likely get asked, so here's an attempt to head them off.

Yes, writing Bree's death scene, and Kael's ensuing sky funeral, was brutal and terrible and I might have shed a few tears. Not that you can prove I did.

No, I do not expect to return to this world in the foreseeable future. There's stuff I could do with it but I think nothing would really top the total chaos and destruction of these first three books.

Yes, Kael and Clara live happily ever after and have a litter of children who also grow up to be Archons and Seraphim. Not too many of my characters get to have happy endings. Consider theirs set in stone.

With all that said, I hope you enjoyed this trilogy. I've

stretched my wings (pun intended) when it comes to world building, magic systems, and unique combat. I loved these characters, and I hope you loved them, too. And no matter what the sales are or how good or bad the reviews, I still got amazing covers by Tommy Arnold for the Orbit releases. Those alone made this all worthwhile. Also, really quick, obligatory thanks to my agent, Michael; my new editor, Brit; the awesome people at Orbit; and anyone else I may have forgotten. You know who you are even if I currently don't.

Most important, thank you, dear readers. You continue to let me live a dream, one I pray does not end for many, many years. I'll see you at the end of my next book, in a brand-new world with brand-new people to love and hate.

David Dalglish
December 7, 2016

extras

www.orbitbooks.net

about the author

David Dalglish currently lives in South Carolina with his wife, Samantha, and daughters, Morgan, Katherine, and Alyssa. He graduated from Missouri Southern State University in 2006 with a degree in mathematics and currently spends his free time leaping around as a giant intelligent gorçla in *Overwatch*.

Find out more about David Dalglish and other Orbit authors by registering online for the free monthly newsletter at www.orbitbooks.net.

if you enjoyed

SHADOWBORN

look out for

AGE OF ASSASSINS

The Wounded Kingdom: Book One

by

RJ Barker

TO CATCH AN ASSASSIN, USE AN ASSASSIN . . .

Girton Club-foot, apprentice to the land's best assassin, still has much to learn about the art of taking lives. But their latest mission tasks him and his master with a far more difficult challenge: to save a life. Someone, or many someones, is trying to kill the heir to the throne, and it is up to Girton and his master to uncover the traitor and prevent the prince's murder.

In a kingdom on the brink of civil war and a castle thick with lies Girton finds friends he never expected, responsibilities he never wanted, and a conspiracy that could destroy an entire land.

Chapter 1

We were attempting to enter Castle Maniyadoc through the night soil gate and my master was in the sort of foul mood only an assassin forced to wade through a week's worth of shit can be. I was far more sanguine about our situation. As an assassin's apprentice you become inured to foulness. It is your lot.

"Girton," said Merela Karn. That is my master's true name, though if I were to refer to her as anything other than "Master" I would be swiftly and painfully reprimanded. "Girton," she said, "if one more king, queen or any other member of the blessed classes thinks a night soil gate is the best way to make an unseen entrance to their castle, you are to run them through."

"Really, Master?"

"No, not really," she whispered into the night, her breath a cloud in the cold air. "Of course not really. You are to politely suggest that walking in the main gate dressed as masked priests of the dead gods is less conspicuous. Show me a blessed who doesn't know that the night soil gate is an easy way in for an enemy and I will show you a corpse."

"You have shown me many corpses, Master."

"Be quiet, Girton."

My master is not a lover of humour. Not many assassins are; it is a profession that attracts the miserable and the melancholic. I would never put myself into either of those categories, but I was bought into the profession and did not join by choice.

"Dead gods in their watery graves!" hissed my master into the night. "They have not even opened the grate for us." She swung herself aside whispering, "Move, Girton!" I slipped and slid crabwise on the filthy grass of the slope running from the river below us up to the base of the towering castle walls. Foulness farted out of the grating to join the oozing stream that ran down the motte and joined the river.

A silvery smudge marred the riverbank in the distance; it looked like a giant paint-covered thumb had been placed over it. In the moonlight it was quite beautiful, but we had passed near as we sneaked in, and I knew it was the same livid yellow as the other sourings which scarred the Tired Lands. There was no telling how old this souring was, and I wondered how big it had been originally and how much blood had been spilled to shrink it to its present size. I glanced up at the keep. This side had few windows and I thought the small souring could be new, but that was a silly, childish thought. The blades of the Landsmen kept us safe from sorcerers and the magic which sucked the life from the land. There had been no significant magic used in the Tired Lands since the Black Sorcerer had risen, and he had died before I had been born. No, what I saw was simply one of many sores on the land – a place as dead as the ancient sorcerer who made it. I turned from the souring and did my best to imagine it wasn't there, though I was sure I could smell it, even over the high stink of the night soil drain.

"Someone will pay for arranging this, Girton, I swear," said my master. Her head vanished into the darkness as she bobbed down to examine the grate once more. "This is sealed with a simple five-lever lock." She did not even breathe heavily despite holding her entire weight on one arm and one leg jammed into stonework the black of old wounds. "You can open this, Girton. You need as much practice with locks as you can get."

"Thank you, Master," I said. I did not mean it. It was cold, and a lock is far harder to manipulate when it is cold.

And when it is covered in shit.

Unlike my master, I am no great acrobat. I am hampered by a clubbed foot, so I used my weight to hold me tight against the grating even though it meant getting covered in filth. On the stone columns either side of the grate the forlorn remains of minor gods had been almost chipped away. On my right only a pair of intricately carved antlers remained, and on my left a pair of horns and one solemn eye stared out at me. I turned from the eye and brought out my picks, sliding them into the lock with shaking fingers and feeling within using the slim metal rods.

"What if there are dogs, Master?"

"We kill them, Girton."

There is something rewarding in picking a lock. Something very satisfying about the click of the barrels and the pressure vanishing as the lock gives way to skill. It is not quite as rewarding done while a castle's toilets empty themselves over your body, but a happy life is one where you take your pleasures where you can.

"It is open, Master."

"Good. You took too long."

"Thank you, Master." It was difficult to tell in the darkness, but I was sure she smiled before she nodded me forward. I hesitated at the edge of the pitch-dark drain.

"It looks like the sort of place you'd find Dark Ungar, Master."

"The hedgings are just like the gods, Girton – stories to scare the weak-minded. There's nothing in there but stink and filth. You've been through worse. Go."

I slithered through the gate, managing to make sure no part of my skin or clothing remained clean, and into the tunnel that led through the keep's curtain wall. Somewhere beyond I could hear the lumpy splashes of night soil being shovelled into the stream that ran over my feet. The living classes in the villages keep their piss and night soil and sell it to the tanneries and dye makers, but the blessed classes are far too grand for that, and their castles shovel their filth out into the rivers – as if to gift it to the populace. I have crawled through plenty of filth in my fifteen years, from the thankful, the living and the blessed; it all smells equally bad.

Once we had squeezed through the opening we were able to stand, and my master lit a glow-worm lamp, a small wick that burns with a dim light that can be amplified or shut off by a cleverly interlocking set of mirrors. Then she lifted a gloved hand and pointed at her ear.

I listened.

Above the happy gurgle of the stream running down the channel – water cares nothing for the medium it travels through – I heard the voices of men as they worked. We would have to wait for them to move before we could proceed into the castle proper, and whenever we have to wait I count out the seconds the way my master taught me – one, my master. Two, my master. Three, my master – ticking away in my mind like the balls of a water clock as I stand idle, filth swirling round my ankles and my heart beating out a nervous tattoo.

You get used to the smell. That is what people say.

It is not true.

Eight minutes and nineteen seconds passed before we finally heard the men laugh and move on. Another signal from my master and I started to count again. Five minutes this time. Human nature being the way it is you cannot guarantee someone will not leave something and come back for it.

When the five minutes had passed we made our way up the night soil passage until we could see dim light dancing on walls caked with centuries of filth. My own height plus a half above us was the shovelling room. Above us the door creaked and then we heard footsteps, followed by voices.

". . . so now we're done and Alsa's in the heir's guard. Fancy armour and more pay."

"It's a hedging's deal. I'd sooner poke out my own eyes and find magic in my hand than serve the fat bear, he's a right yellower."

"Service is mother though, aye?"

Laughter followed. My master glanced up through the hole, chewing on her lip. She held up two fingers before speaking in the Whisper-That-Flies-to-the-Ear so only I could hear her.

"Guards. You will have to take care of them," she said. I nodded and started to move. "Don't kill them unless you absolutely have to."

"It will be harder."

"I know," she said and leaned over, putting her hands together to make a stirrup. "But I will be here."

I breathe out.

I breathe in.

I placed my foot on her hands and, with a heave, she propelled me up and into the room. I came out of the hole landing with my back to the two men. *Seventeenth iteration: the Drunk's Reversal.* Rolling forward, twisting and coming up facing guards dressed in kilted skirts, leather helms and poorly kept-up boiled-leather chest pieces splashed with red paint. They stared at me dumbly, as if I were the hedging lord Blue Watta appearing from the deeps. Both of them held clubs, though they had stabswords at their sides. I wondered if they were here to guard against rats rather than people.

"Assassin?" said the guard on the left. He was smaller than his friend, though both were bigger than me.

"Aye," said the other, a huge man. "Assassin." His grip shifted on his club.

They should have gone for the door and reinforcements.

My hand was hovering over the throwing knives at my belt in case they did. Instead the smaller man grinned, showing missing teeth and black stumps.

"I imagine there's a good price on the head of an assassin, Joam, even if it's a crippled child." He started forward. The bigger man grinned and followed his friend's lead. They split up to avoid the hole in the centre of the room and I made my move. *Second iteration: the Quicksteps.* Darting forward, I chose the smaller of the two as my first target – the other had not drawn his blade. He swung at me with his club and I stepped backwards, feeling the draught of the hard wood through the air. He thrust with his dagger but was too far away to reach my flesh. When his swipe missed he jumped back, expecting me to counter-attack, but I remained unmoving. All I had wanted was to get an idea of his skill before I closed with him. He did not impress me, his friend impressed me even less; rather than joining the attack he was watching, slack-jawed, as if we put on a show for him.

"Joam," shouted my opponent, "don't be just standing there!" The bigger man trundled forward, though he was in no hurry. I didn't want to be fighting two at the same time if I could help it so decided to finish the smaller man quickly. *First iteration: the Precise Steps.* Forward into the range of his weapons. He thrust with his stabsword. *Ninth iteration: the Bow.* Middle of my body bowing backwards to avoid the blade. With his other hand he swung his club at my head. I ducked. As his arm came over my head I grabbed his elbow and pushed, making him lose his balance, and as he struggled to right himself I found purchase on the rim of his chest piece. *Tenth iteration: the Broom.* Sweeping my leg round I knocked his feet from under him. With a push I sent him flailing into the hole so he cracked his head on the edge of it on his way down.

I turned to his friend, Joam.

Had the dead gods given Joam any sense he would have

seen his friend easily beaten and made for the door. Instead, Joam's face had the same look on it I had seen on a bull as it smashed its head against a wall in a useless attempt to get at a heifer beyond – the look of something too stupid and angry to know it was in a fight it couldn't win.

"I'm a kill you, assassin," he said and lumbered slowly forward, smacking his club against his hand. I had no time to wait for him; the longer we fought the more likely it was that someone would hear us and bring more guards. I jumped over the hole and landed behind Joam. He turned, swinging his club. *Fifteenth Iteration: the Oar.* Bending at the hip and bringing my body down and round so it went under his swing. At the lowest point I punched forward, landing a solid blow between Joam's legs. He screeched, dropping his weapon and doubling over. With a jerk I brought my body up so the back of my skull smashed into his face, sending the big man staggering back, blood streaming from a broken nose. It was a blow that would have felled most, but Joam was a strong man. Though his eyes were bleary and unfocused he still stood. *Eighteenth iteration: the Water Clock.* I ran at him, grabbing his thick belt and using it as a fulcrum to swing myself round and up so I could lock my legs around his throat. Joam's hand grasped blindly for the blade at his hip. I drew it and tossed it away before he reached it. His hands spidered down my body searching for and locking around my throat, but Joam's strength, though great, was fleeing as he choked. I wormed my thumb underneath his fingers and grabbed his little finger and third finger, breaking them. I expected a grunt of pain as he let go of me, but the man was already unconscious and fell back, sliding down the wall to the floor. I squirmed free of his weight and checked he was still breathing. Once I was sure he was alive I rolled his body over to the hole.

"Look out, Master," I whispered. Then pushed the limp body into the hole. I took a moment, a second only, to check and see if I had been heard, then I knelt to pull up my master.

She was not heavy.

For the first time I had a moment to look around, and the room we stood in was a strange one. Small in length and breadth but far higher than it needed to be. I barely had time for that thought to form on the surface of my mind before my master shouted,

"This is wrong, Girton! Back!"

I jumped for the grate, as did she, but before either of us fell back into the midden a hidden gate clanked into place across the hole. Four pikers squeezed into the room, dressed in boiled-leather armour, wide-brimmed helms and skirts sewn with chunks of metal. Below the knee they wore leather greaves with strips of metal cut into the material to protect their shins, and as they brandished their weapons they assaulted us with the smell of unwashed bodies and the rancid fat they used to oil their armour. In such a small room their stink was a more effective weapon than the pikes; they would have been far better bringing long shields and short swords. They would realise quickly enough.

"Hostages," said my master as I reached for the blade on my back.

I let go of the hilt.

And was among the guards. Bare-handed and violent. The unmistakable fleshy crack of a nose being broken followed by a man squealing like a gelded mount came from behind me as my master engaged the pikers. I shoved one pike aside to get in close and drove my elbow into the throat of the man in front of me – not a killing blow but enough to put the man out of action. The second piker, a woman, was off balance, and it was easy enough for me to twist her so she was held in front of me like a shield with my razor-tipped thumbnail at her throat. My master had her piker in a similar embrace. Blood ran down his face and another guard lay unconscious on the floor next to the man I had elbowed in the throat.

"Open the grating," she shouted to the walls. "Let us go or we will kill these guards."

The sound of a man laughing came from above, and the reason for the room's height became clear as murder holes opened in the walls. Each was big enough for a crossbow to be pointed down at the room and eight weapons threatened us with taut bows and stubby little bolts which would pass straight through armour.

"Open the grate. We will leave and your troops will live," shouted my master.

More laughter.

"I think not," came a voice. Male, sure of himself, amused.

One, my master. Two, my master . . .

The twang of crossbows, echoing through the silence like the sound of rocks falling down a cliff face will echo through a quiet wood. Bolts buried themselves in the unconscious guards on the floor in front of us. Laughter from above.

"Together," hissed my master, and I pulled my guard round so that we hid behind the bodies of our prisoners.

"Let me go, please," said my guard, her voice shivering like her body. "Aydor doesn't care about us guards. He's worse than Dark Ungar and he'll kill us all if he wants yer."

"Quiet!" I said and pushed my razor-edged thumb harder against her neck, making the blood flow. I felt warmth on my thigh as her bladder let go in fear.

"Look at them," came from above. "Cowardly little assassins hiding behind troops brave enough to face death head on like real warriors."

"Coil's piss, no," murmured the guard in my arms.

"Your loyalty will be remembered," came the voice again.

"No!"

Crossbows spat out bolts and the woman in my arms stiffened and arched in my embrace. One moment she was alive and then, almost magically, a bolt was vibrating in front of my nose like a conduit for life to flee her body.

"Master?" I said. Her guard was spasming as he died, a bolt sticking out of his neck and blood spattering onto the floor. "They are playing with us, Master."

Laughter from above and the crossbows fired again, thudding bolts into the body in my arms and making me cringe down further behind the corpse. The laughter stopped and a second voice, female, commanding, said something, though I could not make out what it was. Then the woman shouted down to us.

"We only want you, Merela Karn. Lay on the floor and make no move to harm those who come for you or I will have your fellow shot."

Did something cross my master's face at hearing her name spoken by a stranger? Was she surprised? Did her dark skin grey slightly in shock? I had never, in all our years together, seen my master shocked. Though I was sure she was known throughout the Tired Lands – Merela Karn, the best of the assassins – few would know her face or that she was a woman.

"Drop the body, Girton," she said, letting hers fall face down on the tiled and bloody floor. "This is not what it seems."

As always I did as I was told, though I braced every muscle, waiting for the bite of a bolt which never came.

"Lie on the floor, both of you," said the male voice from above.

We did as instructed and the room was suddenly buzzing with guards. I took a few kicks to the ribs, and luckily for the owners of those feet I could not see their faces to mark them for my attention later. We were quickly bound – well enough for amateurs – and hauled to our feet in front of a man as big as any I have seen, though he was as much fat as muscle.

"Shall I take their masks off?" asked a guard to my left.

"No. Take any weapons from them and put them in the cells. Then you can all go and wash their shit off yourselves and forget this ever happened."

"I think it's your shit, actually," I said. My master stared at the floor, shaking her head, and the man backhanded me across the face. It was a poor blow. Children have hurt me more with harsh words.

"You should remember," he said, "we don't need you; we only need her."

Before I could reply bags were put over our heads for a swift, dark and rough trip to the cells. *Five hundred paces against the clock walking across stone. Turn left and twenty paces across thick carpet. Down two sets of spiral stairs into a place that stinks of human misery.*

Dungeons are usually full of the flotsam of humanity, but this one sounded empty of prisoners apart from my master and I. We were placed in filthy cells, still tied though the bonds did not hold me long. Once free I removed the sack from my head and coughed out a wire I had half swallowed and had been holding in my gullet. It was a simple job to get my arm through the barred window of my door and pick the lock. Outside was a surprisingly wide area with a table, chairs and braziers, cold now. I tiptoed to my master's cell door.

"Master, I am out."

"Well done, Girton, but go back to your cell," she said softly. "Be calm. Wait."

I stood before the door of her cell for a moment. An assassin cannot expect much mercy once captured. A blood gibbet or maybe a public dissection. Something drawn out and painful always awaited us if we were caught, unless another assassin got to us first – my master says the loose association that makes up the Open Circle guards its secrets jealously. It would have been easy enough for me to slip into the castle proper and find some servant. I could take his clothes and become anonymous and from there I could escape out into the country. I knew the assassins' scratch language and could find the drop boxes to pick up work. Many would have done that in my situation.

But my master had told me to go back to my cell and wait, so I did. I locked the door behind me and slipped my sack and bonds back on. I imagined a circle filled with air, then let the top quarter of the circle open and breathed the air out. I let go of fear and became nothing but an instrument, a weapon.

I waited.

"One, my master. Two, my master. Three, my master . . ."

Chapter 2

I was at twelve thousand nine hundred my-masters.

The man that came for me did not even glance through the bars to check on me before coming in, which made me sure he must be one of the blessed. Few others in the Tired Lands are so careless, or sure, of their lives.

"So," he said, standing in the door and blocking the meagre light with his bulk, "still here, assassin?" I said nothing. Nothing is always the best way to go. It is especially infuriating for the blessed, who expect the world to jump at their whims. "I asked you a question," he said. I still said nothing and would continue to unless they chose to torture me. Then I would say an awful lot of words while still saying nothing.

The man took another step forward, placing his booted feet carefully to avoid the filth in the cell. I could see a few feet of cross-hatched world through the rough weave of the sacking over my face, and he wore good boots, soft leather uppers and thick soles. My clubbed foot often pains me, and I have become a connoisseur of the cobbler's arts. I am often jealous of good boots.

He was the same man who had ordered our masks kept on while his soldiers kicked me in the ribs. He stared at me then looked me up and down before removing the sack from my head and pulling down the mask that covered my nose and mouth. *When I kill you,* I thought, *I will have your boots.*

"I don't think you are an assassin," he said. "The other one maybe, but you?" He had the breath of the blessed, thick with halitosis after too much good food and high with the scent of clove oil to dull the pain of bad teeth. He spat on the floor by my club foot and leaned in close to whisper theatrically in my ear, "What sort of assassin are you? A crippled child makes a poor killer."

"Maybe you are right," I whispered into his ear. "If I were a true assassin I am sure I could slip my bonds and cut your throat as simply as I could kiss your cheek." I moved my head and let my lips brush against the stubble of his chin. He leaped back like a scalded lizard, and I saw the fear in his eyes and, a moment later, the anger.

He beat me then. He used a small wooden club, and though he was no artist he made up for his lack of skill with enthusiasm. As he beat me I reflected on the fact that although, generally, silence is the better option, sometimes it is good to talk. After the beating he replaced my mask and sacking hood then dragged me through the castle.

To the cell door and out to the left and thirty paces on. Up four tightly spiralling staircases. Along an echoing hall running westward and up two more flights of stairs into a large room where the tramp of my feet on the stone floor echoes from a high ceiling. Up two very short sets of wooden stairs to be placed on some sort of temporary wooden floor that echoes hollowly under my feet – a mirror of the echoes from above a moment ago – and I feel vertigo, as if I am suddenly upside down.

A noose is placed around my neck.

Ice runs in my veins.

A scaffold. I was on a hangman's scaffold and as afraid of Xus the god of death as any of those I had brought his unwelcome gift to.

My hood came off.

A vast meeting hall before me, one that had been built before magic and its sorcerers cursed us with the sourings, in a time when people had plenty and great advances were made. The room was four, maybe five times the height of a man, and the black stone walls had been plastered and painted white. In many places the plaster was flaking and yellowed, and no doubt the huge and colourful tapestries that gently rippled in an errant breeze covered more damage. The weak sun of yearsage streamed in through crystal windows set high in the walls, trapping dust, which drifted slowly in the sunlight like insects caught in honey. I felt like an actor in a theatre.

My master and I often travelled as jesters as they are welcomed by the lowest and the highest of the land. Tradition has it a jester does not speak to those who are their betters, so they are often forgotten about and a jester can move unremarked upon through a castle or village. At the same time a jester is a status symbol, and my master's Death's Jester is famous and she, as a jester rather than an assassin, is highly sought after. I have considerable talent myself. My clubbed foot makes me a second-level jester – a clown of deformity – but despite being one of the mage-bent, my foot twisted by the sickness wrought by sorcerers on the land, I understand wordplay and I tumble almost as well as any other. There are very few things in my life as joyous as bringing joy and my dreams are often of the theatre, of letting go of the hand of Xus, the god of death, and walking out to entertain upon the boards and receive the appreciative hand of the crowd.

But in my dreams I do not wear a noose around my neck or play to a grim-faced audience of two – one my master, bound to a chair. The other a woman of similar age but dressed finely in flowing jerkins and gold-threaded trews who holds my master at swordpoint. Both are illuminated by a shaft of light and utterly still like players before the opening of their performance. I wondered if this had been done on purpose. If so there could be no doubt our captors had a flare for the dramatic.

"Aydor," said the woman, her voice husky as if she were aroused, "make sure the rope is tight around the boy's neck, or Merela may not believe I am serious." The noose around my neck snaked shut and the air in the room thickened. "Good boy," she said.

Aydor's foul breath enveloped me as he whispered in my ear.

"You'll regret that kiss you gave me when you're begging for air, mage-bent. No one treats me like a woman; I'm the king-in-waiting."

The woman turned and tore off my master's mask. "So, Merela Karn –" she walked around my master's chair "– who did you come here to kill?"

There was silence then. A long silence. The sort of silence used to underline the drama in the bad theatre pieces that were performed at Festival, the great travelling trade caravan that toured the Tired Lands. This was a bad thing for me as a cripple. A fast rule of poor Tired Lands drama is that the hero's well-meaning cripple friend dies as early as possible in the first act. This gives the hero a reason to continue; it provides them with some impetus. I had never taken the common hack playwrights' work personally until I stood on a stage with a noose around my neck.

"You know me, Merela," said the woman. "You know you cannot lie about your trade. So spare your apprentice some pain. Tell me who you came to kill."

My master said nothing.

"I am the queen now, Merela. Adran Mennix, queen of the whole of Maniyadoc and the Long Tides. You know that; you helped put me on my throne. Aren't you proud of that?" She walked around my master, who ignored her, staring fixedly forward. "Do we not have some bond, Merela? Does our past not tie us together?" She knelt, putting a hand on my master's leg.

My master said nothing and the queen remained kneeling,

searching her face, then straightened. When she spoke again there was a yearning note in her voice.

"Is there nothing there, Merela? Not even in in your code of murder, that says we are bonded?"

My master said nothing.

"Very well, you were always stubborn. Let's see if we can find something you do care about," said the queen. "Aydor, pull on the rope."

"Wait." My master spoke in nothing more than a whisper but it filled the entire room. It was a skill she had taught me in my tenth year, a way of speaking from the bottom of your stomach rather than your throat that fills your blood with energetic fizzing and a room with sound. The queen, at that moment gesturing towards me, gave an imperious smile and let her hand drop. Aydor, who I had decided must be her son as there was a definite resemblance, gave the rope a spiteful tug that had me standing on my tiptoes to avoid choking. I was desperate to hear what was being said by this woman who called herself a queen. My master had always been tight-lipped about her past, and now it turned out she knew one of the most powerful women in the Tired Lands, Queen Adran Mennix of Maniyadoc. If I was about to die then I would at least try to die with my curiosity sated.

"Very well, Merela, I will wait upon you again," said the queen with a mocking bow. "I hope you understand what an honour that is now."

"We were invited here, Queen Adran," said my master, "invited to meet a contact in the castle, and they would tell us our target."

"You came, to my castle, to kill. Even though we were friends once?"

"Yes, I came because we were friends. Once."

"And do you know who brought you here?"

"We both know that."

"Do we?" said Adran.

"Of course we do. You brought us here."

Once again the dramatic silence. Though I knew my master was right because she is always right. I also knew that I had been the only person in the room in the dark about this as Aydor let the tension on the rope slacken slightly in surprise at being found out.

"And," said the queen quietly, "what makes you think that?"

"A night-soil drain designed as a trap. The insistence on our coming through the night soil gate when we all know the blessed keep them watched. And lastly, and most obviously, that I was asked for by my full name."

"Is that so strange?"

"Yes, the number of people who know my real name and what I do can be counted on the fingers of one hand." She looked up then, a big smile on her face. I do not like that smile. It generally bodes nothing good. "All of them are in this room."

The rope creaked, tightening around my neck as Queen Adran stared at my master. Then the queen laughed. She had a beautiful laugh, a chiming girlish laugh that was full of life and pleasure.

"Sharp as ever, Merela. I knew I was right to bring you here."

"And you, Adran, are as willing to make things needlessly complex as ever. You could have asked to see me."

"You would not have come, Merela. Not for what I want."

"And that is?"

"Your advice. Your help."

"Why?" My master tipped her head to one side. She seemed genuinely confused.

"My son."

"Son?" My master raised an eyebrow. "I thought you only ever wanted daughters?" I felt Aydor's muscles twitch through the tension of the rope.

"What was it you always said, Merela? We work with what we have?" The noose tightened another notch. "Nonetheless, I love my son and someone in the court wishes to assassinate him." She nodded at Aydor, a man with breath only a mother could love.

"Of course they do," said my master, and the rope around my neck tightened again, forcing sweat out of my pores.

"Then you know about this? For sure?" Adran – all angles and worry.

I am an assassin, Adran—"

"Queen Adran," she snapped.

"I am an assassin, Queen Adran –" though she used the title my master did not make it sound respectful "– and your son is the heir to the throne so at least half, if not more, of your court would see profit in his corpse. So if your question is 'Does someone want to see your son dead?' the answer is almost definitely yes." Aydor did not take kindly to this news and I felt his indignation in increments as the noose closed further around my windpipe. "The question you should be asking, Queen Adran, is if anyone has the spine to follow through on their desire."

Adran lowered herself to a crouch so she could look into my master's face.

"Or maybe that is a question that you –" she poked my master in the chest "– *you*, Merela Karn, should be asking."

"Me?" It is rare I hear my master sound surprised but she was then. "Why would I do that?"

"Who better to stop an assassination than an assassin?"

"Surely the king has a Heartblade for such things?"

I waited for Adran to reply. It is normal for any of the high blessed to have a Heartblade, a man or woman trained to stop assassins.

"He did have. He died protecting Aydor, though the castle thinks he fell down the stairs, drunk. After all, if it was common knowledge an assassin was already here, you would not have come. But now Festival is coming with all its trade and train, they will flood my castle with people, and . . ."

"You have no replacement to watch your son?"

Adran stared at my master, a smile playing about her lips.

"I have someone to watch him, but not to find whoever ordered this. I want you for that."

"Me?" said my master.

Adran turned to me.

"Your boy is quite talented – the way he dealt with those two guards was impressive. I would have preferred he killed them but that is being dealt with." She stared at me then smiled the way a cat smiles before it pounces on a mouse and turned back to my master. "Let us talk in private, Merela. Aydor!" she shouted. "Hoist the boy!"

What was said between them then I missed as I was choking on the rope. I do not know how long they talked, only that it was for less than seven minutes as I did not lose consciousness and that is how long I can survive on one breath. My eyes streamed as they started from my head, and my tongue swelled to fill my mouth while my master and Queen Adran talked.

As darkness started to close around me an agreement was reached between them. Aydor let go of the rope, and I fell to the floor of the scaffold gasping for air while he laughed, calling me a useless cripple as he slit the ropes binding my hands.

"Go talk to your mistress," he said. "Learn your duties."

By the time I had limped over to my master she was also free. She shepherded me away from the queen and her sewer-breathed son.

"We are to find out if there is a conspiracy to assassinate the heir and, if so, we are to stop it." She spoke loudly enough for the queen to hear.

"But the Open Circle . . . The other assassins will . . ." I said, following her lead and keeping my voice audible.

"Don't worry about them. I have given my word to help. We will have to answer for it."

"Why, Master?" My question was genuine. She did not give her word lightly nor, in my experience, ever go back on it.

"The queen says that if I do not do as she wishes she will expose me. Tell people that the great Merela is a woman and that I am a Death's Jester."

"But then—"

"They will wipe every Death's Jester from the Tired Lands, presuming they are all assassins, and an ancient art form will die. I cannot be the cause of that."

"But—"

"I have given my word, Girton." Sharp words meant to cut me off. She would talk no more about a thing once she was decided.

From the theatre we were taken by a slave to a room where two heated tubs of water waited so we could wash off the filth of the day. The slave did not stay. Adran clearly knew my master well enough to trust her word. I itched to know more but knew that questions would be as welcome as a sorcerer at a crop sowing.

The moment she was sure we were alone my master leaned over from her tub of water and said my name in a whisper.

"Listen to me, Girton. Adran wanted to lock you in a cell as surety. Her son has a warrior called Celot to guard him, and now she has me as well. They see no use for you. I have told them I need you to spy for me if I am to achieve their aims but you may walk away from here. Do you understand? I have given only my word and Adran cares nothing for you; she wants me. You may ensure your safety and slip away in the night and, if you do, you will go with my thanks for many good years of service."

"You mean leave you, Master?" I said.

"Yes. Adran did not get to be queen through kind words

and soft hands. She is not someone you wish to be mixed up with if it can be avoided."

"But what would I do without you, Master?"

"Kill people, Girton. It is what you are trained for."

"But I am still an apprentice."

"Do not play the fool," she said, angry. "You are fully ready and have been for long on long. You are twice the assassin of any other I have met."

"Even you, Master?"

"Girton," she said and shook her head, her anger passing as quickly as the warm breezes that bathe the land in years-life. She reached out and ran a cold wet finger down the line of my jaw. "You are always ready with a joke." She smiled then, her real smile, a small, fragile and seldom-seen thing. "Do not stay out of loyalty to me, Girton. We are not loyal; we are death bringers, cold people." Looking into her eyes I felt the same fear that I had felt when Aydor ap Mennix placed the noose around my neck, the same fear I had felt as a scared child when she first took my hand at the slave auctions. She had found me when I was six and been all I had known in the nine years since. She had trained me in weapons, nursed me through sicknesses, held me when I had nightmares of hedgings coming for me and taught me all I needed to pass in the world. "If I do what Adran wants, Girton, the Open Circle will never rest until I am punished for it. They may overlook your actions, at first, but the longer you stay the more they will see you as my accomplice. So if you stay, be sure."

"I am sure, Master."

Those words, spoken so quickly and without thought to anything but my own loss. I often wonder, now I am older and wiser, if I had paused and thought about what she was saying, if I had considered the facts behind the words, then would I have reconsidered? Because what I did not see, through the selfish eyes of my youth, was that Queen Adran had only one thing she could hold over my master. It was not her identity as a Death's Jester – a new disguise is ten a penny to our kind. It was not that an art form would be lost from the world. That would have saddened her – she enjoyed the work – but she was always a cold realist.

No. There was only one thing my master valued highly enough to betray everything she had lived and trained for. I did not see it then, but now I am older I see it as clearly as the nails on my fingers.

Me.

It was me.

Merela Karn, the greatest assassin I ever knew, gave up everything for me. Dead gods help me. I should have run.

For both of us.

I should have run.